KNIGHTS OF THE LIVING DEAD

Bloodlines

Ryan Holden

RYAN HOLDEN BOOKS

Copyright © 2024] by Ryan Holden

All rights reserved.

No part of this publication may be reproduced, distributed, or transmitted in any form or by any means, including photocopying, recording, or other electronic or mechanical methods, without the prior written permission of the publisher, except as permitted by U.S. or UK copyright law. For permission requests, contact www.RyanHoldenBooks.co.uk

The story, all names, characters, and incidents portrayed in this production are fictitious. No identification with actual persons (living or deceased), places, buildings, and products is intended or should be inferred.

Edition Number: One/2024

About the Author

I fell in love with the idea of writing many years ago. Then I grew up, fell in love with many other things, and had to learn how to be an adult with responsibilities. Two teenage sons later, things didn't turn out too bad, and now I have a little more free time to reunite with my first love... I want to create a world that readers sink deep in and never want to get out. A supernatural detectiverse with intriguing cases and loveable characters. Join me on this rollercoaster.

Contents

Prologue	VIII
Whispers	1
Polaroids	13
Before and After	19
Tape One	24
The Fate of Eckleston	27
The Tape that Keeps Giving	30
The Shadows	33
A seral killer in Willowbrook	36
O'hanlon Crime Scene	40
Church to a Crime Scene	45
The Fate of Patrick Sheh	49
Haunting Ghosts	54
Hit the Books	57
Influence	61
The Sneaky Librarian	64
Hunted Creatures	68
Grace is Dead	73

A Shrill in Time	80
Close Call	84
Return of the Living Dead	88
The Evil Puppet	92
The Escape	96
Help	100
Shadows are Calling	104
Rest	109
Uninvited Guest	113
Dear Doctor	116
Lie Low	121
Here Again	125
It Gets Darker	130
Who Is Ackerman	135
Darkside	141
Scorched	146
Where Am I?	153
Timing Is Everything	159
What's Next	164
Birds of a Feather. Flame Together	169
Cabin in the Woods	174
Death Becomes Them	180
Eye Opening	188
Road Map to Hell	195
Kingsley	204
Face of Death	213
Smoke and Mirrors	223
Light will come from Dark	233

Time Fly's	245
Clinging on	254
A Knight Rises from the Darkness	265
Acknowledgements	280

Prologue

'One week ago,'

It looked like a war zone. Except the dead were the ones rampaging through the streets. We were driving painstakingly slow, zig-zagging hundreds of the undead staggering across the middle of the road and any sidewalk. We passed at least two cemeteries where my stomach churned, watching decomposed bodies punching out the ground. Some had flesh peeling from their bones, oozing black fluid. While others were a little fresher. None of it will leave me for a while.

I was in awe and terrified by how it had happened. Were those creeps in suits that powerful? In that vision through the killer's eyes, he taunted Nathan's father about the gates of hell. George described those guys as demonic knights; could they tap into the underworld? Give the dead a little wake-up call. How else is it possible? The more I thought, the more my brain hurt. None of this should be possible, let alone be my reality. Did my father know how bad things could get? Nathan's father mentioned a plan B. I hoped we would find it at this place marked by a little square on their flesh.

It makes me wish there was a 'do-over' button, rewind to before the accidents, and warn Charlotte and her father to avoid certain things. Maybe ask Father more questions and take an interest. Perhaps I'd be more prepared and, in exchange, warn him about what's to come. I know that's all pie in the sky, and I must start facing what's happening to me. My bloodline is cursed; if I let the darkness in, I'd be the same as the killer. Maybe even do exactly what he is. Was this what I had to come? The reason I keep seeing through his eyes. Or were we connected in some other way?

We neared the end of Wickham Street and exited the village of Billing, Which, much like ours, Maplewood, Melwood and Filton, was drenched in darkness. Not a light in sight. I'd be bold enough to say the power had been cut off on purpose, leaving these villages isolated. This game was getting old. Those fuckers knew what they were doing. Creating distractions and vulnerability, letting the undead terrorise normal life.

This leaves me with the question: Can the undead turn humans? I get they can kill, but what if it's a scratch or a bite? Would that do? I still don't know how that happened when Nathan's father grabbed onto my wrist. It had to be the bloodlines; we're connected like in that photograph. All of them together. It must've been as we swung into another bend; I bumped against the armrest, and a thought came to me. A sickly, stomach-churning thought that I didn't know what to do with.

I'm back at the bar, the two polaroids slide out, and I see that symbol, the moment I'd absentmindedly carved into a coaster moments earlier. The devil star in a circle. Except this was blood on the sidewalk next to my father's body. It couldn't be, not when we'd asked for help. It's not like Nathan was in the right state or frame of mind for me to bother him on this. Besides, it made no sense anyway. Not that it stopped the tired cogs in my brain from turning.

Our wheels rumbled over another cattle grid into an even darker country lane. We continued slow, not thinking there'd be any traffic, and I heard Gerald mention we could end up mowing down some of the dead if they'd made it this far. I could see the logic.

Nathan was slumped as far into the corner of his seat as possible. His expression was pale and vacant. Not the usual happy-go-lucky friend I was used to. Death does that. I would know. I sensed that Detective Reynolds knew that, too. He didn't say anything but empathises and goes out of his way to help while not pushing Nathan or me. I reckon he's been through some version of hell himself. Damn, that word, 'Hell', to think that's what we were trying to stop, the real thing. The detectives had mapped out that weird yet spooky diagram that was somehow printed on Nathan's parents' backs. Fuck, I haven't even thought about how I'm going to handle that. Do I plead ignorance? What good was the truth right now anyway?

Headlights beamed against a black-and-white sign as we swept around another bend, with the sore growing on my elbow feeling like the hundredth one we'd taken. 'Kingsley' was three miles out. Behind that sign, the view would otherwise look picturesque, with trees as far as the eyes could see and hilltops kissing a slightly lighter purple of the sky. Peaceful, that's how it looked, moments that have been few and far between. Reminded me of the girls, praying to god they were safe.

Mother didn't tell me where they were headed; safer that way. It's not knowing if they're okay that worries me. I feel they are, though; I can't say why; it's just a flutter in my stomach when I think of them accompanied by that thought. Hoping they were obliviously sleeping while the world went to shit. This part of it, anyway. Mother would undoubtedly have heard the news; she has 'Radio Two' on twenty-four seven. No sooner had I been comforted by that image. Another came flying in like an express train, the father's head.

Before and after shots. The pleading and a final chuckle of defiance. Then, the yawning, chomping, mindless view rocking in a pool of blood on the table.

I'm looking at Nathan, worried as you'd expect. His world had been smooth sailing as far as he knew. He had a wealthy family, and he got to run around Willowbrook or wherever playing private investigator. Everything he knew had imploded, but that was without the truth. The look on his face now was a man in need of alcohol; boy, could I join him. All of this feels like a never-ending nightmare we can't wake from. We're rolling into 'Kingsley' I'm wondering what's waiting. Nathan is twitching and seems edgy and aggravated. Perhaps his father was lying, hoping to throw the killer off balance. Soon, his father's bloodline will sink its claws in, and all of this dark stuff going on with me will take root. It seems odd he hasn't asked, 'When does this happen to me?'. Does he know something I don't?

I'm looking out the windshield into the darkness, like the black growing within. I see Detective Reynolds's hand change out of the corner of my eye. Dark fur grew thick and bushy; his hand doubled, maybe tripled in size, with his flesh becoming shades of brown. Seeing all this in a surreal, slow motion was scary and remarkable. Then came the claws. Menacingly long, thick, stretching to thin with sharp tips. They were as black as the night around us and just as daunting. I wouldn't want to be on the wrong end of them. Why? That's what I asked myself. The little I knew of this world, I mean their world. It had to mean something, voluntarily changing like that. It feels weird, with the inclination to respect their job as Detectives, but easier when it's less formal. So, I'll call it that way. After all, nothing about this felt 'Law' related. Not no more.

Michael did the same; his hair was lighter, longer, and thinner. No, so werewolf, but more akin to a feral animal. A fox. I'd say. Maybe it's more obvious to obvious, but these moments of the calm before the storm. I was learning as much as I could. Anything to take my mind off what's bothering me the most. Secrets. I don't like them; I was never good at keeping them, and in the last months, I've made it my job, much like Nathan, to uncover the reality behind them.

Look where it got us. George and Michael, though, were bothered right now. I was busy craning my neck and looking for the obvious when something weird happened to me. That bar is uniquely high for me, but this... I was propelled back through the eyes of the killer. Not literally, but those heightened feelings and senses. I could hear heartbeats. That might sound like my stress was getting to me, and it was my hearing. It wasn't. I could hear the double pacing of our supernatural friends in the front. Nathan's was steady, low, almost a sleeping rhythm; he'd withdrawn far into himself and his dark thoughts. Just like I experienced in that vision, George rolled his window down; I watched his head tilt, inhaling to catch a scent. I hate to be rude, but I'd only seen that with a dog. Thank god these were no dogs. His ears twitched, too. My nose began going, too; I picked up on it all. Overwhelming in all its stinking glory. The toxic diesel spewed from our car, a dampness showing rain coming.

That shudder came again; I drifted back in my seat as I felt it. Death. That's what it was. The long, bony hand of death stroking my grave. Vibrant and deadly, it came in ferocious waves carried on the bitter breeze. Death blended with sulphur was travelling toward us, which had George alert. Michael was slower to it, I noticed. Again, why? I asked myself, why was I experiencing this? I shook off the chill in time for another wave. Chills, that is. This was different; I knew what came next. Seems the pre-cursor to our dark standoff.

A finger-like brush of my cheek, then with the usual cold, melancholy, *'Are you ready, Gerald, ready to finally give in? Embrace it because what's coming? You'll need me. Now...Let...me...in. Let the darkness in and own your bloodline and its burden. No crosses need bearing. A curse doesn't need to mean a curse.'*

"I can't; I'm not evil. I've seen evil, and that's not me if I let the darkness in. I become the one killing and looking to turn this world on its head." I whispered but caught George's eyes staring at me in the rearview. Not once have I said yes or embraced it. I came close in the basement, but I didn't. So why am I experiencing what I am? Why did the darkness help me at the farm and the basement, teasing me with all the heightened nonsense?

There's no manual for it, and my father ran from it. Nathan's parents, too. The more I dwelled on that puzzle and startling reality, with that melancholic calling hitching a ride with that ever-present terror bobbing on the tiny boat through my sanity. The river had become a tumultuous sea rife with monsters. All waiting to devour the boat, its passengers become captive to them, beasts.

A world of eat or be eaten. Kill or be killed. To compound my impossible choice in this 'most dangerous game', the boat had lost its steering rudder long ago. Broke loose when I watched Nathan's mother have her jugular cut through and his father, a sword clean through his heart. I guess what I'm saying is that at least two of the four bloodlines have run or attempted to hide from this, and they've ended up dead. Would doing the opposite have the same outcome? That's not me deciding to give in, more 'devil's advocate' playing 'blackjack with a losing hand, deciding whether to stick or twist.

I'm sure this all seems like the rambling of a man who's finally lost his mind, having skirted close for a while. Perhaps that's why the call came at this moment, when morale is low, heading into the unknown, surrounded by the 'undead' staggering through the streets, dripping their decomposing flesh all over the place.

'Why such one-dimensional thinking? If a mundane is inherently evil, it is in their nature that when the opportunity is within their grasp, they will become evil. If a mundane is inherently good, trod a righteous path all of their life, even when opportunities have presented themselves so willingly and that mundane still chooses to walk that righteous path. It will be their nature to be good.'

"So what are you saying?" I said. It was probably my tired brain. I thought I understood the basics and the point, but then I kept looking for hidden meanings. When is evil ever truthful, I asked myself. Nathan continued twitching. I still heard his ultra-calm heart while Michael and George sounded as though readying for that deathly sulphur stench.

'If a mundane is naturally good, like yourself. Look at this crusade for the truth you've been on. I've watched it all; I hear your thoughts, and I know your doubts. I also tantalisingly know your potential. A mundane in pursuit of good. So, why would you think evil would be your path?'

Was I being reeled in? While something approached that I sensed was nothing good, the darkness whispered a sales pitch that made me think. "Are you implying that just because I embrace the darkness, that sounds very much hauntingly evil? I mean, the clue in the word, 'darkness', speaks volumes. It doesn't mean I will become some crazed killer like the other guy. I mean, what the hell is he?"

'Finally, the penny drops. I knew mundanes were sometimes slow, but with you, I had hope. As for him, he has become one of the fallen Knights; there are many other names or titles, but those like him have fallen from the cause, much like the two that hold your detective friend's girl. They were The Knights Templar at one point, until they became Baphoments chosen or the Eternal vigil because at any one time there's two Knights watching over, creating chaos and

evil in the world.- 'I butted in as the last sentence hit me hard.

"What? What do you mean watching over and creating chaos?" I said, forming a picture that these Knights have been the spark for many a conflict that blights our world.

'You see, there's always been that hope, that quest to resurrect all the Knights slain centuries ago when their allegiance to Baphomet was leaked to the King of France. Who ordered them located at eradicated? Including their General Francois, Louis Philip the second. As evil as they come before embracing the devil. There was a belief that one day, the required relics would surface, and one day, a bloodline would give in to the power. Or they will go mad as so many over the years have. Now, there's a hungry killer playing puppet. While thinking he's playing chess. For the most part, in your life, he has. Suppose those Templars are broken out of hell with the demons. There will be an unstoppable army of undead led by some of the fiercest soldiers ever to walk your earth. To answer your question, the Knights need the right environment; they feed off it. You mundanes are easy to manipulate, and by them creating a world ripe with evil, it's like a drug. A highly intoxicating drug that fuels them.' I was stunned into silence. Although I had been whispering, I knew George was listening.

"What would that make me?" I asked. They say curiosity killed the cat. Well, I say better the devil, you know. Corny, right?

'That's one of life's mysteries, I told you; if you let me in, you will experience all the power you can imagine. But... that doesn't mean you have to fall, too. Could well be a true Knights Templar, one to restore faith and order.'

"But in the beginning, you made it seem you wanted me to kill and do bad. What happened?" I asked, thinking back to when the haunting began.

'What's one of those four-legged beasts in the wild? Oh, a LEOPARD. That's right. A leopard has spots. Those spots cannot change—you mundanes and your humanity, those inclinations, mostly to do bad. So, in general terms, you are all leopards, too. I thrived off your anger, pain, and hatred. So, to me, you were just another leopard with power within reach. There is no use in trying to make spots or stripes. Since then, I've watched and listened as you've strived against the pain and adversity. You can be what you want to be. Until then, I would be on guard; something is coming.'

The whispers stopped abruptly, and the chill was gone, but I could still feel that presence this time. I say darkness because it feels that way. If what it alluded to was true,

I had hope, and the girls were swaying me. I could never forgive myself if it went wrong and they came to harm. The reality is, I've been a kite dancing in a hurricane, and lighting was stoking the skies with all its terrifying, strobing might.

Those heightened senses had stayed, too; the nearer we got to Kingsley, the death felt. My ears twitched, which was odd. Getting a taste of what the detectives go through. For good reason, though.

'BOOM, BOOM, BOOM'

My hand tingled; I looked, and I could see real close as the tiny black hairs ruffled to attention, like wind through fields of straw or a forest of trees. Tiny pimples popped across my flesh beneath; My heart was flying, causing my throat to tighten, and Fear was taking over to the tune of a beating drum. That's how loud and what I heard first before each one thinned out. They were wings flapping. Hundreds of them building to a deafening crescendo. Much like the layby, I saw the piercing blue next. It was bloody scary. A horizon was becoming a nightmare. Except for Nathan, who'd stayed oblivious, we all knew what was coming without uttering a word. More importantly, how? Were they following from afar, or did they know much more about this game than we realised?

With everything the darkness preached, I couldn't help but feel disheartened. The lengths to which these evil bastards go to. Manipulating us mundanes, as we're called. Stirring the pot, creating a world ready for them to enjoy. Sure, there's a lot of evil to go around in various forms. What scared me more was letting loose all those Templars and their General. Nowhere would be the same.

George rolls the car to a stop at least two hundred feet from the road sign 'Welcome to Kingsley'. The horde of deathly ravens swooped toward them, their beady eyes glowing brightly before they seamlessly moved, becoming one of those creepy Knights. His face rippled in the moonlight, looking more like a walking corpse. Patches of flesh had long since decayed, allowing his skull bone to show through. I could feel the hatred dripping from his. Stepping slowly, the heavy heels of his shiny shoes clapping against the empty road, echoing a sinister tune.

"What are we doing, Georgie?" Michael says, glancing anxiously toward his friend.

"Fucked if I know. How did they even find us?" George says, thinking like I had while checking on us in the rearview.

'We can end this now. Hand him over with the puzzle piece and the box. He joins us and you lot can go on your merry way. The lovely Ellena included.' The creep spoke as though he were sitting with us in the car; his voice sounded that close. I shuddered again, shaking through the chill. Everything about this morbid freakshow curdles my blood. I had no intention of going anywhere and hoped George was on the same page.

"I trust you can hear me, so hear this. No way in 'hell'." George said. I couldn't resist a chuckle—a poignant choice of words.

"Ooh, nice use of the word Georgie." Michael quipped.

"Why, thank you, I thought you'd approve."

'You think you're so clever. This ends one way, with your death, and the same goes for everyone around you."It may have been a trick of the moonlight or the car headlights capturing in front of us: the street sign, the scenic view of endless trees and the creepy Knight. I could've sworn his eyes changed; pearlescent black became blood red.

"Hey guys, not to rush you or anything? But do you have a plan for dealing with something centuries hellbent on killing us?" I said, noticing George look at Michael as they exchanged smirks as if sharing some inside joke I wasn't a part of.

"Well, we've had a little experience with old things. Michael experiences it every Saturday night down the YMCA chatting up the elderly."

"Hey, you dick. That was one night I volunteered to help run the bar for a friend." Michael said, laughing. I'm looking at these two, so calm and cracking jokes in the face of all this danger. How do they do it? It must be bloody hard on their families. The Knight widened his stance, braced to charge at us; what he thought he would achieve was anyone's guess. His right foot dug into the gravel, twisted, and he powered forward.

"Georgie... erm Georgie. In case you missed it theres a scary looking Knight charging at us, you may want to do something." Michael said, eyes raised, waiting for an answer.

George jammed the car in gear, and with the handbrake on, he throttled the life out of the engine. The car was rocking and vibrating; I shuffled backwards in my seat, feeling the rumbles beneath me; loud wheel spinning filled the air. His claws gripped the wheel tightly. "Fuck it," George says, "Let's go through him." Michael frantically grabbed at his seatbelt, checking he was strapped in. Still, Nathan was oblivious, the three litre engine rocked the chasis some more, I toyed with being brave. There's nothing brave about crashing through a windshield if everything goes wrong.

I'm fighting against the tension to the best of my ability. My eyes dart to the front, the Knight is picking up speed, his coat flails wide, his deathly hand breezes to the butt of a sword. My eyes flick to my belt as I struggle, George unleashes the handbrake and hi BMW beast. The chasis twists and turns against the torque, burnt rubber teases my senses. My eyes dart to the front again, we're flying, the Knight is too.

Finally, the tension releases, and I yank the belt into its lock. I'm looking on in fear and awe that this creepy Knight was taking on a car now doing fifty miles per hour. Bizarrely, the Knight seemed just as fast. Then... everything slowed. Or looked that way. The front of our car connects painfully with the Knight as he draws his sword. A loud banshee shriek rocks the air; thunder claps in the sky. What happened next scared the living daylights out of me. As we plough into the Knight, he crumbles, not into Ravens, but more like decayed pieces of his body. Each part phases ghostly through our vehicle.

His horrifying face was full, gritted teeth, blood red eyes, his sword comes through as the rest of his body is still in pieces. Then I feel it, the darkness rapidly forms a barrier around me, all those gruesome body parts richochet off me. The sword wooshes past, and the scary part is that the Knight smiles as he blazes through, phasing through the rear of our vehicle. George slams on the brakes, screeching tyres roar in the night, and the chassis sways side to side until we stop. My hands immediately pat over my body, checking for wounds while struggling to rationalise what just happened. There's nothing. The detectives swivel in theirs looking shocked, I look out the rear, the Knight is now fully formed, sliding his sword away. Everything went silent.

'Blood...'

I could smell blood—and death and sulphur. But the blood was closer, a lot closer.

"Cuh...Cuh." What just happened, Gerald, I hear beside me. I turned slowly, realising where the blood was coming from. Nathan had a puncture wound to his stomach, his white t-shirt swelling with red and then black. I didn't understand. Judging by their faces, the detectives didn't either. There was another smell, poison I assumed, it smelt rancidly toxic.

'Your friend has twenty-four hours before the poison reaches his heart. Find the box and surrender yourself to the puzzle piece and the box, and we'll let your friend live. You have my word as a Knight.'

"what about your murdering friend?"

'That fool has another quest to fulfil. Don't worry; we'll allow you to uncover who they are. It's only fair to know who has tormented your family after all. Tik Tok.' Before I got to respond, the Knight crumbled into the blanket of Ravens filling the sky. I'm staring at Nathan, watching black track lines spread through his skin as his wound wreaked of the toxin. Twenty-four hours, that's all we had to decide the world's fate. What do I do?

Whispers

1

'Gerald - December 1987.'

'Terror bobs and weaves through my fragile sanity like a tiny boat floating down the swollen 'Willen' river, fighting bravely to right itself against the treacherous murky current and never-ending whirlpools. Whose frothing jaws are eager to drag the tiny boat to the river's darkest depths.'

Fog swept into Willowbrook early tonight like a hungry beast. A bloodthirsty blanket of solemn grey devouring any of Brook High street that stood in its way. Gnawing at that 'swollen river', feeding the fear that I won't see what's coming or see... the 'whispering man' until it's too late. I'm damned to carry this curse and the only person I could or thought deserved my blame is dead. A year has passed, and it feels like yesterday.

The wound is open, festering. An itch I long to scratch. Knowing full well that if it heals, we would've moved on, and I'm left none the wiser... I can't, though. I must know what's wrong with me; perhaps I'm defective. How else can I rationalise what I've been seeing? Or the teeth jaaa... Oooh it's cold. Goose pimples tease the nape of my neck.

'Hush, little baby, don't say a word. Mamma's gonna buy you a mockingbird, and if that mockingbird don't sing, Mamma's gonna buy you a diamond ring.' What the...Charlotte? Is that... No, it can't be. All in my head, that's what it is... Just breathe, Gerald, just breathe. God, that's easier said than done. Right. Where was I?

That's it, the things I'm seeing and, like just then, the teeth jarring voices. So, even before 'him', there have been moments. Always when I least expect it, and fleeting. A passing mundane in the street. I see their faces. For a moment, it takes my breath away, except it's not. A shimmer or a ripple and what should be a normal mundane face is 'death' or the '*dead walking*'. Pale flesh changes to mottled, grotesque grey, decaying, oozing old, toxic blood.

This is the part my mind goes blank or I go to get the attention of someone else, but no words come. I hear the shrills of a pain-riddled yawn without their mouth moving, and their cloudy stare focuses on me. I look behind to be sure, more out of hope they're seeking someone else. They're not, and with that haunting stare, becomes a horrible churning grimace. By the time any of it fullyregisters, or I realise it's not a hallucination,the mundane paleness returns.

In the beginning, those creepy interruptions were now and then, and I can't be certain how old I was when they began. Around eight or nine, I think. And plenty of nightmares, as you'd expect. My mother would roll her eyes, as only mothers do, without trying to be condescending and say, 'Now, now, Gerald, I'm sure it's just your childish imagination. Next week, it'll be dinosaurs.'

Which I didn't argue about because, eventually, they stopped for a while. Until my late teens, I believe. That's when they grew more detailed. Not only 'dead faces' but scenarios. 'Remnants', I called them. Each one, somebody died, sometimes more than one, before fading into a spooky cloud.

Then, the reaper knocked on our front door at the beginning of this year. That is one bastard nobody escapes from; he waltzes in, gets his bony little feet under the table, and says, 'You know what, this family looks too happy. Let's shake it up a little.' And the rest… well, you've got the idea. I won't spoil you with the details; they'll find their way to you soon enough. Since then, I've slowly felt myself sliding, mentally and physically, and it's still happening. A smouldering ember of darkness held within, growing with an evocative sense of déjà vu.

I'm not even sure this moment hasn't happened, and I'm simply reliving the memory. No, it has to be real. The pub door drifts open, but nobody's there. A chill floats through it, biting, prickling my flesh. I'm awake in the now, waiting and hoping my time isn't being wasted.

'Hush, little baby, don't say a word. Mamma's gonna buy you a mockingbird.'
Not again, please stop. Please stop… Breathe, not much longer now.

It's all these things that I'm struggling to handle. I have so many questions and crazy threads to pull on in my search for the truth. The most burning… Why did they leave me stuck somewhere so wicked that the world would sooner forget and so unprepared?

Why didn't Father tell me the truth about all those haunting experiences or that my life would be pummelled until I hit rock bottom and changed forever? There's a neat yet poignant turn of phrase: what is it... Oh, that's it. 'The sins of the father are to be laid upon his son.' Poetic, right, in a nightmare on Elm Street kind of way.

Sure, everything I've explained so far could be rubbish or grief-talking. I assure you, it's not. Okay, perhaps a smidge of grief dripped in for good measure. It's this place. I think it's different, darker. Even old maps have us and the surrounding five villages clustered together, representing the 'devil's pentagram'. I'll leave that to your imagination, but this place isn't right. Us mundanes, going about life, pretending. Not about any particular element, all of it, everything that 'Willowbrook' encompasses.

We hide from the secrets sewed into its dirty fabric. The nightmares we kid ourselves ain't real. If I see behind the veil, surely others can. They have to. I need them too. I need to know I'm not alone. Since 'he' appeared, I have struggled, like moments ago, to discern reality from illusion, nightmare torment from a mental breakdown.

Why can't I escape? Why the constant noise? This differs from any remnant I've experienced before, almost sinisterly tangible. There's no other feeling for it... It scares me. The other stuff is torment. He scares me to the very core of my being.

His eerie whispers saturate our cobbled streets, their sinister melancholy swallowed by the cruel darkness. A shiver coils down my spine at the thought of what's lurking... **'Oh Gerald, why don't you let me in?'** he wails weepily...

I've only caught glimpses—a gaunt, deathly face with wisps of charcoaled flesh peeling from his archaic bones. **'All you have to do is open up and let me in.'** Venomous cries meander mercilessly on the icy breeze: the 'Whispering' man, quite the nightmare name. I know. Until I can say otherwise, that's the best I thought to fit such a menacing thing.

With demonic eyes piercing its deep, garish red vibrancy through the inky veil of night. All framed by the unusual yet intimidating attire of a dirty, bloodstained trilby that's caught the chaotic splatter from what I dreaded to think, previously murdered mundanes. I know... I sound a right barrel of laughs; mock me at your peril.

Or, perhaps in the 'Whispering' man's deranged world, conquests. And a cloak that flutters like torn wings, whipping a menacing symphony against the empty. **'Let me in, and the pain fades.'** He continues toying with that tiny boat, appearing briefly in the shadows, a fleeting 'hiss' in the still air, a ghostly figure in reflections, and when no one else can see the torment that plagues me. In the cold, unforgiving night that smothers our mundane little village. A faded blot on a map, easily overlooked.

Just south of the picturesque Pennines, in the gloomy shadows of the Yorkshire Dales, set amongst rapturous, bounding hills, our 'hellscape', that is, Willowbrook, exists under a near-constant, haunted cloud. Winter lingers here nearly three-quarters of the year, but this season feels colder than before, bringing an icy snap that lingers in the hissing breeze, slicing through to the flesh.

This place would seem appealing to outsiders; other mundanes who didn't have to endure it once 'weeping willow' sunk its hooks in. Shrouded in all the traditional charms of thatched-roof homes from yesteryear and quaint shops, it never harbours over 1,500 souls. It doesn't dare, and no one seems to question it or leave unless it's in a pine box.

Charlotte and I dreamt of escaping, taking the twins and exiling ourselves somewhere far away and warmer. But the grip of this cruel place and Charlotte's sudden death kept those dreams forever out of reach. Oh, I forgot, I lost my wife just six months after my father. Perhaps now you'll see why I hold such disdain for 'Willow' and why I'm barely holding my shit together.

Some say it's because of a hex or dooming omen dating back to the Domesday Book, brought on by bedraggled travellers or AWOL knights running from their troubles, seeking refuge. Only their sins came with them and never left. Others whisper that deep within the hallowed halls of the less than 'godly' ruins of St. Peter's church (trust me, the rumours are bad about what went on), there's an unspoken rule etched in blood, a pact that binds the village to some exaggerated dark omen, one scribed by satan himself. Personally, I believe most of that is nonsense, but the way my life has spiralled, I'm mindful that in every embellished tall tale, there's an element of truth. What our village lacks in its ability to attract fantastical tourism, it compensates with a dark and rather morbid statistic.

It has one of the highest death tolls in mainland U.K., especially from murder. That's why I have so many 'threads' to pull on. 'Murder' has been that dire for centuries. It's probably a little sad that I know details like that, but after hearing the bizarre and horrifying story after the scaffolding crash on the High Street. I got curious about other freak occurrences written off as accidents when the details point to more. Boy, was I surprised. Now, after everything, I'm spooked. Whether any were because of a curse, evil forces, or something more sinister in this godforsaken village remains a mystery. Still, its dark legacy has earned this drearily quaint place the apt nickname 'Weeping Willow'.

I think it was used as a waypoint and secret stash hole for smuggled rum way back when. Or so I'm told. Then, it was home to a rather nice village-brewed cider. Until, like most good things here, they fall foul of the black cloud above. A wise person might say it's merely a village leaning towards what will garner the most attention. But I fear those numbers will grow with every glimpse of him, each sighting a harbinger of more tragedy to come.

The 'Whispering' man's long, bony fingers, covered in decaying grey flesh and tipped with razor-sharp nails, were wrapped in tight, black, fingerless gloves. He drifts on the periphery of my troubled life. My blood runs cold, hearing the desperation as he calls out, "If I let the evil in, my pain will stop," he says.

I don't want to give in. But since Father died, I no longer want to endure the pain; The 'Whispering' man knows it.

Compounded by the secrets rotting within my family like a decaying corpse, or perhaps just cautious half-truths, the old saying, **'Hard to see the forest for the trees,'** springs to mind. These secrets belong to my mother now. How she looks at me now isn't out of pity—I think. It's more like she sees me as a wounded animal or as if I've done something wrong.

She's been a blessing with the girls, allowing me to hold down a job, but her glances, which she thinks I don't notice, truly unsettle me. They carry a frown etched with pain, prompting me to wonder: does she know about Father? About Charlotte? A small voice inside tells me she might. (No, not the whispered one, for a change.)

Because as sure as night follows day, I believe someone is murdering members of my family, making their deaths look like accidents. You might listen to the nonsense the 'Willowbrook' press churns out after the police sprinkle their typical P.R. spin:

'Witnesses mentioned a busy road and a lorry quickly changing lanes beforehand.'

Yet, mysteriously, no one saw where that huge lorry went in the dead of night after causing havoc. It vanished from the M1 and the world, a trick involving no wand-waving or hocus-pocus. Merely a deviant mundane, willing to do anything for their pieces of silver.

This brings me to now—why I'm hunched over in a grubby 'small village' pub—the last place I should be with all these dark thoughts swirling through my brain, wrapped in the oppressive scent of stale cigarettes. If I weren't here, I'd be left with unanswered questions and nightmares—and this thing in front of me, the millstone around my neck, the same fraying newspaper I've carried everywhere. Its date, '17th June 1987,' is seared into my memory until I get justice or something close to it. Three columns down and two across, there's a small, blurry article titled:

'Tragedy Strikes Again for a Family from the Quiet Rural Trenches of Willowbrook after a Fatal Car Crash on M1 - Police Seek Witnesses.'

Mother used to say, *'Gerald, everything happens for a reason, and there's a reason for everything.'* You know what mothers are like—they have a saying for every occasion. But that brings me back to the haunting question: If someone is indeed murdering members of my family, what could be the reason? Who is next? Are my daughters Olivia and Lacey in danger? Then there's the local rumour mill, ever eager to stir the pot with whispers of my father's shady dealings, painting him as a gangster.

True, he wore the 'suits,' but as far as I knew, he was a hard worker and an exemplary manager at the factory where I now work. What a joke... It's more that I clock in and go through the motions. Perhaps I'm being melodramatic, but nothing feels the same—not the place, and certainly not his replacement. There are many reasons I could cite, like grief, or that everywhere I look, I still see my father. Maybe I don't care anymore.

As for my father, he was known for the occasional late-night meeting, typical for his job, and nothing ever seemed amiss. If there had been anything alarming, Mother would have been the first to know—or so I hope. Yet she's given nothing away, which only fuels the frustration gnawing at me. I'm pushing for answers, and she's avoiding reality, giving me that 'side eye' I mentioned earlier, acting as though nothing is amiss. Of all people, I thought she would be desperate for answers. Instead, it seems she's keeping something from me. I need to know what it is.

The road to the truth is never straight, and tonight is about taking a slight detour, even if I fear him catching me off guard.

As the clock inched toward 7:30 p.m. on a chilly December evening, tension knotted my empty stomach—I had skipped lunch. I was waiting to meet Colin Milton, a friend of a friend. Colin was the type who could pass for a librarian or an undertaker: weird and gangly, the quiet sort probably bullied in school. Sketchy, yes, but I hoped he could clarify my nagging doubts about my father's health and the rumours of his drinking. However, Colin had been reluctant to get involved, fearing for his job at the hospital and wary of the local gossip.

In Willowbrook, the mundanes clung to rumours like flies to dung. I knew little about Colin, and whether he could be trusted was up for debate. If he were shady, surely there would be stories? But then, the absence of rumours was in itself suspicious in such a small town. Everything about him was a blank, squeaky-clean slate. Perhaps too squeaky. Only time will tell.

I took another swig of whiskey, contemplating a refill as pieces of my beer coaster accumulated beside the bar.

"Another one, luv?" The question snapped me out of my thoughts, a husky voice tinged with a northern accent cutting through my melancholy. I saw a tall, curvy, smiling brunette in her mid-thirties approaching. Her heels clicked unevenly on the floor—one slightly more worn than the other—creating an uneven rhythm.

For a moment, my mind blanked. I struggled to recall her name, muttering under my breath, "Shit, what's her name? Oh, wait... It's Janice." I gasped as I glanced back at my glass and then up again.

Her face had changed horribly—corpse-mottled grey, with gory, blackened blood oozing from her eye sockets and mouth. It had happened again, truly unnerving.

"S... s... sorry, what?" I stammer, recoiling into my seat, fingernails digging into the wooden armrests as I struggled with the horrific vision. Was this a deranged hallucination?

"I... said... Why don't you... let me in?" Janice's voice became a curdled, agonising wail, blood spewing endlessly from her mouth. I clenched my eyes shut, then snapped them open again, not daring to breathe.

"Hey... you okay? Fancy another one, luv?" Her voice was back to normal. I cautiously met her gaze; she looked just as she had before—no blood, no deathly pallor.

"Um, yes, please, Janice," I croaked, the smoke and nicotine roughening my voice. Unfortunately, I had taken up smoking again after a decade. I needed something—anything—to keep my nerves at bay.

Janice placed a drink on a fresh coaster, glancing at the mess I'd made with the previous one. "So, your day was that bad?" she probed, sensing my discomfort.

"Er... Sorry, what did you say?" I forced a tight-lipped smile, avoiding her gaze. I noticed I'd made a strange pentagram coaster—a design I didn't remember making. Confused, I sank deeper into my seat.

A breeze brushed my cheek, unsettling me further. I shook it off as if it were just a draft. "I said your day was that bad? Isn't this one of those religious star things, you know, what those devil-worshipping freaks are into? You come here every night; this is the most I've seen you do. We exchange small talk, and you keep to yourself, clutching that newspaper. You always look so lost in thought. So, what's going on with you? Especially with this masterpiece?" Janice inquired, pointing at the pentagram.

Again, I shifted uncomfortably, knowing I needed to consider something suitable to deflect further probing. My eyes darted to a rowdy crowd, struggling for the right words. The back of my neck trembled with a constant coat of gooseflesh, feeling that featherlight graze again—this time from below my hairline to the edge of my collar. Doing my best to shake it off, I tucked my shoulder tight as if to make a shield or something. Pointless, I knew that, more a reflex than anything else.

"Uh, I do not know why I did that. I must've seen it somewhere; besides, I like it here. It's your whiskey. You don't water it down," I stammer, wracking my fragile brain to recall anything.

"Water it down? Who on earth would do that?" Janice's disbelief hung in the air. She inspected my newspaper, pointing out that I always have it with me.

"That newspaper you're holding, it's the same one you had yesterday. It's been about six-"

A haunting whisper buzzed past its venomous plea. "Let me in," pierced the silence. My pulse thumped beneath my skin.

My head darted from left to right, looking for who spoke, only seeing oblivious customers happily drinking. "Y... Yes, it's all about the gossip pages and the crossword inside. I've been enjoying revisiting them. I'm a little stuck on a few words, so I take my time. It's my little haven to juice up the brain matter when I'm here." I continue twitching, my right hand trembling slightly.

"But that's a six-month-old newspaper, and I can't recall you opening it once. Not at all."

'Let me in; you got to let me in.' The 'Whispering' man's icy call grated across my earlobe, inducing a temporary numbness. I was unravelling. If there was anything I could

take from this moment, the whispers were different tonight, and it had me spooked. I had to be slipping mentally. How else can I explain it? My eyes lurched at the door, seeing it glide closed with no one there. Then to Janice, who appeared normal.

With an awkward smile, my throat tightened as I struggled for words. Janice's probing was relentless, believing there was more to the story. A glance at the newspaper revealed lines familiar to me and could be recited by heart:

'A tragic accident on the M1 occurred just before midnight; a silver Ford Granada was slammed into the concrete bridge support and divider from the slip road. The casualty, a twenty-seven-year-old woman, a mother and a wife, died at the scene, leaving behind two young daughters in the car, unhurt. And a caring husband. A passer-by states a swerving lorry that had nearly caused several accidents along the stretch rammed her vehicle sideways. Believed the driver may have been drunk or under the influence of drugs,'

'Let … me…in…and…the…pain…will…fade.' The 'Whispering' man cut through again. Stomach churning, a shiver stood my arm hairs on end as a trickle of panic sweat drifted from my uneven sideburns. Life knows how to kick a man when he's down, and right now, I couldn't be any lower.

Janice was busy tidying the sticky bar. She had been around the block enough and heard enough stories in this village alone not to believe any old tale, and she wasn't stupid—that much I'd realised. She sensed something was off, so I tucked the newspaper inside my coat before offering her a cigarette. They were stronger than the ones in my youth, but my bland palate had evolved a taste for them in recent months.

She shook her head, untangling her thoughts from their recent strange and intrusive prodding. Janice didn't pry further; perhaps she thought, what was the point if I didn't want to talk? Besides, Janice—nursing no doubt was weary of scaring away one of the pub's few ordinary patrons. Although, the way I'm feeling at the minute, that's a stretch. And below the age of fifty. A consistent ten-a-day smoker, she jumped at the chance to add to the nicotine fog enveloping the bar.

The buoyant yet ambient-lit pub had become somewhere I could drown my sorrows and escape the relentless torment of my thoughts. That was until tonight—nursing a double whiskey and slinking into the shadows.

Balancing the unlit cigarette between her lips, Janice reached for a blue lighter. Her eyes wandered to the mediocre tip jar, holding a meagre change collection and one peso. "Who on earth tips with one peso?" she whispers, her eyebrows furrowing. With a shrug, she carried on shuffling around the bar, looking like she was re-evaluating her life choices as she exhaled a puff of smoke into the nicotine-laden air.

As Janice looked around, she noticed an empty glass and an abandoned newspaper. It was a far newer one than what I had. Janice slid it over, attempting to give me something fresher to read. It may even distract from destroying more of her coasters. However, when she glanced at the front page, I saw her expression change and darkened. Janice was staring at the main article.

"A 59-year-old man is found hanging at 3 a.m. in his home, which police are treating as suspicious after discovering signs of foul play," Janice read aloud. "Police discovered the full-time scrapyard worker, a father of three and grandfather of two after neighbours complained about an ongoing strange smell from under the door of his first-floor apartment."

Janice paused, her face reflecting a mix of concern and curiosity. "Do you remember him?" she exclaims enthusiastically, tapping the photograph on the article beneath my nose.

Feigning vagueness and slightly irritated by the stink of ink, I begrudgingly reply, "Not really, no. Why?"

"You must do. He borrowed your bloody lighter before the two of you talked like a couple of old women for forty minutes. Then, near the end, you two exchanged a whisper, and he was soon gone," Janice explains, tapping the photo again. Her eyes widened as if trying to force me to recall a memory I didn't want. Not my finest hour. While I couldn't help but notice the little quiver of her bottom lip, anxiety mixed with fear. I could relate to at least one of those.

Playing along, my voice concealing the true nature of the encounter. "Ah, yes. He seemed okay, maybe a little on edge. I can't think why."

'Oh, come now, we both know that's not true,' the 'Whispering' man cooed again, grazing my ear, forcing me sideways, releasing a shudder, eyeballs bouncing, looking for the voice.

Janice nodded, her face still troubled by the news of the man's death. "I know. What a small world. He'd been in a few times before and always seemed nice. Then nothing. Now we know why."

"A small world indeed," I mumble, diverting my attention back to my glass before taking a large sip, scorched by that sharp burning down my throat. It was a momentary respite, but deciding what I was washing away was hard—the grief or the awkward article.

'That won't help. Look at your hands; they're covered. Drenched in blood,' The 'Whispering' man teased, his tone dripping with melancholy. Making me twitch, even looking at the speakers mounted to the ceiling corner above my head as if someone was using them to play tricks.

To be sure, I couldn't resist a look at my hands, a slight gasp escaping my mouth. They were covered in blood. At least, that's what I saw, inducing a frenzied panic. My eyes dart around while shaking. A quick blink and the blood disappeared. Relieved but confused, I lurched for another shaky-handed sip of my drink, this time smaller, my throat tighter.

This bizarre torment had my sanity twisting like a kite in a hurricane. Janice drifted to attend to another customer. Still puzzled and unnerved, I slid my watch under my jacket cuff, admiring it momentarily. It was my dad's, an old silver Rolex with an ivory face, worn with age but with a newer, replaced underbelly. The clasp was sticky, but that didn't bother me. Dad had worn it for five years before that fateful night.

On Halloween last year, at a family gathering, he called me into his study to give me the watch. I thought little of it other than being happy and honoured. Yet Dad was restless, peering out the study window several times after handing the watch over. Besides that, moment and work stress, Dad seemed in good spirits, at least as far as I saw, so there was no need to question why. Years had taught me not to pry too much into my father's business.

We didn't know Father would be gone a year later. A bizarre accident while walking home from the pub. A reason for meeting Colin. Father was said to have stumbled drunk, crashing into some scaffolding, forcing it to collapse. Which was bullshit; none of us had seen him drunk, ever. It wasn't his way. Sure, some wine or a glass of whiskey here and there, but that's it. So, I figured it would be good to get my hands on the real toxicology reports and hope they explain how such a sturdy structure collapses after a collision with one man. The details didn't add up, not that anyone would listen except for a friend who reached out to Colin for me.

'Awe, poor Gerald, if you can't handle the pain, just let ... me...in before it's too late,' each tormenting whisper became more haunting. A shiver rippled over my shoulders.

I remained fixated on the watch in a hazy daydream, fighting to ignore the 'Whispering' man's haunting noise. Weary of the time to get home, I didn't want to be late. Colin was due with the report any moment now. Assuming he had the guts to show up, I trusted Nathan to mediate, and when he said, 'It's in hand,' I believed him.

'Don't pretend, just ... let...me...in, let... me... in,' the 'Whispering' man wailed, tempering my anxiety, merging with the surrounding chatter. The noise became a disheartening background hum. Massaging my neck to soothe the pressure as I stowed away the watch, squeezing my eyes shut for a moment, praying for peace that had been elusive. The anticipation for Colin's arrival added to the unrest. Reflecting on the events of last week, the hours leading to the 'hanging,' the timeline was unsettling if Janice could link the victim to me. How challenging would it be for the police? Lost in that morbid daydream, the haunting whispers broke through.

'Don't fight it; let ... me...in, and let's make the Willows weep. Be on the right side of what's coming.' My head dropped, running a hand through my hair, grappling with the struggle against the relentless calls. If it's not the remnants, the 'Whispering man' is weaving that 'Tiny' boat with unrelenting ease while the swollen river thrashes against the bankside. And now that river flows with blood.

Polaroids

2

'Gerald'

The pub door drifted open, an icy gust ghosted in, stepping on my grave in the process. I jumped,, reaching for the shiver down my neck, hoping it wasn't **the 'whispering man'**. Everyone has something that scares or haunts them. He's my very morbid, very spooky something. Shock soon turned to relief when I saw who it was. The clock ticked to 8:10 pm as Colin shuffled in, head bowed and shoulders hunched. He looked sheepish as he made his way to the bar. His anaemic, gaunt figure was enveloped in a dull brown tweed suit, its drabness only stressed by the dark, almost ominous overcoat draped over his shoulders like a modern-day reaper's cloak. He adjusted the spectacles perched on his nose, briefly scanning the other customers before finally making his way to the bar.

Colin's hands trembled as he gripped the newspaper Janice had shown me—the mysterious death of a 59-year-old scrapyard worker. I tried looking away, motioning for Janice to bring another round of drinks to calm my nerves about the news.

Colin sipped his whiskey, his eyes meeting mine with confidence. He opened his satchel, revealing a weathered, light brown folder with reddish-brown hues that grabbed my attention. Swiftly, Colin removed the folder. He slid it in front of me—a well-organised stack of papers that spoke of Colin's precision and dedication. That or some OCD.

"Have you read it?" I raised a curious eyebrow, knowing how limited my scientific knowledge was and how it may hinder my understanding of technical jargon.

"I have," Colin replies, his voice no louder than a whisper, tainted by foreboding shadows.

"And?" my curiosity danced with dread, their intertwined waltz teetering on the precipice of knowing.

"Would it surprise you if I told you that your father had next to no alcohol in his system?" Colin's revelation hit Gerald like a sledgehammer.

My head tilted, a mix of shock and confusion swirling. "For heaven's sake, you're saying he wasn't drunk?"

Colin nodded, confirming Gerald's suspicions. "He sipped what's left in your glass."

"And he bloody well didn't stagger about in a drunken stupor." I could feel my blood boiling. Knowing the situation wasn't right. Colin helped go some way to prove it.

"No, but something else is happening, and it gives me the creeps. His veins were coursing with adrenaline. I mean off the charts high. It was as though he experienced the rush of an exhilarating climax, but this was the epitome of fear, Gerald. Your father's dopamine, adrenaline, and glutamate levels were through the roof."

My face churned as the horrifying details settled like a suffocating fog. My father, who lost his life because of an alcohol-induced mishap, had fled the pub in sheer terror.

While grappling with the implications, the recent newspaper article, with its ominous headline, seeped into my thoughts. How did a "Hanging Man" earn a front-page feature? I needed the truth and to clear my father's name.

With a last gulp, I drained the remnants of my whiskey, the amber liquid offering some clarity to my fucked up, fragmented world, just in time to catch the trailing words of Colin's warning.

"Be careful if I were you, Gerald. There may be some truth to the stories of 'enemies'; otherwise, how else do you explain the fear?" Colin's once-pallid face now seemed drained of all colour—an unnerving sight for a man who already looked anaemic.

I shuffled the papers, patting one end on the bar; when two small square pieces of card dropped, smooth with a slight polythene coating, I knew what they were—polaroids. No sooner had I flipped them open than I got the shock of my life jabbing them at Colin, reeling in shock. "What the hell are these? Why? What on earth is going on?" The polaroids depicted a small pentagram-like symbol inside two circles, drawn in blood beside his dead father's trapped, outstretched leg—the scaffold accident.

Colin gulped as a bead of sweat dribbled from his brow. "Shit, I'm sorry, that slipped my mind. I found them by chance with the paramedics' papers from the scene that night. I wondered if you knew about them. If not, then that little creepy thing adds to the mystery of your father's terror." Colin settled into his words as he spoke, but I was confused.

"Beats me. It wouldn't seem so obvious, but it's made in blood and crazy enough for photographs to be taken. Yet my father gets branded a drunk and up to no good." My anxiety continues to build, glancing at my watch, on edge.

"I know. But make no mistake. Be bloody careful; this is just the beginning," Colin's disquiet wasn't reassuring with the Polaroids and what Colin knew now. If there were more to my father's terrifying experience, I understood the warning—it seemed I'd opened a can of worms, adding another layer of danger to an already fraught journey.

Our conversation drifted into a sea of whiskey meant to steady rattled nerves as an abrupt chill pierced the air, and a whisper brushed against my neck, teasing. I scanned the unaware pub crowd, but everything appeared normal.

That was until I noticed 'him' in the corner. Hidden amidst the clouds of cigarette smoke, tall and gaunt, clad in that black coat draped over his frame. The wide, dirt-stained trilby made his presence far more sinister. The 'Whispering' man sat in chilling stillness, holding a pint of Guinness with elongated fingers, frozen in a picture of mystery and menace. I didn't need this now. The noise was one thing, but with him sitting there, taunting, while I unravelled. Was too much. Or was it another illusion?

Sparks tingled the back of my neck. I recall another time, a passing moment when life... well... was less unhinged. It was from the hospital—the birth of the twins. It was a weird but happy day, although I almost missed the birth because I'd gone to the canteen for coffee. While in the hallway, I crossed paths with a stranger. I remember his words clear as day. 'Any change for the phone?' the guy says. A chill rushes through my body as if it was happening now.

I was busy stirring my coffee when those words echoed a few feet away. I turned to see a tall man wearing a grubby black canvas hooded raincoat and an unusual-looking dirty black trilby pulled down to conceal his face, leaving only a menacing chin visible.

The man's voice had blood-twisting gravel that would've usually bothered me were it not for the special day. In haste, I scooped a handful of change from my pocket and handed it to the man, who grabbed it with black leather-clad hands. Unlike now, the leather did little to pad out the bony surface or disguise how unusually long the man's fingers were. He'd held my hand for under five seconds, but the impression lasted. Little did I realise I'd crossed paths with the 'Whispering' man.

"What are you looking at? Shit, is anyone watching? Did anyone see?" Colin interrupts, riddled with anxiety.

"A guy in the corner at your six o'clock. He's dressed in all dark clothing and wearing a funky-looking hat." Colin turned his head left, almost giving himself whiplash. His confused expression made me seem like I was going mad, which would've been understandable. I still saw him clear as day. Was it only me? Was I alone, after all?

"Are you messing with me? There's no one there. The symbol may have been a tipping point for you," Colin's words were emphatic, causing an awkward shuffle in my chair.

My heart was thumping against my ribcage. Reliving every vivid detail of that hospital scenario and any fleeting glimpse since, I could taste the sterile, metallic tang in the air, making it difficult to dismiss it as a hallucination.

Moving closer to Colin, I whisper. "Colin, I'm telling you the truth. He was there, you know. The hooded raincoat, the trilby hat—it's too weird to be a coincidence." I stopped short of muttering, 'the Whispering man'.

Colin's scepticism wavered, and he glanced toward the empty corner where I'd mentioned. To him, the place remained empty. He picked his words, sounding worried. "Gerald," he says, "I understand the stress you've been under. Our minds can play tricks on us in times of great turmoil. Hallucinations and delusions aren't uncommon."

That part, I understood; as I said before, I call them remnants, and they centre around death, except for tall and scary. My frustration was bubbling, a mix of anxiety and terror. My fists squeezed so tight that my knuckles turned white. "I'm not going crazy, Colin. I can't be. I know what I bloody saw, and I'm not one to be taken by delusions. That guy is genuine. You can call me paranoid or whatever you want, but I swear, I saw him." I was trying to convince myself more than Colin, at least for now, to get through this meeting and 'abnormal' service can be resumed.

Colin's gaze shifted between me and the empty corner, torn between rationality and fear for my well-being. His analytical mind struggled with the inexplicable, but his empathy drove him to acknowledge the profound anguish I'd experienced.

"We should wrap things up and go," Colin suggests, uneasy. "You need to take it easy, and let's talk somewhere safer and more private—you know, just in case."

I agree, though I wasn't too happy about it. As we finished, I couldn't help but worry that I was the only one who could see the 'Whispering' man. I was determined to dig deeper, no matter how insane I looked or how far it took me into the darkness.

"24 hours earlier - 40 miles away in Rugby."

Moonlight shone through the curtains, unveiling a truly shocking crime scene. A blue and white strip of crime scene tape was draped across door number 17, with silver-plated embellishments and signs of a violent break-in. Forensics moved about detachedly. The constant clicks of the camera reverberated through the room, capturing the brutal details from many angles. A horrid stench of death filled the air. Gagging could be heard around the place. In the background, police radios hummed and fizzed.

DS Michael Dalton and I stood dejected, thinking, why the hell us again? Michael, unable to bear the overpowering stink, smothered Vaseline under his nostrils. No matter how much death he's come across, he was still uncomfortable whenever he got a whiff of a ripe corpse: that and the fact our sense of smell is off the charts since being supernatural.

The scene was a confusing puzzle. A ladder was strung up against the ceiling, a decaying corpse was suspended, and the chaos caused by messing up the lounge. We gawked at the disturbing sight. There are too many perplexing threads to untangle that linked the man's life and who may have wanted him dead. We were supposed to be recovering from our supposed break in Scotland, but that turned out to be anything but. Only to be summoned for another favour. They're bloody stacking up, and I still need a quiet little chat with our Mr Lock. DI Bainton, the man in charge of this constabulary, had an eerie feeling about this murder. It's not normal compared to his years of experience. He was right.

The double-locked front door was the first alarming detail. This confounding factor made it impossible for anyone normal to leave—arrive, yes, but not leave. The ladder was hooked through the gap in the bannisters, but not attached to anything. It defied the laws of physics and reasoning, spanning the ceiling with a noose dangling from it—a horrific call to the now motionless victim. DI Bainton was left wondering, grappling with a mystery that worried him.

Michael led the way for a change. I wasn't in the mood, not so soon. The tough rope fashioned into a noose was thick and strong. It encircled the victim's neck like a squeezing boa constrictor, painting a horrific picture.

Michael whispered as he drew near. "Georgie, do you see what I do?"

"I do, Michael. It's a freaky one."

Michael moved his flashlight across my face, creating eerie shadows as he spoke. "Locke's bill keeps getting bigger. How long do you think?"

I looked at the sick mosaic of death and suffering before us, attempting to understand the nightmarish tale imprinted in anguish and blood. "Judging from the body's condition, I would guess it has been here for about a week. The flies buzzing around the ruptured blood vessels and the bloated tongue that's been partially chewed off—it's fucking awful. This could be personal, Michael. It's possible the killer stayed to watch the life drain from the victim's eyes. And, it truly reeks."

Michael's face furrowed, looking the body up and down. "But, George, how? How could the killer do this? I mean, leave it like this? And why do you think they 'hung around' to watch? Know what I mean? Hung?"

I couldn't stop myself from letting out a low laugh at Michael's morbid humour. His words lingered. "I'm not sure. It's all too weird, and there is no evidence of a fight."

"I noticed that too. The whole thing is bloody ominous, matey, and we're being screwed. So, be careful, Georgie," Michael says, his voice tinged with concern.

My ears twitched, my eyes changing. Fortunately, I stopped before my red grew brighter, feeling something was amiss. "Shit... they haven't left... we are not alone, Michael. I sense it, or them. Something dark, evil, and pissed. I don't know why I'm picking up on it, but I am. The anger... it's terrifying, Michael... There's going to be another victim soon if there isn't one already."

As Michael's jaw dropped, we held our breath with dread as we continued our investigation. My hackles were going haywire, and I kept looking over my shoulder, expecting to see somebody there. As sure as the devil's death knell tolled its haunting chorus, there will be another, maybe many.

Before and After

3

'Present Day,'

Lingering on the image frozen in the CCTV still: a silhouette leaving the warm glow of the pub. But now, the narrative had changed. I knew my father couldn't have brought down that tough parade of scaffolding

Yet, as always with other mundanes, no one acknowledged the truth, which scared me. I've already told you that 'Weeping Willow' is different. Darker. I stand by what I said; I fear the death toll of this place will grow, leaning to what grabs attention by the balls or not.

Colin's medical snapshot had left an unforgettable mark on me, convincing that Father must have been driven to fear by something beyond his grasp. Father was fearless, except for one glaring exception: his arachnophobia, especially those awful hairy ones. Other than that, he was an unshakable pillar of strength, until he left me high and dry, with no answers. Did he even know or suspect that I was different? If he did, my lack of preparation for this dark world was unlike him. Which only deepened the mystery surrounding his sudden death.

Sitting in my car, looking over the file Colin had handed me, I can't shake that nursery rhymne I keep hearing, that's what Charlotte sung to the girls at bedtime. Resting on the passenger seat. Beside it lay Colin's newspaper, an accidental souvenir from earlier. It was the upper class Evening Standard, you know, the one with all the long words. It has immense reach and influence. In stark contrast, the article tucked in my coat pocket had to make do with the local rag, relegated to the thirteenth page, much like my father's tragic fate. Grappling with the cruel irony of why fate seemed so relentless in conspiring against my family.

The clock on the dashboard read 8:55 p.m. I hesitated outside my home before facing the music, still feeling burdened. I hadn't driven earlier, but nearing home, I remembered a half-litre bottle in the glove compartment—something that Charlotte would never condone.

The clapped-out Ford hatchback mirrored the chaos of my life, with empty crisp packets, crumpled newspapers, and discarded liquor bottles strewn inside. My car and life were in disarray, with little hope of redemption. Staring vacantly at the upright of the passenger seat, reminiscing. Charlotte sat there smiling in a bright lemon-yellow cardigan and white dress. Her image soon faded as passing headlights briefly shone against the rear window.

With that memory easing, I reached for the bottle, unscrewing the cap with a sense of resignation, and took a long, burning gulp. Attention returned to the front cover article, now shielded from judgmental eyes. Janice had been on the ball; I remember the man from the article clearly, much more than I'd let on earlier. It was a memory that was the sum of my torment, one I'd tried to bury.

The night air hung heavy with uncertainty as I contemplated the path ahead, knowing that answers were elusive and dangers lay hidden in the shadows.

'Before the hanging - One Week ago...'

I sat alone in the bar, nursing my drink, again wrestling with my thoughts. The pub was quiet and nearly empty. Here, I first noticed the figure in the worn navy coat. A frequent visitor seems to favour the solace of dark corners over the harsh lighting by the bar.

With his tired expression and unkempt look, the man spoke, breaking the silence with a request. "Hey buddy," he says, "do you have a light I can borrow? This thing has given up the ghost," he calls out, his voice carrying the weariness of a life filled with toil and hardship. I'd known of this man for a few weeks, but we only confined our exchanges to quick nods.

Hesitating as I contemplated whether to ignore the request. Careful not to reveal my hand too soon. This place was my secret base after a friend told him I might find the answers I was looking for here. But curiosity got the best of me. Pulling a white lighter from my pocket and handed it to the guy.

"Thanks, these stupid things always fail when you need them the most," the guy grumbled in frustration as he took the lighter. I couldn't help but chuckle, understanding.

"No problem at all. I go through half a dozen lighters a month. Keep it; I carry a spare anyway," I reply with a friendly smile, establishing a subtle connection with the stranger through our frustration.

The man, Frank, introduced himself, and as we spoke, the pub's subdued atmosphere provided a calm backdrop. Frank was drawn to the newspaper beneath my hand, his eyes glued to a specific article.

"Oh, is that today's?" Frank inquired, his eyes fixed on the paper.

My mind, swirling with decisions, shifted. At a crossroads, deciding whether to divulge information from the article to gauge Frank's reaction.

"Not today, I'm afraid. Just an old thing I had in the car. I was working on the crossword, but this article caught my eye," I explain, showing Frank the newspaper, ensuring the headline about a car crash on the M1 didn't go unnoticed.

Frank's reaction was immediate. His face paled, downing his drink in a hurry. I pressed, feigning curiosity, but our power dynamic shifted.

"You, okay? You look like you've seen a ghost," I remark, eyes fixed on Frank. Feeding on Frank's panic.

"Yeah, just tired," Frank trembled as he spoke.

I wasn't backing down and probing further, uncovering Frank's hidden truth.

"Are you sure? Your hand keeps shaking," I pointed, knowing what was happening to Frank while getting a little payback at the same time.

Frank brushed off the concern, but I didn't let up. I used what I already knew, drip-feeding snippets of information to put Frank on edge by highlighting his line of work and the extras he provides—like cleaning up after accidents, crushed vehicles, and dead bodies.

Frank was sweating. His drink was done. I went for the kill. Figuratively, but I was compelled to do it for real. The more I pushed, the faster my heart raced, flooded with adrenaline and anger that seemed to keep rising. An eerie shiver trickled down my neck as each word fired off.

A dark reflection drifted in the mirror, hooded with a large hat underneath. I glanced behind, but there was nothing. An icy breeze circled while my temper peaked.

"You don't know what you're talking about. Talk like that could get you in trouble, could even get you-"

"-what? Killed? Was that what you were about to say? A car travelling on the M1 broke, regaining control as a lorry swerved into their lane. Several curved rubber burns lined the road before the final skid. The car's braking momentum took it straight, and it would've been fine until the last hit. That last one swung left, skidding all the way. The car continued braking, holding straight until one final impact. The lorry's reflectors and part of its green and white side storage compartments lay by debris from the crumpled vehicle as the lorry escaped. Did Houdini drive it? Care to shed some light?"

Catching Frank off guard, with his shaking glass paused at his mouth. Frank didn't answer, finishing his drink before darting to the door. I gave him a moment to create some distance, not making it obvious to anyone else in the pub. Frank looked back, eyes wide with fear, before heading left.

Finishing my drink, I tucked the newspaper into my coat and slid off the chair to follow. The cool air whipped across my face, glimpsing a fast-walking Frank a hundred yards ahead. Frank wasn't a quick runner because of his cumbersome physique, which gave me the confidence to catch up and increased my pace.

Frank kept looking back, getting disoriented, stumbling from left to right before avoiding a lamppost when he faced the front again. Frank veered left, with pedestrian traffic thinning out. My brisk walk turned into a jog, closing in on Frank, who was getting into a white Capri.

"You didn't answer my question. Should I consider your behaviour guilty, or are you late for dinner?" I holler, buoyed by having Frank cornered and nearing. Frank struggles to unlock his door with shaking hands. He shakes and grinds the key on metal.

"You don't understand. Nothing is what it seems; if you push down this sadistic rabbit hole, all you'll find is trouble," Frank stutters, his face red. I rushed him against the car, gripping a squirming Frank by his throat scruff. Filled with hate, face boiling a dark red, on the verge of doing something stupid.

"Trouble ripped away the best things in my life. I may as well say it's already found me. So, what's stopping me from choking you out right now?" Gripping tighter. Flashing images of Charlotte buzzed in my mind, spurring me on. Then I heard the screeching tyres and crumpling metal. I shudder, clenching my eyes to shake off the noise.

"What would your kids think if they heard? Or your dear old mother? There are things in this world you don't want to mess with; this is one of them because this shit doesn't belong in this world," Frank choked on my grip. Stunned, quiet, not relenting in my pressure, nails biting into Frank's flesh, but Frank made me think.

That shiver skated across my neck as the icy wind followed. My eyes drifted near the car window, releasing a gasp of shock. He was there again, his reflection anyway, that scary hooded figure with the enormous hat pulled over the face. 'The Whisper man'. Distracted, I released my grip to turn around.

Nobody was there, so Frank fought his way into the car, jamming it locked. We stared at each other, and the car rumbled to life, filling the air with petrol fumes, with me reeling in confusion. Although I couldn't see anything, my body felt it, and the hairs on my neck shook, sensing a presence nearby.

Frank's car screeched away from the curb, leaving me in the shadowed street, breath visible in the cool night air. The encounter shook me and filled me with an unsettling mixture of anger and confusion. I couldn't believe how quickly things had escalated, and the mysterious figure with the hooded hat only added to the unease.

Composing myself, realising that I'd come close to losing control. My temper had flared, and I contemplated doing something irreversible. It was a stark reminder of the darkness that brewed within, and I needed to be careful.

The icy wind swelled around, and I couldn't shake the thought of being watched. Looking around the lonely street, there was no sign of the hooded figure. I gathered my thoughts with a deep breath, attempting to make sense of everything that had happened. Unable to ignore Frank's warning, even if it was vague. Something deeper at play may have already claimed the lives of those I cared about.

Tape One

4

'present day,'

It was quiet, disrupted only by the 9 o'clock news. Cigarette smoke meandered through the hallway, searching for the draft that was ushered through. I slung my coat on the hook, and keys clattered into a multicoloured dish on the side table that Charlotte dared to make in one of the few pottery classes she stuck to before realising how boring it was. My footsteps betrayed any attempt at sneaking in, creaking floorboards wailing through the hall.

It was 9:01 p.m., a minute past the childish deadline, and I knew judgment would follow soon. Mother's words, "Your priority should be the girls," tormented every step, a reminder of where my obligations lay as a single parent. I can't help but feel a little patronised. I'm the only one who hasn't given up the search for the truth while juggling everything. And the constant, nagging noise in my head.

"Is that you, Gerald?" Mother's voice, half-engrossed in the flickering television, called out.

"Yes, Mum, it's me. Who else would it be?" I reply, weary from a long day and no closer to the truth. I knew what would come next: the well-meaning but stifling advice. The kind I wasn't in the mood for. My experience at the pub went a step further than what's gone on lately. Those photos, I can't believe it. Why weren't we shown them at the time? Bloody sick. I walked slowly, delaying as long as possible.

"Oh, I don't know, Gerald. Why don't you fucking let me in, and let's find out."

Mother's voice was different and cold, like the whispers and Janice at the pub. I stopped dead. My throat dried up; I struggled to respond. A dribble of sweat bobbled on my brow.

"WH... What? What did you say, Mum?" I could barely talk; fear and confusion had set in. Okay, it was more like it had returned home like me, having moved in a while now.

"I said...Your priority should be the girls, not chasing shadows. Christ, are you okay, Gerald? See, I knew all the extra strain you've piled on would get to you." Mother's words echoed, all back to normal but full of worry. The mention of shadows sent an involuntary shiver down my spine, forcing a glance over my shoulder and questioning if I'd heard the different voice at all or whether it was in my head.

I kicked off my shoes, each thud a heavy exclamation of my arrival. Oooh, that immediate feeling of shoeless feet, curling the toes in freedom. It's so soothing, especially after another shit day. A pile of mail on the table beckoned; there was a small, unassuming yellow 'jiffy' package, no larger than an A5 sheet and two inches thick. My name was stuck across the front, a pre-typed label. The imprint around the package resembled a cassette tape, filling me with dread. Who would send a tape? My head was racing, seeking answers where there were none.

"Oh yes, that came around 3 o'clock," Mother says. "I was just returning from the baker's with the girls when I caught a Royal Mail delivery guy about to leave a card. It needed signing for."

Turning the package over, I heard a faint rattle from within. My heart quickened, and I glanced up at the mirror, catching a fleeting glimpse of a dark shadow darting past.

"Did Dad ever mention attending any... private parties or meetings?" I ask, hesitating, afraid of what might be revealed. The package in hand rattled again, and a sense of impending doom settled in.

"Well, he had his nights out," Mother began, her voice carrying the tone of reminiscing, "like anyone else. We weren't joined at the hip just because we were married. But as far as I know, nothing is out of the ordinary. No secret swingers' clubs or anything."

Her words made me recoil at the thought, but I had to ask to delve into my father's past, even if it meant confronting uncomfortable truths.

"Oh, come off it!" Mother retorts, unable to hide her amusement. "We were young once, too, you know. Did you think your generation invented the seedy stuff like sex, drugs, and rock and roll?"

"Again, with the sex stuff, Mum," I mutter, thoughts consumed by the mysterious package. "Seriously, though, has Dad ever seemed worried about anything? Anything at all that struck you as odd?"

Mother didn't respond. She stood by the kettle, her hand poised over the switch, her face a mask of contemplation. Her hand trembled, mirroring the unease that I had sensed.

My fingers gripped an open edge of the package, ready to tear into it. When I remembered Frank's ominous warning: "There are things in this world you don't want to mess with." I had ordered nothing, and my gut tells me I had to continue.

The sound of a spoon clinking against a teacup filled the air as Mother refocused on the clock. She took a deep breath and carried my coffee into the lounge before grabbing her handbag and keys.

"Right, I'm off," Mother announced, her smile forced as she came over to kiss me. I look up from the package to see mother... I jump back, my hand shakes...I nearly dropped what was in my hands. Mother's face had changed. Like Janice, mottled grey flesh, blood oozed from her eyes and mouth. She looked dead, and I was terrified. Not only about what I was seeing, but about everything. My mind was cracking. Or felt so. Mother breezed closer. I could smell the overwhelming stench of decomposing flesh, blood and, oddly but no less scary, the sweet toxicity of embalming fluid. I clench my eyes tight. My feet won't move, and I can't seem to tilt my head further away. It's cold, oh so cold...

"Oi... Come here, you daft sod... You're never too old for a kiss from your mum." My eyes bolt open, Mother was back to normal. My heart wouldn't stop thumping. "Now. Remember to drop the girls off on your way to work and ensure you go. I hear the new boss isn't as friendly as the old one."

I smiled and nodded, shaking off the endless nightmare. My attention went back to the package. Mother noticed and rolled her eyes before heading for the door.

"It's probably just a video Charlotte ordered for the girls," Mother suggests, her voice fading as she leaves. "Don't stress too much about it."

Of course, I knew she was right, but I couldn't shake an odd feeling. I tore the cassette tape open with trembling hands and stepped into the lounge. My eyes widened, staring at an ordinary cassette tape with a white sticky label—one of those you buy to record a show or movie you might miss. But it was the red felt-tip handwriting that left me stunned.

"Things you need to know–Tape One," the words taunted. It was father's handwriting. "What the hell?" I mutter, trying to understand how it was possible.

The mention of "Tape One" has me wondering if more tapes were coming, but my thoughts kept returning to Frank and his ominous warning.

The Fate of Eckleston

5

'One Week Ago,'

Frank Ecklestone finally made it home in the dead of night, fear gnawing at his sanity. His white Capris roared into Berkley Square, Rugby, its engine growling like a beast through the stillness, spewing exhaust fumes into the cold air. Frank swung his door open, his fingers trembling as they fumbled with the keys before he flicked the engine off. Eventually, he summoned the energy to stumble from his seat, drenched in panic sweat, eyes darting left to right, probing the shadows. The harsh streetlight glow revealed his pale, terror-stricken face, eaten alive by paranoia. The confrontation with the stranger at the bar replayed in his mind, a grim reminder of everything he'd been running from, the secrets he dreaded being uncovered, and what he'd had to do.

Little did he know, the killer was waiting, concealed in the inky darkness of the far-right corner just behind unkempt bushes. Their head tilted, a wicked smile dancing at the corners of their lips. The killer relished Frank's palpable terror, savouring every cloudy, rasping breath escaping his frightened mouth. Frank, scrambling and muttering, **"I said nothing; nobody knows anything. He knows nothing. Just thinks he does."** His voice quivered like a leaf in the wind. The car door slammed shut, echoing through the quiet cul-de-sac. Frank stumbled over the curb leading to the communal door of Berkley House. His frantic pace outwitted the sturdiness of his feet, moving as if his life depended on it, still looking behind and seeing nothing.

Inside, Frank made a beeline for his second-floor apartment, number 17. His shaking hands fumbled with his keys, casting nervous glances over his shoulder. Unbeknownst to him, the killer followed, slithering silently at an ominous distance. Frank hesitated at his doorway, eyes scanning the dim corridor behind him. Shielded in the shadows, the killer slipped stealthily along the darkened walls, drifting up the stairs with eerie grace once Frank was inside.

His coat was thrown onto a chair, keys tossed onto a cluttered table, and Frank's trembling fingers reached for a beer to soothe his nerves. He glanced at the ladder and the old gym rope propped against the wall beside the silver fridge, remembering another job he hadn't got around to yet. For the first time in a while, he felt safe—until now. Its presence served as a stark reminder of his constant need to be ready to escape. The end window offered a route down to a flat-roofed bin shed, but he hadn't figured out the logistics beyond tying the rope around the nearest supporting pillar and hoping for the best with the ladder. Handy work like this was never Frank's forte.

He'd managed eighteen months in this place, the longest so far, yet it was his fourth move in five years, as the shadows of his past sins still clung to him. His mind was a breeding ground for ghosts, regrets, and unrelenting torment. The killer understood this all too well, revelling in Frank's plight. With some false reassurance, Frank moved around his flat, checking the place over, muttering like a madman, **"Just a passing phase,"** whispers that lacked the courage of their conviction. Deep down, he knew the stranger's prodding was much more than that. **"He'll get bored and go away ... just clutching at straws, he knows fuck all."**

Frank finally settled into his worn recliner, hoping to relax with any old crap on TV. Suddenly, a loud clap shattered the silence like a balloon popping, plunging the room into darkness. Frank fumbled his beer, spilling it onto the floor. Each drop echoed creepily, teasing the last of Frank's intact nerves. The situation worsened when the fleeting headlights of a passing car cast obscure shadows across the room, briefly revealing the killer's menacing silhouette.

His hand spasmed open in fear, and the beer bottle slipped from Frank's already shaky grasp, shattering into a million pieces. Frank froze. His throat tightened, and his breath became shallow. The ladder he had planned to use for escape was miraculously gone. All Frank could do was mutter, **"I'm fucked,"** a grim truth that the killer savoured. The killer knew they had plenty of time, remaining in the shadows, relishing Frank's rabbit-in-headlights terror. The silence was broken only by the erratic rhythm of Frank's frantic, wheezy breathing. His eyes darted around the room, clinging to the irrational hope that the ladder had somehow moved itself to the window, ready to save him. His pulse pounded in his ears, and cold sweat streamed down his forehead. Frank desperately needed to scream for help, hoping a neighbour would hear, but his vocal cords were paralysed with fear, rendering him a silent, terrified mute.

Amidst his desperation, Frank did the only thing that came to mind. Using a frayed fingernail, he began carving into his arm. Blood oozed from each slice, dripping quicker with each stroke. Finally, he spelt out the word, **"B ... O...O...K,"** his vision blurred with pain. He was too disoriented to notice the gym rope slithering on the floor, manipulated by the killer like a sinister snake charmer. Frank stayed frozen, helpless, resigned to his fate or perhaps too exhausted from years of running to fight. In the looming darkness, he trembled in the face of the unspeakable horror that awaited. The rope continued its eerie dance, its rough twine brushing against Frank's arm before coiling itself around his neck, not once but twice. It tightened with a relentless grip, choking the life out of him. Frank's mouth gaped open, his swollen tongue turning a shade of purple, his eyes bulging with terror. He dangled in the air, suspended by the merciless twine, his life slipping away.

The killer remained unmoved, an embodiment of evil, as they watched Frank's futile struggle. Moonlight filtered through the window, casting irregular ripples of light across the room, revealing a shadowy figure steeped in darkness, focused on their grotesque work. Blood seeped from Frank's mouth, eye sockets, and the gash on his arm, yet no one could witness his agony. No front door slammed shut, and no cries for help echoed through the neighbouring apartments. The killer faded into the night, leaving behind only Frank's lifeless body, swaying in the moonlight like a puppet of horror. Blood dribbled from his pale, swollen face. He'd met a gruesome end, with one last message carved into his flesh. But who was it for?

The Tape that Keeps Giving

6

'Gerald-Présent Day,'

My hands shook, holding the tape. Hypnotised, drawn in by my father's vivid handwriting, I didn't know what to think or feel at that moment other than dread. The room shrank, shadows crawling from every recess as I grappled with the cassette.

With the waning echoes of the news, the onrushing radiance of **"Halloween III - Season of the Witch"** cast an eerie, shifting light across the room. Much to Charlotte's irritation, I have a penchant for horror and gore. No matter how often I'd seen them, my morbid fascination persisted. With how weird my life has been, you'd think I'd be put off by that stuff. Not in the slightest. The urge to immerse myself in the mindless violence of a movie tugged at me. A chance to escape, even for a few minutes. Life had become a nightmarish, low-budget flick, with the mysterious tape occupying the spotlight as a fucked up, ill-timed prop.

Why now? Would I be sent such a thing a year after my father's death? There were no doubts. It was his handwriting, so how was it possible? This played on my mind, begrudgingly sipping tepid coffee, unwilling to let mother's efforts go to waste. Not that she'd know, but I would feel bad. It took all of five minutes before, eventually, I decided there was only one thing to do if I wanted to know. Abandoning my seat, gliding across the cold, unyielding hardwood floor, hand shaking.

An adrenaline surge, it seemed, struggling with the unfamiliar tremors ripping through my body. After all, the situation was hardly normal. I continued, eager to uncover the significance behind my father's decision to make a tape. With the cassette in place, I retreated to the safety of the sofa, fingers wrapped around the remote. Caution to the wind, I mutter, "Fuck it." With an unsteady finger pressing play, the VCR whirred to life, emitting a clunky hum. Unless the recorder's settings were off, Father had recorded this tape a year before he'd died. Making the situation more bizarre than I realised.

The black screen morphed into this fierce, grainy grey and showed Father looking messy. His once crisp blue-and-white striped shirt was now all loose, and a dark blue tie hung loose. His shirt's top button was undone, and his usual slicked-back hair was messy.

"Can you hear me? Can you see me?" Father's eyes darted above the screen, and it appeared he was talking with someone just off-camera. With a forced smile, Father was uneasy as he spoke. Perched on the edge of my seat, my shaking hand urged switching drinks for something stronger.

Pausing the tape, I reached for a hidden whiskey bottle buried under a stack of magazines. It was a reflex, a habit I couldn't let go. Mother had been pouring any bottles she found down the drain. But I kept a few stashed away for a rainy day or a shit one like today. Finding comfort lingering on the memories of Charlotte and father. I poured a shot into my coffee, prepared myself for what would be revealed, and hit play again.

"Hey Gerald, it's your dear old dad. Shit, how stupid of me; of course, you can see me," Father's voice quivered. I imagine a million thoughts racing through your mind, questioning why I sent you a bloody tape. If you're watching this, I'm gone, and it's down to you, I'm afraid.

The tears were coming; I paused again, mirroring how Father looked. I wanted to savour Father's weathered image, still finding it hard to believe, when I noticed an unsettling presence lurking in the periphery. At first, it appeared to be a shadow, but it didn't seem right, though no other voices were heard. The image was faint but detailed enough to resemble a human figure. Hesitating, wiping my face, legs shaking with stomach-churning anxiety before the tape restarted. The unsettling shadow held my attention now. The harder I looked, leaning as far forward as possible without falling off my seat, the air filled with bone-chilling fear. Common sense said to stop, but I couldn't. Maybe there's 'answers I need,' I thought, hand trembling a little more. Before realising it, it was the same as I've been seeing. 'Him'.. Yet, I couldn't figure out why it was on the tape.

Father continues, heavily laden with remorse, "... We tried our best to shield you all, but it wasn't enough. I inherited something from my father when he passed; sadly, it wasn't anything good. Your Nana has all those crazy stories about ghosts and things, but it has been her way of coping with reality. We are fucking cursed, son," Father muttered. His voice grew shakier the more he spoke. Wide-eyed with shock, nausea slowly welling up as those words sank in. 'we are fucking cursed,' Stunned, remembering the village gossip; now it doesn't sound so farfetched.

"From what I know, we're bound to an old book or some crazy connection to its contents—no idea what kind, only that it's full of fucked up demonic shit. The mere idea of it terrifies the heck out of me. Thanks to our ancestors, we were expected to carry out unimaginable acts, but I can't ... I cannot... I... I... I'll stop babbling until I know more. I need you to keep you and your family bloody safe; I love you, son."

The tape ended, leaving me in creepy silence, dropping the remote. How could such a dark secret have been kept for so long? Frank's words of caution haunted my thoughts. And now this. 'Did my father know Frank or of him?' piecing together a nightmarish puzzle, and it terrified me. No matter how freaked out I was, my eyes stayed fixated on the now black screen. With each sip of coffee, the room seemed to grow colder. I briskly rubbed my arms as a shiver rumbled through me. A coat of goose pimples erupted over my skin while I was unnerved by the feeling that someone other than my father was looking back at him through the TV.

My haze drifted deep in thought, only to be abruptly snapped back by a jarring noise—a loud clap. It echoed through the air. Eyes fixed ahead, frozen. The shadow thumped against the TV like a scene from a horror movie; then came its bone-chilling laughter, curdling through my ears. My temporary paralysis subsided, throwing myself backwards onto the sofa. My reflection appeared on the screen, too, warped amidst the shadowy outline.

'**C o m e ... o n ... G e r - ald...I'm...right...here...all...you...have...to...do...is...let...me...in. Henry wouldn't want you to be lonely. Let the darkness in, and you will never be alone again,**'

It was him, the 'Whisper man', but how? How did he fit into my father's narrative? Weeping, mournful cries surfaced, this time rumbling with a crackle through the aged television speakers. Searing heat tormented my eyes at the sight of me in the hood. The surrounding air had turned icy now, and my breath hung like a mist.

'What the fuck is going on?' gasping, breaths caught in my throat. It seemed my father and I may have shared a common torment.

The Shadows

7

'Gerald-The Next Morning,'

The clock's merciless hands clung to 7:49 a.m. I woke with a start, my body riddled with aches from the twisted position. I fell asleep on the tattered sofa. Pain radiated through me, a reminder of the previous night's indulgence—a half-empty bottle of 'Jack' and a drained cup, both accomplices to my throbbing hangover.

Bright wintery daylight pierced through the unshaded garden windows, its merciless rays assaulting my sensitive eyes. With mounting anxiety, I was running late, and the next half-hour became a chaotic whirlwind. Olivia and Lacey were jolted awake from their dreams, scrambling to prepare them for the day. This morning routine was a never-ending battle, especially for me raising two-year-old twins. The mission was to deliver the girls to his mother's house, a mere ten-minute drive, and then navigate the morning traffic to work by 9 a.m.

Luckily, the girls looked so alike that I got away with dressing them in the same outfits. But today, there were mismatched socks, which added to the chaos. The only way to tell them apart was by their hairstyles. Charlotte had always been the one to weave their hair into intricate braids skilfully, a tradition now carried on by Mother. All thumbs, I used hair bands or clips for simplicity, particularly on busy mornings.

Scrambling to collect the last of my checklist and muttering about shoes, coats, and keys. With a weary sigh, the front door swung open, slapped by the cool rush of air against my face. Last night was hazy. Shrouded in a thick fog, especially after the encounter with the tape. Thoughts were tangled, a chaotic web of unanswered questions. With only scattered papers strewn across the mahogany coffee table as evidence of my restless search for clarity. Hoping some memories would pop up during the day. Or after a much-needed coffee boost.

While extending a polite morning nod to Mr Hanson, an older neighbour, I couldn't help but notice the dryness in my throat. Our interactions never ventured beyond these courteous greetings, and I was preoccupied with thoughts of the tape. Fumbling through a jangling racket of keys, my heart raced as I discovered something perplexing.

A small, puzzling detail—a dark red stain marring the surface of my car key. It resembled blood, its sticky texture clinging to my fingertips as I tried to make sense of it. The small pool was deceptive, starting with a lighter hue and gradually turning into a menacing, viscous substance.

Even in the darkened hallway, I would've noticed. Frowning, I swiftly double-checked my hands, relieved to find no cuts or injuries, not even under my gnawed-down nails. The twins were getting impatient and crankier in the morning cold, so I had to get going. The only bright side is the crisp freshness of dewy grass.

I hastily unlock the car, in a hurry to leave. I tuck the twins safely in their chairs, my mind swirling with questions about the bloodstain. Before leaving, I briskly scoured through the street, momentarily lost in the picturesque scene bathed in the morning sun, rooftops shimmering above.

However, an ominous presence lurked silently in the shade. A dark, dirt-caked saloon car with a cracked windshield was trailing behind, its engine growling ominously. A man in his late forties dressed inconspicuously. His facial hair balanced between a 5 o'clock shadow and a beard, giving him a ruggedly indifferent look—with an angry intensity simmering underneath. I caught a glimpse as I swept around the first corner but thought little of it during the ten-minute drive, keeping a two-car gap.

Until we neared the last set of traffic lights just before my turn onto Merkfield Avenue, my eyes darted towards the twins for a split second, making sure they were safe, catching sight of the pursuing saloon boldly running a red light, aggressively speeding up close, too close. The saloon's chassis shook violently as the driver fought to regain control, gaining ground on me.

'What the bloody hell is he doing?' I gasped, hearing the rabid throttle of the engine gaining quickly. My stomach tightened, approaching my parents' home.

With no idea what to do, my heart was pounding. Mindful with Olivia and Lacey in the car. 'It's okay, babies; daddy will have you with Nanna soon.' I cooed at them through the rearview, albeit with gritted teeth, catching sight of the saloon again. I was sweating buckets.

'Let me in, Gerald. We can end him and you won't need to be scared.' I twisted up my neck, shaking it off, I didn't need him right now. It was hard enough to concentrate as it is.

Nobody in their right mind would take such risks during the day, yet I was being chased by some maniac on four wheels with a death wish. 'He's flipping crazy.' I mutter, tightening my grip on the steering wheel. Fear and disbelief buzzed inside a horrible hive of emotions.

Nearing Merkfield, this was the one opportunity to outrun the relentless saloon. 'Hang on tight babies, Daddy's got this,' Bracing myself before throwing the car into a sudden tyre-screeching left turn. The saloon followed suit, misjudging the angle. A loud crunch of metal rang out as the saloon smashed my bumper. Tyres squealed with pain, and the saloon was sent into an uncontrollable spin.

In seconds, the narrow street was filled with the loud chaos of rubber tearing across the concrete. The saloon gradually regained control, veering right, ploughing over a metal signpost and dragging it underneath them. Turning into the spin, my body tossed around like a rag doll, the smell of burnt rubber filling my nostrils.

My car stopped, crashing into a tree, the nearside door wedged tightly, refusing to budge. Olivia and Lacey were shaken but thankfully unhurt in the back seat. 'Who the hell was that?' breathing a sigh of relief, knowing it could have been far worse. The pursuing saloon vanished into the distance, leaving behind a trail of shattered glass, twisted metal, and a broken lamppost.

'It's okay, babies. We're at Nanna's now,' I reassure the girls. Even if they didn't understand, I felt guilty they'd been caught up in whatever this disaster was—sitting there, struggling to compose amidst the chaos consuming the once-serene Merkfield Avenue. Within moments, Mother sprinted from her home at number 18, hurrying to lend a hand. She knew I was due soon with a habit of running late, but she didn't expect to find me sprawled by a tree, face pale and sweaty.

A chilling fear took root as Mother drew nearer. Her eyes darted left to right toward the main road, looking for more. Of what, though? Either way, it felt darker and more terrifying than I expected—Father's cryptic warning had become a nightmare.

A SERAL KILLER IN WILLOWBROOK

8

'Gerald,'

My agitated pacing back and forth echoed through the kitchen. Trembling hands shattered any appearance of composure I tried to maintain. When we were done with the wreckage outside, and safely in Mother's place, it wasn't hard to sense an already thick tension in the air.

My worry intensified. For a while now, I've battled with the feeling mother knew more than she was letting on. Now though, she was on edge. Everything seemed to happen at once—the cryptic videotape playing on repeat, the car chase growing more intense by the second, and the whispers echoing in my ears centred around my glimpses of 'the whispering man'.

My judgment felt 'skewed', but I held onto a glimmer of hope that Mother would finally give some answers I desperately needed. Things could've ended far worse, especially having the girls with me. But she wasn't talking, though, not yet. Her eyes darted nervously around the room, looking anywhere but at me.

If Mother wasn't forthcoming, I had to find out for myself. Snooping around to satisfy curiosity. I'd always considered myself open to supernatural and bizarre things, but this experience surpassed my wildest imagination.

In the video, Father had hinted at a mysterious legacy, speaking about a book handed down through generations. I wondered where the book might be. Curiosity grew as I considered the possibility that it was real. The sight of Father's shaky hands and wide eyes clarified it had to be. So, where was it? And what exactly did he mean by 'bound'? Compelled or obligated to follow certain rules or expectations? My head was all over the place trying to piece the information together when I saw an envelope among the rum bottles.

It had been opened recently and had a peculiar crimson wax seal with a mysterious symbol. Everything about it seemed eerie, and judging by the smudged lipstick on the glass, the contents weren't much better. It was early, and Mother had already started drinking. That wasn't her; she'd lectured me enough lately. For her to crack open, the rum was bad.

With a loud clanking that broke my stare, Mother returned to the table with two cups of coffee. She'd seen me looking at the symbol, causing her lips to tremble. She went to speak but paused before taking a deep breath. "You might as well see for yourself," she says, slowly sipping her coffee. Her cheeks became flustered.

I quickly grabbed the envelope. Its texture beneath my trembling fingers had a certain elegance, a sophistication that was absent from the typical cheap ones from the post office. But as the symbol on the seal caught the sunlight, its design appeared eerily captivating.

A goat's head was nestled within a five-pointed star in the centre of a double-lined circle. Perhaps there was some truth to his theories on occultism. The inner and outer rings are filled with mysterious glyphs and symbols, adding an air of mysticism. My eyes dart to Mother for inspiration, any signs of recognition or understanding in her expression.

Mother's voice shuddered as she finally spoke up. "It's not what you think," she gushes, her eyes filled with a haunting sadness that seemed to linger.

My finger delicately traced the seal's smooth contours, savouring the anticipation before cautiously opening the envelope. Inside, there was a slender slip of paper, and then I found what caused Mother's need to drink. Gruesome was an understatement and defied belief—a two-inch by two-inch piece of flesh scarred with the same sinister symbol—bloody human flesh.

"Goddamn," I choked out, reeling at the horror. The raised lines formed a grotesque pattern that had me at a loss. 'What the hell were my parents into? And why now?' That was all I could think about. I turned to Mother, looking for answers.

"I wouldn't call it 'godly.' But you're not far off," she whispers, her voice heavy and emotional. I could see tears bubbling at the corners of her eyes. "I'm so sorry, Gerald. We didn't want this for you."

"Whose flesh is this? How did this happen? Why?" The questions poured out, each more bewildering than the last.

Mother struggled to find words, her voice barely a whisper. "While I may not have all the answers, I know that mole. It was on his lower back. Your father shielded us from so many things for our well-being. He'd been better prepared for this world than you before his father's passing. With a deep loathing, he grappled with the idea of this legacy becoming your responsibility, striving to break the curse that had haunted his ancestors. Shortly before his death, he mentioned a searing, burning sensation in his back. Still, he refused to let me or anyone look at it. Now we know why," she says, stuttering, holding back the urge to full-on 'ugly cry.'

My mind spun. Thoughts shifting towards the safety of Olivia and Lacey, they, too, could be at risk.

"I got to protect my daughters." If all of this is true, I can't allow the same darkness that had consumed my father's life to threaten what's left of my family.

Mother retrieved a newspaper hidden in a drawer and placed it before me. The headline rocked me backwards in my seat: "A Serial Killer Stalks Willowbrook?" it read. The article detailed a second gruesome death in less than two weeks—a trucker with ties to Willowbrook was torn apart.

My heart thumped as I saw the truck fronts in the accompanying photograph. It was one of the rowdy group from the pub, one I'd suspected of Charlotte's accident.

"Gerald ... Did you go out last night?" Mother asks softly, her heavy voice sounding worried.

"No, never; why are you asking and showing that?" I reply, unease deepening. Not that I could remember after the horrifying tape. "Do you know who tried to kill me today?" I ask, thoughts returning to the car chase and the blood on the key. Then the newspaper again.

"I do not know, but all of this terrifies me. Are you sure you didn't go anywhere at all?" Mother asks again, her voice quivering. I didn't understand why she'd ask.

Feeling confused. "I'm bloody sure; why the hell are you asking that? You don't seriously think I could do that?" Did my mother suddenly think I was a killer? She'd never questioned me before. Why now? Whether it was that emotions were running high or she was holding something back. I found her behaviour odd and slightly unnerving. Considering I held an envelope containing human flesh, that said a lot.

"I don't know. It's odd timing, and the little I knew from your father made me think he was some contract assassin or something. But I can't bear the thought of anything happening to you and the girls. This family has already endured too much loss." Mother gushes while she refuses to make eye contact. There was more, but I didn't push. The idea of my father as an assassin brought a slight chuckle. The only thing I'd seen him kill was a fry-up on a Sunday. However, there was more to him than I'd realised. Perhaps I never knew my father if he could keep these secrets for so long. A curse and a strange wax symbol. What's next?

O'Hanlon Crime Scene

9

'Détective Reynolds,'

Here we were, on the way to another crime scene. If there's one constant in my life, it's murder. I needed time before more of it. My head was still in Scotland, taking on vampires. How that ended has me in limbo and I fear they're not done with us. All I wanted was to go home, invite Ellena over and lock ourselves away for at least a week. Seems the moment we get close, death pulls us apart. There's no escaping it. Now was no different. Our unmarked rumbled through the rugged, twisting streets of Newport's industrial estate, tyres thudding against the pavement. The atmosphere in the car was tense as Michael and I exchanged worried glances. We were on our way to O'Hanlon's Haulage, a well-known company in the village and the transportation industry.

Our arrival in the small village has so far been met with a cautious silence, the lingering unease of the first murder casting a shadow over the community. The local folks were left bewildered by the murder, unable to grasp its bizarre nature, as a growing dread filled the air.

As we approached O'Hanlon, there was no hiding our apprehension. It was already 1 in the morning. When security patrolled, they saw the company gates wide open. In the cold, unforgiving night, the security team stumbled upon the lifeless body of a forty-five-year-old man. He was torn in two, his lifeless limbs bound to the merciless grills of two massive lorries.

I gazed at the path, my thoughts consumed by fear and curiosity. I questioned whether we were walking into a nightmare from which there was no escape. For such a small place, it's attracting a hell of a lot of trouble and I fear a repeat of Scotland. Not that I'm telling Michael that. This case was already pushing me to my breaking point.

The silver spikes, resembling skeletal fingers, cast eerie shadows as we loomed closer to the gates. I rolled down my window, picking up on the putrid odour that overwhelmed my senses. It was the smell of blood, thick and cloying, saturating the air.

"You getting that, Georgie?" Michael asks, his voice tense, his nostrils twitching as he revels in the stink.

"Afraid so. Lots of it, too," I reply, unable to hide the strain in my voice.

"You sensed anyone or anything else yet?" Michael inquired, his eyes scanning our surroundings.

"Sadly, Michael," I sigh, "this is strikingly similar to the previous one. Aside from the chaotic chemo signals standing around waiting for the miracle of a body reattaching itself, I haven't picked up on anything else. Not even faint."

I was tense and full of frustration. My unique abilities have been a double-edged sword, captivating and tormenting me simultaneously. Sensing things that others can't isn't always a good thing. However, this gift has become a burden of late, darker since all the bone crunching I had to do. Michael and I made unique partners in our fight against all that goes bump in the night. If only we could catch a break.

"You're making it sound like the victim strapped himself to both trucks, and the lorries magically reversed on their own," Michael's scepticism was clear, but he was also in denial. Scotland got to him, too.

I smirked at Michael's comment, even allowing a sly smile, but my eyes betrayed a lack of joy. It wasn't only the vampires that raised the bar; it was Ruth and the magic she could do, which meant the lorries magically assisting wouldn't seem so far-fetched. Only I wasn't so sure Willowbrook wanted their supernatural sins laid bare.

When we arrived, the coroner's van was already on the scene, casting a long shadow over the gruesome picture. A short man with a slightly larger build, the coroner appeared uneasy, his face reflecting the horror before him, looking anxious. He, no doubt, has seen many things in his line of work, but this was different.

Stepping out of the vehicle, Michael and I swiftly flashed our warrant cards at the police officer managing the scene cordon. The Blue-white tape parted, and we slinked forward, our senses on guard for a repeat of the last scene, being watched. Something evil drenched the ground we walked upon in blood.

I whisper to Michael as we approach the body, "Nothing yet." But then, an involuntary shudder courses through me, and I reach for the back of my neck. Michael experiences it, too, a disquieting sensation that makes his skin prickle.

"That was strange," he says, his eyebrows furrowing in confusion. Wait up, check out your 9 o'clock. Michael whispered, his eyes darting around the scene as he noticed the two guys in black suits and ties who did not look like detectives.

I followed his gaze and saw two mid-thirties men dressed impeccably in dark suits, their polished shoes clicking on the pavement. They stood out, and their presence was a strange one, considering the morbid scene. I couldn't shake the unsettling sensation that something was off about them, Michael too, causing a chill to creep down our spines.

A distance away, the two men watched the unfolding scene with fixed eyes, acting as if they were mere onlookers, rather than the feeling I was getting. One held onto a small black book with obsessive enthusiasm, while the other jotted down notes in a black pocket-sized notebook.

I ask, whispering, "Are they watching us?"

"Yeah, but trying not to be obvious," Michael replies, his voice filled with caution. "But begs the question, how long they've been here, watching the body? It doesn't seem to faze or concern them."

My unease was growing, the hairs on the back of my neck standing on end. "I don't like this, Michael. I don't like this at all. We are missing some big 'dots.' This village isn't as innocent as it appears. I need to check whether there is a heat path around the cabs and body."

To most, the yard appeared indistinguishable from its gravelly surface, marked by the haphazard footprints of officers and onlookers. As I looked around, I could see the heat signatures left behind by others, giving me an insight into what was fresh and what was not.

"Hurry," the old git whispers, his eyes flickering to the watchful, unknown figures. "Photographs are being taken, and the flash is dancing like a playful toy."

Crouching down, I shudder at the chill of the cold ground against my fingertips. My eyes flashed blood red, and I could suddenly see the hidden world beyond the perception of anyone else. This was one trick I was glad to have in my supernatural arsenal. Heat streaks marked the raised layers of crumbled stone, a haunting reminder of the violence and brutality unfolding. I could see the power, the force that had torn a man in two, and it churned my stomach.

While investigating the scene, I wondered, 'What will it be this time? The Kanaima was dangerous, the vampires thought. They're the deadliest and I still think the big battle is still to come. "

Michael was about to turn back to me, thinking he had given me enough time, when I saw him check out those two guys. He'd noticed movement. One of them adjusted his suit jacket collar, causing his shirt cuff to slide forward. Unusual cufflinks were unveiled, showcasing a round symbol depicting two knights on black horses, each carrying shields decorated with crosses.

However, what stood out was the circular black pin or badge discreetly tucked under the collar lapel of a particular man. The emblem, an old-style Red Cross, mirrored the design on the cufflinks.

Watching Michael's face, deep in thought (that's when his forehead wrinkles clap together) he thought they were familiar but couldn't recall its meaning. Michael leaned close to me and whispers, "Georgie, have you finished?"

Still crouched, I reply, "Yeah, still nothing, and it's getting annoying ... wait... the blood splatter, the pattern changes. Fuck, it's everywhere because the killer wanted it to be. The blood is in a symbol, the five-point star in a circle. Satan." My voice stretched an octave in shock.

"You've got to be kidding me ... and as if things couldn't become any stranger or worse... there's another factor we may need to explore," Michael remarked, his voice low and tinged with exasperation. "If that's about the devil, do you know anything in that encyclopaedia brain of yours, on the intricacies of religious beliefs?"

I shrug, but intrigued. The cross, Christ, and the church. Why does it seem like this case has taken a strange and unexpected detour? I wonder to myself.

Michael subtly gestured towards the two mysterious men, their presence cloaked in an unsettling veil of curiosity. At least one of those guys has knights, shields, and a cross as hidden emblems on his cufflinks and lapel.

With a frown, my instincts were on high alert. "Should we say hello?"

"It would be rude not to. I speak, and you listen. We can start deciphering their symbols once we're back at Willowbrook station. They could tell us something, especially about this crap on the ground. I can't believe we came so close to missing it."

His eyes locked onto the two men. Michael's suspicion grew stronger with each passing moment. He sensed something was awry with them, and they had secrets much darker than the night enveloping them. Willowbrook's secrets were about to unfold, taking us on another journey, as long as it's not like the last one.

As we cautiously approached the mysterious figures, Michael tightly gripped his leather warrant card wallet. He caught their unsettling gaze and spoke without hesitation, "Excuse me, do you have a minute?"

The two men shifted their gaze towards him, their faces calm, but their eyes said otherwise.

Church to a Crime Scene

10

'Détective Reynolds,'

In the chilly, moonlit night, the two guys in suits glared at us without flinching. The one on the left possessed a broad, imposing frame, his chin jutting forward beneath a meticulously groomed goatee. I looked him over, seeking details to help us. Something to fill in the blanks. I was getting a bad feeling, sensing something different that prickled my neck.

Every facet of their appearance radiated with a creepy menace, casting eerie shadows over the scene. The man's shoes, gleaming with military precision, told a story of discipline and order. Layers of ash and charcoal clung to the soles, hinting at an affinity for contemplation by open fireplaces. The faint scent of tobacco, not from common cigarettes or cigars but from a pipe, suggested a certain importance, though not necessarily from a legal standpoint.

My thoughts raced back to Michael's cryptic mention of knights and crosses, with the blood-dripped 'devil' symbol across the gravel by the body, which made me think of religion. A gold ring on the man's pinkie finger, a subtle effort to conceal it. Its oval top bore a raised logo, while his tie, fashioned like a sword with a small black emblem at its centre, added another layer to the mysterious puzzle.

As I took in the sum of these eerie details, a shiver rippled through my hackles, causing the fine hairs on my neck to stand on end. They might appear to be churchgoers, but I didn't like what I was reading. Unsettling dots connected in my mind, setting off alarm bells that reverberated between my bloody ears. Why would representatives of the church be present at a crime scene?

The man on the right, shorter and leaner with sharp facial features, echoed the meticulously catalogued details. But it was his accent that intrigued me the most. A twang, perhaps French or Italian, concealed beneath a veneer of something other than English. Each word was spoken with measured precision, a deliberate effort to mask their origins. Michael's ears pricked at the peculiar intonations, too. The Wiley git was never slow on the uptake.

Neither of us suffered fools or lies, but when Michael's 'gut' tells him something was wrong, he listened and wasted no time cutting to the core. "What's your interest in the crime scene?" Michael demands, his voice laced with a hint of venom.

The man's response, a claim that the deceased was a loyal parishioner, did little to sway my scepticism. His heart remained eerily steady, starkly contrasting with the lies in the air. Since when did the church send representatives to pay their respects to the deceased?

Michael, not mincing his words, covered his nose to shield himself from the stench that clung to the scene. His gruff, Cockney-inflected tone dripped with cynicism as he probed for answers. "Is that right now? Excuse me for a minute as I digest the thick stench that wafted up. What's his name?"

The man's response veered further into deception as he painted a portrait of Mr Patrick Sheh as a troubled disciple, often expelled from casinos because of his mingling with the wrong crowd. It was a story that didn't align with the facts, and my intuition refused to accept it. Why, if Sheh was such a nuisance, would these guys come to view his body? Their eloquence and intelligence suggested a deeper layer of deception.

My patience was wearing thin. I took a bold step forward. "And you appear under the impression we were born yesterday. As you called him, Patrick Sheh meant more than that to you. Otherwise, you wouldn't be here. Now, respectfully, I would like to see some identification, please."

Tension drifted between us as we faced off, eyes darting like shadows in the moonlight. I knew that the answers I sought wouldn't come easily. Then, the man on the left, his smile chillingly unnerving, produced a white business card from a Bible. Its thick, textured paper exuded an air of luxury; on it, a cross was inscribed unlike any seen in typical churches. Below, a phone number, "913, 0309," stood without an area code.

I exchanged a perplexed glance with Michael, who wore a furrowed brow. A gust of wind, laden with the scent of blood, swept through the night, causing both of us to tip our heads instinctively. I wondered if the card was some twisted form of humour, a way to throw us off track.

Suddenly, as moonlight washed over their faces, my heart quickened. I stepped back, muttering, "Just when I thought it couldn't get weirder." I caught an unsettling image—a distortion. No trick of light but a nightmarish shift that rippled across their features. Their skin withered, like that of a long-buried corpse, only to revert to its smooth, living state in the blink of an eye.

My heart raced, and a sickly sensation settled in my gut. Something darker and far more ominous was at play in the quiet town of Willowbrook, and it had little regard for the trappings of the church. The two mysterious men who had taken an interest in the crime scene harboured secrets that didn't bode well for the murky road ahead.

Before we could probe further, a voice called out from behind, startling us. Our eyes darted briefly, a natural reaction. The mysterious duo had vanished by the time we looked back. A sinking weight settled in my chest, adding another air of strangeness to an already crazy night.

We approached a nearby Portakabin, where a uniformed officer awaited. Michael was dwelling on the sudden disappearance of the two men, causing him to reflect on Scotland again. I knew that was the case because I'd done the same. Now I grappled with the darkness that now entrenched my life. The involvement of 'the Church' only deepened the riddle, leaving us with more questions than answers.

A simple business card, an unusual cross, and a phone number devoid of an area code—details that seemed ominous were leading them down a twisted path of the unknown. All the details bothered me; the cogs spun in my mind, piecing everything together, wondering if Willowbrook's constabulary was corrupt or just blind to everything happening. I knew there was no way in hell some random dead guy would get a visit from the church, except the Pope, of course.

"Hey, detectives, it's not much, but it's enough to confirm something fucking strange. They realised the concealed camera, and it went off," the officer called out, holding the cabin door open for the detectives.

I paused at the threshold, my gaze lingering on the carefully recovered sections of Mr Sheh. The wind whistled through the yard, carrying an eerie chorus that seemed to echo through the pipes and barrels. A tingle prickled at the nape of my neck. It was happening again; we were being watched. Had the two men merely strayed further out of sight? Even up close, the trouble was that neither I nor Michael read anything from them other than a heartbeat, and that didn't sit right.

Inside, the tape played on a grainy black screen, revealing tantalising fragments of a sinister image. Two looming lorries flanked a stricken man on the ground, caught in the throes of an unnatural spectacle. A hooded figure materialised, their arms weaving intricate patterns as chains slithered from the lorries to ensnare Mr Sheh. The realisation that nobody touched those chains churned my blood, and no one appeared to be driving the lorries.

The hooded figure turned toward the camera, a veil of darkness concealing their face, and with a deliberate movement of their arm, the camera abruptly ceased its recording. We were left in stunned silence, senses overwhelmed by the puzzle we had just witnessed.

The Fate of Patrick Sheh

II

'*Killer,*'

The killer waited patiently for the right time to choose their prey in the crowded, dirty tavern.

The rest of the group had called it a night and hopped into a shared taxi, leaving only the middle-aged man standing by the door. His bald head shone in the dim light, and he was dressed in faded blue denim jeans, a worn 'Michael Jackson' T-shirt, and a navy blue parka casually draped over his arm. His shirt inched upward as he grappled with the rebellious parka, exposing a protruding gut and a symbol etched upon his flesh, sending icy tendrils of dread through the killer's veins.

An insatiable thirst for the unholy consumed the killer's vengeful mind as the cryptic and foreboding emblem resonated deeply. After draining the last of his drink, the man staggered out of the 'Bull and Barrow,' clumsily crashing through the rickety door and shattering the previously calm atmosphere. The night had reached its conclusion for his friends, but for the hunter, it marked the start of an exciting journey.

The killer loomed in the night's darkness, their intent solely focused on one singular purpose. Deep down, they knew certain souls would never find redemption, no matter how hard they tried or how much they wished for it in the eyes of a god. The killer's faith was of a peculiar kind, one that had been forged in the fiery pits of hell and yearned relentlessly for vengeance.

While the man was stumbling forward, the killer silently pursued him, concealing themselves in darkness. The man was headed towards a sprawling car park filled with the sights of cars, a blue van, and his white truck without its trailer. Completely oblivious to everything except his erratic thoughts, the trucker desperately held onto the frigid silver handrail, his foot stumbling awkwardly on the unforgiving metal step.

Overwhelmed by the weight of his past, his face flushed with guilt and intoxication. With a sudden, ungainly leap, he lifted his cumbersome body upright as he forcefully yanked open the door of the "cab". Whether driven by stubbornness, lack of care, or being drunk off his ass that clouded his judgment, the man's intent was clear, and the killer revelled in the certainty of it.

A pregnant pause filled the air, creating a temporary veil of apprehension that caused the windows to mist. It made little difference to the killer. The man's fate was sealed in the killer's evil narrative as the 13-litre diesel engine erupted with a thunderous roar, breaking the silence and setting the stage for the tragic events. The deserted area was filled with the resonating rev of each engine, creating a reverberation that permeated the lonely night, save for a few stray souls.

As a drizzle replaced the earlier dampness, the killer's determination in their pursuit remained unwavering. Their cloaked hat heavenward, they inhaled deeply, taking in the intoxicating blend of falling rain and acrid diesel fumes—a mixture that carried the ominous promise of impending evil.

A commotion momentarily stole the killer's attention from a nearby side road. A couple, barely in their mid-twenties and intoxicated, carelessly stumbled along their raucous rendition of 'We Will Rock You', disturbing the night's tranquillity. The innocence that clung to them spared them from the killer's cruel intentions. Tonight, all of their attention and focus were directed towards one man.

The killer watched patiently as the man's lorry careened recklessly through the car park, mowing down car mirrors and scraping by recklessly. Unless their prey left a trail of anguish and death in its wake, they knew exactly where it was headed. As the night unfolded, darkness and evil united in a shadowy tapestry, orchestrating a chilling reckoning.

The entrance to the haulage and recycling yard, marked by large spiked metal gates, had been violently smashed open. In the howling wind, the broken chain and padlock appeared to be beckoning the killer inside. The yard stretched out vulnerably and alluringly ahead as the killer crept toward a motionless truck. The engine hummed softly as the driver, deep in thought, took a moment to relieve himself by the front.

Wearily against the truck's engine grill, the unsteady man struggled to coordinate, unaware of the killer's watchful gaze. The recent downpour had finally stopped, and if the killer had their way, the next few minutes of their prey's life would be equally fleeting. The darkness was filled with incoherent whistling that echoed while the guy lazily wobbled, and his head bobbed limply, showing no concern.

In the wake of a thoughtless journey, the street became a mess, with rubbish and the remnants of vehicles littering the area - broken wing mirrors, a mobile bin knocked over, and a motorcycle left in a mangled state, all abandoned at the curbside. Thankfully, no one else was hurt ... at least not yet. As the trucker staggered away from the vehicle after answering nature's call, the wind carried showers of gravel dust that stung his eyes and coated his skin. He stood wistfully gazing at the line of trucks, trailers, and the imposing sorting shelters for recycling. From twenty feet, the killer watched as the wind gently ruffled the man's worn parka.

In the pale moonlight, their sinister black eyes glistened with an intense fury, sending shivers down the trucker's spine. Thoughts of murder and how to execute it swirled in the killer's mind. They noticed a nearby truck with a heavy-duty towing winch as their gaze shifted. The sight of its thick chains, coiled with lethal potential, ignited a sinister idea in the killer's imagination.

Both trucks had chains that glistened like ghostly Christmas lights, presenting a chilling surprise for their unsuspecting victim. The trucker, totally oblivious, finally turned around. He spun clumsily and stumbled again because he couldn't stay steady. His blurred vision made it even more remarkable that he found his way to the yard. The misty darkness slowly dissipated, unveiling an eerie and unsettling scene.

Fear gripped the trucker's throat tightly, causing unease to fill his stomach. In all his years, he had never come across anything like this. He entertained the thought of running, but fear held him steadfast. He stood face-to-face with his worst nightmares; every fear and dread he had ever harboured had manifested into this shadowed figure and had him firmly in its sights. His trembling hands were slick with clammy sweat, causing his cherished 'M J' T-shirt to cling uncomfortably to his skin. The patient and unrelenting killer could practically taste the fear of their helpless prey.

"L ... look, I don't know what you want, but the yard is closed. Y ... You are not supposed to be here," stammers the trucker, clinging to the faint hope that he was imagining the horrifying scene before him.

The eerie silence remained, broken only by the occasional rustle of leaves. The trucker attempted to flee, but his escape was thwarted as he lost his balance and landed with a loud thud on the ground.

"Look... if it's money, there's a small safe in the office, petty cash mostly, but have at it," pleads the trucker, his efforts in vain. Gravel crunched beneath the weight of the killer's heavy boots, each grinding of stone against stone, sending a shiver down the trucker's spine. Every hair on his body stood on end, tingling with a deathly chill, as the killer continued to approach.

Little did the trucker know chains with chunky red hooks were hanging ominously from the underbellies of the trucks, creating a haunting sight as they weaved through the gritty and moonlit landscape. Resembling, poised cobras ready to strike, they swayed with an eerie anticipation.

The killer, with a sinister silhouette that contrasted against the eerie glow of the moon in the backdrop, ominously stood over the unsuspecting trucker, who could only make out the menacing black eyes that gleamed with a terrifying and unnatural grey glow, piercing through the shadows of the killer's sinister mystique.

With a sudden, ghostly movement, the killer's arm slashed through the air, and the chains from both trucks came to life with ferocious intent. They lunged forward, their movements quick and calculated, wrapping themselves around the trucker's arms and legs like vipers on the hunt.

As the other truck roared to life, the helpless trucker was yanked away, suspended by his arms, creating a furious cloud of dust. He dangled like a grotesque piñata, his body slowly stretching, bones snapping, and cartilage tearing, all accompanied by a symphony of agonising sounds that filled the night air. The trucker's wails of pain, haunting and dreadful, echoed throughout the desolate yard, much to the killer's dark joy intensifying with each piercing cry. By their belief, revenge was a pleasure that carried both bitterness and sweetness, and they revelled in the suffering they had caused.

Amidst the heart-wrenching 'banshee' wails, tears and saliva sprayed from the trucker's contorted face. Below the grinding wheels, the dusty earth quivered, and the chains groaned under the immense strain of the grotesque mess. Each agonising second brought fresh torment, bones snapping like brittle twigs, as the trucker's body was tormented and tortured.

Dripping with desperation, the trucker clung to life, his eyeballs popped, dangling by slender threads of optic nerves, swinging and flopping with each struggle, while his enormous belly flipped from beneath the torn T-shirt, revealing the gruesome tearing in his flesh. The horrifying sight compelled the killer to shift slightly, momentarily taken aback by the sheer brutality of their 'bloody' orchestra. Frothing cries for mercy echoed in the night, but went unanswered as the killer remained unrelenting.

Then, the last act of brutality unfolded with a sudden and violent whoosh. The trucker's torso was ruthlessly shredded from his lower body, releasing a gruesome torrent of blood and organs that showered the gritty yard. Each end of the severed body clapped against the fronts of the waiting trucks, creating a sickening and chaotic spectacle that the killer savoured in slow motion. The metallic scent of blood hung heavy in the air, whipped around by the wind beneath their hood and the hat's wide brim. A second victim was claimed, and as the torso flopped to its side, casting a spinal cord trail through the dirt, the killer saw the 'cross'. That fire behind the eyes burnt bright with so much more to do, a question of who would be next.

With an air of mystery, the killer stepped back from the gruesome scene, their face completely obscured by a hood that concealed their menacing expression. Blood splatters painted their boots and clothes as they watched the grotesque aftermath of their brutal act.

Now lifeless and mangled, the severed body lay sprawled on the ground like a grotesque work of art. The eerie glow of the moonlight showcased the macabre details, creating a chilling ambience. The chains used as torture instruments now dangled ominously, still dripping with the trucker's blood.

The killer's heart raced with a mixture of exhilaration and satisfaction. They revelled in their power over life and death, relishing the fear they had instilled in their victims. The 'cross' they had seen etched on the trucker's body symbolised their mission to cleanse the world.

The killer looked at the lifeless body one last time before fading into the darkness. Their brutal quest was far from over, and there were more sinners to be judged and more blood to be spilt. The wind whispered their chilling laughter, creating an eerie atmosphere in the desolate yard and a chilling reminder of the horror that unfolded. The village should sleep uneasily, their dreams haunted by the eerie whispers in the night breeze.e.

Haunting Ghosts

12

'Gerald,'

I stood before the mirror, hands trembling. Cold water gushed from the tap, its rhythm a haunting melody that splashed my palms. Lost in the maze of my thoughts, I watched with dread as beads of condensation raced down the spout.

My reflection, drained of colour and contorted with fear, stared back at me from the foggy glass. The whirlwind of the morning merged with the night's terrifying revelations; weaving a nightmare, I was desperate to escape. The memory of father's severed flesh, wrapped in the envelope with a bizarre wax seal left in the kitchen, weighed heavily. It was a puzzle piece more unsettling than the tape, gnawing at my sanity like a starved rat.

Why didn't Colin mention the missing patch of flesh during Father's autopsy? That's all I kept thinking about. Surely, he would've noticed. The air in the bathroom was thick with tension, made eerier by the low hum of the fan, casting long shadows that danced in the corners of the room. Life had taken a nightmarish turn, thrusting me into a world for which I was ill-prepared, burdened not only by my father's ominous legacy but also by the haunting whispers that coincided with the ominous presence of that cloaked figure that seemed to stalk my every move, especially earlier.

The image of the figure's dirty, black sleeve wielding a sharp, gleaming knife against mother's throat sent a chill crawling down my spine. The overpowering atmosphere of the bathroom was getting too much; every breath created white plumes in the soapy air. I twisted the tap shut, still shaken.

Suddenly, a strange sound sliced through the silence. My heart thumped hard. I knew the sound, and what followed had me frozen in place. Lines slowly etched themselves into the condensation-covered mirror, gradually speeding up with creepy intent. Each stroke deepened my apprehension as they formed the very symbol I'd just been thinking about a double-lined circle with a five-pointed star. The dreaded goat's head was the only element missing, leaving me struggling to understand what the hell was going on and how it was possible.

Terror tore through my veins. I wanted to run but couldn't, so I remained rooted to the spot. Making matters worse, an invisible presence drew nearer, smothering the air behind. Cold brushed my earlobes and cheek, pimples rippling over my flesh as a heavy breath whispered close.

I could feel someone close, yet no one could be seen. My stomach churned, and a faint tug at the front of my shirt brought my neck hair to attention.

"Why do you stand there so helpless, Gerald?" a grating, melancholy whisper, cutting through the silence like a hot blade through flesh. I spun frantically, desperate to see where.

An unmistakable woman's voice gradually penetrated my consciousness until I finally twigged. It was Charlotte. Sweat trickled over my temples, and my eyes darted to the mirror's reflection as a blast of wind swept past. My gaze followed as streaks materialised with dread and fascination until three ominous words stared back.

"Kill... For... Me."

"Do that for me, Gerald. I need you to do that for me."

There was no doubt it was Charlotte's voice. Yet, the undeniable truth lingered—she was gone. Recent talk of demonic curses had screwed with my faith in what was possible and rational.

"It's alright, Gerald. It's me. You can trust me. It's your Charlotte," she whispers soothingly in my ear. Was this happening? How?.

I wanted to talk to her so badly. To tell her what I didn't get to before she died. I yearned to apologise for not standing up to my boss that fateful night. I should have been in the car with her, and Charlotte wouldn't have been driving so late. And maybe, just maybe, that lorry wouldn't have smashed her off the road.

I wanted to share the bizarre, harrowing events that had unfolded since her death, the revelation that my family was cursed. Strangely, perhaps Charlotte had a fortunate escape from the spiralling madness that now consumes me.

Staring into the mirror, Charlotte's voice echoed in my ears. My heart was pounding against my chest, throat parched with terror. Because the painful truth remained—I couldn't have those conversations I yearned for. Charlotte... was... dead. It wasn't her speaking.

I was soon wide-eyed with dread as reality drenched itself in this unsettling truth that rapidly twisted and warped hauntingly. Looking back from the mirror was the imposing, cloaked figure, its dirty hood concealing any view of its face. An enormous hat cast a shadow that added to the horror.

"Gerald, if you loved me, you would seek revenge upon those responsible. Let the darkness in. Your father would agree—they deserve punishment, all of them. Baphomet demands that you paint the streets with their blood, and the pain will fade like the dead leaves in autumn." Charlotte's voice reverberated chillingly from the looming figure. Rigid, unable to do anything except mutter, 'Baphomet demands it,' as my blood curdled with fear. I tried blinking repeatedly, hoping to clear the horrifying illusion, but the steam persisted, as did the disturbing symbol.

"Gerald, are you alright? I know this is all so overwhelming," Mother called out, concerned yet tinged with a curiosity that left me questioning how much she truly knew. Her shrill was enough to shatter the surreal trance I was in. Left with a bewildering question: 'What the bloody hell is happening?'

"I... erm, yeah, I think so," I stammer, throat dry and gravelly, unable to understand the reality that had just unfolded. The steam quickly dissipated, and the messages ceased haunting, but the sinister symbol remained etched into my mind, compelling a need for answers about so many things. For now, I'd settle for the unique wax symbol and strange blood on my car key for.

Hit the Books

13

'Gerald,'

I hastily abandoned my mother's vehicle half on the High Street pavement. Even though mine was still usable, I couldn't take the risk. With the chase and all the weirdness that's gone on, I couldn't rule out being watched. That may well be my fear of talking, but putting anyone else in danger, especially my two innocent daughters, I had to play it safe. They depended on me for everything, and I couldn't let them down.

Yet, there was also a need to unravel the mysteries of what was happening. What better place than the library, a towering fortress of knowledge and creepiness, with its unsettling steps. I hadn't set foot in the place since my school days, a time I'd rather forget. The idea of going back didn't appeal, but inside those fancy walls, there had to be answers to the weird symbol on the envelope and the creepy message on the foggy mirror.

Charlotte's eerie voice continues to occupy my thoughts, its echoes carrying, *"Kill for me."* It triggered a vivid image from my school years, during which I'd endured religious education lessons. It's boring as hell. But now I wished I'd paid more attention. Although, I remembered enough to recall some of the devil worship stuff. Thoughts that come with a wave of dread. The envelope's wax seal had a goat's head, supposedly linked to 'Baphomet' - a name messing with my mind.

The tape talks about a curse - a mysterious puzzle that made me think the library was a good place to learn more. It's not the curse itself, but theories about its links to the devil and other weird stuff. I'd also made plans to catch up with my buddy, Nathan Hartley, who was following his passion as a private investigator.

After we chatted about Colin, Nathan has been investigating father's hidden past. Not being related, his snooping wouldn't set off any alarm bells. We're hoping he'd discover something to silence the gossip and protect Father's flawless reputation. I always saw father as a perfect example of virtue, unable to do any wrong. However, Colin mentioned his fearful escape from the pub intensified concerns about the unsettling rumours.

Making my way up the imposing staircase, I cast a final, apprehensive look behind me, expecting something or someone to come from the shadows. As I entered the library, a gust of warm air brushed against my face, bringing the comforting aroma of old books. I couldn't help but appear like a fish out of water approaching the librarian's desk. Grace, a middle-aged woman with greying black hair tightly pulled into a bun, sat peering over her glasses with a serious expression.

"Excuse me," I began, my voice hesitant, "could you guide me to the section on religious history, specifically regarding Baphomet?" He paused, grappling with how much information to divulge. Grace's response was swift, causing a tangible shift in the atmosphere. With suspicion etched in her narrowed eyes, she paused momentarily before uttering a word.

"Certainly," she replies, her voice tinged with caution. "You'll find what you're looking for on the first floor, row twelve."

I suppressed a reluctant groan, eyeing the endless flight of stairs ahead. The library's intimidating layout gave the impression of a whole other universe. The mahogany wood and blue-grey carpet drew me in deeper as I mutter, "Thank you," avoiding Grace's penetrating gaze. Heading up the creaky staircase, my unease mounted, and I felt I was being watched.

Eventually, at row twelve, the books looked even older than I'd expected. Their spines were all tattered and cracked. A cloud of dust and a choking, musty scent accompanied the sound of pulling out a crusty one. The book had the intriguing title "Occult Symbols and Their Origins." Not a terrible place to start, I thought.

The book opened, and bizarre symbols on brittle pages greeted me. I delved into the history of Baphomet, learning about its shady ties to secret cults and ancient orders and its mysterious role as the nemesis of the Knights Templar. Each word left me scratching my head.

My eyes got all watery from the strain. I couldn't believe any of it was happening. The same goes for the unsettling sounds and the jumble of spooky nonsense. But every time I stumbled upon an answer, more questions surfaced.

'With its intricate and dark persona, Baphomet became a symbol of intrigue and dispute, its history cloaked in mystery and controversy. The name "Baphomet" initially appeared during the early 14th century and has since become intertwined with many esoteric traditions, secret societies, and occult practices throughout the centuries. Like a tapestry, the story was a mosaic of different threads, each contributing to the overall picture.'

The Templar Connection:

'Arguably, the most infamous affiliation was with the Knights Templar, a medieval Christian military order established in the 12th century. In 1307, King Philip IV of France started a persecution campaign against the Templars, accusing them of heresy and criminal activities. During their trials, some Templars confessed, under duress and torture, to worshipping an idol named "Baphomet." Historians still debate the existence of such an idol and the veracity of these confessions.'

Occult Symbolism:

'Baphomet often appeared as a horned, goat-headed entity, blending male and female attributes. Its right hand pointed upward in the "As Above" gesture. In contrast, the left hand pointed downward in the "So Below" gesture, symbolising the union of opposites and the equilibrium of spiritual and material forces. The symbolism surrounding Baphomet was rife with occult elements, including pentagrams, torches, and serpents.'

Occult Revival:

'Baphomet experienced a resurgence in the 19th century during the occult revival. Secret societies and magical orders incorporated the figure into their rituals and symbolism. Figures like Eliphas Levi, a French occultist, contributed to its popularisation through writings and artworks.'

Modern Occultism:

'Baphomet continued to hold significance, particularly within traditions like Thelema, founded by Aleister Crowley. In Thelema, Baphomet symbolised the union of opposites and attaining spiritual enlightenment. It was also linked to positing gnosis, which is direct spiritual knowledge.'

Pop Culture:

'Baphomet appeared in literature, music, movies, and video games, cementing its status as an enduring symbol in the realms of the occult and esoteric. It was crucial to acknowledge that interpretations of Baphomet varied, with its meaning changing depending on the context.

To some, Baphomet symbolised spiritual transformation and enlightenment; to others, it stood for heresy and the occult. Regardless of its origins, Baphomet's presence loomed large, enveloping those who dared to seek its secrets in an ominous shadow.'

Each paragraph was getting harder to understand, and I was unsure which claims were credible. The interpretations were different, but none nailed what I needed.

INFLUENCE

14

'Gerald,'

As I was about to lose hope, I found something unusual—a hard, dry, dark green book with only the symbol I'd seen earlier.

Within its pages is a story about the devout Knights Templar, a faction eventually fragmented when its members succumbed to the irresistible allure of darkness. Their rise had been unstoppable, but their tactics had become twisted. With many a horrifying picture left in their wake.

The Templars' influence peaked during the twilight of the 12th and 13th centuries as they amassed great wealth and power. However, not everyone in their group was satisfied solely with piety and chivalry. The Lord Aldric, leading a renegade faction, desired something beyond the humble life of devotion.

A pact was struck in the dimly lit room, the words carefully etched in sinister ink. Their voices barely above a whisper, they invoked the name of Baphomet, an unholy deity of dualities, the words hanging heavy in the air. They traded their souls for riches, power, and a life of luxury, transforming into harbingers of death. Baphomet's desires became the catalyst for their intertwined destinies.

Their identities were forged by their crimes, hidden away in the shadows. With deadly precision, the assassins fuelled their dark patron's thriving. As riches poured in and their influence grew, their hearts turned cold.

Despite everything, with time, the cursed Templars transformed into something far more sinister—the infamous "**Eternal Vigil.**" A cult of malice, they revelled in suffering, seeing it as a tribute to their goat-headed deity.

Yet, the curse extracted a toll. Souls have withered, lives have crumbled, and minds have spiralled into madness. Lord Aldric, who was once charismatic, transformed into an empty shell of a man, plagued by visions and tormented by the relentless demands of Baphomet.

Whispers were brought to the attention of the Church, compelling the faithful Templars to undertake a cleansing of their order. Amidst a hidden war, brethren betrayed one another, engaging in combat for the very core of the Templar Order.

The story of the Baphomet's Chosen is a chilling reminder of how power, greed, and unholy bargains can corrupt. It exemplified the depths to which humanity could sink while striving for material wealth and the nightmarish outcomes that awaited those who dared to violate the laws of nature and morality.

My fingers trembled with anticipation as I read the pages of the weathered book. Each word hit me hard and made me sweat. A worrying sensation of darkness closing in had me increasingly uneasy.

The story spoke of the "**Eternal Vigil**," a haunting presence that lingered in the shadows, remnants of the original Templars. Heart pounding, all I could picture were these cursed figures, trapped in some limbo between life and death, burdened by the weight of centuries of grave responsibility.

The description of their eyes, once filled with devotion to the Church, now haunted by an unending torment, made my legs restless, riddled with anxiety. In their spectral existence, the Templar Cross played a macabre and eerie role, symbolising their eternal allegiance and a stark reminder of the sins committed by their cursed comrades. I imagined a heavy, ominous cross, tarnished and unsettling, hanging around their frail necks.

With each passing moment, the tale wove a more unsettling narrative. In its tireless quest for righteousness, the Church was determined to rid the Templar Order of the curse that plagued them, a stain on what they created for, believed to be from Baphomet. The need to confront the evil presence that had infested the order turned to its most devout and unwavering members, the **Eternal Vigil**.

These Templars, bound by an unbreakable oath, embarked on a harrowing quest, their hands gripping tightly onto the hilt of their sacred artefacts. The detail in this book was crazy, if at all true. It spun my mind, vivid pictures of their covert activities, their ghostly figures stealthily navigating through history, leaving no evidence behind.

I was getting into the story and questioning if the Eternal Vigil was still around, lingering on the fringes of the modern world. In the legend, it is said that they would appear in deep despair, manifesting as ghostly figures or undead that embodied the Church's righteous anger. The idea of coming across these creepy enforcers made me sick.

The uncertainty surrounding its existence only added to the chilling aura of the supposed legend. Were they real, or were they a nightmarish fable? The line between reality and myth blurred, leaving me in a state of disquieting unease.

The tale's conclusion left him with a haunting reminder—a battle between light and darkness that persisted through the ages, with unwavering forces ready to defend against the encroaching evil. It was a story that was sure to stick with me, an unsettling narrative I didn't like, much like everything that's happened so far.

THE SNEAKY LIBRARIAN

15

'Gerald,'

Slumped against the foot of the bookcase, I grappled with conflicting emotions as I closed the old book. My anxiety heightened at the thought of father's potential involvement with some twisted cult, real or otherwise, as it would mean the curse alluded to on the tape was about to bite me in the arse.

With the pale glow of flickering overhead lights, the library had an eerie feeling toying with my nerves. It's like watching a horror movie. You know it's all acting and makeup. Once it's finished, you're no less scared. That's how I was feeling after that book. Not helped by the silence, only interrupted by the rustle of pages and the occasional cough of someone downstairs.

I had the best view from where I was—seeing everyone reading but Grace. She couldn't stop staring at me, but now she's on the phone. Worry lines etched throughout her face, emphasising the furrowed expression in her eyes. Her glances had me on edge. The car incident had me on guard, warranted or not.

Grace appeared elegant like butter wouldn't melt earlier, now emitted an unsettling presence that clung to her like a bad smell. Her phone call seemed to carry a sense of urgency while the rest of the library remained calm.

That's when I spotted Nathan breezing through the library door, and paranoia tightened its grip. Nathan appeared visibly worried, his head swaying from side to side, his face turning red. As he glanced upwards, he met my eyes staring back at him from behind the metal bars. Nathan hurried past Grace without uttering a word.

Dressed in a casual brown suede jacket, blue jeans, and white trainers, his otherwise nearly crafted blonde hair had been battered by the same crosswinds I'd endured. With each stride, he cleared two steps at a time, his six-foot athletic frame gliding Gisele-like with a slightly anxious head swivel before pouncing to my side.

Grace was glued to her phone, looking concerned and keeping a close eye on me and Nathan, worried about what it could mean. Nathan leaned in close, his voice barely a whisper. "Gerald, we need to talk. I'm being followed,"

My mouth dropped. "By who?" I say, glancing at Grace.

With sweat on his forehead, Nathan looked toward the door and then back to me. "Two guys in black suits. "I've seen them everywhere," Nathan says, his voice trembling with worry.

I was spooked. As Nathan's worry grew, so did the sense of unease in the library, and my mind immediately turned to the words I'd read. The cool breeze from the air conditioning rippled against his skin as I anxiously checked around the library. The air was thick with the musty aroma of old books, and panic added an eerie undertone to the unfolding situation. Nathan's tormented look mirrored everything I was feeling.

"What do they want? Did they ever say anything?" I whisper back; my voice is barely audible.

Nathan leaned in real close, murmuring. "I don't know, but they've been following me for days. They never get too close, but I can sense their presence. Ever since I began poking around in property records looking for links to your father,"

My mind was going crazy, figuring out another piece of this enormous mess of a puzzle. The connection between the symbol on the envelope, the mention of Baphomet, and the mysterious men in black suits became increasingly clear. I couldn't help but wonder how much father was wrapped up in that creepy cult to have put them in danger.

Grace's voice crackled over the phone as she continued her conversation, her eyes darting between us. She wasn't leaving us be, and that's unsettling.

"We need to get out of here," I say, eyes flicking toward the exit. The thought of confronting whoever was following Nathan in this crowded library filled me with dread. Nathan nodded in agreement, his face pale. "Agreed. But we can't let them know we're onto them."

As we slowly rose, Nathan glanced at Grace, who was still engrossed in her phone call. The two men in black suits had yet to enter the library, but Nathan's instincts told him they were getting closer.

We made our way toward the exit, acting as casually as we could, but purposefully. Every step could be a trap, and the weight of a potential curse hung heavily. I was riddled with guilt for involving my friend.

Just as we reached halfway to the library's entrance, a shiver ran down my spine. I turned to steal one last glance at Grace, who was now off the phone and watching us intently. Her expression was a mixture of concern and something else, something that kept a constant icy breeze running through me.

With us caught in 'no-man's-land,' Grace stood up as if she was about to move and cut off any chance of retreating. The double brown doors swung open with intimidating menace. A looming shadow filled the doorway. Just as Nathan had anxiously explained, two men in black suits.

The once bright but windy outside suddenly became full of grey gloom, further enhancing their shadowed mystique. An occasional light from the library would glimpse the haunting twosome. Their paleness had me and Nathan shook, heads swivelling as we wrestled with our 'flight or fight', looking for another way out. After all, it's not like I knew them or what they could or couldn't do.

My clammy hands brushed across a heavyset, dark-stained table to guide us as we stepped back slowly, trying not to draw attention from anyone else. The two men stepped ominously forward; they appeared normal. If scarily worn, it could be called normal. The one on the left clutched a Bible close to his chest while their deathly black eyes narrowed on Nathan and me, as if penetrating our souls.

Meanwhile, Grace had manoeuvred herself from the desk to a huge bank of switches on the wall. I read what she intended. To put us in darkness and make it easier for the two in suits. My heart pounded as we fumbled backwards; the library's lighting flickered ominously.

Nathan's voice quivered as he mutters, "We need to get out of here now, Gerald." I nodded in agreement, mind racing for an escape plan. The library was filled with unsuspecting patrons engrossed in their reading, still oblivious to the unfolding drama.

The two men in black suits continued their slow, deliberate approach, their eyes locked on Nathan and me as if we were prey.

I turned to Nathan, whispering urgently, "Follow me, but stay low and quiet." Nathan nodded, his face pale with fear. We crouched behind the table, shielded from view by the library's towering bookshelves. The dimming lights added to the tension, casting elongated shadows across the room.

Grace continued her deliberate approach to the wall of switches, aiding the two men whose menacing eyes seemed to glow, more so the darker it got. I knew we had to hurry, with a wave of worried heads perking up before reaching for their table lamp switches.

With Nathan close behind, I made a daring dash for the emergency exit to our left, just past the librarian's desk, my heart pounding with each step. The door was heavy, but I pushed it open just enough for us to slip through. The brisk wind outside was a welcome relief, and we stumbled into the library's back alley. It was a narrow, gloomy space cluttered with discarded, dirty old furniture and overgrown shrubs.

We kept low, our breaths coming in shallow gasps as we hid in the shadows. I watched the library's lights flickered and went out completely, plunging the building into darkness.

The two men in black suits were moving quicker but momentarily lost sight, giving Nathan and me a chance to slip away. We needed to find answers and uncover the truth behind the supposed curse with two creepy guys chasing us.

Huddled in the alley, I wondered about Grace's role. Her actions were calculated, and her being on the phone while keeping me and Nathan in her view before the creeps arrived raised even more questions.

But for now, the priority was to stay hidden and evade the mysterious figures relentlessly pursuing us. The day was far from over, and the darkness would soon be upon us. Before then, safety and I needed to find out what Nathan had uncovered to draw such dangerous attention. My world was unravelling quicker than I liked, and it seemed all roads led to the 'Bull and Barrow' for a well-earned pint. With the contents of the books still fresh in my mind, I had to decide which was fact or fiction because my life and others could depend on it.

Hunted Creatures

16

'Gerald,'

Like hunted creatures, we huddled closely in the grim shadows of the pub corner, our senses acutely tuned to the unsettling aftermath of our recent ordeal. The library, somewhere that should've been safe and quiet, turned into a nightmare.

Nathan absentmindedly traced the condensation on his beer glass, like the sweat on his forehead. My family's secrets consumed his mind, or should I say my father's, filled with both uncertainty and a sense of foreboding. He had a hunch that something fishy was happening, and the danger was getting bigger.

My hands wouldn't stop shaking, holding onto a whiskey glass, calming the storm inside. The recent revelations have been one blow after another, and now I'm losing my grip on reality. The unsettling figures in black suits now intersected my life. Thankfully, for now, they were nowhere to be seen. One of them held a Bible as a talisman and a damning puzzle piece.

We had solace, even if only for a moment. The other customers were busy chatting about sports, sex, and politics, which served as a raucous backdrop. I was in awe of their obliviousness while I sat, fearing something off was lurking nearby.

I was just about to take a sip of my drink when my attention was grabbed by a figure outside the window—a bloody raven. I wouldn't have minded, but it looked weird. Then it twitched, tipped its beak skywards nonchalantly, and let rip with a loud screech; the windows were thin, and the door was closing slowly. So, it was piercingly damming. I recalled from a passage in the books. It's a creature as ominous as the devil, looking equally haunting.

The raven's ebony plumage contrasted with the dull surroundings, and its beady eyes bore into my brain. Each tap of its beak against the windowpane reverberated through my bones. The bird's neck twitched in rhythm with its relentless pecking, intensifying the unease hell-bent on surrounding me and Nathan.

However, what had my spine quivering was the unnatural brilliance of the raven's eyes—a piercing blue that summed up their day, eyes that delved into the darkest corners of his mind. While the pub's patrons continued being oblivious in their fun-filled night, the intrusion of this demonic-looking creature consumed Gerald's senses.

Others soon joined in, descending upon the ledge with an eerie chorus. Their relentless tapping crescendo into a deafening din, and I could picture the window shattering into a thousand jagged pieces.

Overwhelmed by the torment that built up much like everything else recently, I buried my head in arms, seeking refuge from a high-pitched tinnitus—a maddening symphony I wasn't sure was real. Then...

'Hush, little baby, don't say a word. Mamma's gonna buy you a mockingbird, and if that mockingbird don't sing, Mamma's gonna buy you a diamond ring.' An almost polyphonic sirenesque torment. High pitched and squawky, a change from 'Charlotte'.

Thankfully my pain was finally broken, Nathan's low and uncertain voice dared to speak first. "Gerald," he began, eyes staring vacantly outside the window. "We've been through hell, and it's time we talk."

I turned to Nathan, still drawn to the unnerving ravens. "I'm sorry, Nathan," I say with resignation. Everything had happened quickly, and the last few days had spiralled, yet I'm no closer to understanding why."

Nathan mustered a reassuring smile, though his composure hung by a thread. "Well," he began, "What I've uncovered might add fuel to the fire. You know I've been digging into your father's past, into Henry's secrets. There's more to him than meets the eye, something a little on the dark side, tied to your family."

My dread deepened as I thought about the implications of Nathan's words. With their eerie blue eyes, the ravens temporarily faded into the background of my thoughts.

Nathan continues, his voice strained: "There's a farm in the remote Cotswolds. It isn't much on the surface, but it's jointly owned, and your family name, the Ackerman's, is on the deeds alongside other family names. It goes back bloody decades, perhaps even longer."

My scepticism surfaced. "How many generations are we talking about here? Did you find the farm's address?"

Nathan hesitated; his tone was heavy with uncertainty. "I can't say for sure, but it might span at least half a century or more. And here's the kicker—the documents are sealed with a strange wax emblem. Correct me if I'm mistaken, but didn't they stop using such seals with Henry the Eighth?"

Puzzled, my eyes narrowed, trying to understand the implications of what Nathan was saying. The trouble is, I don't remember my parents ever mentioning such a place. Yet, the strange wax seal ignited my curiosity, especially after the envelope at my mother's place. I had to know more, particularly about the other families involved. "After what I witnessed this morning," I whisper, barely audible above the relentless tapping of the ravens, "I can't ignore this as a mere coincidence."

Nathan's curiosity deepened. "What else happened?" he inquired sharply.

I recounted the unsettling events of the day—the envelope with the cryptic wax symbol, the gruesome patch of father's skin branded with a pentagram, mother's mysterious behaviour, and the attempted vehicular assault. Nathan's face paled as the gravity of their situation knocked him sideways.

Nathan finally spoke, his voice weighed down by the mounting dread. "With everything that's gone on—the surveillance, the librarian, the pursuit—it's clear this is more than we ever imagined. When people go to such lengths to conceal history, it's seldom for innocent reasons. Gerald, this is a fucking tangled web, and I fear it leads to something we would never imagine in a million years. Common sense tells me to distance myself, to flee from this bullshit nightmare, but you're my best friend, and I can't abandon you. -

- "A part of me is inexplicably drawn to uncovering the truth. Whatever path we choose, we must tread cautiously, perhaps even consider gaining bulletproof vests." Nathan's attempt at humour couldn't mask the gravity of their predicament.

I nodded, Nathan's ominous words weighing heavily. I had to protect myself and the girls from the rapidly consuming darkness.

'Later That night,'

Leant against a bookcase's cold, unforgiving surface, bathed in the ghostly glow emanating from the mysterious leather-bound book in my trembling hands. A title remained conspicuously absent from its cover, replaced by the etching of a double-ringed symbol—a sinister goat's head within a star. How I had this book was a mystery, but I was compelled to read it.

The cryptic passages within the book, written in a language I frustratingly didn't understand, writhed and pulsated before my eyes. Words danced and twisted, weaving intricate occultist theories that fascinated and repelled me. The library's atmosphere grew heavy, saturated with a silence that had me on edge.

Then, with a startling abruptness that made me jump, the library's lights flickered and dimmed, casting a never-ending darkness. Panic surged within, clawing at my chest as I desperately sought a lifeline—a book, a shelf, anything to help pull myself from the floor. My trembling fingers groped at thin air, searching for purchase.

Moonlight pierced the night through the window, revealing Grace, the librarian, standing at the towering wooden doors. Her hesitant steps betrayed an overwhelming sense of suspicion.

The air grew cold, and an unnatural draft chilled the library and everything in it, me included, extinguishing the remaining lights with a sinister hiss as power was severed. My heart thundered, and I watched in paralysed horror as Grace was no longer alone. A towering figure appeared from the shadows, cloaked in a tattered, filthy hooded coat that billowed like a grim reaper. I recognised the figure with a sudden jolt.

The figure's face remained obscured beneath a wide-brimmed hat, but its intentions radiated intense terror that even scared me, and I wasn't as near as Grace. The air thickened, shrouded in wisps of ghostly white mist that slowly wove through the space, setting an eerie atmosphere. I could not move or utter a single word to warn Grace.

Her voice quivered as she stammers, "I ... I tried. Please don't do this." Her pleas hung mournfully in the air, but they went unanswered, falling upon deaf ears that belonged to the sinister presence looming over her.

Then, in an instant, everything shifted. I was up close and looking at Grace's terrified face, my arm covered by the grimy black coat's sleeve. With deliberate, evil intent and a gloved hand raised, I was now a passenger in the killer's mind or body; I don't know, but it was as if I was an unwilling accomplice. Barbed wire, wickedly jagged and dripping with the sinister lure of blood, cruelly crashed through the fire exit door with unrelenting ferocity.

Much against my will or control, I drifted toward the trembling Grace, the barbed wire coiling through the air with horrifying menace. Agonised screams tore through the library, blood showering from the thick, fleshy, sliced wounds as the barbed wire tore through Grace, staining the floor in puddles of crimson.

I couldn't believe it, and fighting the urge to 'throw up', I lived every ounce of the killer's sadistic pleasure, an insatiable thirst for suffering and death that coursed through his very being. The killer manipulated the barbed wire with an unnatural precision, moving with ruthless purpose. I could do nought but bear witness to the horrors unfurling before me—Grace was being torn asunder, her life extinguished in a nightmarish onslaught of violence. As the barbed wire finally relented and Grace's life faded, my vision blurred, and the horrific view faded into darkness.

'AAARGGHH,'

I awoke with a gasping start, bathed in a chilling sheen of cold sweat, the memory of the horrifying murder still fresh in my mind. It was an experience filled with brutality and evil that defied explanation and reason. It was almost a nightmare, yet it felt and looked so real. Considering what we'd escaped, I understood why it may manifest in my mind, but this was different in so many ways.

Sat upright, shaken, as I replayed the details, trying to catch my breath. One thing was for sure: I'd been given an unholy glimpse into the darkness—an evil presence lurking in the shadows. Its insatiable appetite for violence and death resonated deep within my unwilling occupancy of the killer's body. To compound my fear, it became apparent the killer was the same mysterious figure who had plagued my thoughts and haunted moments of my 'day-to-day', not that Colin saw, whoever this person was had changed the library into a theatre of horrors with terrifying ease, leaving me a trembling, sweat-soaked mess, clinging to the fragile hope that it was my overactive imagination.

Grace is Dead

17

'Détective Reynolds,'

We were exhausted wrecks, Dalton and I, clinging to our coffee, minds a mess, trying to make sense of the fucking nightmare we'd been thrust into. That's two bodies now, one so soon after another. I should be used to it all by now, especially after Scotland and the blood spilt there. Yet, here we were, another gruesome murder waiting in the wings; not even the Kanaima case in London seemed this busy so soon.

The absence of forensic evidence made it even more unsettling, leaving us with no leads. All it did was bring our awareness of the murders into a world we knew well. The only thing that could have killed Mr Eckleston was something supernatural. There was no other way to justify the scene. However, we needed another theory to sell to the locals if we didn't want to spread any more fear than had already been circulating in the press.

Tight-knit communities like Willowbrook enjoy gossip; anything out of the ordinary would be rife by morning. Michael says it best, 'treat them like mushrooms', at least for now. In other words, keep them in the bloody dark. Some days I wish I could be the same, sadly that luxury is long gone.

The library stood eerily silent, its polished floors now stained with a thick river of blood that, even drying, still stirred the senses and the air heavy with the overwhelming metallic scent of death. Eyes scanning the surroundings, I approached the uniformed officer who had the misfortune of maintaining the crime scene cordon. "What do we have here, Officer?"

The young officer looked visibly shaken, his pale face whipped by cross winds, but he tried to maintain his composure as he explains, "It's ... it's a real fucking mess in there, detectives. The victim, Grace, the librarian, she's ... well, you'll see for yourselves. It's like something out of a nightmare." The officer didn't seem like he'd seen much death before. For us, it was just another day at the office.

Dalton nodded, his face grim, like always, at least until the caffeine kicked in. "Alright, we'll take it from here. Has anything been touched inside?"

The officer shook his head. "No, we've kept everyone out since we arrived. As instructed by the DI, he said you two have the experience of h ... hundreds like this...I... I don't know how you handle it all, but the scene's all as we found it."

Michael sensed the officer's unease. "It's alright, matey. You'll develop a cast iron stomach before long. It'll soon be water off a duck's back," he says, forcing a smile for the officer's sake.

We left him be, donned our cheap-looking latex gloves, and entered the library. The overhead lights were flickering ominously, catching my wandering eyes, prompting short flashbacks to some of the shitty visions I've experienced over the last year—the basement ones. We were greeted by a sight that was nothing short of horrifying. Grace's lifeless body lay sprawled across the floor, surrounded by a gruesome pool of blood and gore. Her once-neat bun was now matted with blood, and her glasses lay shattered beside her. I could picture how she would've looked beforehand. Sweet and wouldn't say 'boo to a goose' type of lady.

This one was on me. I lost the coin toss on the way to the scene, meaning I would take the lead. However, I still think Michael is trying to 'school' me, too, in his way of doing things. Don't get me wrong, he's a brilliant detective, and I've learned loads, but sometimes, the old git needs to relax. Anyway, we'll need to use our 'other' unique skills if we want to make any headway. I knelt beside the body, eyes narrowing to examine the scene. "It's another word one, Michael. Look at the precision of these wounds; they're too bloody, brutal and deep. They had complete control and no remorse, hundreds of tears in her flesh, yet there was no sign of a struggle. How on earth does that happen?" I say, pointing out the wounds and noticing that they appear to have happened simultaneously.

Michael shuffled around, surveying the area, his attention drawn to the barbed wire covered in blood. "And this wire? How does it happen without the killer getting hurt, too? Rings a little too much like the flipping haulage yard."

I knew what he meant. "This doesn't sit right ... Nothing about this is natural, Michael.

The way the wire would've moved, it could've danced through the air like the chains ... just as we saw on the CCTV from that place; I'm not reaching for straws here, we both saw. It's as if the killer had a supernatural ability; I'm going on a limb to say the same happened here. The fucking killer can end a life without laying a finger on the victim; how the hell do we manage that?" I fired off, frustrated and bewildered.

Michael frowned, eyes bulging like they do when his thoughts were racing. "We've been through this crap repeatedly. We always come out on top, especially Scotland, but I agree with you; this is different. We must find out who or what could do something like this."

As we continued to examine the crime scene, I noticed something peculiar. "Look at this, Michael," I whisper, trying not to draw too much attention because of how weird these scenes have been. Clear they belong firmly in our secretive 'supernatural' wheelhouse. I gently parted Grace's clothing, revealing a gruesome branded cross, barely above her skirt's edge, carved into the flesh on her back, seared with precision and brutal intent. The surrounding skin was charred black and blistered, looking extremely painful.

I leaned in closer, his expression etched with grim determination. "Michael. It's the same symbol on the torso of the last scene. We need to get the hanging victim, Eckleston, re-examined, looking for the same, aside from him clawing the word 'B.O.O.K.' into his flesh; I fear this 'Cross' could be what connects the victims."

Dalton nodded, his eyes flickering a little yellow while keeping them hidden. Fixated on the branded cross, he tried to look closer. "Matey, it's got to be a mark of a cult or something weird. Just when we thought we'd got a handle on the weird."

I quickly sketched in my notebook, fearing this wouldn't be the last time we saw it. Or should I say, the last time we found it on a victim? It was a horrible reminder of just how dangerous the killer was and the nature of what was at play could be our worst case yet.

We continued to search, and our attention turned to the shattered bookshelf nearby. Books lay strewn about, their pages torn and their covers scorched. Michael quickly picked up one of the damaged ones, flipping through its pages. "Again, the sick bastard has staged the scene, ransacking the place in another attempt to confuse us."

I agree, eyes sweeping across the chaotic shelves. "We both know how easily you're confused, don't we, Michael? Seriously though, the killer wants to throw us off by desecrating places like this; they'll be in for a shock because we aren't buying. What I don't get, considering the savagery of the murder with no evidence, why bother? On one hand, showing off, and on the other, hiding. It's like they're conflicted, or someone is covering up," I attempted to sum the mess up, daring to delve into the killer's mind. Not a nice play to be, considering all I imagined there'd be was blood and anger.

The details led us deeper into the maze-like aisles of books and up the stairs, covering all bases, each step bringing us no closer to a truth that so far kept evading us. We were shuffling through when I spotted a dusty old book on the floor with nothing but a strange, faded symbol that looked a little familiar. At first, I was drawn in and went to open it until Michael grabbed my attention. I placed the book neatly on the shelf and walked away.

We neared the stairs; I got that familiar, unnerving rumble that we were being watched; that last murder had me paranoid, waiting for those two men in black suits to appear. The library is having my wolf's senses go haywire. Something was off.

We returned to the library's entrance with the branded cross lingering on our minds. The weight of the unknown and how dark it could get before we got close enough to stop the carnage niggled away at me. But unravelling these stories is what we do best.

Outside the library, the world remained oblivious to the horrors that had unfolded within its rustic walls. The streetlights continued to flicker, their distant glow finally going out as a new day began. We were entangled in a narrative different from what we'd experienced so far, and that's saying something considering our brush with vampires.

Michael looked unsettled, probably thinking over my comment about the victims being connected and cast an eye over the branded cross on Grace's back again; if any of my habits had rubbed off on him, it was that the details mattered. And there was a detail about the cross bothering him. Like I had, Dalton traced the charred lines with his gloved fingers, his mind racing to connect the dots, when a grim realisation washed over him. The symbol seared into Grace's flesh resembled the emblem he had seen on the cufflinks and pin badges worn by the two scary-looking men in black suits the other night.

"Georgie," Michael says, his voice low, "remember those blokes the other night? The symbol on Grace's back is like the one those men had."

I nodded solemnly. "It can't be a coincidence, Michael. We need to see if this dear lady was also one of their 'parishioners', as they called it."

We exchanged a distressed, knowing look, our thoughts intertwined in the mysteries surrounding them. Both dreading what might happen next while watching for the two haunting men in black suits.

'Grâces last moments,'

In the darkened stillness of the night, Grace, the librarian, began closing up, her mind lingering on her failings earlier on with worried glances over her shoulder. Grace feared repercussions, knowing all too well what happens to anyone who doesn't fulfil their task. The air was laden with the musty scent of books, and the feeble lighting cast eerie shadows that writhed along the towering shelves. Grace had always cherished the peace and normality of this place, but on this night, there was no escaping the rapid heartbeat and panic sweats.

She normally moved through the narrow aisles, checking for stragglers and straightening uneven books. The hushed whisper of her footsteps reverberated in the silence. Her greying black hair was still neatly secured in a bun, even though tiredness wanted to dictate otherwise. Her semi-oval-shaped glasses perched atop her nose, magnifying her aura of order that didn't suit her earlier participation. Grace had been an unassuming custodian of the town's library for many years. Flying under the radar to most who saw her, Grace had secrets.

As she neared the grand wooden doors that guarded the library's entrance, her footsteps slowed, and an unsettling chill crept over her. A sudden draft penetrated the hallowed space, making the overhead lights flicker ominously. Grace's heart quickened, but she dismissed it as Gremlins fucking with the old-ass electric again.

Grace reached the imposing doors, briefly sweeping her eyes over the quiet high street. The world outside was a complete contrast to the busy bustling of daytime, nothing but distant, flickering lampposts. Satisfied that she was alone, Grace locked the heavy doors with a jingling of keys and turned to return to the front desk.

But as she took her first step, an unexplained gust of frigid air surged through the library, extinguishing the remaining lights in a chilling breath. Panic surged through Grace as she stood trapped in the darkness, her heart drumming frantically.

Twisting her head, frantically adjusting her eyes amidst the suffocating blackness, Grace quickly realised an unwelcome presence—she could see nothing, but a tall silhouetted outline that seemed to appear out of thin air. Grace strained her eyes for all their worth, fear causing sweat to pool around her plunging neckline and brow, but was met with an unyielding void. A tremor of anxiety with a sense of impending doom coiled around her chest as she fumbled for the landline, her trembling hands struggling to flip the lamp switch.

Grace's breath caught in her throat as her eyes were attuned to the darkness. She looks up to see the faint outline of a towering presence shrouded in a filthy, hooded cloak. They were smothered in the horrifying coppery scent of blood and putrid death; its hood and wide-brimmed hat imposingly obscured their face, leaving them shrouded in a sinister shadow. The mysterious killer had chosen Grace as their next victim.

Terror rendered Grace's voice a mere whisper as she stammers, "I ... I tried. Please don't do this."

Not who Grace feared they were. The killer remained horrifyingly silent; slowly, it raised its gloved hand. Her shallow breaths filled the air with ghostly plumes as Grace watched in paralysing horror as a length of barbed wire cruelly whipped and stripped from the alleyway fence and ripped through the fire exit door with heart-crushing ferocity.

The vile killer advanced toward a shaking Grace, the barbed wire teeth dripping with the eerie promise of blood twirled through the air, guided by its perpetuating puppeteer. Grace's voice rose in frantic desperation, but her pleas were in vain. The imposing killer manipulated the barbed tool of torment with unnatural grace; every movement exuded a devastating purpose.

With no need to lay a gloved bony finger, the killer began torturing Grace, the barbed wire dancing around her, slashing ferociously like a morbid marionette's strings. It sliced through her flesh repeatedly, hot-knife-like, invoking agonised screams within the library's walls. Blood gushed across the floor as Grace's body writhed in unbearable pain.

The killer seemed to revel in her suffering, not for the first time, its sadistic cruelty boundless. The once-sacred library had become a chamber of horrors as Grace's life ebbed away.

In her last moments, Grace's anguished cries were drowned by bloody gargles and the killer's presence, which had violated the sanctum of learning and fictional escape. As the last threads of life seeped from her, the killer had the barbed wire ripped from Grace's grated flesh, leaving behind a ghastly tapestry of death and devastation.

The slaughterhouse wreaked with fear and death. Its polished floors were now painted in blood. The killer had claimed a third victim and Grace's life, lingering in the shadows, an ominous harbinger of horror, claiming another victim while remaining shrouded in darkness. It stepped back with a cold, calculating menace, allowing the room to be consumed by a deathly silence.

The dimly flickering lights cast eerie, disjointed shadows across the crime scene. The air was heavy with the metallic scent of blood, mingling with the ever-present aroma of stale dust. The library had been defiled, and Grace had been made to pay; the venom that lingered in the shadows seemed to feed on the terror it had sown.

Outside the library, the world remained oblivious to the horrors that had unfolded within its rustic walls. The streetlights continued to flicker, their distant glow offering no solace to the sadistic darkness that had descended.

In the aftermath of the gruesome murder, the killer retreated, its purpose fulfilled. The world would soon awaken to the horrifying truth of what had taken place in the night's heart, but for now, the killer remained hidden, waiting to unleash its terror once more; its dirt-black hooded cloak had become an embodiment of evil. Some might say, even supernatural. Their relentless pursuit of revenge as death continues.

A Shrill in Time

18

'Gerald,'

The shrill ringing of the house phone in my study jolted me awake, causing a startle upright in bed. With tired, sore eyes, I jumped up in case it was mother about the girls. Considering everything, I thought it would be safer if they stayed with her, even if it was just for the night. My heart raced as I dashed for my desk, fumbling for the receiver, still dazed.

"Hello?" my voice wavered as I answer the call, my nerves still raw from the bloody nightmare. It was horrible and far too real for my liking, as if I were there.

"Gerald, it's me, Nathan," a familiar voice crackled through the line, bearing an urgency that cut through the early morning haze.

"Nathan?" I blinked, shaking off the remnants of the nightmare. "What's going on?"

I sat hunched over my desk, clutching the phone tightly, although my hand kept shaking.

"Listen, buddy," Nathan's voice crackled through the receiver, "you need to grab a copy of the morning newspaper. Something fucking awful has happened."

My curiosity mingled with dread as I glanced at the clock. It was far too early for a phone call like this, and the uneasy fear from the dream still clung to me.

"I don't understand. What's going on, Nathan?"

Nathan sighs heavily. His voice sounded scared, and he was holding back out of that fear. "It's about Grace, the crazy librarian from yesterday; well, Grace Lipton is her full name, but that's getting off the point. She's dead, Gerald. bloody murdered."

Nathan's damming words formed a dark cloud over my head, and my heart sank as my mind flashed back. I was going to be sick. Grace tried to fuck us over, but didn't deserve to die. I replayed every detail of what happened and didn't know whether or how to tell Nathan.

"Murdered?" I repeated coyly, my mind struggling to process how it had gone from the dream to being real. "How? Why?"

Nathan's tone was sombre. "All I know is in the morning newspaper. They're calling it a brutal killing. Lavished all over the headlines."

My surprised gaze darted to the side table beside the desk, where a newly folded newspaper lay untouched. My papers are delivered and usually come early, but I hadn't been up yet, let alone gone to the front door—not that I remembered, anyway. Quickly, I snatched at it and unfolded the pages to reveal the gruesome headline that confirmed Nathan's words. The image of Grace's serene face stared back at him, a stark contrast to the horror I'd seen.

"Police are investigating," Nathan continues. "They found her body at the library. It's a fucking sick buddy. Yeah, her motives yesterday were questionable, but this?"

I couldn't tear my eyes away from the article. The details of the murder were scarce, but the brutality described had my stomach churning. Hoping it had been a one-off.

"I can't believe it," my voice raspy, not wanting to utter the words. "She was just ... she was there yesterday. As you say, questionable, but...."

Nathan's voice softened. "I know, mate. It will shake the town, and we need to be careful. There's something crazy happening in this little place, and it looks like we've found ourselves in the middle of it."

As we spoke, one thing was on my mind, first seeing Grace and the looming figure, then becoming the killer's eyes. The murder of Grace Lipton was ominous because a pattern was forming. She was another person I'd crossed paths with, and now she's dead. It wouldn't take long to find that detail and connect the dots.

With a heavy sigh, I finally gathered the courage to share the haunting details of last night with Nathan.

"There's something I have to tell you ... I was in the library," I began, slow and deliberate. "I saw Grace ... she was there, just as she always is, closing up for the night. But then, the lights went out, and I watched ... I watched as she was murdered."

Nathan's silence on the other end of the line was deafening, and I understood the level of my friend's concern.

"It was like a nightmare, Nathan," I continue, a little paranoid, scanning around me. "I couldn't move, couldn't do anything to help her. And the killer ... they were shrouded in the shadows, wearing a hooded cloak. It was the same figure I've been seeing in passing reflections or sitting in places, but nobody else can see them. It's like they've been haunting me. Then, the dream. The worst part is, at one point, I was viewing through the killer's sadistic fucking eyes."

Nathan finally spoke, his voice filled with unease. "Gerald, this is more than just a spooky coincidence. We must get a handle on what's happening with you because that shouldn't be possible unless you've developed some crazy psychic ability, bullshit, you lucky fucker. I suggest we keep quiet about it for now, but we need to tell someone if it happens again before people put two and two together and come up with you as the suspect. Besides, we will have our hands full, uncovering the seedy secrets about this town and your father. I don't mean seedy for your father, but he's got some skeletons, that's for sure. Just tell me if any more weird stuff happens, okay?"

I nodded. It was weird, considering Nathan couldn't see me, but struggled to reply. The past days' events rattled me badly, and I knew we were on the cusp of uncovering something we may wish we hadn't.

My paranoia wasn't letting up, eyes pinging back and forth, expecting to see that figure. Ironically, I could still smell Grace's blood and the killer's sick scent of death; the view of Grace's shredded flesh on the floor in a dark crimson 'bloody' swimming pool sent bile surging into my mouth. Leaving me with a genuine fear swooshing around in my head that more bodies would drop, and I hoped they wouldn't land at my feet. Yet, I got a horrible feeling...

I sat, reflecting in the silence of my study, my man cave, as Charlotte would call it. The antique clock on the wall ticked away the seconds, each in time with my heart. I didn't know what to do next, other than not going to work. My excuses were ready. The after-effects of the car crash were lingering. At least, that's what I'd say. Whiplash can linger a day or so, and the way I saw it, why the hell not?

Just as my thoughts drifted to the current boss and then the former, being my father. A thunderous banging echoed through my quiet, semi-detached home. Loud enough to make my heart leap into my throat and my blood run cold. The pounding on the front door was relentless, as if someone were breaking through.

Fear took over, sweat bubbling over my forehead as I slowly rose from the chair. My footsteps echoed in the peaceful hallway. Dread grew with each step toward the front door, and my imagination cooked up some nightmarish scenarios.

I reached the door, a shaky hand hovering over the doorknob. The pounding continued, growing louder and more urgent with each passing moment. With a deep breath, I summoned the courage to twist the knob and swing the door open.

What met me was not the nightmarish figure in the cloak I'd feared, but a postman standing on the doorstep, looking confused. The man held a parcel wrapped in a yellow jiffy package, contrasting with the ominous and needless thumping on my front door.

"Parcel for Mr Gerald Ackerman," the postman announced, his tired voice droned as he repeated himself with each delivery.

I sighed in relief, my heart still racing from the initial knock. Nodded and took the parcel from the postman's outstretched hand. The postman tipped his cap and departed, leaving me with the perhaps not-so-mysterious package, as I suspected it could be. It felt flat and solid, yet also light. The morning was about to take another turn, not for the best.

The door swung closed, and I carried the parcel back to the study, where the desk lamp lit a pool of light in the early morning gloom. Carefully, I unwrapped the yellow package, revealing what I feared: another VHS tape—much like the one I'd received before. 'Things you need to know–Tape Two,' the same red felt tip handwriting, too.

It made me wonder, though. Why did father have to resort to tapes? Why couldn't he say something? And why the hell did it have to be our family entrenched in this web of darkness that is on the verge of shaking the Willowbrook facade? If it hadn't already. Quiet on the outside, darkness underneath, is what I thought of the town now.

My hand hung in the air and paused. I didn't want to do it, but I had to. With the VHS stowed, the screen flickered to life, and grainy streaks covered father's-tired image filling the screen. It was another recording, another glimpse into the past and what other bloody secrets my parents had. What did Henry have to say this time?

Close Call

19

'Gerald,'

The grainy image flickered to life, casting an eerie glow that seemed mesmerising. The video abruptly paused, freezing on an image that had tormented me since the first tape. Father nestled in a darkened room.

I was fixated on looking for clues, anything to tell me where they were filmed. The man who had been my unwavering pillar of strength now resembled a shadow of his former self, haunted by a past I needed to uncover. His wrinkled and soaked in sweat, pale blue shirt displayed the look of a man under pressure. The top button was left undone, and a navy blue and white striped tie encircled his neck like a noose waiting to be tugged tight.

Tears were bubbling as I absorbed the image of my father. To see him struggling so badly and he hadn't let on was a bitter pill to swallow. What led to this harrowing decline? He looks burdened by guilt. Why didn't any of us notice Father's silent suffering? Unless Mother had, and she's holding back more than I thought. The symbol cruelly etched into Father's flesh left a physical and emotional scar, and many unanswered questions swirled in my fragile little mind. Who could do such a sick thing? For what purpose? Was it a warning or an omen? Or something different altogether.

However, a familiar and haunting presence harshly interrupted my thoughts. The hooded figure's faint, ominous outline lingered menacingly behind father in the footage.

Pushing on, I pressed play again. Father's voice echoed from the speakers, each word full of sadness.

"Hey Gerald, it's me, reaching out to you from beyond the grave." Father's voice quivered. "I'm sorry, but this is your reality now. I can only imagine the strange things you've experienced, perhaps even run-ins with certain individuals. Listen carefully; avoid the men in the black suits at all costs; they are far more dangerous than they appear, and deception lurks where you least expect it."

My jaw dropped as the words sunk in. "Strange and unexplainable things will happen, tightening their grip on you," my father cautions. "Some will inflict unimaginable pain. I sought ways of escape and hunted for loopholes, but life kicked me in the balls. The answers exist, but I realised it was too late. My Father, your grandfather, kept our family's darkest secrets from me; if only he'd been more forthcoming, we may have stood a chance."

This was a Pandora's box of nightmares. "Understand this, Gerald. Your world is changed forever," Father continues, urgency lacing his voice. "Our family name..."

Before Father could utter another word, his gaze snapped towards something in the room, and I followed his father's line of sight. The shadowy figure lurking behind his father had shifted, raising a menacing arm to point ominously. Father's panicked reaction sent a jolt of dread coursing through.

"Oh, damn it," Henry mutters, his voice tinged with fear. "I must go now. I will update you soon. Remember, I love you, my son. And above all, stay safe. Knowing you, you're probably already digging into this. If so, remember, a picture is worth a thousand words."

The recording abruptly ended, leaving me deciphering the cryptic message at the end. The figure in the shadows lingered on the screen; its presence plagued me. Scratching my chin inquisitively, holding off from swallowing a mouthful of saliva as I approached the TV screen. Slowly, I traced the outline of the shadow, feeling static beneath the tips, widening around the head area. 'The bloody hat,' I murmur, eyes widening, reflecting the frozen screen. My heart was beating two to the dozen after the last time the figure whacked against the screen, even though I hadn't rationalised an answer for everything happening.

'You ... got...to...kill...them...all,' Ice drifted down my back, finger glued to the TV screen when I heard father's voice again. This time, not from the TV and scarily high pitched.

My head turned slowly as I heard his father's voice echoing from the hallway. 'There won't be peace until you kill them all,' the voice continues. Each made me shudder a little.

The footsteps that followed were heavy and deliberate, each step drawing closer. I was paralyzed, unable to comprehend what was happening. Father's voice and the ominous message were all too much to bear.

And then, as the shadow in the doorway became clear, my world unravelled completely. It was his father, but it couldn't be. It was impossible, yet he stood there, his eyes absent and ghostly.

'Do it, Gerald, end them all. End the cursed, and you will be free. There's no escaping your fate.' Henry raised his hands, showing blood-covered palms. 'We all have blood on our hands in this family, but you can wash it away.'

My eyes bulged in shock, watching the blood drip from his hands, fixated as each drop fell, and then I noticed something that snaps me back to lucid. The drops weren't showing on the floor, and there was no puddle, but I was no less scared.

The words were going over in my mind. *'Do it, Gerald. Kill them all.'* How was it happening? I kept asking myself, thinking back to my mother in the kitchen, wondering if this was what his father meant about seeing things. I shook my head, hoping it would disappear, but Father remained. Suddenly, a series of thunderous booms resounded against the front door, each impact more menacing than the last. I wasn't expecting anyone or anything else. Then again, I wasn't expecting another tape, and the relentless pounding woke me up. I look down the hallway, where the haunting image of his father had vanished, leaving behind a trail of unanswered questions. 'Boom, Boom, Boom,' the thumps echoed again, my neck hairs bouncing with worry.

I sprang to my feet as sweat trickled down his cheek. I glided silently to my bedroom, hastily dressed in jeans and snatching the nearest T-shirt. As I slipped into my trainers, a low, rumbling like distant thunder echoed from the front door. It didn't sound good.

I threw a load of bits in a holdall and got ready to leave via his study window. It would take me to the pathway at the side of the house, and from then on, it's a fifty-feet dash to the car. It seemed not even home was safe now.

"We know you're in there," a skin-grating voice called out, an accent, possibly Italian, 'What the fuck? How could they?' as I continue my hazy attempt at stealth, vindicated by not having the girls with me just now.

"Come on now, give up, and we will spare the pain, and anyone else in your family, and your curse ends with you quickly. Don't, and all hell will rain down on you and everyone you know and love," an unfamiliar voice this time, much like the last, pitchy with a squeal of chalk grinding on a blackboard.

"Arrenditi traditore, abomination," sounded off in a language I didn't know, yet it was scary. I was desperate to understand why I was being hunted down with such ferocity and wondered how deep the trouble father had got himself into.

I sneaked toward the hallway, hearing the vibrating louder. The front door knocker rattled against the wood. Their silhouettes loomed in the frosted glass. I was about to dash to the study when he saw the strangest thing: a black-suited arm passed through the door, and then, one by one, more limbs followed; I was frozen—no other way to put it. I froze in awe and fear. Their heads drifted through, but they didn't look how I'd seen them at the library. Not in the beginning, anyway. Both appeared like 'death', with skeletal faces littered with decay. They'd pass as zombies or similar if I didn't know better. Not that I believe in such things. At least, I didn't until this.

Both displayed menacing grins as their pitch-black eyes gleamed in the shower of daylight being cast through the windows. Finally, I returned to the task and ran to the study.

'Crap,' the window stuck, doing its best to resist my efforts.

Their footsteps were heard moving through the hall. They were in. At this rate, I was going to need a pacemaker, the way my heart was being made to work. Pounding so loudly as I yanked with all my might, sliding the window a little.

The steps were close, "come out, come out, wherever you are," one shouts, sounding confident.

The window juddered a little more. "you have nowhere to go," they called again.

A loud squeak gave me away, but the window loosened more; with a final yank, it slid upward sharply. The haunting men were in the study doorway. I flung myself through in the nick of time as they lunged forward. My body hit the rough stone path hard, drawing blood across my palms and knees. Their horrifying faces drifted between the window gap; with a deep breath, I dragged my body up and ran as fast as my legs could carry me to the car. All the while, their steps could be heard. My hand was shaking, unlocking his mother's car. The front door crashed open without them breaking stride.

My car door flung open, and I dived in, bag in hand; thankfully, the key slid into the barrel at the first time of asking. The engine cranked to life, screeching away as the two angry men reached his door. There was no knowing where I was going or what to do next, as long as those monsters were fading in his rearview. It was a close shave. Far too close. The bigger question is, who the hell was hunting me? Other than two guys that look like they've been dug up from a cemetery.

Return of the Living Dead

20

'Détective Reynolds,'

Michael's footsteps reverberated through the darkened corridors of the morgue, each cumbersome step echoing. His mind was elsewhere the entire journey—no doubt cursing our luck. Angst harboured against A.D.I. Locke for trapping us in this nightmarish town. For a change, I was lagging after a hurried call to check on Ellena. Aside from the bloodshed, there were moments of normalcy in Scotland, momentary glimpses of normalcy amidst the horrors we had now unravelled. Yet, the ominous presence of murder dragged me away, imposing its sinister interference in our lives.

The recent murder of Grace at the library had left us with more than just a chilling crime scene. It had planted a seed of unease in our minds, a cryptic symbol etched upon the victims' flesh. A cross, both intricate and ominous, had left an indelible mark upon two of the three bodies we'd encountered. Frank Eckleston, a hanging still full of mystery, loomed worryingly. I had my suspicions, and they were far from comforting.

We were headed for the autopsy room, where Frank's corpse awaited us, thanks to Michael calling ahead. The circumstances of the recent murder had left a bitter taste in old Micky boy's mouth. I was busy wrestling with the eerie discrepancies that defied the conventional more than we'd experienced so far. That speaks volumes, having been blindsided by a witch, gone toe to toe with vampires and survived a Kanaima demon. We shared an aversion to returning favours that involved confronting horrendous corpses, and the prospect of a third had us uneasy.

The morgue's harsh fluorescent lights, casting menacing shadows across sterile tiles, exhaled a morbid ambience. The scent of formaldehyde, clinging to the air, tainted our every breath. An unsettling, chilling, unforgiving atmosphere enveloped us as we entered.

Dr Emily Thornton, the morgue's resident pathologist, was already at work, her gloved hands busy with the grisly task of examining Frank's lifeless body. She looked up, her eyes reflecting curiosity and unease as we approached.

"Detectives Dalton and Reynolds," she murmurs, her voice bearing the weight of years spent alongside the dead. "I hadn't expected you so soon. I understand your desire to see this mess firsthand, but I had hoped to spare you the ordeal and offer you a report."

Michael's response was stoic, his sombre tone matching the unenvious task. "Thank you, Dr Thornton. However, we believe there might be more to Frank's death, just as there will be with the other two."

Dr Thornton nodded, shifting past us and viewing Frank's corpse. As she slid past Michael, the scent of Chanel No. 5 ruffled his senses, masking the otherwise morbid stink. Frank's lifeless body lay naked on the cold table, with a white sheet covering his modesty. His neck was distended and bruised, with dark purple swelling below the jugular. We looked on with apprehension; I hated this aspect of our investigation. We have seen enough death to last a lifetime, especially recently. I was still haunted by some things that went down and what I had to do, images of blood seeping over the pavement; now we're in another mess.

Leaning in, my eyes narrowed to focus before slowly drifting over the body as Dr Thornton manipulated Frank's dead limbs. As Thornton manoeuvred a tree trunk of a left leg, I glimpsed what we'd feared yet assumed would happen: the cross was etched into Frank's calf. The cross was vibrant, with most of the skin a cold, mottled white and purple, which seemed odd.

It matched exactly the one found on Grace's lifeless body and the dismembered body of Patrick Sheh in the haulage yard. The intricate design seemed to shimmer hauntingly, its meaning and purpose still a mystery to us, only that the two strange blokes had similar markings on their cufflinks and badges.

"Aside from that bloody thing, have you found anything else unusual? Is there any sign that he may have put up a fight after all?" Michael asks, a little distracted as he takes in the cross's view, too.

Dr Thornton hesitated, her gaze shifting uneasily. "I've seen nothing like it, no pressure marks or bruising other than the carving in his arm. I swabbed the dried blood under his nails to be sure, but it was his; I don't understand who would have the mind to tear **'B.O.O.K.'** into their flesh while hanging themselves?" she admitted with an air of confusion. "The 'cross' wound appears charred as if seared into the flesh. There's no sign of infection or external trauma. It's ... unsettling."

I shifted to face her, dreading what else the doctor would spill. "He didn't hang himself," I paused, glancing at Michael, who shook his head 'no'—not to tell her. He had help; we just don't know who, I finished reluctantly, holding back that it was supernaturally induced. That would make the Doctor's toes curl.

As we contemplated the cryptic cross, an eerie silence enveloped the room. The air seemed to thicken before a sudden faint whispering echoed hauntingly in the background. Michael and I stepped close to Dr Thornton and clenched our fists to hide our claws that had slid forward on guard.

A cold draft swept through the room, encompassing everything in its path. It extinguished the overhead lights with a frightening flicker and plunged us into darkness. With the look of 'not again,' Michael reached for his tiny flashlight, but the cross on Frank's calf glowed blood red before he could flick it on horrifyingly.

Frank's body suddenly writhed, and his dull eyes readily snapped open, glowing a haunting, ghostly grey. His fingers twitched at the sound of bones breaking. Each snap made me shudder, and a low, growling moan escaped his stern purple lips. It was a sound that skated a chill through us all. The Doc's scowl of distress spoke volumes.

"Frank?" I stammer in disbelief at what I was witnessing, unable to hide the shake in my voice. "Is that you?"

Frank's response was far from human. He sat up abruptly, his movements jerky and unnatural, his bones clicking and with more jarring snapping, only louder. His spooky, glazed eyes fixed on Michael and me with a venom that scared us, even with our unique abilities. I could hear all our heartbeats throttling like a Ferrari. We still held off, not wanting Dr Thornton to know what we could do. If the doctor knew I was a werewolf and Michael... well, let's say 'shifter' for now until we get to research more., she would run away screaming.

The room felt alive. Equipment rattled, and cabinets creaked open of their own accord, haunted house-like. Dr Thornton backed away; her fear resonated as her pale skin turned ghostly.

The reanimated corpse confronted us in the deathly cold ambience of the morgue. We were in the middle of another weird twist in this web of mysteries that showed no sign of relenting. We stood frozen in the middle of the morgue, shielding the doctor. Our rapid breathing was visible with white clouds in the frigid air. Frank Eckleston was dead, now defied his brutal hanging and the laws of what I knew about life after death and all that jazz. Those ghostly eyes seemed to gleam, with a sinister smile twisting across his lips.

"What in the unholy hell is happening?" I gush. Fingers tensed as they fought their unnatural instincts, fighting back the claws.

Frank's voice, dripping with a ghastly cadence, slithered through the air, each word a chilling revelation. "You seek answers, detectives, but answers have dangerous consequences for you and those you love. Answers your fragile minds aren't ready for."

"Tell us ... what do you bloody want?" Michael implored, his voice trembling. All Frank did was glare back menacingly. I was distracted by the glowing symbol, wondering if that was how Frank's corpse was being manipulated. Farfetched to most, maybe not when I know magic exists. Not the good kind, either.

The Evil Puppet

21

'Détective Reynolds,'

Frank's eyes bore devilishly into us with an intensity that had us on the back foot and worried for the Doc. If she wasn't here, it may have been easier to handle. "We will bring down retribution, the unleashing of darkness upon a world that has forgotten and spurned the gift of life. The cross is our awakening and will be your undoing."

"Who are you beneath Frank's flesh? What do you stand for? Why are you doing this?" I summoned the courage to ask. Glancing nervously at Michael.

"We are the harbingers and the beginning of the end. All your bodies will be conduits for evil's army, and soon hell will erupt into a frenzy, spreading into your world like a plague. And there's nothing you can do," Frank hisses, the cross eerily shimmering brighter than before. "The blood-bathed reckoning is coming."

"We're not buying, I'm afraid. Tell your friends we don't need any visitors; the world is overpopulated enough already," I quip, putting up a front as I look at Frank's overweight flesh. More symbols suddenly sliced their way through Frank's body until he looked more like a 'bloody' patchwork quilt.

Frank's head juddered, twisting his broken neck, the bloated flesh stretching as the head circled around and around, blood drooling from his mouth as the head was now backwards, looking directly at me.

"You insignificant cockroach. I highly recommend you to run home now. Kiss Miss Ellena Walker goodbye before it's too late. Mr Dalton, you and the doctor should get a room. You both want to; how better a way to spend your time seeing out the end of your world as the streets become rivers of red? The skies will smother you in eternal darkness, and the dead shall flock from their graves to embrace a new world and regime," Frank snarls, gargling blood through decaying teeth. I stood in shock, questioning how this dead thing could know of Ellena, let alone the dooming premonition.

"Piss off, you're not the first morbid doom bastard, and I'm sure you won't be the last," Michael fronted up, attempting to ease the doctor's visible fear.

"The knights are on the March, beacons of death, and there's nothing you can do," Frank cackled loudly, his shrills causing us to shuffle back a few steps.

The room shuddered as Frank spoke, and the morgue's lights fluctuated faster with fear-inducing regularity. A wild wind howled through the hallways, carrying Frank's words repeatedly, as shadows converged upon Frank's continuously deforming body, churning up the symbols, swirling and merging into a nightmarish cloak of darkness.

"Is this guy for real, Georgie?" Michael hisses shakily. I didn't have an answer to this question. It was real, in the essence, that it was happening before our eyes, while common sense told me it couldn't be.

I whisper in terror, "We need to get the fuck out of here now!" We looked to the doorway, braced to run for it.

But it was too late. The room convulsed; the very walls pulsed. The morgue's cold steel tables and gleaming instruments rattled and clattered as if they, too, were being controlled. The fluorescent lights overhead flickered wildly, casting eerie, strobing shadows that danced across the white tiles that now seemed sprayed by blood.

Once a corpse, Frank's body was fast becoming a grotesque canvas upon which evil painted its horrific masterpiece. His limbs contorted and twisted in ways that defied the laws of anatomy, bones snapped like brittle twigs, and his flesh rippled and writhed. The air thickened with the sickening stench of decay and burning sulphur; a foul aroma toyed and clung unnaturally to our senses.

As Frank continued changing, he filled the room with a morbid laugh that echoed around us, a haunting symphony reverberating deep within. It was a laughter devoid of the semblance of humanity. It was coming from all directions simultaneously as if the walls and floors were mocking us.

Michael and I stumbled backwards; our eyes locked on the freak show that had once been Frank Eckleston. His skin took on a sickly pallor, veins of oily blackness snaked beneath the mottled surface, and his eyes glowed with unholy light. Jagged, needle-like teeth protruded from his misshapen jaw, and a guttural, inhuman growl emanated from his twisted throat.

The room seemed to writhe in agony, leaving us and the Dr trapped in a nightmare. The walls oozed a dark red that dripped and pooled on the floor, with Frank using everything around him to torment the life of the doctor and us. Considering what we'd seen, that took some doing. The blood had a mind of its own, catching my attention, slithering across the sterile cream stone floor with grotesque patterns becoming strange sigils and a familiar symbol, the one Frank's corpse wore, as did the two men in black suits, blood-red crosses, whose lines curved ornately. The temperature had long since plummeted to bone-chilling depths, and that thick air was now heavier, making it harder for everyone to breathe.

Amid this dreadful nightmare, Frank's twisted body levitated hauntingly above the morgue table. He hung in mid-air, a scary marionette in a nightmare puppet show. The sinister cross upon his calf pulsed with an intensity that matched the frantic rhythm of our pounding hearts.

With a growing horror, little Willowbrook was covered in a dangerous darkness that may be the beginning. As we backed away, our footsteps echoed in the chamber of horrors. Evil hungered for death and chaos. In my mind, the sinister cross was the connection.

The morgue groaned in protest, and the ceiling above wept blood. Its once-sterile walls now bore the scars of an unspeakable terror. The symbols on the floor and the cross had multiplied, forming a grotesque mosaic of evil. Their meanings remained a mystery, yet we could not tear our eyes away from the sinister sigils, whose lines curved, resembling ancient scripts or similar, with Michael assuming them to be Latin.

Then, with a sudden, violent lurch, Frank's crazy contortions ceased, and the grotesque spectacle that had once been a man floated motionless at the centre of the morgue. His eyes remained fixed upon Michael and me with an unyielding, evil gaze that penetrated our souls.

Our breaths hung in the frigid air, visible puffs of fear and worry. The icy shadows that had crept across the floor now coiled around our legs, threatening to drag us into the nightmarish darkness that had consumed the morgue.

As we grappled with understanding the 'if's and how's,' Frank's voice began spouting off strange words, an incantation that sounded like nothing we knew, perhaps in a film or a book, but nothing else. The eerie utterances lingered, a chilling torment that rattled our very being. Frank's twisted and grotesque corpse let loose a loud, piercing scream that echoed through the morgue, only to cease abruptly, leaving a disturbing silence in its wake.

The blood and shadows encircling Frank's body abruptly disappeared. The symbols on the floor faded, leaving the morgue in eerie stillness. Frank lay motionless on the metal table.

Reeling from the horrors we'd witnessed, our senses exchanged bewildered glances. Whatever evil had gripped the room, whatever irrational nightmare had unfolded, was gone, leaving us in disbelief.

Dr Thornton, who had watched the nightmarish events unfold with a mix of fascination and terror, cautiously approached Frank's lifeless body. She examined the cross on Frank's calf, which had once blazed unholy fervently, but now seemed inert and ordinary.

Her composed demeanour, shattered by the inexplicable events, could only shake her head in bewilderment. "What the hell just happened?" she asks, her mind grappling with the unexplainable. "It's as if ... as if that flipping dead body came back to life, possessed even."

Michael could only mutter in response, his voice bearing the weight of confusion and dread. "I do not know."

The room was now silent and unyielding, its walls and floor bearing the fading scars of a bizarre, evil or other supernatural essence, which made me worry over who or what could be next. As we left, our minds were haunted, as the investigation had taken a sinister turn that could lead us deeper into the heart of darkness and the unknown.

The Escape

22

'Gerald,'

My heart was going like the clappers as I escaped through what seemed like the endless bloody streets of Willowbrook. With each turn, each glance in the rearview mirror, I half-expected to see those spooky-looking men in black suits closing in on me. This was no joke. I feared for my flipping life, the fear coursing through my veins like a chilling toxin, struggling to understand why I just leapt through my study window. Every blink, every glance, I felt haunted.

I kept seeing the shadowed figure in the hooded cloak, an eerie reflection haunting every surface, intensifying my paranoia. Every time I checked, there was nobody following; he glimpsed that hooded shadow in the car's rearview. Father's tapes needed to spill the beans quicker than they'd been so far; drip feeding, the story left me hanging, especially as whatever father escaped in death was now ravaging my life.

My nerves were shot to pieces. Blood dribbled from my knees and palms, but that was nothing compared to the sudden rush of searing pain; I tore around a country lane, being forced into a muddy ditch by a lorry too wide for the road. This route was to loop around town in case those men were more than they appeared. As my heart fell back into my chest, that pain was tearing through my bloody back. Perhaps I'd hurt myself by jumping through the window worse than it seemed. Fearing adrenaline had been masking the extent of an injury. This was steadily becoming agony, but I couldn't stop.

Desperation gripped me, and I needed to get somewhere safe to call Nathan first to ensure he was okay, and then for help. So far, Nathan was the one ally in this search for hope and answers, consuming my thoughts. As I sped through the grim streets, my eyes desperately scanned for a phone far enough away. What else could they do if they could blow off a front door?

Finally, there was one just off the bend, towards the end of the high street, tucked behind a wall by an alley. It was the perfect escape route if I needed it. With trembling hands, the car screeched to a stop, leaving it looking abandoned with a small cloud of smoke from the engine that caused a slight concern as I lurched from my seat, fumbling for change. The last thing I needed was to be without a vehicle right now; I'd be a sitting duck. With a fistful of coins, fingers clumsier than normal, uncooperative, as nervous energy coursed through.

'NATHAN'S RESEARCH,'

Meanwhile, Nathan Hartley was poring over some disturbing revelations in another part of town - through not-so-legal channels - he got his hands on copies of the crime scene photos; there was another connection he feared but hadn't told Gerald yet. Here, a little flirting went a long way because he worried that if he could spot the link, the police would too. Nathan had put Gerald on the trucker's trail because of his wife's crash that killed her. Nathan found Patrick Sheh, who supposedly drove the truck that night and was now dead. He'd uncovered that the haulage yard has a habit of scraping vehicles involved in incidents like that; a few rumours were knocking around, and they made certain bodies disappear, too.

The go-to guy was Frank Ecklleston; he's dead, too. Then there's little old Grace, the librarian, who seemed to aid the two in black suits; she's dead. Nathan connected it all, made worse by Gerald telling him he witnessed the murder through the killer's eyes. Nathan knew Gerald wasn't a killer, but coincidences were one thing; this was a pattern, and Nathan wanted to help protect his friend while his own hands may also be slightly questionable. Their connection with a certain symbol had Nathan spooked and shocked. His hands trembled as he lined up three clear pictures; each victim had a symbol etched into their flesh, each a scary burnt cross.

Nathan's gaze remained fixated. The crosses were hauntingly familiar, echoing with a sinister significance that made Nathan take notice. They weren't just random symbols; they held a dark secret. One that was centuries old, entrenched in nothing good, and Nathan wanted to know what they meant and why now.

Intrigued, Nathan recalled his father, Jack, who had a penchant for collecting ancient dusty relics and historical works. Jack's obsession with history had left Nathan with the bug and a treasure trove of books. Among them was a crusty-looking one about the medieval French military, a subject Jack had been particularly interested in.

Nathan suspected these symbols held a connection to the old military, called the Knights Templar, the ancient order shrouded in mystery. The further he read, the more he realised that this wasn't necessarily the Templars he or history knew of. These crosses were different, twisted, and darkened, reflecting a sinister divergence from the norm.

The Templars, originally known as the Poor Fellow-Soldiers of Christ and of the Temple of Solomon, emerged in the early 12th century during the Crusades. Their primary mission was to protect Christian pilgrims travelling to the Holy Land. Over time, they became a formidable military and financial force, amassing wealth, land, and influence across Europe.

Nathan discovered their red cross on a white field emblem, which was deeply symbolic. It represented their commitment to defending the Christian faith and their willingness to shed blood in its name. The cross had taken on a darker meaning in their recent investigations, as it was tied to forbidden knowledge and supernatural forces.

As he read through the accounts of their history, Nathan uncovered the Templars' connection to the Holy Grail, a legendary relic believed to possess divine power. The Grail was said to be the cup used by Christ during the Last Supper, and the Templars were rumoured to have searched for it during their time in the Holy Land.

Their quest for the Grail led them to discover ancient texts, and arcane rituals delved into the occult. During this period, a splinter sect of the Templars emerged, seeking to harness forbidden knowledge and wield dark forces for their gain.

Nathan's research also revealed the Templars' ultimate downfall. In 1307, King Philip IV of France, in league with Pope Clement V, ordered the arrest and suppression of the Templars. They were accused of heresy, idol worship, and other crimes, leading to the brutal persecution and dissolution of the order.

However, rumours persisted that some Templars had escaped persecution, carrying hidden knowledge and relics of immense power. These survivors allegedly went underground, preserving their dark secrets and continuing their clandestine activities. Nathan was hooked, getting carried away with the enchantment of his reading, nearly forgetting what drew him to the books.

As Nathan returned to the task, he compared the crosses in the photos and the books when his house phone suddenly rang, making him jump out of his skin in the tobacco-clouded silence. Nathan reached for the handset in the book pile, his heart racing like a Formula One engine as he answered it. He heard a desperate voice crackling through the line.

Help

23

'Gerald,'

"Nathan, I need your help. I'm in trouble and being chased by those men in black suits again. They bloody found my house; they're not flipping normally. They walked through my bloody door, for Christ's sake. We need to meet somewhere safe. I'm out of the way for now, but this shit has me paranoid. There's so much more to this than we realised." I say, twitching with nerves, my head on a swivel.

Nathan's voice surged with urgency as he responded, "Gerald, I've uncovered something too ... It's about crosses. And a lot more. Meet me at the old St. Peter's church ruins on the outskirts of town. It's isolated and the only place close enough to talk safely. But for god's sake, be careful, Gerald."

With that, I hung up the payphone and returned to the car. I pulled away from the high street, my mind racing with fear and anticipation. The church ruins on the outskirts of town were a gloomy location for a meeting, but it seemed like our best option for now. I navigated the winding roads, eyes darting around, searching for any sign that I was being followed.

The pain in my back continued, a searing reminder that made me look in the mirror. Still there, I saw the hooded figure again, as if it was me, who was the shadowy menace, and as haunting as it was, it was the least of my worries. My hands tightened on the steering wheel as I drove toward the unknown, wondering what Nathan would tell me.

Meanwhile, Nathan had gathered all the information he could about the Knights

Templar and their dark connection to the crosses. It was a history that had been buried beneath layers of secrecy, and Nathan was determined to uncover the truth for his friend's sake, even if it led them into the heart of darkness.

'Gerald,'

I headed to the church ruins. My mind was all over the place, even if I was a little curious. The fear was genuine. Judging by what Nathan alluded to, our meeting could change everything. My car pulled up to the desolate church ruins and stepped out, eyes scanning the eerie surroundings. The place seemed old, centuries maybe. There is no telling what secrets this place holds. I waited anxiously for Nathan.

When he finally arrived, Nathan seemed full of dread. Eyes bulging, bouncing around in his head. There was no turning back now. We were on the cusp of a revelation that could either save us or damn us to a fate darker than we could imagine.

Wind whispered through the crumbling arches of the grey ruins. We stood in the heart of this relic, our faces partially obscured by the shadows cast by the fading sun.

"We need to sort out what the hell is going on here," I say, unable to hide the quiver in my voice. "I keep seeing that fucking hooded figure in my reflection; it's everywhere I bloody go; it's beginning to seem like it's me. I'm cracking up, and I don't know why. And those creepy guys in the black suits are bloody hunting me as they followed you, Nathan; I don't know how, but they did; they found my home. I'm just lucky the girls were with my mother because they blew the front door off with a wave of a hand. Oh, did I mention those creepy bastards walked through the door on the way in?"

Nathan nodded, his eyes never leaving my anxious face. "I've been digging into this madness and some history. This rubbish has precarious links to you; each body has crossed your path recently. I'm not saying it's you, but the police might, and I helped put you onto them, except the librarian. I'm worried the police might sniff around you after making the same connection."-

- "Also, each of the murder victims had a cross burnt into them. I thought it seemed familiar, the shape of one of my dad's books. It's the Templars, fucking medieval knights, and what I've found fascinating and terrifying. The cross, the one burned into the bodies, is not the typical traditional Templar cross; the shape is. It's the colour; it's darker. The darkening of the red represents 'Hell', their fall into corruption and evil, into darkness and their hunger for blood."

I shudder at the implications of Nathan's words. "So, you're saying each murder is linked to me, that I may have done them?" My eyes widened, face churning with disgust at the thought, "I didn't, I couldn't, you know that. And those two creeps are supposedly Templars? Yet, in the same breath, it sounds like they aren't the virtuous knight's history portrays them as?"

Nathan's expression grew grim. "I know, mate, but you seeing through the killer's eyes takes explaining. We should keep that quiet for now. As for the murders themselves, that's how it seems; the marks on the bodies would suggest that symbolism. But I'm not sure about the two blokes unless they're secret agents; I can't think of another solution for them other than somehow, they're knights or descendants. After what you said about the door, those bastards could've had their wish centuries ago. Delving into those crazy forbidden rituals, seeking power beyond their wildest dreams. Seems the root of all evil, anyway, right? This symbol could be a beacon for their return or a warning. But what I can't figure out is why now. Why here?"

My paranoia resurfaced as I glanced around the desolate ruins, the sense of being watched intensifying. "We need answers, Nathan. Before more people die, I still can't get over how I dreamt of seeing the librarian murdered. I'm scared out of my mind; my father is sending tapes recorded a year before he died telling me something. My mother is sketchier than a married man getting caught soliciting a hooker, and it seems my father was haunted by that same hooded figure, too. In the footage, their shadow stands behind him. It's bloody crazy."

Nathan extended the folder he brought. "This is how I knew what was on the bodies and connected the dots. Don't ask how, but I owe a certain lady dinner. But look closely, Gerald, see if you noticed what I did. The crosses aren't just symbols burnt into flesh for the hell of it; they're runes. If you focus hard enough, you will notice each one has a slight shimmer about them; even in death, the marks seem alive. They're being used for something dark that we must find out quickly because it's unnatural."

My heart raced as I examined the photos, the realisation sinking in that we were way out of our comfort zone, and Nathan was right. "We have to find the link, Nathan, whatever it takes. The stuff you found on my father and the farm. Who else could be involved, and why are people suddenly dying? But also, how? How do we dig into all of this, something supposedly lurking in the shadows for centuries?"

Nathan's eyes gleamed with what looked like an idea. He gets this over-excited puppy look when he thinks he has something. It's a giveaway in poker. Not that I'd tell him. "We have the advantage of knowledge, Gerald. We know more about their symbols; now, we uncover exactly what it does or means. First, we need new wheels and somewhere safe off the grid."

As the last of the sun gleamed, casting long shadows over the ancient stones, we knew the path ahead was dangerous. Still, we had to uncover what was behind the darkness and, if they were real, just how dangerous the Templars could be.

Shadows are Calling

24

'Gerald,'

We lingered on a stone path within the church. The gloomy atmosphere and the sun going down gradually gave the place a haunted feeling. The once-hallowed walls exuded an eerie presence that sent neck hairs tingling. There was a peculiar scent, not the sterile cleanliness of a hospital, but something that would resonate with Sunday churchgoers who walked into a place marked by the remnants of holiness.

I clutched the folder of photographs tightly, each image of a burnt cross etching into my mind. As usual, I was staring into the shifting shadows of the windowless arched openings, my flipping imagination running wild. Nathan seemed captivated by the place, too, lost in thought. We came here with a secretive purpose, but the haunting ambience had taken us by surprise.

The wind howled through the decaying organ pipes mounted against the back wall, a creepy melody that made Nathan wonder why such valuable relics hadn't been plundered like vultures on a sacred corpse. Surely, they held a fortune, but perhaps some things were deemed too historical to defile and were left to decay with time.

The roof above us had succumbed to the ravages of time, reduced to skeletal beams covered in the refuse of countless birds. Pigeons, brave enough to land, took flight whenever a fragile wooden door slapped shut, causing the adjacent crumbled wall to quiver in response to the strength of the breeze.

My eyes darted nervously, shadows playing tricks on my senses, each morphing into the symbols Nathan was eager to tell me about. We had pulled a thread, which led to the creepy men in black suits. Nathan and I had overlooked a crucial detail—were more of them? So far, the encounters with those two had been nothing short of terrifying.

My gaze shifted to the shadowed crosses on the wall, unsure whether it was paranoia or something else. In the far corner, one cross seemed to shift and contort, taking on the form of a person. Scared, I tried to turn away, hoping to shift focus elsewhere. We needed to figure out our next move rather than stay in this place longer than necessary. My stomach was churning with frayed nerves.

Shadows danced along the colossal, crumbling wall, the human figure growing in size. A phantom arm extended from the shadowy body, reaching toward me, while the creaking timbers above groaned in response against the swirling winds outside. I was freaking out inside. I tried looking away, but it was as if the shadows had some crazy grip on me.

The hairs on my hand jumped as the shadow brushed against my hand, an icy grip accompanied by a melancholy, sobbing voice. "Let it in... Gerald. You... must... let... it." Its whimper rippled down my spine with a tormenting purpose. The voice sounded like Charlotte's, just like in Mother's bathroom. Why the hell was I hearing from her?

I was frightened, no hiding that, and I hadn't dared to respond. It must've only been a few seconds, but it was like an eternity before I finally ask, "Let what in?" I discreetly checked on Nathan, who remained oblivious to the unfolding eerie. The crosses on the wall continued their haunting dance. "You must let the darkness in."

Every whistle and creak made me jump. Feeling hypersensitive, deafened by the weeping choir. The shadow's clutches seemed all too real, dismissing any notion that I might imagine it. "Who ... what are you?" I whisper hoarsely, trying not to alert Nathan to my distress, who was still lost in his thoughts.

"I want to come home. We're all alone, and we want to come home," Charlotte's voice echoed, and I could see an outline that looked like her shape and height. Yet I knew it couldn't be her. I tried to pull my hand free from the shadows, but it held firm, and a searing pain shot through my flesh. With every struggle, the grip tightened, drawing blood that stained the church's stone floor. The shadows on the wall continue to wail and weep. "You must let it in." Their grip grew even more suffocating. My heart quickened, pulsating in my temple. I was desperate to flee, to escape. How did my life come to this?

"Why should I? How can I?" I question as I listened to the eerie imitation of Charlotte's voice beckoning me to embrace a bizarre darkness. "If you want us to be with you again, you must let it in and finish the book," the wailing continues, tugging at my heartstrings as the bloody puddle beneath me grows.

The shadow's grip loosened slightly, allowing me to snatch my arm back. It tore through my flesh, leaving a trail of blood in its wake. "You're not her. What do you mean by letting the darkness in and finishing the book?" I ask, my wounded hand trembling as blood dripped to the floor.

Finally sensing something amiss, Nathan quickly turned to me, moving cautiously as he watched me struggle with something Nathan couldn't see.

"Who are you really?" I utter meekly.

"I am Gerald, of course," the shadow whispered from the depths of the womanly shape before branching into something taller and wider.

"Come now, Gerald. Let's put an end to all of this. The sooner you embrace the darkness, the sooner we can return home," the voice had suddenly changed. It was my father. I was shaking uncontrollably. My mind was numb, struggling to string a thought together.

Riddled with panic, I faced Nathan. "What in God's name are you talking about?" I say, backing away from the shadows. Nathan looked at me with genuine concern, hearing my disjointed words but seeing no one else in the room.

"Fill the book, and the gates can open. Then we'll come back to you, silly," Charlotte's shadow danced forward. I jumped back, colliding with Nathan, whose face twisted in worry.

"Gerald, are you okay?" Nathan shook my shoulder, snapping me out of whatever trance had taken hold.

I stared blankly momentarily, an unsettling presence closing in. A chilling breeze caressed my neck, causing my already rapid heartbeat to thunder. The shadowed figures drew nearer, and my eyes bulged with terror.

Then Charlotte let out a mournful, crying moan that pierced my mind. "You must let it in, or else you'll end up stuck like us. Nobody wants to be stuck, Gerald. It's full of sadness and pain. You don't want me to be sad, do you, Gerald? Let the darkness in. Fill the book, and the harbingers will bring us back to you." a tear rolled down my cheek.

"They guide us by the cross. You know the cross is good, everything that's holy. It's safe. All you have to do is let it in and trust no one. Nobody will understand, not even Nathan," Charlotte's voice continues to echo, weaving its melancholic narrative through my wavering resolve.

I kept checking my hand, seeing deep slices dripping blood. Nathan, still baffled, watched my erratic movements.

"What do you mean?" I quivered.

Charlotte's wailing intensified, bouncing off the walls. A thumping echoed deep in my eardrums—the relentless pecking that had grown louder and more frantic. I couldn't escape it. The church beams were now a congregation of scary-looking ravens, their piercing blue eyes fixed on me, just like at the pub.

"If you let it in, the darkness will reveal many truths. It will show you many things. Don't you want to know the truth?" Charlotte's voice, now high-pitched and unsettling, prickled my skin.

I tilted my head, torn between fear and curiosity. "The truth about what?" I tentatively inquired.

"The darkness says, when is a friend, not a friend?"

"When they're an enemy."

"And closer than you think. The darkness can help you exact revenge on those who pretend to help. Look at him, faking interest, when all the while he seeks hidden treasures. The things obscured by history. Why do you think he was eager to tell you about the knights? He wants to twist your mind into believing they're evil. But that's not the worst part—he helped kill your father," Charlotte's voice, dripping with accusation, rattled my soul. Hate was brewing inside, but it didn't feel like mine. I was being made to feel and brew on something I didn't want to. And my body was allowing the hate to take over. I glared, but suddenly, my arms moved involuntarily, becoming a puppet.

"Let us show you what to do. It's so easy. Once you know, you won't stop. There's no point in resisting. Submit to the darkness," the shadow's voice coaxed... I had no control; the rational me was a passenger in my body. Without warning, I lunged aggressively at Nathan, my hands closing around my friend's throat.

Nathan gasped, struggling to breathe, his face turning red. "Gerald, snap out of it. What's happening?" Nathan fought to free himself from my grip, vision growing dim.

"See, Gerald? Life is slipping away under your grip. Revel in the power. Just let it in, and we will come home," the shadow urges, its presence tightening its hold on me, and I was fucking powerless.

I heard Nathan's muffled pleas for help deep, and my thoughts jumped to my twin girls and the rest of my family. Then, the image of father struggling on that old VHS tape played into his mind. I knew in my heart that Nathan wasn't responsible for their deaths.

With a clenched jaw, I struggled for control, pulling against the shadow. "No, I will never let it in. Leave me be. You aren't Charlotte or my father. Someone murdered them, but it wasn't him," I mustered all my strength, tearing my fingers free from Nathan's throat. Slowly, I slid my arms back, and with his eyes gaping, gasping for air, Nathan spoke, "Gerald, wake up. What's going on?"

The shadows that had taken over now retreated, unleashing a final horrendous wail. The ravens scattered, their ear-splitting squawking, vying with the shadow's cry. I had broken free completely, struggling for breath and watching the shadows recede from the walls. They left no trace behind—except for one haunting sight.

"Gerald, are you okay?" Nathan finally regained his composure, rubbing his throat.

"I'm so sorry, Nathan. It wasn't me," I reply, regretting what I did.

"I know. It seems there's no escape, and someone wants to send a message," Nathan says, his gaze fixed on the back wall. A large, burnt cross loomed ominously, its presence haunting and alarming, symbolising the mysterious terror we had unwittingly uncovered.

Rest

25

'Détective Reynolds,'

The side lamp was off but still warm, and a bundle of case papers rested beneath, looking a dishevelled mess after I'd spent the last couple of hours poring over them, fighting for clues. Hope. My eyes were as worn out as the rest of me was and were still no nearer to answers other than one massive blood-riddled mess. This case is far more complicated than me or Micky boy bargained for. At least with the other cases, we had a trail to follow. Right now, we have fuck all.

Michael and I did our best to piece together the chilling events in the morgue, with those symbols grabbing the most attention, though a heavy black cloud still lingered overhead. I, in particular, carried the weight of recent horrors deep within, bubbling to the surface, bordering on self-pity; mostly, I needed to keep my thoughts to myself, not even sharing them with Micky.

I don't feel like myself, not since Scotland. Barely a week had passed, and the memories haunted me. The relentless image of the vampire horde, the gut-wrenching sight of Michael sprawled lifeless on the floor before morphing into the elder, followed by finding Michael safely recovered at the B & B–it was a never-ending loop of nightmarish images that played in the circus of my mind.

I couldn't shake the lingering fear, a gnawing suspicion of the horror still to come from that one. Ruth's escape and the possibility of the elder's body-switching ability had me dreading them showing up in London and turning it into a bloodthirsty playground for evil.

The smoke and mirrors fight scenes while the vampires fled the supernatural onslaught only deepened my worries. But above all, my painful memory of taking a human life haunted me the most. It's making me feel I must hold back the other side of me. Though the victims were not innocent by any stretch of the imagination, and desperate times called for desperate actions, our plunge from the window stained the pavement and my conscience. There was no making the bloodshed disappear. It's been keeping me awake at night.

As I lay in bed, dwelling on all this, most of the room was dwarfed by darkness, except for a slender sliver of moonlight sneaking through a gap in the curtains, casting a glow across my crisp white bedsheets. The Willowbrook constabulary had been gracious enough to provide lodging for me and Michael at a Holiday Inn hotel while we continued to work on this baffling case. At this rate, it seemed we might be stationed here for some time, especially since what had started as a single body had multiplied, with the unexplainable resurrection of one corpse still haunting my thoughts. In contrast, the symbols and the glowing cross had thrown us a curveball.

Was I cursed to keep landing all these horrific cases, or was it purely that we were best equipped to sift through the bullshit and handle the supernatural? My hotel room, although comfortable, provided little comfort for my troubled mind. The flickering of the muted television in the corner was distracting as I tried to calm the chaos.

Even with heavy eyelids, the eerie silence of the night had me on edge and restless. The soft rustle of curtains in the moonlit breeze and the distant hum of the town beyond were the only sounds that dared break the stillness.

A sudden chill made me shiver beneath the sheets as my eyes finally closed. I hoped to sleep and get some temporary respite from the relentless images that spun through my mind. The rustling curtains beat louder by the second. It wasn't long before my body was heavy, and I had given up for the night...

'Knock, knock, knock,'

A muffled tapping echoed through the room, and a dreadful, light rapping of knuckles vibrated against the wood. My eyes shot open, and my senses heightened as the wolf in me came alive. With a frustrated dash, I ripped open the door, heart pounding, but the hotel hallway remained empty. With my feet barely touching the ground, I returned to bed to try again.

'Knock, knock, knock,'

The tapping came again, growing more insistent and louder, as though someone urgently wanted my attention. I cautiously rose from my bed, footsteps soundless on the carpeted floor. With every step, the tension intensified. I reached out, hand trembling towards the doorknob. The hairs on my knuckles waved in a light breeze. Just as I grabbed a hold… 'Thump, thump, thump,' it came again, far harder… I dragged my hand sharply away.

Silence crept in; I counted five seconds before trying again. Finally, I twisted it slowly; the door creaking open, revealing the empty hallway again. The never-ending shadowed walkway stretched left and right. No one was there. I lingered in disturbing silence, confused and becoming slightly fearful, knowing nothing good usually happened next.

I peered into the uninviting hallway, grappling with what was happening. There was no normal reason for the persistent tapping, with no one to be seen. I was no stranger to horror films, where there'd usually be a ghost or the killer had somehow already got inside. Only me and Michael were on the second floor, which should make it difficult; sadly, our world was drenched in things that seem to do the impossible.

I hesitated, deciding whether to wander for a look or return to bed and try again. The moonlight, now shaping eerie shadows along the hallway's walls, piqued my curiosity. I took a tentative step outside; the door closing softly behind me.

The hotel corridor seemed longer, with me fully immersed in its blandly stretched carpets and pale walls, decorated with nondescript artwork and poorly lit candle bulbs. There was something undeniably unsettling about the atmosphere. A subtle but intrusive odour lingered a damp, earthy decay. And dare I think it, 'death'. The putrid stink rampantly swept through the imposing halls and worsened my fear.

Further down the corridor, my hackles rumbled, eyes were on me. Or, at least, felt that way… I couldn't tell where or why; my werewolf senses gave nothing. If I didn't know better, I would swear a young officer had been goaded into hazing their visitors. But then I would've heard them already. It was a frantic spin to look, and still nothing but space. The rumbling stayed strong enough to drag my claws forward. My pace quickened, footsteps echoing off the walls. There was intense silence, broken only by the distant, evocative hum of the hotel's ventilation system.

Then I glimpsed movement from the corner of my eye. It was a flicker, a shadow darting across the hallway, just beyond the reach of the dim overhead lights.

"Who's there?" I called out, a little rasp in my throat. There was no response, only the sound of my rapid and shallow breath, my pulse thumping beneath the skin. I took another step, eyes scanning the corridor for movement, my heightened hearing reaching far and wide. And then...

Uninvited Guest

26

'Détective Reynolds,'

A soft, inaudible whisper carried on the swirling draft drifting through. The words were indistinct, but the tone was familiar — an eerie, haunting wailing.

The ghostly lament grew louder as I continued, reverberating through the dim hallway. Curiosity gripped me, driving me closer, seeking where it came from.

My footsteps quickened. The shadows smothered the surrounding space until I could barely see my hand before my face; they shaped and danced at the edge of my vision. Unnerved, my throat withered, telling myself, 'I'm a fucking werewolf; I'm a werewolf, for Christ's sake; I shouldn't be afraid of anything,' but I also knew there was no fighting what I couldn't see. Common sense went out the window, and I kept walking.

Moving closer to where the haunting wails were coming from, the shadows writhed toward. They twisted, reaching to grab a hold with their phantom hands. The mournful voices grew piercingly louder and anguished, filling my ears until I was ready to burst or bleed, whichever came first.

I tried to slither away, to escape, but the corridor stretched endlessly in every direction. Panic set in as I realised they were suddenly coming from both ends; there was no way out, no escape from this nightmare.

Desperation forced me to race through the shadows to my room, my heart pounding like a drum in my chest. I dug deep into my tired supernatural reserves, moving fast, but the shadows pursued me relentlessly. Their ghostly fingers brushing my skin struck shivers through my body. I lunged into my hotel room, slamming the door behind me.

Breathing heavily with relief, I scanned the room for more bizarre shadows that could've made their way in; the room was full of them, but none were moving. Until I saw a slither of moonlight cast across the shadowed corner...

As if the night couldn't have been any more frightfully stranger, creepily sat in a rickety brown wooden bloody chair, one of the hauntingly gaunt men in black suits. The figure was draped in darkness, the bony contours of their face obscured. But I remembered enough from our first encounter.

Shaken, I locked eyes with the mysterious intruder. First, the shadows, and now this, "Who are you?" I demand, my voice shaky, riddled with fear and anger. The intruder remained silent, their gaze unwavering; a gleaming black pierced the night.

Eventually, the intruder finally spoke in a reverberating voice from the darkness, "You would do well to leave this be."

Threatening words, I stood in no-man's-land, questioning how the guy got in my room, let alone serve a warning. Cautiously, I stepped forward; my eyes stayed on the shadowy outline in the chair. Weary of what he could do, I held my claws out of sight, surrounded by an electrified tension smothering the air, a brewing storm; so far, I'd resisted my primal instincts.

"We are not your enemies, not right now, Detective Reynolds," the intruder continues, their voice a haunting rhythm vibrating within the walls. "But we will be; if you insist on pushing down this road, you won't like the horror that found you. This is your watershed moment; do you stick or twist, be a thorn or step aside."

My voice struggled, mind racing, to comprehend what was happening. Seeing ghosts was one thing. I don't know what to label this other than weird. "What horror? What are you implying?" I finally found some courage. My words were barely more than a whisper.

The figure leaned forward slightly, a subtle shift in the shadows revealing a glimmer of piercing, haunting eyes. "There's a darkness coming, and you're getting in the way; you have a job to do, but I warn you, don't dig too far; you won't like what you find," they reply cryptically. "You have glimpsed, but a fraction of the evil in this world, Detective Reynolds, and there is much more than history hid; it's time to let nature take its course or get swept aside. You don't want your friends, or dear, sweet Ellena, dragged along in the wake of the impending darkness, do you?"

I was a mixture of fear and fascination. The scarily calm intruder's words struck a chord with the unique events Michael and I had encountered recently; I knew there was more to the case than we'd seen so far. But the man in the shadows was there to hand out a warning, and no, I didn't want anyone else to get hurt or understand how they knew of Ellena; I also wasn't in the habit of heeding sinister warnings. Especially ones in the middle of the fucking night having been chased by, of all things, a shadow. God, Michael will have a bloody field day when I tell him.

A small part of me urged going toe to toe right there and then used my claws to peel the morbid flesh from the creepy bastard's gaunt bones and see what was underneath. At the crime scene, their faces shimmered to look different, and I wanted to know what they were. Regaining composure, thanks to the mystery man pushing my buttons, "Seeing as you know about Ellena, that tells me you know a fair bit about me; you should have gathered that I don't just stand aside and let creepy fuckers like you get your way, even if you appear to be men of god," I fired off, feeling the anger brewing.

At first, there was no response until the guy began laughing; he let out an evil, rumbling laugh that curdled my blood. "See, you don't even have that right," I nervously looked over my shoulder after hearing a rustling outside my door, a humming slowly growing louder. Wind whipping curtains back and forth, each slap louder in the chilly air...

'Knock, knock, knock,'

"Urgh, w ... what the hell," I bounced upright, the moon beaming through the window, my sweaty vest clung to me. With an erratic breath, I gradually got a grip on myself.

'Knock, knock, knock,'

"Georgie, you, okay? I'm living every bloody ounce of your anxiety. What the hell is going on with you?" Michael shouts from the other side. I sat bewildered, questioning if I'd experienced a strange and haunting dream. It had to be.

I spun to face the chair, looking for my deathly guest from the dream. The seat was empty, as expected. Almost anyway, I was given another surprise...

A large burning cross blistered through the wooden seat, still smouldering a little. The stink of burnt varnish on wood got up my nose, leaving me questioning my sanity—and not for the first time. It wasn't a dream. Far worse, in fact. It was darker, and we were still on the back foot.

Dear Doctor

27

'Détective Reynolds,'

Dr Thornton hadn't given up, working long after everyone else had gone. She toiled endlessly in the cold dullness of the morgue. A chamber of secrets concealed behind rows of silver doors. Each door hid a cadaver with untold stories etched into their cold, lifeless bodies.

Her fingers moved rapidly, a ballpoint pen tracing an inquisitive path along her quivering lower lip. The autopsy notes sprawled across the steel table formed a haunting mosaic, revealing fragments of a tragic puzzle.

The room carried an unrelenting chill, yet it was a frigidity that Dr Thornton embraced, mirroring the relentless curiosity that gripped her. This curiosity led her to question the very essence of the human soul and what happens to it once the flesh dies.

While the bizarre horror earlier in the day would have driven most to the brink of terror and flight, Dr Thornton remained dedicated to finishing her files for the detectives. However, her unyielding curiosity pushed her further into the unknown. How was it possible? Frank Eckleston's miraculous resurrection and horrifying suspension in mid-air had not only piqued her curiosity but had unleashed a torrent of questions in her mind.

She longed to confront Mr Eckleston, to glean answers from him, even though their encounter had been far from ordinary, marred by eerie symbols and malevolent taunts. However, the pragmatic sensibilities of her profession prevailed. She had agreed with the detectives to keep the details of the bizarre incident locked away from prying eyes, though few would be inclined to believe her account, regardless.

Outside, the world was already in darkness, the silence of which carried an eerie weight. It was the ungodly hour of 2 AM. Thornton should've been at home with a glass of wine and her ginger tabby, 'jinx', curled beside her. Instead, three lifeless bodies lay sprawled on cold, metal gurneys, waiting for her eager eyes, hoping to get the answers Dr Thornton ardently sought. Her nimble fingers drifted over the cool steel, gloved hands reaching out to compare the grotesque crosses etched into the flesh of the deceased.

Each cruciform Sigel bore a disturbing resemblance to the others, yet Dr Thornton's perceptive eyes detected subtle divergences. The patch of skin encompassing the seared symbol pulsed with an eerie glow, and the flesh surrounding it appeared oddly preserved, if not entirely alive. The gruesome remnants of Patrick Sheh, severed and dismembered, elicited a queasy sensation in her stomach. However, being in charge has its perks; a discreet sip of whiskey concealed within her coffee gleefully provided a temporary respite.

Guided by her unwavering quest for truth, Dr Thornton allowed her limited artistic skills to manifest in the pages of her notebook. She sketched the intricate cross with meticulous penmanship, noting the distinct nuances that set it apart from the traditional ecclesiastical symbols she had previously encountered. As the ink flowed across the page, something was happening. Thornton's eyes were glued on the symbol in a hypnotic state, while the pen seemed to move with a mind of its own. Her hand lurched and scribbled relentlessly without Thornton doing anything, mirroring the disturbing nature of the symbols on the deceased.

Until she finally snatched her hand free from the pen...

Only to watch it continue dancing across the page. Thornton gasped, trying not to swallow as her confused, churned face soaked in what was unfolding. Before her clinical brain could rationalise the free-flowing pen as anything other than spooky, the morgue's sterile lights flickered, making Thornton jump, initially just once, as happens sometimes, then it happened again ... and again... each time picking up speed, causing Thornton's heart to thump louder and louder...

Until that's all she heard between her ears. For a moment, Thornton was lost, struggling to pull herself together, when she realised the series of flashes appeared to be an unorthodox morse code, which Thornton nearly dismissed out of hand as too weird to be possible. But it continued forming patterns, so she attempted to decipher. Finally, getting to prove 'Girl Scouts' wasn't a complete waste of her youth. The flashes had a particular sequence, 'like a short sentence,' she muttered, hastily grabbing a pencil and some scrap paper, partly eager, partly scared. **'Y ... O...U... W...I...L...L...D...I...E,'**. By the time the words were complete, she was terrified.

Thornton dropped the pencil on the floor. The colour drained from her face, repeating what she wrote, **'You will die'**. The lights danced, repeating the taunt before the room suddenly plunged into nerve-wracking darkness. Thornton shuddered, twisting and looking while overcome with turmoil. An icy breath whispered across the nape.

The hairs on her arms shot to attention, quivering. Dr Thornton's eyes strained to pierce the darkness, her mind reeling from the message. Thornton could sense someone nearby as the cloudy breaths persisted until she realised the looming presence behind her—a tall, intimidating figure clad in a deathly black suit, exuding a fearless aura of evil that penetrated the marrow of her bones.

With a sinister, blood-curdling grin catching the fluctuating light, the once-tranquil morgue transformed into a haunted theatre of horrors, orchestrated by the ghostly figure's bony hand.

Thornton lurched away, tumbling off her stool as she tried to put as much space between her and the uninvited guest as possible. The figure didn't need to move. Instead, he gruesomely summoned the corpses at the centre of Thornton's intrigue.

The dead bodies of Patrick Sheh, Frank Eckleston, and Grace Filton, who had been mere cadavers' moments before, suddenly stirred. Their limbs flopped against the sturdy metal, then jerked and spasmed like morbid puppets, with their bones breaking and echoing around the room; their bodies were slowly being manipulated, as if being pulled by invisible strings. Dr Thornton was horrified yet slightly fascinated as their eyes, once dulled by death, flickered with an evil, ghostly glow.

The haunting figure in black masterfully orchestrated this dreadful nightmare. He wove his ghoulish tapestry with no apparent purpose or reason, not that Thornton could tell, transforming the dead into nightmarish marionettes, their movements grotesque and beyond understanding. Dr Thornton stood at the cusp of a chilling torment, her unyielding curiosity luring her further into the heart of this supernatural darkness, even as the boundaries between life and death blurred ominously before her eyes.

Thornton's inner torment intensified as the haunting figure in black continued to commandeer the undead for his sinister pleasure. She, a rational scientist rooted in empirical evidence, found her world unravelling before her eyes. Cold beads of sweat formed on her forehead.

Her trembling fingers clung to the notebook bearing the sketch of the mysterious cross, symbolising her descent into realms that could lead to her death. She wanted to scream and flee from this unholy mess, but she couldn't move; whether the sinister puppeteer or her relentless curiosity, her body was stuck.

The undead puppets, now eerily animated—became instruments of madness, their bodies twisted and tormented. Every movement was a grotesque reminder 'that curiosity killed the cat', and the signs were looking ominous for Thornton.

Her breath came in ragged gasps as she experienced their agony as if it were her own, their anguished yawning cries reverberating in the darkest recesses of her mind. The room seemed to constrict around her, its walls pulsating with evil.

The haunting figure in black, his predatory gaze now fixated on Dr Thornton with unnerving intensity, whispered words that sent shivers down her spine. "You, Dr Thornton, bear witness to but a glimpse of what will come. Your insatiable curiosity has led you to a path from which there is no return; you could've gone home to play with your pussy ... Now, poor little Jinx will be motherless, all because those detectives piqued your interest. Unfortunately, we can't have people meddling with destiny."

Her rationality shattered like fragile glass, and the world around her blurred into a nightmarish phantasmagoria. Thornton realised she had reached a point of no return, consumed by the unravelling horror. She had become a prisoner of darkness in the cold, unforgiving confines of the morgue. "Please, I can help you; I can spread your message. If I'm spared, I will forget anything I saw."

"My dear, you will already help us. And your message will be resounding, although there is one last thing for you to do for us," he taunted. As the haunting figure in black continued to exert his sinister influence over the undead, their lifeless eyes flickered with an unholy gleam, and their movements became more purposeful, more horrifying.

The atmosphere grew thick with dread...

Dr Thornton, trapped in the suffocating embrace of the room, trembled with fear of the once-lifeless bodies...

Her heart raced, and her breath quickened, spreading cloudy white plumes as an icy hand of terror clutched her...

"What's that?" Thornton, her voice weak and raspy, finally asks, dreading the response.

"All ... you have to do is...die," he let out a curdling laugh and forced tears down Thornton's cheeks.

With uncanny coordination, the corpses lurched forward, their movements grotesque and unnatural. Patrick Sheh's pallid fingers reached out like elongated claws, Frank

Eckleston's eyes glowed with insatiable hunger, and Grace Filton's lips curled into a wicked, sadistic smile. The toxic stink of mottled death filled the space between them and Thornton.

Dr Thornton's mind screamed in fear as they closed in on her, their footsteps echoing with an eerie rhythm. She attempted to retreat, to find an escape route, but the room had become a nightmarish kill box, each path leading to a gruesome dead end.

Desperate to elude the advancing horrors, she stumbled backwards, inadvertently knocking over a metal tray with a resounding crash. The metallic clang reverberated through the morgue, an ear-splitting death knell.

The haunting figure in black, his looming presence unwavering, watched with sadistic delight as the undead descended upon Dr Thornton. Cold as the empty night, their hands tore into her flesh. Thornton's screams rippled through the air, and her lungs bulged to burst.

The dead, shredded piece after piece of flesh, flaying her body to reveal the glistening pinkish-red meat underneath, inflicting searing agony that had Thornton on the verge of passing out. Her anguished wailing relentlessly reverberated within the lifeless chamber, but nobody was around to hear her.

Dr Thornton's vision blurred as she fought to cling on, powering through the pain, and in her final, gasping moments, she mustered the strength to utter a hoarse, trembling question, "Who the fuck are you?"

The sinister figure leaned closer; his terrifying grin was barely visible in the darkness. With a voice that had her spilt blood bubbling, he whispers, "Gerald Ackerman."

Summoning the last ounce of her strength, Dr Thornton's trembling fingers dipped into the pool of her oozing blood, and, in an act of defiant desperation, she scrawled the word "Ackerman" onto the cold, unforgiving morgue floor. As darkness enveloped her and her life slipped away, the word remained—a chilling ending to the horror she had endured. A message was the only way she could. Hoping the right people found it. While evil had snuffed out Thornton's life and any possibility of meddling.

Lie Low

28

'Gerald,'

A run-down cabin stood amid the heart of a spooky forest, nestled amongst an army of bounding, warped trees, nicely concealed by tall, menacing oaks and elms that stretched their branches across the meandering, gravelly road that led to somewhere safe for me and Nathan. Inside, the rustic fire ablaze gave us the warmth and cosiness needed. The room was full of shadows cast by the flickering embers I couldn't escape but desperately wanted to avoid, especially after the church. This was somewhere nobody with cruel intentions should've known about. While a sense of mystery and danger still had us on tenterhooks.

The logs in the fireplace crackled and popped, providing a semblance of comfort that's been sorely lacking recently. The firelight dancing across weathered walls, those shadows that seemed to shift and sway with a sinister life of their own, had me paranoid. Surrounding them were towering stacks of books, their spines faded and a little torn, but we hoped they could contain some semblance of answers. Their pages were filled with many passages that I struggled to understand. We delved deeper into the literary mountains, driven by the unsettling events that had shaken me earlier. It felt so real. I was powerless in my body and could've seriously hurt Nathan. Maybe even killed him.

Most talked about dark rituals, occult practices, and evil entities lurking in the world's darkest corners. The pages seemed to throb as I stared, their words pulling me deeper into the unknown. Nathan was busy, too. His fingers traced cryptic symbols within the pages;

his face etched with fascination and apprehension.

The cabin used to be a getaway home of Nathan's grandparents, and for now, the coincidentally named Church End Cottage offered a temporary respite from the endless cycle of darkness that seems to follow me wherever I go. Unable to escape that, I'd been marked by more than just some strange story of a family curse. The shadows that taunted me, the voices that imitated Charlotte and, occasionally, father, all hinted at a daunting agenda that seemed to have chosen me as its pawn in a dangerous game. And it scared me senseless.

Mother's hasty agreement to take the Twins away for a few days left me with unanswered questions. It was as if she, too, expected trouble. Something ominous, something I would have money on, that she knew more about than was letting on. Perhaps she hoped that with father's death, she wouldn't have to repeat the same terrifying past mistakes. But these questions would have to wait another day as more pressing matters loomed.

The night outside was as hauntingly dark, without a streetlamp in sight. My paranoia was getting worse by the minute, steadily feeling we were not alone in this place after all. My eyes darted to the shifting shadows, dreading more whispers like earlier.

As Nathan and I continued exploring the books, a chilling pattern emerged. They were brimming with stories of dark rituals, occult practices, and the existence of evil entities that dwelled in the darkest recesses of the world, surprising Nathan, who had never imagined his family being involved in such matters. Not once had he got a clue that they'd been into that stuff. Every family has secrets, and Nathan dreaded what he might find next.

My fingers traced the words on the page, looking for anything relating to symbols, particularly that incessant 'cross'. Like earlier, my back continued to ache with a burning sensation; as much as it was annoying and I should have seen what was causing it, there were too many bigger problems to handle, and I assumed it was stress-related. Like I get in my neck sometimes. After all, being tells to 'let the darkness in and fill a book' wasn't the easiest problem for me to wrap my head around.

"What kind of bloody book requires filling with the blood?" I muse aloud, a little shaky, simply by saying such crazy things.

Nathan, his face etched with concern, looked up from his research. "Is that what you heard at the church?" he replies gravely. "Over the years, certain cultures and religious sects have sacrificed blood for spiritual wisdom. But what you heard goes far beyond anything I've encountered. It's as if we've stumbled upon something too dark for the typical library or bookstore shelf. There was a man I used to consult for information who delved into the strange and the dark. If you catch my drift, he might have some insight into this."

I shivered as a cold draft swept through the room, rustling the pages of the books like a chorus of eerie whispers. "A plan as good as any because other than that, I'm stumped about what direction we should take next," I say, my eyes fixed on the deepening shadows that filled the cabin, twitching nervously. "All I know is that we need to unravel this nightmare quickly. I saw Grace murdered in a dream as if I'd done it, which terrifies me. Then I was strangling you. I had no bloody control. Again... I'm sorry, buddy."

Life would get worse before it could get better, and so far, it has involved mysteries surrounding my family. If I fail, if we fail, it could plunge me into a darkness from which there would be no return. Though disturbing, the voices from the shadows had forced their hand on what we had to face first. It was only a question of how.

As the night pressed on, Nathan's brow furrowed as he continued to research, his fingers tracing more cryptic symbols and incantations within the pages of the books. "Shit... It's not just about filling a book with blood, Gerald," he says, his voice tinged with apprehension. "It's about something far darker that goes beyond our understanding. It's more literal. If I'm reading right, it says about filling with souls. I don't get how, but as weird as it sounds, it makes the most sense. In some ten degrees of separation kind of way."

My heart raced as I ran that idea through my brain. What in god's name have we got ourselves into? More importantly, what the fuck have my parents done? The pain in my back, the nightmares, the voices from the shadows—all of it was connected to a crazy plan that had 'doomed' written all over it.

The swirling storm brewing outside mirrored the turmoil within the cabin. It was as though the fabric of reality was unravelling, and we were caught in the storm's eye. But we were determined to uncover the truth and confront the darkness quickly becoming apparent.

"We need to find that guy you mentioned, the one who knows about this crap," I declare. "He may hold the key to understanding what we're up against and how to stop it. If not, we're screwed."

Nathan nodded in agreement, his gaze fixed on the flickering flames. "Agreed, Gerald. Maybe have a little faith. Eh. We'll check out the guy and see where it leads us. And we'll cross the bridge for the rest when we come to it. Until then, try cheering the fuck up a little, will you? I don't want to deal with this crap and you being a 'mopey dick'—you daft sod. Oh, and forget the stuff at the church, please. I know that wasn't you. As long as I can punch you in the mouth if it happens again?" Nathan chuckles, breaking the tension.

"Okay, okay. If you must, aim for an eye if you don't mind. Rather not lose a tooth or something," I say, breaking a brief smile in return.

If only it weren't fake. No amount of jokes or smiles can hide how bad things are. A question of how bad it's going to get and whether there will be more death.

Here Again

29

'Détective Reynolds,'

I t's 4 am, and we're back at the cold, unforgiving morgue. We got a call from Thornton's assistant, who'd been woken by a milkman doing his rounds. Mr Brian Lancaster drops off two pints of full fat and a pint of fresh orange juice every morning around 3.30 am. Never in all his years delivering here had he come across it insecure. So, he called Miss Danielle Fenshaw in case of a mistake or something.

The Willowbrook control room called through to Michael just before my fucking night terrors fed through to him. I'm still not used to this 'pack' connection dynamics. Or, at least, I forget since we've been here. I put that down to what I've been going through since Scotland. Well, it's more about beating myself up over what and how things went down. All the holding back that I'm doing. Two baby steps forward and a huge leap backwards.

This place, though, last time around, was eerie enough. I hoped we'd be coming back for a detailed report the doctor had been working on. Not this abstract work of 'blood art' covering the once sterile autopsy room, and another statistic to the list.

I can't decide whether it's the early hour or the constant chill making it feel all the more hauntingly damming. I can't decide. But the nature of this murder is devastating.

As far as we knew, the doctor was innocent, trying to do her job like she's done it for the last ten years without a problem, according to my notes. So, why now? Was the doctor collateral damage or doing it to emphasise the point made by my creepy guest earlier?

Another crime scene and the fourth murder. Poor old Dr Emily Thornton. Looking at her flayed corpse, I was lost in a little daydream, picturing the story told by 'Skip' and what happened to his wife. Skin was shredded from her body and mounted to the wall and made me wonder. Did the Doc have a partner, a husband or wife, a boyfriend or girlfriend? I couldn't see a ring on her finger from where I stood, but that could've easily slipped off in the savage melee.

There was a lot of blood, too much for Michael and me. I could feel my claws edging forward, and now and then, the tips of my fangs caught my tongue. After a lot of hand waving, huffing and frowning, and contorting his head in positions I didn't imagine possible. Michael's eyes flickered yellow, but I don't think he noticed. He was too busy with his notebook.

Thankfully, that meant the other officers were also too busy to notice our involuntary shifting. Sadly, that's one element I'm still struggling to get a grip on the intoxicating lure of blood. It has been the case ever since I first discovered what I was.

Meanwhile, taking a few steps back and to the right by a row of corpse cupboards, Michael pulled his face from the book long enough to stand open-mouthed, surveying the carnage in its gruesome entirety.

Thornton's pinkish-white corpse glistened under the fluorescent lights that weren't flickering this time. She didn't have an inch of flesh left intact on her body. How? Even with the supernatural beings we've crossed paths with so far, such brutality would be too difficult for any of them, even the Kanaima. It was hard to tell what parts of her scattered, flayed flesh belonged where. Between that and the swamp of blood, it was truly horrifying. I watched in slight amusement as Michael attempted to sketch the scene in his notebook when a thought crossed my mind.

"Hey, Michael, without thinking, what's the first answer that springs to mind for this question?" I say, watching the cogs whirring to life. "Remember, without thinking. Should be easy for you, usually blank anyway." I jest, smirking, knowing I would piss him off.

Michael's hands drop to his sides, eyebrows raised with a straight-faced look of 'what the fuck did you say?' expression. "Fuck off, come on, I'm trying to work, in case you haven't noticed?"

I glance over the body and the copious amounts of torn flesh once more before facing back to Michael. "How many did this, and it's not one?" I ask, watching Michael's eyes ping wide. The open mouth look returns before a momentary glance. "Maybe three or more," Michael says, his voice pitchy, as if asking without fully committing to his answer. He was on the right train of thought and exactly what I was thinking.

"I'm leaning to three. It's fucking brutal, and I can't see the slightest trace of flesh intact. Even her hair was striped in one complete section." I say; no sooner had I responded, I look at the gurney tipped across the floor. There are three of them. Suddenly, a sickly cold sensation ripples in the pit of my stomach. I could almost feel the colour draining from my face and worrying enough to prompt Michael to breeze to my side. His ears were twitching, picking up on the quickening of my heart.

It was bizarre that I was even having this thought, and before today, it would go against anything I knew and had learnt of our new world so far. Resting a tentative hand on my shoulder, Michael scans the area before me like I had. Each long silver gurney displays traces of bodily fluids and debris. It was Michael's turn to let the weird realisation sink in. I hear his heart speed up, too...

Michael's head slowly turns sideways to face me while his body stays forward, fists balled to hide the sudden appearance of his claws. A slight hiss of pain escapes his mouth, his palm flesh pierced, allowing thin trickles of blood to push out the creases between forefingers and thumbs. "Are you thinking what... what... I'm thinking?" Michael says again, and the yellow of his eyes sparkles briefly.

"If those tables had on them what I think they had, then that fucking circus freak show we witnessed come to life earlier pales compared to what went down for this murder," I say, thinking of my run-in with the Creep show that seemed a nightmare.

"All three murder victims were brought back to life, or the 'undead' to kill Dr Thornton. This begs the question." Michael says, pausing for me to fill in the blanks.

"Where the hell are they now?" I say, coming to terms with the notion that one creepy bastard occupied me while the other ran this morbid puppet show.

We're looking around. I'm watching Michael and his little changes when I notice a patch of pooled blood by Thornton's outstretched left arm. It's hard to see clearly with smears and parts of where her blood trickled. It looks like symbols, but I can't move close enough with how widespread the carnage is.

"Michael... Oi, you old git. I need you to block the view to me." I say, taking a second to register my words with him.

"Huh? What?" Michael Says, moving forward without thinking to block the line of sight from the doorway. "What's wrong?" Michael peers to the officer at the cordon tape and back to me, whispering.

"I need a better look at Thornton's hand. It might be nothing, but it could be something." I say, keeping my voice low in case it leads to something less in the remit of the normal local officers.

"Get on with it then, and be quick. SOCO have just arrived and are already getting click-happy with their camera," Michael says, tilting his head as if to hear better. They were down the corridor by the main entrance, capturing the route and distance to the morgue, which tells the whole story, especially with no damage to the door.

My eyes flash wolf red, zooming in on her hand. It's not symbols, but Thornton scrawled an attempt at a message. One word only. I go to snap Michael back to tell him what I found when I feel a chill drift across my shoulders. I shudder and tuck my arms in tighter. There was no draft, although the morgue was already cold. This felt different. Enough to force my claws out. I quickly hid my hands in my pockets. My senses were going haywire. Suppose I were a betting man, which I'm not. I'd say we had company. My feet pivot on the spot as I soak up every detail and persons around us. No one stood out as different.

The chill came again, the breeze ruffling my hair. Michael is staring at me as if I'm going mad. Whatever this was, I didn't like it. Then I catch a scent. My nose twitches in disgust. It's almost a sickly 'off egg' stench. 'It's fucking sulphur', I mutter aloud. Michael catches on, inhaling deeply. His face screws up in disgust, and he searches like I had.

'Having fun there, detectives?'

A haunting voice snaps through the air with a scary cackle trailing. It sounded everywhere and yet nowhere. Michael and I stare at each other. Everyone else was still going about their business, for our ears only. They knew what we were or had half an idea. Even worse, I recognised the evil reverb within the shrill tones. It was one of those creepy fuckers in black suits.

'Is this your doing? You sick bastards,' I whisper back, assuming I'd be heard. Sure enough, I was.

'Well, as you like to say, 'the devil is in the details'. Have you found those details yet? I'm sure when you do; you'll find out who is responsible. Oh, in case you wonder what I know of you... Let's say... the file is extensive.' I look back at Dr Thornton's body and at what I was about to tell Michael. More worrying was the so-called 'extensive file' he goaded with that familiar cackling shrill trailing off.

"Michael, in the blood, Thornton wrote 'Ackerman', and that creepy fucker wants to push us down that line," I say, still twitching nervously, checking around us again.

Michael had his usual puzzled expression; the cogs were turning, and I was waiting for the penny to drop. Or he would come up with an alternate theory.

"So, those fuckers manipulated the dead and gave that name to the doc, who in her last moments thought she was helping,' Michael says, with a sudden smug grin stretched across his face. He may have more police experience than me, but he's quickly catching on to the warped and crazy thinking of the sick supernatural. Trouble is, it's the idea of bringing the dead back to life and making them kill. More importantly, where was the 'undead' now? And who the hell is Ackerman?

It Gets Darker

30

'Gerald,'

"Mmm, dark roast with a hint of hazelnut," I murmur as a warm waft teases my senses, making my nose twitch. My eyes reluctantly open. Sleep had been elusive, my mind overcrowded, and the howling winds outside straining against the chimney hadn't helped.

I had crashed out on a dusty sofa in front of the fire, an old book sprawled across my chest. Slowly, I hoist myself upright into the sofa's corner, each movement punctuated by clicks and squeaks from my aching body. Tucking the red tartan blanket around my waist, I see Nathan looking equally tired and unkempt. Despite his dishevelled appearance, his pale face, shadowed with stubble, is alight with excitement. He must have news, or perhaps he's already had too much coffee.

Nathan thrusts a steaming mug of rocket fuel under my chin. "Here, come on, take this," he says before darting over to the rustic round dining table and snatching up a small black phone book. "You won't believe this," he says, bouncing back before I sipped my drink.

Before indulging Nathan's antics, I gulp a mouthful and take the book from his jittery hands. "You found a phone book. Congrats," I say, smirking in jest. Yet, Nathan stares as if expecting me to read his mind.

"Just flip it open, you idiot," Nathan urges, tapping the hardcover enthusiastically. I'm too tired for his puppy-like excitement; my eyes have barely cleared, and Nathan wants me to dive in cold turkey. I only hope it's worth the drama.

I part the pages between sips, and my finger catches a paper sticking out from the top. My eyes dart to Nathan, who looks even more bug-eyed than before, silently urging me. A quick flick reveals yellowed pages and an old black-and-white photograph, weathered, creased, and, dare I say, haunting. I don't speak immediately.

"I know, crazy, right?" Nathan gushes, snatching his coffee from the table. I'm still digesting the sight of my young parents among a group of perhaps twelve others. I scrutinise the background, turning the picture in my hands—it was taken in this cabin. Coincidence? Maybe, but I've never been a fan of them.

"Yeah, that's my mum and dad," I finally respond as Nathan sits.

"And mine," Nathan blurts out. "My grandparents, too," he continues while I inspect the other faces.

"Who are the rest, and more importantly, what the fuck were they up to? Please tell me it wasn't some wife-swapping bullshit," I joke, lightening the mood and causing Nathan to choke on his drink.

"Well, I hope not, but you want to know what's even weirder? That's Colin's parents, maybe grandparents, and a few others that look familiar, but I can't place them," Nathan says, regaining his composure. Did Colin know more than he let on? "Wait until you turn it over," he adds while I'm lost in thought, uncovering more secrets my mother kept quiet about.

"You've got to be kidding," I say, inspecting the back of the photo as Nathan suggests. The idea of Colin's, mine, and Nathan's parents together in some secret group is unsettling.

"You know what that's meant to represent, right?" Nathan whispers, lowering his voice even though no neighbours are within a mile of the cabin. He nervously checks the front door.

My fingers trace the line work of a symbol on the back. "This was on the wax seal and the flesh my mother received," I whisper back, feeling a chill creep up my spine.

"Baphomet, right? You know, the devil, demons, and whatnot," Nathan says, eyeing the piles of books around us. The more I think about it, the more I realise we should've judged a book by its cover on this rare occasion.

"The goat's head and that cross symbol, yes. But there's something different about how the image is encircled—just a feeling," I say, my neck tingling with a foreboding sense that all is not right.

Nathan examines the picture again, his eyes narrowing. "I get what you mean. It's a bloody coin," he declares, a smile spreading across his face as he hands it back to me for another look.

He's right. The image, drawn long ago and faded like the photo, shows detailing around the edge that matches a coin, complete with a series of sigils within an inner ring, reminiscent of hieroglyphs but slightly different.

"You think it's a talisman of sorts? Maybe those creepy guys are after it?" Nathan muses. The cogs in his head are spinning. When they came after me at my home, it seemed they wanted more than just any old trinket. All they had to do was knock and say, 'Hey there, we might look like the Walking Dead, but I wondered if, by any chance, you had a weird-looking devil coin.' Then again, maybe not. Surely, there'd be simpler ways to handle the situation if that were the case. What about the guy who tried to ram me off the road? How did he factor into this? Were we being hounded by two different groups with a vested interest?

"Honestly, I don't know. But our parents are entwined with whatever this is. Except those creepy sods have a target on my back," I say, trying to piece together the clues.

"Our backs now. They followed me, remember," Nathan replies sharply, just as the wind hisses through the cracks in the cabin's wooden structure.

"Crap, look," I say, pointing rapidly at the image again after noticing another curious detail.

"Oh god, you're right. There are drawn cracks dividing the image—as if..."

"As if it's been split into four sections," I interrupt before rereading the photo to look at the group.

"Correct me if I'm wrong, buddy, but does that look like four families to you?" I ask, spotting my family, Nathan's, Colin's, and another set.

"What? And you think each family has a piece? How? Why? Surely, one of us would've known. Wouldn't we?" Nathan asks, his face reflecting my feelings of being left out of the loop, expected to handle it all on our own.

It makes sense, but to what end? And what did the coin or talisman belong to? How did it coincide with the expectation of filling a book with blood?

"Oh, Gerald... let me in, and we can find the key together. Let's paint those pages and open the gates," a sudden cold hisses by my ear. I twitch; the whispers are back, toying with my sanity. Nathan notices me shifting awkwardly.

"Fuck off... Leave me alone," I fire back, staring at the empty far corner. My body is boiling, sweat dripping, soaking my T-shirt, yet my face remains clammy and nauseous.

"Erm... Gerald, are you okay?" Nathan asks, hovering over my shoulder, not touching, just lingering there, shaking. His face is screwed up with worry. Our church incident has been more damaging than we'd realised.

"Let...Me...In... destiny demands it. You must let me in. Open the gates and set your family free," the whisper transforms into a more melancholic cry.

My body throbs, and my hands slide over my thighs, balling into fists. I'm moving them; I have no control. It's surreal, something within me pulling me toward it.

"G...Gerald... block it out. Think about the girls. Think about Charlotte. We will break you free for them. Find peace for them. Remember, you are a father and still a husband; Charlotte will watch over you. Don't give in," Nathan's voice is softer, calmer. Every time he mentions Charlotte, I pull back. Whatever is going on inside feels powerful. Charlotte is my anchor, and Nathan is right; I must block out the noise.

"Leave me alone. Leave me be. Find someone else to be your puppet," I snap sharply, regaining control over my hands.

"Oh...Gerald, it was always going to come to you. You are bound. We are bound as one. Your ancestors made it so when they took the book. Your family line and their rebellious companions caused all of this. Now, it's your duty to set history right again. The chance of power, fame, and fortune could've laid the foundation for a prosperous future. Instead, conscience interrupted. Now you owe, and it's time to pay... So... fucking... let... me... in," the voice persists.

Again, with the book and the past. Whatever my ancestors did has landed me in deep trouble, but I can't give in. I can't surrender. I feel Nathan's hand grip my shoulder reassuringly.

"Leave me be, leave all of us be," I say, venom in my words. Pulling away more and more until I regain control over my body. I turn to Nathan. A parting breeze whips past my ear.

"Gerald, thank God. You look like yourself again," Nathan says, allowing a small smile.

"What do you mean??"

"Your eyes. They turned black. It was bloody freaky." That would explain my lack of control. More worrying is just how much pull the whispers had. It's getting stronger and harder to resist. The church was a warning. I fear I may have inadvertently allowed them room to take over. I don't know how many more times it can happen before I lose. We need answers fast.

"I'm struggling, mate. Every time, it's worse. This time it mentioned my ancestors, power, and stealing a book being the causes of this," I say, quickly downing the rest of my drink to compose myself.

"Well, our next stop is that guy I mentioned. You know, the one who knows about this shit. But let's show him that symbol and see what he says," Nathan suggests, returning to his drink.

I sit and replay the weird conversation. I don't want to let the darkness in. I can't, but the struggle is real. I hope the guy Nathan knows can shed some light before it's too late.

Who Is Ackerman

31

'Détective Reynolds,'

It barely reassembled a door. What would've been a thick beast was shattered into several pieces, with the bottom quarter just about clinging to its hinge.

We ran down a list of 'Ackerman's' in the directory and any known police databases. The first place was Merkfield Avenue, a quiet cul-de-sac, nobody home. It seems we're on the right track with this one. 'There's no smoke without fire' Michael likes to say and my 'dots' weren't adding up. We stood at the doorstep, and I had issues. A feeling we were being led down the garden path.

First, the word 'Ackerman' is scrawled in blood at a crime scene, and then we find a front door obliterated. Voter's check showed Mr Gerald Ackerman listed, while police reports show the family has been through wars lately. First, Henry Ackerman dies after a freak scaffold collapse on the high street. Then Mrs Charlotte Ackerman is a victim of a 'fatal' traffic accident.

I don't know how the local constabulary works, but both reports contained no information, follow-ups, or further investigation—just closed cases. And now we've followed the 'Blood crumbs' to Geralds's home, a setup.

"Hello... anyone home?" Michael leans past the debris, calling through. There is no answer. My heightened hearing is in full flow; all I can hear is a ticking clock.

"Michael, this doesn't feel right," I say, grabbing his shoulder as I step forward to catch up. Michael frowns. We both go to move when I feel it. Then I saw Michael react. His eyes flickered yellow, and my hackles rumbled with a chill.

Another day, another bloody set-up. My claws slid forward. Michaels, too. We made it to the hallway, and my senses were going haywire like no other time. Not even Scotland. I was feeling defensive and a little fear. Whatever we were about to confront had us, particularly me, at a disadvantage. I wasn't ready to 'go there' again. To embrace all the werewolf part of me, not so soon.

Michael would joke about 'performance anxiety', but this was more than that. There were boundaries crossed in Scotland that I can't wash away just yet.

We shuffled along the wooden floors, relieved nobody else could see us part-shift. We'd reached the lounge doorway, my red eyes scanning the floor, able to see footprints. First, there were men's size ten or eleven. Then I caught a scent, just as a little trail of black smoke whispers on a breeze surrounding further prints.

"Michael, sulphur," I say, noticing Michaels's nose twitch.

"Yeah, I caught it too, just like the morgue," Michael says, which means trouble—confirming my worst fears. Those sulphur-scented prints came in two sets—those creepy guys in suits.

'De.... tec... tives. Ooh, detectives. Nice of you to join us,' a chilling voice hissed around us. Sounding everywhere yet nowhere.

"Show yourselves. And stop bloody interfering with our investigation," Michael growls with venom, fully on guard. I'm busy trying to catch a location.

'Oh now, now, you don't sound very grateful for the nudge in the right direction,' the voice chuckles at our expense—the cheek of the creepy bastard.

"A nudge? A misdirection more like," I say, pointing to the VCR, noticing a VHS ejected with the words 'Tape two' in red felt tip and another VHS in the coffee table saying 'tape one'. Both were ringing all sorts of alarm bells. In my experience, and based on what we'd discovered so far, they were old family memories or messages. Then I noticed the padded envelope with the same handwriting on the sofa arm.

We had enough of these details in the 'black widow' case. God, I can still visualise how Inspector Bamford was murdered, drained and mummified. That forked tongue. All in der an hour. Fucking awful.

'How so? We gave you a name, didn't we? You no doubt looked up the family enough to realise they've been through some trauma, and now revenge is sought.' The lack of conviction in the 'tale' was so telling, and my bullshit meter was getting overwhelmed. Michael was pissed, too. He needed a target to cut loose on.

"No, you want us to track the guy down for you, hoping to do the dirty work so you can swoop in. The revenge part is understandable, but from what we've seen, he's not the one doing it. And the theatrics at the morgue. I have a sneaky suspicion that's your handy work," I say, waiting for a response, but nothing. It fell eerily silent.

Our senses were still going haywire, but it appeared I struck a nerve. We stepped further through, moving into the lounge. I wanted to check out the tapes. Something was telling me I should. A little niggle. We'd gone a few feet past the fresh hold, and everything darkened. Every instinct was screaming danger. Shadows crawled from the floor, encroaching on the walls, forming human-like shapes, flailing and writhing, painful screeches slowly built in time as the shadows moved until the dark smothered us.

There was no light through the window, nothing through the smashed front door. It was pitch black, except I was seeing in shades of red and grey. Michael was fully enveloped in that yellow aura as his eyes blazed. For a change, we were both stumped. What was once a door frame from the hallway gradually crumbled into dust. Anything normal was now gone, and I couldn't see a way out. My body was on fire with trepidation. Before long, the screeching became low sobbing. Strong, emotional sobs from a woman that echoed around us.

'Why Gerald, why won't you leave it be? Why?'

"Helen?" Suddenly, the wind had been taken out of my sails. I was hearing the voice of my dead wife. It couldn't be so.

"That's not funny; pack it in," I say, firing back through gritted fangs and looking around us, hoping to see the creepy guys.

'What do you mean, Gerald? You missed me for so long, and now I'm here. If you leave everything alone, I can stay.' My head was spinning. I could hear Michael whispering to me, but I was too gone to understand. They were toying with my emotions, trying to hit me where it hurt.

"You're not real. Helen died years ago. This is bloody sick, stop it,"

"Georgie, Georgie. Don't bite. It's a fucking game," Michael says, his words finally breaking through. It's easier said than done when it's pulling at the heartstrings and opening the old wounds created by Charlie.

'What about me, Georgie? Will you stop for me? I don't want you to get hurt or worse… dead.'

I was rocked on my heels, panic-sweating to the tune of Ellena's voice. At least the imitation of her. Each time the creepy bastards spoke, they tried to get under my skin, pushing my buttons. More dimming was the fact they knew who to use.

"Knock it on the head, will you? I don't understand what you're trying to do here, but you're in the way of our investigation," I say, attempting bravado with a lack of conviction in my voice. Which is quite hard, considering I was part-shifted with fangs on show.

Ripples in the darkness, warped and writhed, the air stifled, my ears twitched, sensing movement around us. Michael's yellow aura was frighteningly illuminating, and so were his eyes. I'm still not bloody used to it, to him like that. The glow really brings out the wrinkles below his eyes. (Not that I'd tell him.)

'Oh, Detective, if you were half as intelligent as I thought you were, you'd understand the bigger picture here is far bigger than you could imagine. Far scarier... and, let's say... unholier. Is that a word? Okay, let's say unholy. And someone of your standing should root for it. Instead, you're becoming a blip, a stain. A fucking inconvenience.' They cut the act momentarily, back to the usual sinister gravel travelled. (Think I preferred to hear it from Ellena's voice).

My mind was stuck on two things other than the horrible feeling the room was closing in on us. Michael felt it, too. Shifting nearer to me. I digress... where was I, right, two things? My standing and the unholy. He sure as shit was referring to skin colour, which brought me to my other affliction.

"So because I'm a werewolf, I should stand by and let people get murdered?"

'More so than you're part demon. Did you think we didn't sense that the first time we met? We're more alike than you think, and that's why I say unholy. Allow this story to unfold, and we won't kill you and everyone you hold dear. Get out of the way, and you will be rewarded.' their confidence was growing. A bone-jarring chuckle clung to the end of his words.

"Fuck off. And stop these theatrics. Getting tired or listening to your horse shit, matey. Speaking of which, ever heard of mints? I get the impression you may be dead and all, but fuck me, your breath is mingling," Michael says, firing back. I glared at him, trying not to laugh. He shrugs as if to say... What? It's true.

The room fell silent, but our senses were going crazy. And then...'If you insist,' the darkness began deteriorating rapidly. Fading back to the lounge. Revealing a picture that stole my breath for all the wrong reasons.

'You see, detective, we figured you may need some motivation. A little incentive. So we brought you some.'

My eyes clenched, fighting back the anger. The pain. And the emotional hand grenade

I'd been thrown while I listened to a woman squirming with cries of pain. One creep had Ellena suspended mid-air by her throat.

His long honey fingers pierced the sides of Ellena's jugular, causing blood to trickle. Her face was bright red; she couldn't breathe. Tears bubbled at the corners of her bulging eyes, building and building, until they boiled over her puffy cheeks.

I edged forward, my brain racing, factoring in how fast I would need to move to make it in time before he suddenly ripped Ellena's throat out. Suddenly, Scotland felt like a walk in the park compared to this.

'Uh uh uh.' the creep tossed Ellena around like a rag doll responding to my movement. Her squeals were higher pitched. I was so goddam helpless. I was fast, but they knew my every move and then some. In that vein, we couldn't stand by and let the world go to shit. Although, some may say, that horse bolted long ago.

"You bastards. There was no need. Supposedly, men of god and you do this. It's sick,"

'Once... maybe. Us? Sick? That's rich coming from a beast that needs flea treatment and crushed a man to do death in Scotland.' again, I was left stunned. How did they know all of this, all of that?

"Let her go,"

'Not yet. She is our leverage. Bring us Ackerman and your Ellena will be released. All in time to witness greatness. Speaking of which, maybe you'll need to see the depths of darkness we're capable of for yourselves,'

"What do you mean?"

"Now, now. You pesky werewolves aren't blessed with patience, are you? Okay, he's a clue...When is death not the end? Understand that and know what's coming, only a taster, might I add?"

This time, Michael dared to move. The room rumbled, electricity charged the air, and the two creeps disappeared with Ellena, crumbling into blankets of crows with bright blue eyes, hundreds of them dissolving into a black cloud, leaving the room back to normal. Michael and I were stunned, traumatised, and, did I say, stunned? We've seen so many things in a short amount of time. Yet, anything supernatural like what they did in the smoke. Defied rational thought, even in my case, irrational.

"Georgie? Georgie? What just happened? How the hell did they get Ellena? Fuck... why does this keep happening? What on earth do we do now?"

I didn't respond, not immediately, anyway. Was too busy reeling from being blindsided—a quick sweep around us. I saw the VHS tape again. We had to start somewhere other than angry.

"Get the fucking tapes. They have Ellena, but if they get this Ackerman, there'll be a shitstorm that my little lamb would tear us a new one for, and you know this all too well, Mickey boy... There's something else, too: when is death not the end? That's what he said,"

"Don't I just... not the end? Fuck... When they come back to life. You don't think... like the morgue?"

Michael bent down to grab the tape from the recorder bus and accidentally knocked it in. The TV flicked on; the tape roared to life.

An older guy in a pale blue shirt came into view, sitting on a chair in front of the camera. He looked stressed, sweating and shaky.

'Hey Gerald, it's me, reaching out from beyond the grave. I'm sorry this is your reality now. I can only imagine the things you've experienced, perhaps even run-ins with certain individuals. Listen carefully, avoid the men in black suits at all costs. They are far more dangerous than they appear, and deception lurks where you least expect it.'

Michael tapped pause. I stared at the screen. There was more to see than just a guy who is Mr Henry Ackerman, a man who died in a scaffold accident. In the background, there's a shadow, an outing of something wearing a large trilby-style hat. Only a shadow but hovered behind Henry. It's bloody weird, but perhaps our first proper clue. We needed to find Gerald Ackerman, and fast. If the creeps alluded to more of the dead coming back to life, we would have our hands full. For such a small village, I've seen at least three cemeteries already. The locals will be traumatised, and the dead cat will be out of the bag.

DARKSIDE

32

'Gerald,'

"Hey... Mason... you there?" Nathan calls out. We'd made fifteen miles outside of Willowbrook, and I didn't have a nosebleed for leaving my comfort zone.

The small village of Melwood was much like Willowbrook, only... well... smaller. Which seems hard to imagine, considering our not so quaint place has a population of little over 2000. The last I knew, anyway. Everything leading up to the shops screamed 'retirement', the place to go when life has reached that point of needing calm. Much like mine now.

The place we wanted was called 'Kooky Comics & The Dark Side,' which was quite fitting considering our situation. Hearing a flustered Nathan call out the guy's name, 'Mason,' was the first I'd heard of it since Nathan suggested it. Inside, the decor was quite basic and low-maintenance. Standard plywood flooring and the walls painted blood red on the top half and purple-black on the bottom half.

Floor to eye level were rows and rows of comics in protected covers, some even in display cases, and tiny figurines. I quite liked comics as a kid and had a half-decent collection, too. Then, one year before senior school, we moved, and I think Mother was tired of the clutter and ditched the box. To this day, I'm sure I packed a big brown cardboard box full onto the moving truck, but they never arrived, and Mother claims I must've thrown them out by accident. 'Yeah, right, mother? Pull the other one.'

Seriously, though, the shop seemed quite cool, making me reminisce. Then, I noticed a few strange objects and symbolic statues on some shelves behind the counter. There was a dry muskiness to the place, perhaps to keep the comics in mint condition.

"Yo Mason, you there," Nathan calls again. I could see out to the back, and nobody was there. It was feeling like a wasted journey. Then I heard footsteps. Heavy ones on wooden, creaking steps, but I couldn't see where. Or how was it possible? There didn't appear to be another corridor, only a toilet and a tearoom by the looks of it.

I was fidgeting and getting antsy, but Nathan seemed more confident. Out of nowhere, a large bloke popped up from behind the counter, giving me a start. Similar age to us, six foot three, more on the overweight side of the scales, receding dark brown hair, a thick matching beard and a pair of specs. I'm not sure what I was expecting, but Mason's face kind of fitted without being rude or slightly nerdy-looking.

Happy about that... Or not. Maybe he was a walking encyclopaedia of all things dark and weird. We didn't have a choice or room to manoeuvre. Didn't stop my arse puckering a little at the thought of us wasting time.

"Well, well, well, look what the cat dragged in. Been a minute, Nathan, what's up?" Mason says with a big grin as he gets comfortable on a stool-height chair.

"I know. Listen, we have a little issue. You're into all the freaky occult crap still, aren't you?" Nathan says eyebrows raised, seeking confirmation.

"Freaky occult crap! Not quite how I'd put it, but yes. What's going on?" Mason asks, leaning toward the glass counter. His thick arms pressed over the view I had of some rare Superman editions.

"Gerald, show him," Nathan says, waving an arm and prompting me to get the picture out of my pocket.

I slid the photograph free, unfolding it before tentatively handing it to Mason with the faded drawing facing him. I didn't know Mason, and it's a big ask to trust someone I don't know. So, I was watching him closely. Nathan was too caught up in the moment to be careful.

Mason's eyes widened, and the smile vanished. I thought he recognised it, but how our luck has been. Mason would no doubt lie. He went to speak, jaw flapping in the breeze, with no words coming.

Nathan shuffles forward. "Well, do you recognise it or what?" he says, waving his arm impatiently.

"I, er... Bloody hell, Nathan, what do you think I am? A bloody encyclopaedia?" Mason says, with a little fire in his tone. It was behind that I had reservations about. A little quiver. He knew it.

"What do you know?" I wasn't standing on ceremony, not with those scary blokes in black suits chasing us and so much more crap going on.

"I never said I knew anything. With respect, I know Nathan, but we aren't close. I sure as hell don't know you, so don't make assumptions," Mason says, shaky throughout. I was getting a bad feeling. The whole time, Mason's eyes drifted to the drawing.

"Come on, Mason, as you say, we aren't close, but I know you enough to tell when you're holding back. What gives?"

Mason stared at the drawing, panting. His hands kept fidgeting. After several gulps of saliva, Mason quickly turns tail and marches behind the counter. I hear keys jingling.

"Come on," Mason says gruffly before dropping low. Then, the thuds on wood we heard earlier. Nathan and I looked at each other, shrugged, and followed.

There was a large hatch on the floor. Mason was a big guy and looked thin compared to the hole and steps down. There was a rattle and a ping near Mason, a bit of the way down. A light flashes on, showing us dirty, damp lines of brick to either side, with rickety handrails. With each step Mason took, an echo grew. It must've been thirty feet down before we reached the bottom. Had me wondering if Mason made it or if he got lucky.

"What is this, Mason?" Nathan points to a large metal door seen on walk-in safes.

"You'll see." Mason jams the keys in the door with a loud clunk. Each twist made me jumpy. Ten seconds later, the door groans open, releasing stale dust. Mason pings another light on, and I am blown away. We were still at the doorway, looking into a room at least 15 by 15 feet. Drawings and pictures were covering the walls like wallpaper. Bookcases rammed with old-looking books, older than what I'd seen at the library. More statues and ornaments, all quite bloody weird.

"What the hell, and this is related?" I'm scanning for similar images.

"Why don't you go look? Nathan, can I have a word?" Mason summons Nathan toward him.

I moved inside unthinkingly, a little overawed. So many symbols, 'crosses' that differed from the usual seemed familiar. 'The Templar Knights' was scrawled below an image. Then, four feet to my left at eyeline height, I find an old page torn from a book. The paper was a yellow-brown, almost leathery-looking. The image was something else, nothing I could imagine. The appearance of a puzzle box is shown in two forms: unfinished and complete. The completed one made me step back.

A large round symbol is in the middle, exactly like the coin in our photo. Four quarters moved and twisted until each part lined up. Reminded me of a Rubik's cube and I bloody hate those. Beside it, there's a piece of pad paper with a handwritten paragraph.

'Believed to be Pandora's box. With many rumours circulating that there's more than one. This one opens a secret hiding place of a long thought lost, Book of the Dead, which requires four sections of a stolen Baphomet coin. Centuries ago, a sect of four Templar knights split from the cause to forge their path. One filled with bloodshed and pain. They sought control and power, dividing the coin between them and knowing the true location of this Pandora's box. While another rumour is that it's simply the master key to unleash the gates of hell, and the book of the dead is used to summon the rarest and most dangerous demons or spirits, too terrifying and uncontrollable, they're banished to pandora's void or the empty. A place only opened by a particular incantation whilst possessing the box configured as described in the book. At present, it's unknown if either ever used the book or where the box is, let alone the puzzle pieces. Suppose they fall into the wrong hands. Evil could be unleashed upon the world. Like with anything, there's always a counter method if the worst happens, a way to reverse it. Or so they say.'

"What the hell?" I mutter, wondering if Nathan's parents and mine knew about these boxes. The drawing from the cabin shows all four parts together. They had to have seen it.

"Hey Nathan..." I turn to call Nathan over, swivelling in time to see the door swinging shut with a resounding thump.

"Hey guys, this isn't funny." I dash to the door, banging loudly, but no one responds.

I'm paused, ear to the door, straining to listen. There's a loud hissing, but not from outside. I look back into the room, 'fuck there's gas' I see thick clouds of musky yellow gas streaming through vents near the ceiling. My heart thumps wildly. I'm trapped and don't know what's happened to Nathan. Only someone shut the door on me. Mason was a little sketchy when he called Nathan away, so the money was on him.

The room was filling quickly; I had nowhere to go and could already feel it in my lungs, burning. Every inhale caused it to tear deeper within. I was choking, having and struggling to breathe. After thirty seconds, I could barely keep my eyes open.

'Let me in Gerald... Let me in. I will protect you.'

A cold whisper cuts through the cloud across my cheek. It was the last I needed, fighting on two fronts.

"N... Not... Now," I barely got my words out.

'Come now, Gerald, let me in. Everyone has abandoned you. I won't. I'm always with you, Gerald. So, let me I, n and we can rip out some fucking throats and get revenge.'

My willpower was at its weakest, and I was unsure if I could hold out much longer. It's taking everything I have to stay on my feet, and now the whispers feel their closest to taking over me.

Heavy, ever so heavy. I stumble, legs turning to jelly. One step left, two steps to the right, legs tangled together. I couldn't keep upright. Until, finally... crash. A fallen tree in the woods. I crash hard. I couldn't move. I lost all feeling and control of my limbs. A final twitch, my eyes slam shut...

'Time to open the door, Gerald. All you have to do is say yes,' the when whisper felt foggy through my eardrums. My head pressed against the cold stone floor.

"Y...Y... Ye,"

Scorched

33

'Détective Reynolds,'

The skies were already darker, being winter and all, but thick grey-black billowing smoke was swarming the space overhead, obscuring the incoming quarter moon.

We hadn't even got out of the car yet, and we were gagging—charred human flesh and, if my senses were right, a fair amount of it. I'm still licking my wounds, reeling that Ellena has been swept up, like us, into someone else's problems and held captive to force my hand and flush 'Ackerman' out. Those creepy men in black were so much more than we'd yet to figure.

Those tapes seized from Gerald Ackerman's home were unsettling, to say the least. In Michael's words, "Fuck me, the guy looks like he's been put through the wringer, matey". He wasn't wrong. Whatever Henry knew or was into before he died scared him. Fear painted his face and suspects his death has been covered up and written as an accident. While his demeanour and warnings would prove anything but.

More unsettling was the shadow behind him, the figure in a hat. Then, the spooky silhouette thumped the screen. Michael nearly wet himself, and not much scared him. Even I jumped a little. Whether it could only be seen by the supernatural is anyone's guess. We haven't dared to show anyone else yet. Not least the local plods. If this case shapes up how I think, then there's so much not to trust about Willowbrook and its people.

We were given 'Kooky Comics & The Darkside' after a sudden fire was killed. I didn't understand why a fire would concern us. After all, most arson to business premises turns out to be insurance jobs. Yet, what we were smelling said otherwise. However, Michael and I benefit from heightened smell and hearing to distinguish the stench inside, making it doubtful whether a normal human would smell anything else. Bringing me back to wondering why us?

We abandoned our car on Elk Street beside the shop's parade. The fire was the second shop along and tearing through unabated. The water fairies were fighting hard. The blackening smoke didn't inspire confidence. Blue lights lit up the street, and hordes of people were escorted away from the buildings as a precaution. The last thing we needed was for it to spread through the parade.

Michael and I made our way toward it; the closer we were, the stronger the burnt flesh stunk. Pausing on the pavement at the corner, my hackles began rumbling. Michael shuddered. We exchanged knowing glances. This had all the fingerprints of something supernatural going down. Yeah, I get that. It sounds like a stab in the dark. After all, it could be a fire where some unfortunate soul got trapped inside if I've learnt anything by now other than to expect the unexpected. It's trusting my werewolf senses. They generally hit the mark when something was off.

Michael sifts a cigarette pack from his jacket, 'Bensons,' before flicking one in his mouth and turning to me. "How many?" he says without breaking his process, cupping the cigarette and a lighter to spark up.

I shake my head at the slightly poor timing, considering we were at a fire. "I didn't know, but the stink is strong," I say, gazing at the bouncing flames. My mind wanders, mesmerised momentarily. I think back to the stories of my childhood. The house fire at the foster home and how badly I was supposedly burnt. I say it like that because I still can't remember everything, relying on Skip to fill in the blanks. There's a lot of them.

Michael waves a hand before my face to snap me back to reality. "You okay matey? Look, it was a real shit move on their part, but we'll get her back.? Ellena is built differently from the standard woman. You know that," Michael says. He was right, of course. Ellena was probably already giving them grief, making the creeps rethink their life-or-death choices.

"I know, mate. The trouble is, Scotland did a number on us all. We need to find how these evidence puzzle pieces fit together. Why did it have to be us here? The CAD sheet was vague, much like everything we've been told. Doesn't even mention who called it in."

"Perhaps it's what's sold inside, matey, not necessarily the comics. But any name that includes 'The Darkside' hints at something a little less than normal matey. Now, I'm not counting my chickens, but I guess the locals know exactly how weird and felt it suited our current case," Valid points, and I hope he was right, something as straightforward. If only we didn't need to keep reading between the lines. It's like trying to box with one hand tied behind our backs. Or a game of chess wearing a blindfold.

We were getting carried away with ourselves without noticing the tide had turned. The fire was being pushed back, squeezed, and squeezed until it was on its last whimper. So much. I grabbed two sets of latex gloves from my pocket, handing one to Michael.

"Jumping the gun a little, aren't we?" Michael says, killing off the last of his cigarette beneath his rather expensive-looking, shiny black Italian shoes.

"Or just being prepared. You and I both know we're going in the regardless."

"What if the 'water boys' say it isn't safe?"

"What? For the overpriced leather? Just put some cover shoes on."

"Fuck off. You and I both know what these structures are like after a fire," No sooner had Michael says, his than eyes rolled, tilting his head to the sky, muttering 'fuck'. He assumed I'd take it wrong, but I knew what he actually meant.

"Relax, old man. And yes, but we both smell that shit, so we go in as detectives or sneak in as a werewolf and whatever the fuck you are. A were-Rat or something," I poked Michael's beer gut, messing with him. I didn't want him to think the worst. In truth, he was a mystery. So far, he appears a variant of a Kitsune, although he wasn't at the start; in the black widow case, they messed with his supernatural side. Judging by his yellow aura. A thunder type, too,

Near the first cordon, the officer looked fed up. Again, he was young, like the previous ones. I can relate, given how often I got stuck at a crime scene when I was new. His name badge said Officer Kirby.

We flashed our warrant cards, trying the good way first. "Hey lad, we're detectives working your murder spree in these parts and have been sent here. What's the crack? Any chance we can have a cursory once-over," Michael says, waking the young officer up,

"Yeah, you've been expected. I'm surprised how quickly word spreads around here. How you two get to work all the spooky ones. Kinda envy you, to be honest. Instead, I have a scene log and a pen. But yeah, happy trails. Just be careful. We're lucky the floor is solid stone under ply boards," Kirby says, resigned in his voice. Yeah, it can be fun working on these weird ones, but with everything we've survived, I'm not sure he'd be so keen if he knew.

We dipped under the tape held aloft by Kirby and made short work of the pavement to the front door. All the glass was smeared black, and the dampness of burnt wood soaked in water was overpowering. It wasn't long before the stink changed. Around us, what had been comics and other items were nothing but burnt debris and melted plastic. The glass counter was blown out.

"Michael, take the left quarter. I'll take the right. Use your other eyes. This place feels all kinds of off." I say. With everything still smouldering and cloudy, it was hard to find the exact source of the burnt flesh, but any dead bodies would give off a unique signature under U. V than the standard burnt crap.

There were footprints everywhere. A gasoline trail, too, spray marks up the walls, over the stands and a long trail around the counter to the door behind us. My wolf's eyes worked the right-hand wall when I saw some odd symbols. Not the sort ordinarily visible, especially without the fire. These were meant only to be seen a certain way (black light) or by the supernaturally inclined.

I got so fixated on what I saw. I was paying attention to where I stepped. Another 'goat's head in a star', just like Scotland and anything linked to Satan or devil worship. The other symbols were more like the sigils at the morgue when 'Frank' first came back to life. While he was busing being 'living dead', sigils formed from the shadows and in blood. I couldn't translate them, and sure as hell, Michael couldn't either.

My feet scuffed through the burnt plywood and puddles, still fixated on the walls when I stub my toes. I jumped back in a panic. Not something I would've done had it been some wood or the counter. My heightened hearing heard a crunch. One all too sickeningly familiar. The fragile cracking of burnt flesh with fluids beneath the skin scorched away. Leaving behind a fragile burnt shell. The tips of my shoes must've gone an inch deep.

A full-grown adult male. I swivel on the spot. There's three other corpses scattered nearby. My stomach flipped., It's okay; everything I had was not to spew my guts. Michael saw it, too.

'Three... two...one,' I counted, watching Michael dash to the far corner in time to spray the walls. Two bodies had the limbs ripped off, thrown wildly in the tragic aftermath.

"Not one word, you hear? Not one," Michael says, looking up and wiping his mouth.

"Who me? Never. If you're about done, princess, we need to connect these fucking 'dots'. In a comic store of all places,"

Michael tip-toed around the body parts with all the grace of a drunk ballerina. He was about to step past a Chunky arm when he froze. His bright yellow eyes bulged wide, his mouth opened, but no words came. Not immediately, anyway.

"Fuck... fuck... fuck, matey, this isn't" Michael looked shaken, and he's been good with most stuff like this, but he was rattled.

"What?"

"From where I am, I can see those cross things. You know, the glowing ones on the bodies in the morgue," Michael pivoted around the arm, face churning as he skipped across the puddles to where I stood.

The bodies where Michael was had a slight glow, getting brighter and bringing that symbol through the burnt shell. I check the one near me. Or what there was. Upper right of what had to be the back began cracking and splitting. That glow fighting to push through.

"We can't let anyone else in, Michael. I have a bad feeling." I looked through the gap in the scorch marks across the glass. The numbers were growing. The only thing on our side was that it had got dark. I was doing the math, and it didn't work.

To handle what I feared would happen and stop outsiders coming into the firing line. We'd have to split our attention. To do that, I'd have to unleash the wolf properly if the shit hit the fan.

"I know, matey, I'm still digesting what happened at the morgue,"

Loud snapping in unison took us by surprise. A twitch here. A scuffle, crackle and groan there. We had movement to bring that fear I mentioned to the forefront. All four corpses began crunching the char-grilled shells, slow robotic movements. Then, the inconceivable happened. Compared to the crap I've seen, that's saying a lot. If coming back from the dead was bad, watching on in awe as torn limbs slowly slithered through the burnt debris.

Michael and I were gobsmacked, mouths hung open, stomachs flipped with bile surging through mine. Those limbs made a beeline to the relevant corpse. My wolf's eyes zoomed in to see them reattached themselves, crusty flesh sewing the pieces together.

Each corpse pulled itself upright. Puppets on strings, minus the strings. They appeared mindless and vacant yet moved military-like. Loud, melancholic groans oozed through their burnt jaws, with scorched blood frothing over the edge. My heart was a runaway train. Michael's not much better.

"Michael, no matter what. Go to the door and don't leave it. Don't let anyone in or anything out,"

"But,"

"But nothing... If we don't and these things go out there, picture what was left of

Doctor Thornton. I'm not saying that's what these want right now, but we have to prepare,"

"What if they are being controlled and summoned back?" Michael says, making me think. For every argument, I had a counterargument.

"What if they had been normal before the fire? Once dead, thanks to those symbols, the corpses are reanimated." Michael had that rabbit in headlights look again. In fact, we both did because I just realised something, too. What if that's the plan? Anyone killed with a symbol becomes the living dead—an unstoppable army of death. We didn't know how many mindless followers had that symbol.

All four corpses were on their feet now. Staggering forward slowly. Their arms strained toward me. Whether they simply needed a target or were running off a memory beforehand. I couldn't take the risk.

I caught a glimmer of the moon through the window, enough to give a little boost, prompting a 'shift' not fully evolved but even to scare the shit out of anyone coming in. I slowly backed away, sliding behind the counter. The corpses followed. There was a trapdoor open on the floor, steps going down. If I could lead them near, they'd fall.

The plan was working. I slid near the edge before the first step. I leapt backwards just as they leaned forward. They'd be off balance and drop. I was rocking on my heels. Michael watching on with fear. All four groaned hauntingly loud. I didn't budge. It had to be the very last second. It was about to happen when a loud clap rang out. Shop filled with a thick black cloud that swarmed the dead, whipping a cloudy blanket around them and another loud clap. They were gone. The fuckers had been summoned back.

Breathing a sigh of relief, I was glad the dead were gone but worried about what would be next. More importantly, what the bloody hell happened? Michael scooped an arm around my shoulder, happy it was over, too. Then h, e clocked the trap door, too.

"So, matey, the elephant in the room,"

"Eh, your ex-wife isn't here,"

"Oi, you cheeky twat! Although it is a fair point. Anyway, I meant, what do you think is down there?"

"Only one way to find out," Michael nodded before stepping down into the next unknown.

At the bottom, there's a large open metal door, a big safe one. I'm scanning with my wolf's eyes. There was drool on the stone floor within the room. Somebody had been down here. Aside from a little smoke damage, the fire hadn't touched its contents, and boy, oh boy, were we surprised.

Those sigils were nothing compared to this. More crosses were just like what we saw on the creepy guys. My attention went straight to an old parchment or an old page taken from a book—leather appearance.

"Fuck... Pandora's box. This says they're gateways to hell."

"You're shitting me? Those things are real? I thought that was a myth," Michael says, shuffling beside.

"This one is a puzzle that requires coin pieces. Once solved, it opens a gateway to where the 'Book of the Dead' is hidden. Oh god, a band of templar knights split away, taking pieces of the coin with them. Four Knights,"

"Could those knights have bloodlines alive today, matey?" I was getting an eerie feeling. The kind that meant I was reaching for straw or going mad. A knot in my stomach made me think Gerald Ackerman's family could be a descendant. I know, quite the jump. The details made sense. Then there's the shadow on the TV screen. It's not quite the far-fetched theory, especially as the creeps had a similar link with those symbols. "Why else would they want Gerald? I guess so,"

"Georgie, we both know I'm no genius in this stuff, but I have a hunch or a shot in the dark. But what if that Gerald guy was one of those knights? His family line. The creepy fucks suspect he has a coin piece, and they want it. For all we know, they've recovered the other three pieces. Then they discover the box wherever that may be." -

- "Then they get the Book of the Dead, who knows what it could contain. Perhaps the key to bringing forth the big bad guy himself. Complete with an army of the living dead," I interrupt. Michael made a hell of a lot of sense. The question is, what actually happened here today?

Where Am I?

34

' Gerald - Melwood 8 PM,'

"Cuh, cuh. Where am I?" My eyes were slow to open. I can feel pressure on my wrists. Wait... my arms are above my head. I can't move them. God, my head is killing me. No hangover has kicked my arse this bad.

My brain was slow to catch up, trying to process what had happened. Why I can't move? Then I remember the room below the floor in the shop. Hissing, a gas came through the vents. Bloody hell, I was locked in and knocked out by that gas.

Oh no, those whispers called to me when I was on the floor—telling me to let it in. I didn't, did I? Please tell me I didn't. Damn, where's Nathan? Where the hell am I? That pressure on my wrists gradually became apparent that it was metal shackles. They were biting into my flesh. My eyes were open, but I still couldn't see.

Every breath feels warm and stifled. There's something over my head. A cloth hood or similar. It smells musky, can't pick up on any other scents around me because of it. I try moving my legs. The tips of my toes barely grazed the floor. I scrape some dirt, but beneath felt solid. If I hedge my bets, it's straw over flooring. I was in a barn.

I could barely hear muffled moans. Sounded at least ten feet away. It could be Nathan, but if we're both trapped, then Mason screwed us over. I remember him calling Nathan out of the room not long before I was shut in. Surely, Nathan wasn't in on the act. Fighting back a wave of sickly emotions, needing to have a rational mind if I stood any chance of escaping.

"About bloody time you're awake." I hear a voice from the shop, abrupt but sounding a little like Mason.

"Who are you? Where am I? Where's Nathan?" I say, my throat still feeling the after-effects of the gas.

"Be bloody quiet. We'll ask the questions if you don't mind. More importantly, we want to know what you are. We have our suspicions, but we want to hear it from you. How you are a sick, killing machine." What? A killing machine. They must have their wires crossed, assuming I'm guilty when I've done nothing yet. Have I? Fuck, what if it is me?

"I'm not the one you want. It's not me, we're trying to find who too. They killed my father and wife. So, who are you?"

"Oh, but you are. How about we start simple? Where's the puzzle piece?" What the hell is this guy on about? I knew even less than whoever this guy did, and yet he's asking me for some bloody piece of a puzzle. Had me thinking they were on about Pandora's box—the image on the wall. In the photo, it showed four sections, but I had none.

"Hey, come on, buddy, you really have the wrong guy. I didn't know what you're on about. Now, where's my friend?"

"Nathan is fine. You two stroll into my shop, start enquiring about things only certain people will know of. My guess is you have a piece and want to know how to unite them to find the book. Well, newsflash, it's our destiny. Only those loyal to the cause of ushering in a new world. One where there's no pain or suffering. I witnessed the brutality because of your presence. The carnage you cause."

"What do you mean?" the guy was going off on a tangent while I was using the time to wiggle my wrists, hoping I could drag them free.

"Don't pretend, you sick bastard." His tone turned angry, stomping up close, whipping the hood off my head. True enough, there was Mason. We were in a large farm barn suspended from beams. Nathan was across the way and seemed out cold still.

Behind Mason, there are half a dozen blokes, only they're all wearing pointy black hoods with the Templar cross on the front. Mason had started some crazy cult. To what end? What did he think he would gain? His comment about ushering in a new world stuck with me. Did those creepy guys promise them power and riches or whatever the going rate is for stringing up two guys trying to prevent more death?

"Hey, I'm really not into whatever you and Brady bunch are, so how about you? Let us go, and we'll leave you be."

"No way. All you bring is death. Now, you have to make amends. We called others that are really interested in you and we would've been in their good graces. I can't believe you don't remember. Perhaps this will jog your memory."

Mason brawls his fist, draws back, and lets rip with a punch to my left cheekbone. For a fat guy, he packs a whack. It bloody hurt. It worked, though...

A quick burst of images, jumbled, trying to form a memory, then...

"Y...y...ye... No... I can't let you in."

'My head is heavy. I can lift a little from the floor. I hear a loud groan, metal grinding against metal. I tilt my head on my chin in time to see the door drift open. I can hear banging from upstairs. The air is clearing. I can pull myself up, but I'm so woozy. My eyes were bleary, like a sheet of fog in front of them, but I saw enough to stagger toward the door.'

Then I lose the bloody trail...

"Wow, is that all you got, big boy? My kids can hit harder than that... Hate to crush your ego; they're two," I goaded, watching Mason's face turn bright red.

"F...f... For Christ's sake, Gerald, don't.... You don't know what you're doing... I mean, Mason is sensitive about his weight. He can't help being a fat double-crossing bastard," Nathan came around just in time. A little groggy but alive and with it enough to follow my lead.

"I know, right, Maid Mason and his merry band of six misfits?" It was my turn to return the favour and give Nathan the gist of what we were dealing with.

The barn was larger than I'd seen before. Enough to have a ground and first with ramps going up left and right to a big platform that has a hatch with a winch. The Bradys formed a loose semi-circle wall behind the main man, Mason. If we could get free of the shackles, we stood a chance. Although Nathan was groggy and I'm not much better. It's pitch black outside, and we didn't know where we were.

Our choices were slim. Play along, piss Mason off enough, so he slips up and gives us what we need to know. That starts by taking another hit, restarting that trail.

"You both think you're funny. Just because you killed those thugs, there's no way you're leaving here until we get what we want. As for the 'fat' comment. Have this, you arsehole,"

'Thump,'

"Fuck... What was that, a wet fish?" My bravado was cashing cheques my body hated paying. He packed a punch alright. But...

'I'm gripping the door frame. There's a commotion getting louder.'

'Come on Gerald, let me in. Your friend needs us. We can save him if you let me in.'

'The whisper came, but I hadn't let it in. I shook my head and continued up the steps.'

'Okay Gerald, if you're playing hard to get, how about an audition?'

'I didn't answer. If the darkness needed me to let it in, how could it do anything? At least that's how I thought. I'd made it halfway. There's nothing but darkness, and suddenly, a large outline of a man appears. He's moving quickly. There are others, too. Nathan is on the floor already. The silhouette tears relentlessly through the group. I'm on the top step, then 'ouch', I feel a sharp pain in my neck. I turn to see Mason holding a needle. Then I crash to the floor.'

I'm back in the present at the barn with memories intact. I didn't know whether to be scared or emboldened. Mason was half right, yet I don't do it. Just the darkness trying to impress, and then Mason knocked me out.

"Cheers for that, you sneaky bastard. Skulking in the corner to inject me. You were wrong, by the way. I killed no one,"

"Well, how about this, Gerald Ackerman? Yeah, I know your name thanks to this driver's licence. You're the descendant of the late Frederick Ackerman, a traitorous knight of the Templar order. So I know exactly who and what to expect. That's why I called these guys again."

Mason slips a white business card from his pocket. Nothing but the same cross I saw in Mason's basement and the number '913. 0309. Which was weird, not the usual numbers I'd seen, but I fear he called those creeps in suits. Whatever I was going to do, it had to be quick.

"So what, I have a famous relative, a bit like you're related to 'Jabba the Hut' and what's that? your prostitute hotline?" I say Hearing Mason chuckle under the hood.

That was the straw that broke the camel's back. Mason stormed up close, kneeling me in my stomach, taking the wind from my sails. He leaned close, sweat streaming off his forehead, bright red and pissed. He leans close.

"Where's the fucking puzzle piece?"

"Bloody hell, Mason, the breath. Would you kiss your mother with that mouth," I say, feeling the singe on my stubble.

"Come now, Gerald... It's well known Mason has been kissing his Mother since he hit puberty... Congratulations, by the way. Last month, right... Now you're a real boy!" Nathan ripped into Mason. His words were a bit slurred and a struggle. Funny, though, and Mason was livid.

"So, now your secret is out, Mason. Get it in your thick head. I didn't know what you're talking about," I say, dropping the smile and glaring at Mason's fat, red face.

"They will make you talk. Funny, really, I was so creeped out when they first came to the shop, but their vision for the future is exactly what this world needs. To think you're a Templar 'bloodline', what a joke,"

There was me digesting Mason's talk again about a new world and the creeps when I heard a 'click'. The shackle on my wrist felt loose. Mason stayed close, and somehow I could move.

'You're welcome,' a low hiss breezed down the bend of my neck. The darkness had auditioned for the second time. A compelling argument. Since when did something that could kill so ruthlessly ever turn out well?

Mason's head bobbed in front of my face. I took my chance. I yanked my hands free and swung an elbow square on the bridge of Mason's nose. Blood spurted across his face. I kicked him in the bollocks before snatching keys from Mason's belt loop. The Bradys were stunned, and Mason stumbled, struggling to regain composure. I unlatched Nathan's shackles, tearing the hood from his head.

We still had much to do. Nathan was a dead weight hanging from my shoulder. We shifted to the right. Nathan kept flinging his arm up, catching me in the face while trying to speak, but he was quite groggy still.

"G... Ger... Gerald.... The lantern. Get the blubby, I mean bloody lantern. No smoke without fire. He has the smoke coming out of his ears. Let's give them the fire. Look." Nathan threw his arm to point at the straw throughout the floor. I got what he was selling. And could be the perfect aid to our escape.

We scurried a cross to a lantern hanging from a support beam, knowing we should be lucky they're still using flame ones. Mason and his Brady bunch had regained their composure, darting toward us. With a quick flick of my free arm, I sent the lantern spinning through the air. I don't know why, but was standing and watched, twisting through the air seemingly in slow motion. Two of the Brady's dived, attempting to catch it. Others flung themselves in opposite directions.

A loud crash and 'whoosh' fire ripped through the shattering glass across the straw. Within seconds, the entire section of open floor went up in flames. They couldn't get to us. I hoisted Nathan up higher and shuttled us to the doors. I couldn't hear anyone outside, but that didn't mean a thing. I'd be foolish to think there were only a handful of sycophant cultists deluded that evil would do anything for them, which brings me to my issues. Why was this darkness, this strange whisper, so hell-bent on being embraced that it helped us?

There's a dark panel van to the left with headlights on. We may have just got our first lucky break. We were definitely on a farm, a huge one, all in darkness. If we had time, it would be worth digging a little and seeing what else is here, but time wasn't on our side. I threw Nathan in the back. He was still very drugged, which puzzled me because I took the gas and an injection and still more with it.

I dived in the driver's seat, thanking my lucky stars that the keys were there. First, turn... fuck... it didn't turn over... second... still nothing... third... it roared to life. With a quick rev, I chucked it into gear and was about to go when the night sky lit up with a flashing blue. An unmarked police car came tearing through the farm's muddy road, skidding to a halt in front of us.

My lights shone directly on their windshield, two guys in suits. Thankfully, not those creepy ones. An older, seasoned guy in the passenger seat, the driver much younger. I thought about fleeing, a quick reverse and spinning the van right. Until I caught sight and something weird... Considering how high my bat for that has gone lately, that speaks volumes.

Their eyes changed... one flashed red, the other yellow. I should have been scared. Oddly, my sixth sense was telling me they were going to help. I don't know why. We needed all the help we could get, even if I could be suspected of murder.

Timing Is Everything

35

'Détective Reynolds,'

We flew through the farm, throwing our car to a halt just in time to stop a dark panel van from leaving. We discovered a house near the shop service road had CCTV that captured two guys bundled into the back. Both were limp and out cold. The van was registered to the shop but stupidly set off half a dozen speed cameras, tearing through red lights.

The bloody trail led us to Maplewood, thirty miles outside Melwood. We still had three farms to choose from, so it was a little potluck. The lights gave it away. Looking at the two in the van was like startled rabbits wrestling with flight or fight.

My senses tell me it was Ackerman and a friend. We couldn't take any chances. My ears were twitching to the tune of a commotion inside. We were reading all sorts of wrong, setting our eyes off. We were in a standoff. Michael grabs the mic for the loud hailer.

"Switch your engine off and step out of the vehicle slowly," Michael says, his dulcet tones screeching out of the speakers, jarring my nerves.

"It's not what you think," I hear the driver shout out the window. His heart remained steady, elevated from the situation—no blip during his words.

"Step out of the vehicle," Michael says again.

"We need to get out of here. What you want is there,"

My hearing drifts past the van, through the doors. There's a crackling from a fire and raised voices.

"Michael, he's telling the truth. And I think that's Ackerman,"

"Really?" Michael says, looking at me, puzzled.

"Yep, but there's trouble,"

We stepped out of the car. I watched the driver, still listening inside. The driver was on edge, and his foot tapped the accelerator. He wanted to go, but suddenly opened his door. His face was more of fear and worry. I didn't get a guilty vibe from him.

"Are you Gerald Ackerman?" I say, on guard as he steps in front of the van's headlights, projecting a silhouette over our car bonnet. That's when I noticed... The silhouette was the same on the tape, the one that loomed around Henry and smacked the TV screen.

"Y... Yes... Look, we were drugged and kidnapped. My buddy is in the back. In that barn is a bunch of weirdos into some strange cult."

Everything he said matched what we saw on the CCTV. There's still so many vague 'dots' to figure out, like why those creeps wanted him.

"We saw. We've been to your house, too. In fact, we know a little more than you'd expect. We're going to need you to fill in some blanks, though," I say, still listening for changes. I heard fire extinguishers being sprayed.

Ackerman raked his hands through his hair, gasping in distress. "You wouldn't believe me if I told you," Ackerman says, glancing nervously over his shoulder.

"We would. And now we have a vested interest. We know about the two in black suits,"

"Them creepy bastards. They blew my front door off, followed my friend Nathan, and chased us."

"What happened in the shop, the dead guys and the fire?" I ask. Ackerman pauses, thinking about what he should and shouldn't say.

"We went there looking for answers, was looking at some old papers when everything went wrong. I was gasses, but it wore off. I climbed from the basement to find Nathan passed out on the floor and some thugs in the shop. It was dark. Somebody attacked them. They ripped them apart. Before I could do anything, the owner of the shop jabbed a needle in my neck."

Most of what he said, but his heart jumped when spoke of the thugs being attacked. He knew more, but not in a way he was guilty.

"Well, if this little get-together is done, maybe we can get the fuck out of here?" Michael says, looking irritated. I sensed it, too. There was a change in the air. Nothing good.

"Right, you follow us. Do anything stupid, and everything you have said so far goes out the window," I say, checking for a flinch of uncertainty. Unfortunately, the lights were on, but nobody was home.

I stepped toward Ackerman, hands held up to show no harm intended. I needed him to get on board my train of thought and fast because something was brewing in the barn and the winds were sweeping in something far worse. My hackles were on fire. Michaels, too, I was loathed to show a mundane the other me unless push came to shove. The wolf prefers to do the shoving.

"It's okay, relax," I say. He wasn't relaxing, instead he kept looking toward the barn.

Wind hissed between the barn planks, whipping up an eerie frenzy. The extinguishers stopped. My hackles bounced, and then... 'chuh chuh' Michael and I looked at each other. He jumped beside me. Several shotguns just chambered.

I could feel it coming. Michael was watching me. "Mr Ackerman, I know there's more going on with you. But something bad is about to happen and what you'll see may scare you, but don't worry," I say. Ackerman stood open-mouthed at first.

"What do you mean??"

"Your shadow shows the hatred silhouette that's on your tapes. My guess is your father was cursed or afflicted. His death passed it on to you. Am I close," Ackerman nodded.

A stampede of footsteps rushed the barn doors. I was fifteen feet away with Ackerman in the way. Several thugs burst into the open. Fingers pressed triggers, I dug deep and powered forward. The muzzle flashes were in slow motion. For me, anyway, hurrying. I ditched. My jacket flared my claws and phased on the fly, pouncing over Ackerman onto all fours, fully shifted and without pain. Michael, using his speed, whipped Ackerman out of the firing line.

First guy went down easy, disarmed, and I didn't hurt him too badly. I didn't want to. Figured a good scare should be enough. Until I caught a stray bullet, one ripped through my thigh. Thankfully, it wasn't Wolfsbane. Hurt like hell, though, and really pissed me off. My claws tore through his stomach. As the guy fell, his finger stayed on the trigger, firing into his friends and taking down three others. I prowled upright, growling, teeth bared and claws dripping with that venom. I've never appreciated just how big I am until now, looking at my shadow on the barn. The rest of the gunmen fled into the vast, empty fields.

There were four dead on the floor, and I was bleeding. Only when the adrenaline eased did I appreciate just how bad. Slowing down, I phased back. Michael threw his coat over me. I was limping badly. The bullet grazed my femoral artery.

"Fuck matey, you pissing blood. You, okay?" Michael looked worried. Ackerman was too shell-shocked.

"Yeah, I'm okay. I can feel it trying to heal, but the artery is pinched. I need to cauterise it to speed up the process." I say, slumping against the van.

"Flares... yes, a flare. I saw some in the van," Ackerman says, running to the passenger side to grab one. Within seconds, he was back. A quick click, and it's lit up like a Roman candle.

"Do it!" I say through gritted fangs. My claws latched onto Michael's shoulder. With a swift move, Ackerman plunged the flare into my wound. My eyes bulged, searing heat tore through my leg and then my body. I let rip with a deep, bellowing roar that shook the barn to its foundations.

"Fucking hell, mate. I know it hurts, but do you mind leaving my shoulder attached?" I looked to see my claws were buried deep. Even worse, the venom was killing his flesh. I quickly retracted them and checked out the wound. Much to Ackerman's astonishment, it had completely healed.

"That is so cool," a voice blurts out from the van. Ackerman's friend was awake and had his head out the door. How much he saw was anyone's guess.

"I have to agree with Nathan. I should be scared shirtless, but that was awesome." Ackerman had finally settled and seemed confident and unafraid.

"Well, with that in mind, we need to make like a tree and leave. There's something else coming, and we're on the back foot," I say. The others nodded in agreement. Just as we were stepping away, me getting dressed on the move, I heard stirring. A familiar groan we'd heard earlier.

All four thugs were coming back to life. Each had that glow emanating under their clothing. Their eyes were jet black, skin a mottled grey-white. All back on their feet, moving as if riddled with rigour mortis. Not even a normal corpse sets that quickly. These stumbled like zombies.

"For fuck's sake, not bloody again," Michael gushes.

"As much as it would be great to go again, let's just go. Let these disappear like the others. I'm sure they'll come again." I say, ushering everyone to the car.

The living dead's numbers are growing. Those creepy church fuckers are hot BB on our heels, and they have Ellena captive. We have Gerald Ackerman now chalking a point in our win column for a change.

A storm is brewing, and it's threatening to rain blood. Before we know it, the streets will be swamped with the undead and their sadistic puppeteers. We need to punch their ticket permanently. All this rinse-and-repeat nonsense is wearing thin.

WHAT'S NEXT

36

'Gerald,'

I'm back at the farm. I don't know how. I'm headed back to where we left off. I'm in the driver's seat but not in control. It's happened again. Dust is kicking up along the muddy trail. Every crunch under my feet is too noisy compared to the stillness around. Tallgrass line the path left and right, boarding weathered picket fencing. Not a streetlight in sight. Instead, there's a motion-detected halogen in the front of a barn in the distance.

The air was icy cold, and white clouds bellowed in front. An owl echoes a hoot to the left, high in a tree, showing all the ravages of winter. There's shadows jostling, animated, full of rage, breaking from some fields toward the barn. One slightly bigger one burst through the doors.

I'm walking slowly; the air feels off, musky. I'd made it within twenty feet. Three guys and 'Mason' twist. They're running towards me. I don't stop. Edging forward. Each had a shotgun, chambering loud enough to send my arm hairs to attention. Nothing. I'm moving without control.

"Who the fuck are you? What you doing here? Did they send you?" Mason is spitting venom. He doesn't recognise me.

Anger quickly became a look of fear. Mason jumps backwards in line with the others. He snatches at a gun from one of them, raising it to the front, followed by the rest, but I continue forward. Shaky hands slide to the triggers and press. With a unified click, I dive forward.

Swooping beneath the first gunman, I lash upwards, gripping an arm. I hear a loud crunching of bone; I tear an arm clean off with the gun still held. Blood sprays skyward. Curdling screams filled the air. I wasn't in control, but I didn't stop.

The arm is tossed to the side, and I notice my hands. They're long, thin and clad in gloves. My arms are covered with black coat sleeves that are now dripping blood. I was seeing through the eyes of the shadowy figure again. The one that haunts me. It's 'Grace' all over again.

My menacing, bony fist powered through another guy's chest, clutching his heart, smashing out of his back, squeezing the heart to splatter everywhere. The guy drops in a heap before I blur through the rest; limbs scatter across the ground that's rapidly pooling with blood until the last man standing is Mason.

He staggers backwards, stumbling over a torso that's gushing a crimson river. Mason has backed himself against the thick barn door. The halogen light above paints his frightened face. Pale round flesh dripped with panic sweat and dribbles of his friend's blood. His mouth flaps open, but no words come. Until I reach out an arm.

"Pleaseees don't," Mason begs. "Tell them I will make amends. I promise". Mason continues. I close him down like hunted prey, trapping Mason against the huge structure and a gruesome massacre mosaic.

My fingers puncture either side of Mason's windpipe. It's bony and a little squishy, toying with it like violin strings. Mason's eyes bulge, fit to burst from their sockets. Pale white blended with checking red. His body flailed against my grip. A little pressure and I'm squeezing Mason off the floor, sliding his fat frame up the door. His chunky legs trash wildly.

A little tug. A little flex and pull, a quick yank, and my hand flies free from Mason's neck, his jugular still clutched between my blood-drenched fingers. With a loud gargle, Mason spurts a red fountain as he drops in a dead, bloody heap. A quick squeeze and I toss Mason's mess over my shoulder before soaking up my looming silhouette cast across the wooden doors to the sound of the owl hooting hauntingly once more.

"Oi, wake up,"

"Huh, what?" My eyes jump open. I'm in the back of the police car, and

Nathan is shaking my arm. My head was reeling from what I'd just seen. I was drenched in sweat, my heart going two to the dozen.

Nathan stared at me as if I was the second coming of Christ. The car wasn't moving, and from what I could tell, we'd stopped in a layby. Both detectives were twisted in their seats, staring, too. I quickly pat around my mouth, checking for drool. After all, why were they all boring holes in me with their eyes?

Maybe I was sleep-talking, I thought. Until I noticed both had bright red and yellow eyes. Their hands gripping the seat top had claws. Which brought me back to the farm and what I saw. It was fucking crazy.

How on earth had my life come to this? Knowing there are other things out there. Dead-looking blokes that can blow my door off with a wave of a hand. Coppers that can turn fully into werewolves, and a haunting whisper that somehow breaks me out of shackles. None of it was rational, and I'd call bullshit. But with the devil symbols popping up, me seeing murders happen in my sleep and those bodies... They bloody came back to life.

The only place I felt fit for was the loony bin. Now, I had to break it to the others that Mason and his cronies were likely dead. I had the front-row seat—a place I wish for nobody.

"Gerald, you okay?" Nathan taps my arm to grab my attention.

"Er... yes and no," I say, watching in awe as the detective's claws fade along with their eerie eye glow.

"We guessed, judging by the frantic muttering and the other weird," The driver, Reynolds I think, spoke up, and sounded on edge. Who could blame him with the crazy going on?

I edge back in my seat, fully awake. "Other weird?" My head flicks at Nathan and the detectives.

"Gerald, it was nuts. I'm talking full-on out-of-body experience nuts. Only what came out of your body wasn't you. At least, I don't think." Nathan was clawing at the flesh of his hands. He was on edge. Any shuffle from me had him flinching.

"I don't get you,"

"Someone in all black, with a hat, long bong hands, gaunt, deathly features. Your eyes fluctuated from red to black. You had some upside-down Templar cross carved into the flesh of your forehead. And it floated like a cloud from your body, with ripples of black smoke.." Nathan says, his tone trailing into one filled with worry, maybe even fear.

"Gerald, it was just like the silhouette at the barn and what we saw on the tapes," Reynolds spoke softly as if that would be reassuring. Nothing I'd heard so far was settling me down at all.

I was dreading what my impending news flash was going to do to the atmosphere and the palpable tension I was picking up on. If they saw that projected from me, imagine their faces when I say, 'Oh hey guys, guess what, that thing you saw, I was it, in my sleep, and I filleted Mason and Co,' No doubt those glowing eyes would come back quick. They had to know, though. I owed them the truth, considering the mess we were in.

"Well, I was dreaming. That thing you saw, I was it. A passenger of sorts, being carried along for a '*bloody*' ride. I was back at the farm. And ran into Mason again." I paused, seeing just how spooked everyone was. Surprisingly, not that much.

"Come on, matey. Spill the beans before I reach pension age," the other detective spoke up, smiling in a weirdly unsettling way.

"Aren't you there already?" Reynolds piped up, busting his friend's balls. Considering what they could do and see, they didn't seem fazed, as if was second nature to them. I dreaded to think just what they'd seen in their careers to be so relaxed.

"I was just how you described, minus any control, as I ploughed through Mason and any remaining friends. I literally had Mason's jugular in the palm of my hand as his corps dropped to the floor. Blood gushed everywhere. What was weird, though, other than the obvious? Mason pleaded as though he thought my visage was sent from those creepy guys," I say, without coming up for breath. I felt a little lighter sharing the load. Instead of shock, I saw the detectives facing each other, exchanging a knowing look.

I got the impression they'd experienced similar before. That I didn't envy, I can't wait for life to return to normal. Only, I had a feeling it wouldn't be the same again.

Silence fell between us, nothing but the low hum from some cheesy music on the radio and the sound of traffic whizzing past us. I was lost in a daydream, staring out the front windshield. Nathan had settled into his seat, half asleep. The detective's mouths were moving, but I heard nothing. A perk of their condition? Super hearing, maybe? God, how I dumbed that down, 'condition' like it was a sickness. Not that I knew what it was.

Sure, I'd seen the movies—the low-budget horror flicks. You know, the ones, town folk with pitchforks and fires. Oh, and silver bullets being the one thing to kill one. I had so many questions I wanted to ask but now didn't seem the right time. Although it was like an itch, I desperately wanted to scratch. Their faces spooked me a little.

Subtle twitches. I slid forward in my seat, watching their ears oddly changing. Something was wrong, and the detectives were picking up on it. Bloody, weird, but oddly fascinating. Out came the claws next. I can't lie. I was puzzled, and Nathan was, luckily, oblivious.

Looking out the window again, a low glow the size of a pin caught my attention against the night sky. A star, I thought. It was getting bigger and brighter. The detectives swivelled their heads slowly to see it, too. The hair on their necks ruffled like strange fur waving. How a dog's hackles would stand on end?

The glow was a bright blue, bolting me back to the pub after we escaped the library being chased by the creeps. Within in seconds, the glow had landed on our car bonnet. A raven. Its freaky, bright eyes peered directly at us. Its neck twitching. The detectives were freaked out. One after the other, more came swooping down until the bonnet was full of them. Again, much like the pub. Hundreds of needy, haunting eyes glared through at us. I'm no fan of coincidences. By the looks of it, neither were the detectives.

Suddenly, Reynolds speaks, but he's talking to the ravens. "What do you mean?"

"What's going on?" I ask the other guy, Michael, I think,

"It's fucking weird, mate. They keep saying, turn on the news, turn on the news. All in bloody unison. It's flipping spooky,"

My jaw dropped, and I slumped in my seat. Just when I thought the night was crazy enough. Dreams and all. Reynolds twisted the dial on the radio. Silence had been abruptly interrupted.

'Calls are flying in from the residents of Willowbrook—talk of seeing the dead walking the streets. Wait, now neighbouring villages, Melwood and Tilling, are reporting the same sightings. Some are saying arms can be seen busting out of the ground in cemeteries. More to follow in an ever-changing situation,' the radio gets flicked off again.

All the ravens were tapping on the glass, "End it now, before anyone gets hurt" Reynolds was angry, growling even.

Then Detective Reynolds turned to me with a look of horror on his face but said nothing.

Birds of a Feather. Flame Together

37

'Détective Reynolds,'

"What?" Detective Reynolds looked like a man wrestling with a problem. One that involved me.

"Well, aside from the dead coming back to life. They've threatened to resurrect your wife and father. Make them endure the pain of death all over again. That or... and I phrase this word for word. We will bring back what he held dear, put them on display outside the village church surrounded by the living dead and news broadcasters, and have them torn to shreds by hell hounds under the watchful eyes of the world,"

"W... what? Surely, that's not possible. Is it?" I say, feeling the colour drain from my face, sinking to my feet. I felt physically sick.

"I get the impression it is. They won't if you surrender yourself with the puzzle piece and the box."

I didn't have any puzzle pieces or the bloody box. I wish I had, would give us some semblance of bargaining power. Why would supposed men of god want a 'pandora's box', in particular the one that, I can't believe I'm even mentioning it, is a gateway to the Book of the Dead?

Not once has my father mentioned it, nor my mother, for that matter. Although, what she was keeping from me could fill a book of its own. I'm still a little slow on the uptake with all this weirdness, but I got the impression that Detective Reynolds was holding something back. His voice was riddled with emotion, and not because of the threat to bring Charlotte and Father back from the dead.

That radio announcement was unsettling, but not what bothered Reynolds, though. I mean, I'm sure in his line of work, it would. This was different.

The ravens were still tapping away. "I don't know what they're on about. That's what drew us to the shop. The owner 'Mason' who is now dead, was an expert in weird relics and the occult. We had this photo and wanted to know more," I say, handing the paper with a group picture on one side and a drawing of that coin in four pieces on the other to Reynolds.

Reynolds toyed with it. Flicking from one side to the other and back again.

"Who are these people?" Reynolds says, not taking his eyes off the group image, while the other guy was getting edgy over the haunting ravens.

"From what we could work out, mine and Nathan's immediate bloodlines. Parents and grandparents with the parents of Colin Milton. A friend of Nathan's,"

"Hey, that weirdo isn't quite a friend. I just know him enough to ask for help." Nathan cracked his eyelids open enough to interrupt groggily.

"Okay. So that's this lot. What about the fourth cost huddle?" Reynolds tapped the picture. I didn't recognise them. Nathan didn't seem to when we first found it at the cabin.

Michael turns in his seat, smirking, raising his eyebrows at Reynolds. "Georgie, be gentle, will you? You can see they're fragile with all of this. Stop playing games and spill what you've figured out," Michael says, getting a slight smile from Reynolds in return. These two are quite the characters, and don't get me wrong, I'm glad they're on our side, but I wasn't in the mood for games.

"Okay, okay. Well, did you geniuses stop to do the maths? How many bloodlines do you see here?"

"Er...Four?" I say sheepishly.

"Exactly. Why do you think there are pieces on the back of this photo? "

"But, Nathan? He's not going through what I am," I say, now looking closely at Nathan, second-guessing everything we've been through so far. Looking for inconsistencies.

"Well, I'd assume his father is still alive. For the time being, at least. The bigger issue is tracking down the other two bloodlines and seeing what they know about a box and coin pieces. Where's this in the picture?" Reynolds points out the cabin.

The tapping on the windshield was louder, a slight crack rippled just above the steering wheel. "I, erm, well, that's Nathan's grandparent's cabin. But shouldn't we, erm, do something about that before we're, er, I don't know, pecked to death or something?" I kept shuffling in my seat. Each peck was deafening, like what had happened at the pub.

"He's right, Georgie. Those demonic-looking fuckers will be in here shitting all over the place. Spray the screen wash or something. I read somewhere it's flammable,"

Reynolds pressed the crap out of the stick by the wheel, pissing all over the little demons. They weren't budging. Instead, began morphing, phasing into each other. Again, spooky yet fascinating. An outline of a man was forming, one of those creepy guys. I look at the car roof, noticing the sunroof. Then to the armrest by my feet. There's a press in lighter, beside me a newspaper. I quickly push the lighter, ripping several pages and wrapping in a wad in time for the lighter to pop out.

I jam the red-hot glowing end on the paper, sparking it to life. "Detective, roof," I point to the ceiling. Reynolds presses a button, allowing a rush of icy wind to whip through. I shielded the flame, chucking my aversion to beady-eyed ravens to one side and stood up through the roof. Meanwhile, Reynolds throws the car into reverse. A finger pressed firmly on the screen wash, smothering the flying rats.

I face hundreds of bright blue eyes fixed on me. *'If you just let me in, you wouldn't be afraid. Now, just let me in.'* A chill skates down my back. The darkness chose its moment, and I shudder, shaking it off. The flame was barely alive. The ravens continued to merge. Soaked, I tossed the bundle down, engulfing the birds in the fire. I drop in time for the roof closing. Reynolds floored it, and the fire whipped and swirled. Feathers blistered to the winds. We watched the ravens fade to dust…. Screeching tyres set the tone as the flames blew out with the eerie.

'Reynolds'

We were in the middle of nowhere, downright spooky. The entire journey, I'd focussed on the sky, waiting for more of those blue-eyed demons. Towering trees lined a gravel road, a little like the farm where we found Mr Ackerman.

I slowed us down, weary, as we neared a really old cabin—something out of a horror movie. Our headlights painted the weathered porch. No sooner had I clicked the handbrake on than I felt a familiar chill—a rumble through my hackles. Ackerman didn't tell me or Michael just how far back their families were connected to this place. That chill was telling me there was trouble. Or had been.

I was daydreaming, and without thinking, I rolled down my window. Instinct had my senses coming to life. Silence, nothing but the stirring of the woodland nocturnal. An eerie wind rode past us with haunting ease. It was carrying news. Not the good kind. Michael caught the trail, too. A giveaway is always his eyes, the little rumble of yellow. Death was here or had been.

Michael and I exchanged glances. Both are on the same page. We had to be careful for the sake of Ackerman and Nathan. Playing it cool, we stepped out casually; I swept the right of the Cabin, Michael the left. Then the chill came again. This time, more of an icy shudder from someone stepping on my grave. I knew what was coming next, and they'd been a little less lately. Ghosts, a man and woman in their late fifties, gave me a horrible, sickly feeling.

'Michael, I have a bad feeling before we go in,' I whisper, looking into the woods and the never-ending darkness.

'Let me guess, ghosts,' Michael hisses quietly.

'How?'

'Your eyes. They went black again,'

'Well, I think something bad has happened.' No sooner had those words left my mouth than we heard a slight shuffle inside. My claws flew forward. Michael's, too. Keeping it from the others wasn't easy now. Ackerman seemed a little too keen on our 'shifting' side.

"Right, you two hang back a minute," I holler to Ackerman and Nathan, who looked puzzled until they saw the claws.

Slowly, we shuffled through the gravel. Michael stepped on the porch, and rotten boards creaked. Louder in the eerie silence. I flash my red eyes toward the window. Thick grime festered around the pane. Carefully, I trod forward. At first glimpse, I thought it was a ripple. The Dirty curtain moved. A draft, perhaps. No lights were on, and if it weren't for my supernatural vision, there'd be nothing but darkness.

'I think there's someone inside,' I whisper, catching Michael with his face hovering millimetres from the other window. He was on edge. I noticed a tremor in his left hand. My ears strain to listen. There's a heartbeat. Very faint and slow. Far slower than I'd read from mundane humans. Vermin, possibly. The place was old and dirty enough.

I'd crept up close to the window, holding my breath. Everything was still... my heart pounded between my ears until...

Cabin in the Woods

38

'Détective Reynolds,'

My attention snapped back to the window at the faintest tap—a nail rapping against the glass. The oval, head-shaped silhouette remained, fingers now elongating from its top, moving up and down as if counting or waving. I stared, perplexed by the silent show unfolding before me. My chest tightened with each breath I held.

The figure moved again, slightly but enough to make me jump at the sound of crunching, accompanied by a gelatinous, squelching noise that set every arm hair on end. I closed my eyes briefly, tilting my head skyward as I rode out the chill coursing through my body. I knew the sound all too well—a sad fact, but true, always in super high-definition thanks to my acute supernatural hearing.

Opening my eyes, I noticed again the absence of the moon against the purple-black sky. The tall trees and dense clouds thankfully obscured the half-lunar light; the full moon was still a few days away. Reluctantly, I looked back down at the window, digesting the realisation that I had just heard flesh and bone being severed. I caught Michael's grimace out of the corner of my eye; his eyes seemed unnaturally bright.

The oval head moved again, hauntingly slow, like a taunt, mocking our hesitation. In Scotland, we charged in, fangs blazing, achieving little—story of my life. Blood trickled down the other side of the window, dropping ominously into a puddle.

Now, the head had been ripped from a body. With a cautious glance to my right, the ghosts remained. Whether they belonged to the unfolding horror, I dared not guess.

Instinct whispered the worst—they were Nathan's parents. The head rose higher on the window, fingers gripping a scruff of hair, tossing it around like a macabre ball. We had to act. The grotesque display was more than my stomach could bear.

'Michael, come quick,' I called. His footsteps thundered towards me as we charged the door, smashing it against the wall. We landed in a large, musky, open-plan room lined with books. It was dark, but we used our other senses.

Over by the window stood a menacing figure, just a shadow, tall and imposing, silhouetted against the creaking, weathered walls. It let out an evil chuckle before hurling the head at us, the blood spraying wildly. Michael reluctantly caught it. The face belonged to a man in his late fifties, with short, greying hair and a patchy beard, his face contorted in pain and shock.

I had seen one ghost outside, and now my list of supernatural encounters was growing—more consistent than the U.K. weather, which varied from shades of dry, occasional sun, and frequent rain. The latter, I didn't mind; something was soothing about rain pounding against a window. Ghosts, however, were far less comforting. These had been dead for a while.

Either the Freakshow in front of us took their time, or they expected us to come. Michael placed the head respectfully on a table—it hardly seemed right to toss it aside like something insignificant. The body was slumped against the wall, oozing what blood remained. One might wonder how blood could 'die,' but it can. It carries a musky rot, distinct from its usual coppery scent. Then I saw the woman's corpse in all its grotesque glory.

We had been so distracted by the shadows and the head being thrown at us that neither of us had looked by the fireplace. Hung by her ankles from a man-made deer antler chandelier was a woman matching the other ghost. She had been stripped to her underwear, drenched in blood. The amount of blood was too overwhelming to determine where the wounds were, though a dark line circling her throat suggested a fatal cut.

While grappling with the scene, I flicked my gaze between the menacing figure by the window and the horrific spectacle hanging near the fireplace. Michael stayed near the door, keen to avoid interruptions to our grim discovery. His mouth fell open, pointing at the lady. "Fuck, her eyes are so cloudy it's fucking spooky," he exclaims with a mix of horror and disgust.

As I turned to the gloom by the window, something dangled from the bony hand of the shadow—a string or something similar. "You're bloody sick," I spits out, grimacing at the sight. A slight clanking sound echoed faintly in the eerie silence.

"Two down, two to go," the figure declares with a sinister chuckle, sending a chill through my blood.

"Two what?" I demand, trying to discern what was on the string. The occasional glint under my U.V. light only revealed metal.

"Oh, you'll see soon enough. It'll probably be too late by then. Since when has that stopped you, Mr Reynolds?" the sinister voice snarls, its cockiness unnerving me. "That's right, I know who you are. And your little friend there. Not to mention your fondness for the full moon."

"Who are you, and what's all this for?" I ask, shifting cautiously closer to the body hung from the chandelier.

"To change history. Stop all the hiding and embrace the power that was so obvious to everyone who came before. All they had to do was open a gate," the figure replies, his voice echoing like a distant storm. We were like chess pieces, each taking turns moving around the board.

"And you think that responsibility falls on you? Where do you fit with the two church guys in suits?" I pressed, eyes darting to Michael, who had slithered inches from the door, blocking any potential escape route. I rocked on my heels, treading carefully to avoid any noisy floorboards. Unfortunately, I wasn't as stealthy as Michael. A creak from underfoot caused a stir in the shadow. The clinking sound came again.

In my head, I plotted a swift leap across the room to the window, possibly to grab the killer, though I was still unsure how dangerous they were. Odd, considering I'm a werewolf. It's the new, over-cautious me—thank Scotland and its gang brigade for that. That mess has a lot to answer for.

"Responsibility? Never. A calling. To finally step out of the shadows after being seen as a fragile weakling or undertaker and be noticed. Everyone else ran for so long when all they had to do was accept fate. I'm going one further. Call it reinventing the wheel," the figure boasted, his confidence knowing no bounds. The wheel? Really?

"What do you mean, 'everyone else'?"

"Bloodlines. And all it would take is to drop a few bodies, ready an army, and find the book. Instead, they hid behind secrets and wore the keys like jewellery. What a sacrilegious joke," he scoffs. It was what I saw in the basement—a Pandora's box needing four pieces of that coin, which Gerald had a drawing of. I heard the clanking once more. They had at least two already. I was next to the dead woman, my eyes blazing over her flesh under

U.V. light, catching strange lines. Not tattoos, but something only visible under U.V.—a diagram... No, a map. At least part of one. Did the killer know?

"Have you found the book? What even is it?" I ask, ready to continue, when I heard movement outside. Footsteps trudging through the gravel. Gerald and his friend were approaching. Michael twitched his head, hearing it too. We couldn't let them in, not yet. Not with these being Nathan's parents.

"Soon enough. Right now, I'm enjoying myself. Leading everyone on a merry dance while, bit by bit, little by little, on this 'bloody' journey of discovery, I remove the obstacles that have held back change for centuries. All the while, others are too weak to embrace the darkness and become gods in a new world," he boasted.

I stood there, the sickly taste rising in my throat, déjà vu hitting hard. Another maniac, with a touch of the supernatural, wanted to rule the world or wield more power. It may sound weird, but reflecting on the simplicity of my past encounters—like with Charlie or Ethan, as he was actually known—felt almost nostalgic. Ethan's straightforward murderous rampage had been horrifying, yet he was undeniably human. This wasn't even our home soil; Locke had truly landed us in a mess, yet this village had an eerie charm. The demon within me sensed it, too—a dangerous darkness lurking, waiting to be unveiled. The population was sparse, and they certainly didn't need wannabe gods stirring chaos.

"You know that won't happen, so how about we end this little standoff, and you come down to the station? You can tell us more about your grand ideas there," I suggest, trying to sound more confident than I felt.

"Shame I have to disappoint. It's time darkness took over. After all, this village was made for this. Why do you think it's called 'Weeping Willow'? Not just because it sounds good. No, if only you knew the secrets. But you'll see. From what I gather, it's already begun," the figure retorted, shifting the man's dead body, likely searching for something I had seen on the woman.

The killer checked the flesh; his movements were meticulous. The radio reports of the Walking Dead echoed in my mind as we avoided the main routes to sneak here. I didn't doubt his words.

"Weeping Willow was an interesting choice for a nickname," I admitted, the huge, old tree on the outskirts of the churchyard giving the name some creepy validity.

We needed to take him down, and I was close enough to attempt it, but Michael seemed caught between decisions when a loud thumping at the front door interrupted our stalemate. Nathan and his friend were a dangerous distraction.

This was going to have to be on me. We couldn't afford for Michael to let collateral damage interfere. I felt a surge of supernatural PTSD—if there was such a thing. My senses were going haywire, and I had a dreadful feeling that this figure could be far more dangerous than any vampire. As the demon part of me picked up on the strange vibe, I slinked along the fireplace. The closer I got, the more menacing the killer appeared, the stench of blood almost overpowering—not just from the recent corpses but splattered across his black cloak.

One final step forward, while the killer appeared distracted, searching the body. That step got his attention. A loud creak from one of the few loose boards I'd found making my hackles jump.

"Tut, tut, tut. I was happy to leave you be for now. Just finish what I came here for, then I'd be gone. You couldn't wait, could you?" Long, bony fingers drifted from the headless corpse, reaching toward his hip and beneath his cloak. I caught a glint amid the red haze—the hilt of a sword with a Templar cross. Its grip was bound in what seemed like leather—a quick inhale confirmed it was flesh, old, mixed with another substance.

One... two... three...four... Almost decay-like bony stems rippled around that grip. I heard the metal blade grate in its sheath as the killer drew the sword upward slowly. Only a few inches, enough to intimidate. For reasons I couldn't quite grasp yet, the killer wasn't looking for a face-off. We weren't on the menu for the time being, which unnerved me even more because it alluded to a grander plan.

I was fixed on the hand, watching for sudden movements. Everything was quiet except my heavy breathing and the thumping of my heart. The killer seemed cornered—I emphasise 'seemed.' Experience tells me he wouldn't allow himself to be trapped without an escape plan. The problem was that I couldn't shake the thought of what he was searching for and whether it was the markings I saw.

The silence was deafening, a fitting saying, until a pain-riddled groan unnervingly shattered the quiet. Michael and I exchanged worried looks. It seemed to be a theme lately. Only my ears had pinpointed exactly where it was coming from, and I was too scared to look—the crusty old table.

"You got that, Georgie?" Michael says with a sheepish smile, his eyes darting to the table as well.

The decapitated head began moving, its soulless grey eyes creaking open and oozing blood. Its jaw jutted with the groans, making the head wobble, gooey entrails squelching with each sway—a horrifying surround sound. The dead were coming back to life.

"Yeah, cheers, Michael," I responded, watching Michael shrug in resignation as if to say, 'What can I do?'

I jumped, a shiver running through my legs. I felt a tapping on my thigh, a brush of my pocket. At first, I thought it was just the wind or perhaps a draft from the howling fireplace. Then it happened again. Reluctantly, I glanced down and nearly choked on my saliva in shock. The lady's corpse was writhing in the air, her drooping arm not so droopy now, her hand twitching against my leg.

I scanned her face: vacant, ghostly grey, dead eyes. Her mouth wouldn't stop moving, twitching as if she was trying to speak but had been muted—the lights were on, but nobody was home.

"Fuck, Georgie, look," Michael says, pointing to the corpse near the killer. The headless torso lurched forward, its arms waving for anything tangible to grasp.

I looked at the killer, who slid the sword back into its sheath. His tall, deathly presence pivoted slowly, taking a step backwards. His shielded face swivelled menacingly, allowing me a glimpse of parts of his face. A surge of bile flew through my throat. Taunt, bony contours, similar to the two church creeps. His face appeared rotten and dead. Before long, his eyes breezed through the haunting shadow—blood red set amidst endless black.

"And on that note, it's my cue to leave," the killer says, oozing with a confident menace.

"I don't think so, matey boy," Michael retorts, screeching from the door, slamming shut every time Gerald and Nathan tried to enter.

"Come now, detectives, this isn't the dance for us. Soon, though, that I promise. Until then, I have a puzzle to complete. The gates won't open themselves. Good luck with... all of this... well... death. I'll leave more for you to find," the killer taunted, waving at the moving corpses before my brain could engage to get my body moving. A black cloud smothered the floor around the killer's feet, consuming any vacant space, and in the blink of an eye, the killer faded into the cloud and then disappeared up the chimney. He had escaped, leaving us more on the back foot than ever. Gates... Not only did we have to stop more deaths. We had to stop the gates of hell from being opened.

DEATH BECOMES THEM

39

'Détective Reynolds,'

Michael let the door swing open, and Gerald and Nathan came rushing in, skidding to a stop. Nathan crashed into Gerald's back, who had already caught sight of the carnage. I remained by the fireplace, my thoughts consumed by the macabre theatrics that had just unfolded. The burning issue of Ellena being held somewhere dark and equally terrifying tormented my mind.

Gerald's jaw hung open, his gaze fixed on the head of Nathan's father, who groans and yawned with all the grace of the undead—Christ, even to think it, 'the undead.' Not so different from vampires, I suppose, minus a brain, fangs, some aversion to sunlight (some of them, at least), and the raging bloodlust. Yeah, it's not much different at all. Gerald turned to me, visibly stunned, now confronting the sight of a dead woman hanging upside down from a chandelier. Her throat slashed. Like the other body pieces, she writhed, unable to form words, a shell of a corpse waiting for a soul. Her eyes showed nothing at all.

I noticed a slight glow inward from her right side, that same creepy symbol. No coincidence there; it was symbolic to whoever brought these back. To what end? That's what I kept asking myself. The Killer hinted at an army or something similar—could that have been some sadistic truth? With the dead marauding the streets as we hid in a cabin with two more, what would we do with these? We couldn't just cut them down; the head was proof the limbs would stay alive. Nathan looked shell-shocked, a trauma that would undoubtedly worsen. Did he even understand the connections?

I didn't have time or patience for sympathy. There was too much at stake. Michael put an arm over Nathan's shoulder, casually turning the stunned young man to head back out for some fresh air. Gerald didn't move. I was busy trying to get a closer look at the lines on the lady's back.

It was incomplete, half a map or a crude attempt at concealing a secret location. The lines warped and snaked. As I moved closer, avoiding the flailing hands, I noticed a familiar pattern, at least part of one. Then, even weirder, several small crosses appeared, looking similar to Templar crosses but too small to make out. I was distracted by raised voices outside while trying to find some rhyme or reason. Nathan was hysterical and understandable but not helpful right now.

"It's the village," I blurt out, finally realising the shape. I caught Gerald's attention.

"Sorry, what?" Gerald says, startled.

"I can see lines on her back and weird crosses. It's the village. Well, part of it and the surrounding area, leading to other parts of the country," I explain, recalling the A-Z I used to give Michael directions on our way to Willowbrook. God, I wished I could turn back time, take the first slip road off the motorway, turn around, and never take this case. That was going through my head, but I would never say it aloud.

"Crosses like the one in the photo, with the goat's head?" Gerald asks, eyebrows raised inquisitively.

"Could be. Hard to tell, really," I reply, looking again. The map outline was correct, yet I couldn't see more. As I drifted in thought, I heard a thump against the wall. It was the father's corpse, flopping around. Then it hit me: what if he had another part of the map? An undead tied up was one thing, but he was all over the place, and I certainly didn't want to get too close with its flailing neck cartilage.

"Do you think Nathan's dad has the same?" Gerald was surprisingly on the ball, considering the nightmare he was in the middle of.

"Possibly, but the way the body moves, we don't want to get caught in its clutches. God knows how strong an undead could be or if it can spread a disease to make others like it," I say, thinking like a normal person for a moment, forgetting I wasn't. While having that little epiphany. What if they could turn the normal living into the dead? Like a vampire bite, its toxin is injected into the bloodstream, all but killing the victim to resurrect as another bloodsucker. Or me turning others into werewolves with a bite. Christ, this supernatural world is crazy.

"Yeah, but aren't you some sort of super beast or something?" Gerald remarked, simplifying it quite a bit.

"Not exactly, but yeah, something along those lines," I reply, noticing more rope by the sofa.

"So, what do we do next? We can't leave them like this," Gerald wondered aloud, echoing my thoughts.

"Grab the rope and help me secure him," I instructed.

"Okay," Gerald responded, weaving past Nathan's mother to grab the rope. He threw one end to me. There was a cushioned armchair near the window line in the left corner. Using the rope, we could wrap around to secure the arms enough for me to get a look at his back. Then, we guided the walking corpse backwards to the seat, where we hoped to tie him up, sparing Nathan any further emotional stress. It was all going to plan when we crossed paths on the wrap-around.

The corpse flailed an arm wildly at the wrong time, catching Gerald off guard. Gerald dodged and flipped the rope upwards, attempting to lasso the arm back down. But the corpse suddenly gripped Gerald's hand. Now, I'm used to weird stuff happening to me, all the conversations about my eyes changing different colours. To see it was something different altogether. Gerald froze, not out of fear or anything like that. His body went rigid, and his bloody eyes rolled backward in his head before turning a horrible, spooky grey. Gerald's jaw yanked open before letting loose with a high-pitched scream that had my hackles firing. Reality hit: Gerald had somehow been yanked into a fugue state, and there was nothing I could do. Gerald was on his own...

'GERALD,'

The bloody corpse snatched at my hand just as I thought I had the rope clear to yank down again. I felt a strange static shock, strong, a sudden jolt that had my body spasming. I couldn't stop from twitching and convulsing. Then it all went dark. It had happened again, only this time I wasn't dreaming. I'm sitting in the armchair, hiding in the shadows, waiting. The cabin is dark; only slithers of the night sky through the dirty window help give a view of the front door. I'm incredibly calm until I hear a car pulling up, wheels grinding through gravel before stopping.

My hands, I mean the Killer's long, bony hands, rap impatiently against the arms of the chair. I can feel my heart speeding up, shit... the Killer. I can't get used to seeing through the scary fucker's eyes. Grace's murder was hard; at least, I was dreaming. This felt every bit as though it were me. I was living with all the emotions, apprehension, and then impatience. Nathan's parents were excited and even happy. They laughed, making their way from their car; it sounded a longer walk than ours; they must've parked to the side or around the back.

My left hand drops to my side; I feel the dirty, bloodstained material of the cloak, its thick and coarse between my skeletal fingers. A little flick and the cloak is clear of a glinting metal 'butt-end'. A knife, possibly a sword. It feels weighty against my long, muscular, yet lean legs. It's a sword; I look down to see the grip, but it's hard to tell if it's wrapped in leather or flesh. One detail I notice is that even in such a dark, haunting environment, my vision is enhanced, everything is clearer, I can home in on minute details with ease, and everything is a lighter black with shades of red. My heart is calm. The Killer feels calculated, and his beats jump slightly upon hearing their footsteps draw closer. Then, there was a loud creak of tired old wood; they stepped onto the porch; I now felt excitement—a small adrenaline rush.

'We', slid forward in the chair, yep I say 'we' It's easier to explain just how goddam strange this experience is. Simpler, I guess, although, let's get this clear, in no way, shape or bloody form was I in control of anything. It was the complete sensory, unwilling passenger experience, and I couldn't wait for it to be over, as I knew what was coming next. Keys clunk heavily, unsteadily in the lock. They'd been drinking. Fuck, I could smell it. How is that possible? I'm on the other side of the door, and I can smell it, even a hint of asparagus and tomato soup. Holy hell, this was a new level of weirdness, and that's saying something. Then I wondered if this was how it feels for Detective Reynolds. Whatever that man is, I'm glad he's on our side; seeing him change like he did was scary but impressive. He must have super senses, too, like what I'm experiencing.

Oh god, my mind wanders; what if someone farts? I know, timing, right? I was about to experience the merciless massacre of Nathan's parents, and that's where my head went. Anyway, the lock finally turns, and with a chilling creak, the door yawns open. We don't move, not yet. The parents stumble over the threshold, and the loud creaking of the floor makes my teeth itch. The Killer's heart was pumping now; he couldn't wait to get going.

Nathan's mother clumsily thrashes for the light switch to her right, connecting her third attempt... Nothing. They exchange confused looks; the father reaches and taps a nearby wall light, but nothing.

"I'll ch... check the fuse box." He says, slurring his words. The father could barely walk straight, crashing into the back of the sofa and the table.

"That won't do you any good." We say gruffly, with a bone-jarring gravel to the tone.

"wh... who said that?" the mother says, her voice high-pitched and shaky. Slightly more coherent.

We reach inside the right pocket of the cloak, retrieving a lighter. A snappy flip, then a click sparks a flame. We hover it intimidatingly below our face. I can smell the light fluid strongly. Nathan's parents look on, shocked, mouths wide open. Even with the low light, I could see the colour draining from their faces. Neither looked capable of moving. Easy pickings and the Killer was thriving because he had them right where he wanted them. Even if they ran, the Killer oozed confidence. It was a most dangerous game, and the Killer revelled in it.

"wh... which one are you?" The father finally croaks up.

"The only one that matters, the only one willing to embrace what you all run from. To think all you had to do was let it in. The darkness can fulfil everything you wish, yet you squandered the opportunity and power. Even worse, you anger those who gave you this gift."

"It's not a gift. It's a bloody curse that tormented our bloodlines for centuries. And you think it's something to be happy about." The father became aggressive wearily; I could sense the tiredness in his voice. Not from a night out. No, this was a burden. There's more to Nathan's parents; that much is clear. They know more than I was told in the tapes so far or by my mother. Now they're dead. Well, not exactly now, you know what I mean.

"Oh, but it is; the world is fucked and needs a do-over. All these years, all the wars, death, hate and financial crisis. Now, it's time for someone to shake things up." I didn't like the sound of what the Killer was selling, nor were the parents. Their hands wouldn't stop shaking. They knew their fates were sealed. This was one last drunken stand. I hated every moment. Poor Nathan, how do I tell him what happened? I Can't, surely?

"Humanity makes mistakes, sure. It doesn't need evil incarnate running the show."

"O, it's more than running. It will be hell on earth; I intend on opening all the gates, unleashing a demonic army and seeing how quickly countries want to go to war." The Killer said, unleashing a blood-stirring laugh while ever so slowly we're edging closer to falling off the chair. Now that would be embarrassing for the creepy fucker.

"you can't do that besides if you know anything about the occult and the devil. Demons need vessels. They can't drift aimlessly; they will burn out and die. No, returning to hell, they will be gone." Well, that's new, a little tit-bit for the group. Sick, but it's something we didn't know.

"That's where you one-dimensional cowards have been failing. You're afraid of destiny and can't see the bigger picture. Did you not know that everybody dropped by the darkness becomes a ready-made vessel in waiting? And believe me, I've been so fucking busy. It's great. Sometimes, all it takes is a wave of a hand to let it happen. You know, I picture it, and things happen. The best part is that the party has begun, and the undead are swarming the streets as we speak."

"Wait. What? You don't know what you've done. You're nothing but a puppet. Don't you understand the curse? It's because our ancestors rebelled and grassed up the locations of the Templars, who were executed without mercy. Suppose the rest of the knights are set free. There'll be no putting the genie back in the bottle, and you will be dispatched as soon as you've served your purpose." Nathan's father was so scared, reaching to grab his wife's hand and pulling her closer. They knew it would be soon but attempted a last go at reasoning in the thin hope of breaking through to the Killer. It wasn't happening; I could feel the Killer ready to move.

"I will be a god beside them. I've been told so. All the power and freedom to do what I want. No longer seen as a weakling, someone only useful for information when they're desperate. Speaking of which, it's time to cough up." For a moment, I was stunned by the need for the information part. Why did that feel familiar? Our hand dropped to the sword, slowly swirling the grip for extra menace.

"No. You can't, we won't. Anyway, did you think there wouldn't be a backup plan? We know there's one of us strong enough to break the curse, break what they're meant to become and will use it to stop your stupid, reckless and suicidal plan." Nathan's mother finally spoke up, leaving me more confused than I was. This vision, or whatever, had to have happened for a reason. No accident, but who could she mean?

"Makes no difference; I believe I have them on a string; in fact, I reckon so far I've led them perfectly on a nightmare trail; soon, they'll be too scared and traumatised to do anything. I can't wait to see his face when I tell him how many pawns have been moved through his life to get to this point. People willing to get their hands dirty for the promise of power. The trouble is, I share the limelight with nobody and have to do a little spring cleaning; call it a tale of two halves. Now give over the piece and tell me where the box is."

"Never." Nathan's father snaps back.

"Persuasion it is."

We dug down our left foot, ground into the floor, and spun on tiptoes; in what felt like a blur, we breezed over the sofa in a single stride, whooshed past the parents, drawing the sword and was back near the chair within seconds. We faced the corner as the room fell silent. Then, 'thud', a loud crash on the floor. We'd moved too quickly for me to see who it was. The Killer was ecstatic with himself, and then came the loud, guttural scream of pain and anguish... from Nathan's father.

We spun to face an emphatically crying father, who'd dropped to his knees and was now holding his wife's motionless body in his arms, blood spewing waterfall-like. There was no putting a band-aid on that.

"Sooo, about that puzzle piece and the box. Are your memories coming back to you? Feel like sharing now?" The Killer goaded. His laugh seemed to grow more menacing and evil if that's possible. I can't truly describe how it was deeper, bellowing with a confident snarl. I could smell the intoxicating coppery aroma of blood—lots of it flooding the floor.

"Why... Why... Why, there was no... bloody... need." The father screamed at the top of his lungs, face gone a brighter red, flooded with tears. The Killer just laughed.

"Don't pretend you weren't expecting this. Now, how the rest plays out... Well, that's up to you. We have all night, we're in the middle of nowhere, and there's a million ways to make you scream in agony that I'm happy to explore. So, what's it to be? Easy, quick. Or a stubborn bastard, tortured until the end?" I needed to be sick. I was desperate. I couldn't take being a passenger anymore. It was downright inhumane. What's worse, it's another human being who succumbed to evil and allowed the darkness to take over. Everyone has a bit in them, some more than most. That doesn't mean you have to let it win.

"Here, take it. Useless without the rest, anyway. As for the box, I don't know; I didn't get entrusted with those details. Now, please, let me be. Let me bury my wife, and you'll never see me again." The father ripped a chain from his neck, tossing it to us before pleading through sobs for his life. I wish I could stop this; the whole no-control part of this adventure was awful, gut-wrenching, even.

"Aww, look who's pitiful and weak now, begging. Is that how you think this works? I appreciate the co-operation. I'm afraid it's too little too late. Besides, I may have been born at night, but I wasn't born last night. If I let you go, all you'll do is finally let it in and come after me. I can't be having that now, can I? Don't worry; when it passes on, your son will get the same treatment."

"No, you won't. You'll never find him; we made sure of that." The father allowed himself a brief chuckle, a slender one up on the Killer. I was impressed and confused because Nathan was their son.

"What little old Nathan, that's easy. I hardly call that hiding. Fuck, were you ever good at games in school? That's bloody awful." The Killer said, oozing smugness. I so wanted Nathan's father to turn the tables, let the darkness in and put up a bloody fight.

"You know the saying, don't put all your eggs in one basket? We didn't. Nathan is adopted; we desperately wanted a child and had one, but we knew the dangers. So we had our child safely adopted with a plan, set up for life and instructions for when the time comes. Nathan? Well, we had friends who'd just had a baby. Then, one night, somebody broke into their home and murdered the parents while they slept—leaving the baby fast asleep. This happened just as we gave our baby over, so it was sad but perfect timing. We adopted Nathan, and he's none the wiser. So go ahead, do your fucking worst." Nathan's father laughs again, this time a full-on 'I don't give a shit,' laugh. The Killer became enraged, a quick shift of weight and boom, a blur up to and in, impaling the father's heart on the sword. He paused, drifting his head down to the father,

"Looks like I have the last laugh. I can't wait to see the look on their faces. Especially when you become an 'undead'. It looks like death becomes you, old man. Sweat dreams." The Killer slowly withdrew his sword, basking in his murderous mayhem. Until we heard a car, damn super hearing too, still a mile away; it was coming quickly.

We grabbed some old rope off the table and quickly stripped the mother before stringing her up by her ankles to the chandelier. Then we grabbed the father by his hair, dragging him to the window. In no time, we heard voices. It was us, as in Nathan and me, and the detectives. The Killer quickly smooshed the father's face against the wall. And then... I feel a surge of electricity... Before nothing... It's darkness.

Eye Opening

40

'Détective Reynolds,'

"Hey, wake the hell up. Come on, snap out of it." The eyes were bad enough between the 'undead' groaning. Nathan's understandable hysterics and Michael being about as useful as a paper bag in a rainstorm, I was edgy. Gerald Ackerman began writhing as if at the onset of a seizure.

Whether the vision or fugue state could instigate that, I dreaded to think. He had me worried, though. My eyes never went like his, and I have seen no other instances like it. Gerald's face contorted, jaw twisted, or appeared to, his eyes remained. The guy looked in a hell of a lot of pain.

Gerald had already mentioned seeing murders through the killer's eyes; my bets were the poor sod was enduring the torture of his best friend's parents. I've had my share of similar; I tell you, it's no fun. I'm still reeling emotionally from all the bloodshed in Scotland, and that had to happen, experiencing it while helpless as if it's you committing the atrocities. That's going to need a shit tonne of therapy.

I'll tell you a little secret: I have my first session booked for when we return to London. Michael doesn't know, nor does Locke, Only Ellena. It was her that twisted my arm. I just don't know how to explain or talk about the trauma I've gone through, considering I can't tell them what I am or what we face. How the hell do I juggle that? For Gerald, though, it could be a little easier, although I don't know everything about him all too well.

I've sensed that he's a good man, but that demonic element is really getting to him. We don't need another loose cannon. Bad enough, I had to carry a pensioner around. (sorry, Michael). Jokes aside, this is one big cluster fuck of mess I'm struggling to wrap my head around. Thank god, there are no nematons or telluric currents to worry about. I hope.

"What the hell is going on, matey?" Michael breezes in, the scent of his Armani aftershave softening the bloody stench, only slightly but enough to quell my tastebuds that begun watering. Yeah, I forgot to mention I haven't kicked that craving yet. The longing for the taste was made worse by the vampires. I'm no savage or anything; it's just a bizarre apex predator issue, especially on a full moon, which is two days and sixteen hours. If my math is right, it's quite possible it's not, but you get the Jist. I hope we have Ellena back by then, but I don't want to fight to snatch her in the heat of the moment. Michael still needs to be chained up, so god knows how that will work.

"Honestly, I don't know."

"Well, fuck me sideways. The great Detective Reynolds doesn't know something. Only messing, but he looks like he's being given some hedonistic bondage shit."

"Piss off, Mickey boy, he doesn't have your proclivities or alternate personality."

"Hey, you leave Sharon out of this. That's only on the weekends. Anyway, seriously, what the hell?"

I went to speak, mouth poised and open, while looking at Michael, who'd been flitting his attention between Nathan, who was still outside, and us. When the writhing suddenly stopped. Gerald was laid flat on the floor; I had to when he fugues out; otherwise, he would have collapsed. Blood pooled around us and drifted tantalisingly close to Gerald's arm. Even had my werewolf eyes blazing brighter. Everything was still... Nathan hung in the doorway oozing pain and anger but suddenly looked concerned for Gerald. All I could hear were our heartbeats thumping almost in unison, except for Gerald. It was racing. Full on v12 engine, pedal to the metal, going for it.

I didn't say it. I wanted to. Only knew it would amplify the worry, especially for Nathan. I feared Gerald was in trouble—some existential fugue crisis. Suppose there's such a thing. What does it matter? Not much of anything has a label these days. Except me. Lycanthrope. I mean, who sits around thinking of these things? What would they name the killer? The grim reapers twisted cousin?

We all waited, expecting a sudden shock. Geral didn't disappoint. He bolted upright, eyes pinged back to normal. "Hell, the gates." Gerald gasps, panting wildly, his head thrashing left to right, looking disoriented. I can imagine why, suddenly yanked back from seeing what would've been blood-riddled trauma. His heart continued rapidly, nearing dangerous levels. Gerald kept attempting speech, strands of saliva jetting free at each try.

"You okay there, matey? You had us a little worried."

"N... no, the gates. The killer wants to open the gates of hell. Demons will possess the dead." Gerald was frantic. Sweat dripped from his brow. I listened closely, especially when his eyes darted to Nathan, and he paused. It appeared Gerald had more to say. Then again, he'd just watched how Nathan parent's murders went down and thought better of it.

Somehow, I didn't think so. The little wince and a brisk judder by his Adam's apple, there was something else and bad. Gerald caught me staring; he dropped his head meekly to avoid eye contact. I had to know.

"Did they suffer?" Nathan pipes up, surprised with his question. "That's what happened, right? What you were doing? You saw something. Like how you saw Grace killed. I mean, I get it wasn't nice; just look at them. But did he toy with them?" Nathan continues, looking solemnly toward his mother and father, moving in their 'undead' way. Tears streamed down his cheeks.

Gerald didn't answer straight away, eyes searching the cabin for an escape he would never take before finally. "It didn't seem so. He asked a few questions before anything, and then... Well, you can see." Gerald's voice was low and soft, hating what he was doing to his friend. A curse of this world, I'm afraid.

"Then why? ... Why the hell did they have to fucking die?" Nathan gushes with pain, his face red, eyes bulging fit to pop out of their sockets while tears rained down. That pain was rapidly turning to anger. I know what comes next. 'Hate' I've been there, and watching Nathan now, I feel for the guy. Gerald has his battle scars, too. The VHS tapes tell part of the tale.

"In our line of work, matey, it's not nice at all, but bloody often, these sick fuckers have no reason. At least none that makes sense to us sane people. Mostly, it's for the thrill or wrong place and wrong time." Michael says, shuffling calmly to Nathan, placing a reassuring hand on Nathan's shoulder.

I looked at Gerald while Michael spoke; he was uncomfortable. None of this was made easy by the 'undead' groaning and rocking in the background. Noticing Nathan's headless father, I still needed to check his back. My hunch was that he had another section of a U.V. map. I couldn't fathom why, though. What was the purpose?

Gerald shook his muttering to himself, something like, 'For fuck's sake, why me? Why us? All it will cause is pain'. Then he raked his fingers through his hair, the whites of his knuckles beamed as he gripped clumps, riding through the stress.

"It's Okay. Breathe. I will listen when you're ready," I say, facing Gerald down, my voice low enough to evade Nathan. Michael looked, though.

"I was him. Bloody him. I felt it all, but I couldn't move. Yet, everything was ramped up; I could hear our car coming from a mile away; yeah, that's right, he heard us well in advance. I could smell everything down to detecting the metallic essence of blood and my eyesight, well, it was mixed shades of red and black but I could zoom in, everything was high definition. While that all felt good, I didn't like feeling helpless enough to stop it. All he wanted was some box and the puzzle piece." Gerald says, his voice crackling through waves of emotions. I could smell the salty texture of his brewing tears.

"Was there anything else? Even if it's small, it could be a detail that helps us." I say, carefully prising while cautious that the night was slipping away from us.

"He has two pieces of the coin puzzle. Doesn't have my father's yet and I don't know where it could be. So that leaves one more. He knows you're on his case; he is letting us follow. We need to be careful of a trap. If the gates get opened, he boasted that he'd already killed quite many people. – Vessels, he called them.." Gerald paused, his eyes darting to the left. I could almost hear the cogs turning. He was grasping at a theory, a detail stuck with him. I get them a lot; call them my 'dots,'—the connections in a case that need to sync up. If any are out of line, it can really mess with your head.

Believe me, inside my head, that's not a pretty place to be. What Gerald is enduring. Being lured into the darkness. Haunted by whispers and having to sit within the killer. That's got to be tough right now. We needed everyone switched on, and Gerald had to open up sooner rather than later. Especially with the thought he was wrestling with.

"Gerald, just whisper, I'll hear," I say, hoping he'd feel at ease.

He looks at Nathan again. "The father boasted that the next in his bloodline was hidden away. Nathan was adopted after his real parents were murdered. Their baby sent away to be safe, taking Nathan as their own." As Nathan breezed past his father's juddering, yawning head, Gerald paused. Nathan hovered his hands on either side of his cheeks. Nathan continued crying, his face churning with pain. That bombshell didn't need to drop right now.

The problem we had, there were no other elements we couldn't control. Would the killer take those words seriously and go hunting for the true bloodline heir? Or simply look to catch Nathan when he's distracted. Who may or may not begin experiencing the troubles Gerald is...

I left them alone. Nathan's father was pushing against the ropes, almost leaning forward, edging to the left of the chair along the window line. My werewolf eyes blazed. A flick of my claws, and I plucked the edge of his shirt loose and up. He had lines, too. A section connected to what I saw on the mother. More small crosses, a tree, and then three quarters up his back, a small square with a badly drawn face.

Gripping the back of the chair, I shoved it across the wooden floor, grating loud—enough to get all eyes on me. The chair was near the writhing mother. Arms were already bound. One hand on the piece by her midriff, the other I ripped a claw through what was tied to the light. Her body dropped quickly. Flipping her on her feet, still writhing against my grip, I had the backs side by side.

"Michael, get your book out and come here," I say, beckoning him to hurry.

"What?"

"Use your other eyes and just bloody draw. These undead are strong." If anything, I'd undersold it a bit. We didn't want to get tangled up with them. They may be empty shells, but what brought them back has given them an upgrade, supposed for the impending opening of gates.

"What the hell? Do you think the killer was looking for this? After all, it's bloody weird, ain't it?"

"Honestly, I'm not even sure he knows it exists. Can only be seen under U. V anyway."

"Next question, what's it about?"

"A map, I guess. Willowbrook and the surrounding villages, even further afield." Michael was busy sketching quickly, too. When he just stops. His pen stayed pressed on the paper, causing a small bubble of ink. His expression was one of surprise.

"You ain't going to believe this," Michael says, which was surprising coming from him. He drags the pen slowly, one line, then the next. Several lines later, I saw what had him startled. They formed a symbol. That star of 'Baphomet', at least the pattern without the goat's head. Lo-and-behold, in the centre, was that tree. They had to be gates with ley lines, but the tree was a mystery. And that square... I had a horrible gut feeling; that's where we needed to go next. Wherever 'there' might be. Once Michael had finished his masterpiece, we secured the mother in another chair. It was the only emotionally painless thing we could do until we discovered a way to enable them to find peace—a way to disconnect from the power that feeds the symbols on their backs.

Nathan, looking detached from reality, was busy wrapping them in quilts, tucking them in as if they'd be resting. The rabid, 'undead' groans gnawing at the air made him flinch now and then, but he still found it in him to stroke his mother's cheeks. He'd placed his father's head securely under an arm. A longing, sorrowful look drenched the air in pain. My heightened senses were reacting to it, and Michael's, too.

I sidestep the morbid show, treading near the fireplace; I hear a creek—my foot wobbles. I looked down to see one wooden floor strip different from the rest. Lighter and less weathered. My claws were still out, so I jammed one into the thin crevice. There's a slight draft ruffling the hair on my wrist.

Eventually, the board comes free, releasing a musky dampness and a shower of dust. A pit of black revealed nothing, so I reached inside. About a foot deep, I brush a rough canvas bundle. I quickly retrieve it, unfurling the dirty green wrap across the floor. It was my turn to be surprised. An ancient dagger. Its blade was twenty centimetres darker than the typical silver. It had a strange smell to it, too, blood. Not old from being used, but infused with probably Damascus steel. There're symbols or sigils along the blade's edge. Some similar to what we saw at the morgue.

Its handle was a mix of ivory and brown deer antler wrapped in old-looking leather. My hand drifts close; I get a bizarre prickling sensation like static. My finger skims the blade; it glows blood red through the edging. And each symbol is illuminated. Michael and I exchanged looks. Surprise mixed with a little shock. It didn't hurt me, instead more of a belonging or familiarity.

"Bloody hell, Georgie. Oh, look, there's a note," Michaels says, pointing to a small pocket beneath the blade. I slip the leathery parchment free. It reads...

'What you fear is always near. Light leads the way to keep the demons at bay. -The Demon Blade.'

No wonder it glowed; it was reacting to me. To my blood. I'm no genius, but I assumed that Nathan's parents had this in case the worst happened and what the killer was hellbent on doing. Only, I couldn't wield it. Trust is an issue for me, and if this were to be used for the battle ahead, I'd want Michael to weald it. His supernatural speed and strength would work well. The outside bet was Gerald. We know little about him but seem focussed on the task at hand. Michael and I have our shifter abilities to help us. At least the mundanes would be armed. Not that I wanted it to come to that point. Because that would mean we're royally fucked.

"Michael, take it, for now, it's reactive to me." Michael nodded; he'd read what I had. Now we pray. Cling to hope we won't need it. First, find a map to plot what Michael had drawn. How it looked, if all the gates opened at once, releasing all that evil, what's stopping those ley lines ripping a demonic pathway through the country, tearing apart the earth's crust? There'd be so much death, more than just what demons possess. For reasons I couldn't understand, the tree at the heart of the symbol occupied my mind. How did these evil 'dots' connect?

Road Map to Hell

41

'Gerald,'

It looked like a war zone. Except the dead were the ones rampaging through the streets. We were driving painstakingly slow, zig-zagging hundreds of the undead staggering across the middle of the road and any sidewalk. We passed at least two cemeteries where my stomach churned, watching decomposed bodies punching out the ground. Some had flesh peeling from their bones, oozing black fluid. While others were a little fresher. None of it will leave me for a while.

I was in awe and terrified by how it had happened. Were those creeps in suits that powerful? In that vision, through the killer's eyes, he taunted Nathan's father about the gates of hell. George described those guys as demonic knights; could they tap into the underworld? Give the dead a little wake-up call. How else is it possible? The more I thought, the more my brain hurt. None of this should be possible, let alone be my reality. Did my father know how bad things could get? Nathan's father mentioned a Plan B. I hoped we would find it at this place marked by a little square on their flesh.

It makes me wish there was a 'do-over' button, rewind to before the accidents, and warn Charlotte and her father to avoid certain things. Maybe ask Father more questions and take an interest. Perhaps I'd be more prepared and, in exchange, warn him about what's coming. I know that's all pie in the sky, and I must start facing what's happening to me. My bloodline is cursed; if I let the darkness in, I'd be the same as the killer. Maybe even do exactly what he is. Was this what I had to come? The reason I keep seeing through his eyes. Or were we connected in some other way?

We neared the end of Wickham Street and exited the village of Billing, which, much like ours, Maplewood, Melwood and Filton were drenched in darkness. Not a light in sight. I'd be bold enough to say the power had been cut off on purpose, leaving these villages isolated. This game was getting old. Those fuckers knew what they were doing. Creating distractions and vulnerability, letting the undead terrorise normal life.

This leaves me with the question: Can the undead turn humans? I get they can kill, but what if it's a scratch or a bite? Would that do? I still don't know how that happened when Nathan's father grabbed onto my wrist. It had to be the bloodlines; we're connected like in that photograph. All of them together. It must've been as we swung into another bend; I bumped against the armrest, and a thought came to me. A sickly, stomach-churning thought that I didn't know what to do with.

I'm back at the bar, the two polaroids slide out, and I see that symbol, the moment I'd absentmindedly carved into a coaster moments earlier. The devil star in a circle. Except this was blood on the sidewalk next to my father's body. It couldn't be, not when we'd asked for help. It's not like Nathan was in the right state or frame of mind for me to bother him on this. Besides, it made no sense anyway. Not that it stopped the tired cogs in my brain from turning.

Our wheels rumbled over another cattle grid into an even darker country lane. We continued slowly, not thinking there'd be any traffic, and I heard Gerald mention we could end up mowing down some of the dead if they'd made it this far. I could see the logic.

Nathan was slumped as far into the corner of his seat as possible. His expression was pale and vacant. Not the usual happy-go-lucky friend I was used to. Death does that. I would know. Detective Reynolds knew that, too. He didn't speak but empathised and helped while not pushing Nathan or me. I reckon he's been through some version of hell himself. Damn, that word, 'Hell', to think that's what we were trying to stop, the real thing. The detectives had mapped out that weird yet spooky diagram that was printed on Nathan's parents' backs. Fuck, I haven't even thought about how I'm going to handle that. Do I plead ignorance? What good was the truth right now, anyway?

Headlights beamed against a black-and-white sign as we swept around another bend, with the sore growing on my elbow feeling like the hundredth one we'd taken. 'Kingsley' was three miles out. Behind that sign, the view would otherwise look picturesque, with trees as far as the eyes could see and hilltops kissing a slightly lighter purple of the sky. Peaceful, that's how it looked, moments that have been few. Reminded me of the girls, praying to god they were safe.

Mother didn't tell me where they were headed; safer that way. It's not knowing if they're okay that worries me. I feel they are, though; I can't say why; it's just a flutter in my stomach when I think of them accompanied by that thought. Hoping they were obliviously sleeping while the world went to shit. This part of it, anyway. Mother would undoubtedly have heard the news; she has 'Radio Two' on twenty-four seven. No sooner had I been comforted by that image. Another came flying in like an express train, the father's head.

Before and after shots. The pleading and a final chuckle of defiance. Then, the yawning, chomping, mindless view rocking in a pool of blood on the table.

I'm looking at Nathan, worried as you'd expect. His world had been smooth sailing as far as he knew. He had a wealthy family, and he got to run around Willowbrook or wherever playing private investigator. Everything he knew had imploded, but that was without the truth. The look on his face now was a man in need of alcohol; boy, could I join him? All of this feels like a never-ending nightmare we can't wake from. We're rolling into 'Kingsley' I'm wondering what's waiting. Nathan is twitching and seems edgy and aggravated. Perhaps his father was lying, hoping to throw the killer off balance. Soon, his father's bloodline will sink its claws in, and all of this dark stuff going on with me will take root. It seems odd he hasn't asked, 'When does this happen to me?'. Does he know something I don't?

I'm looking out the windshield into the darkness, like the black growing within. I see Detective Reynolds' hand change out of the corner of my eye. Dark fur grew thick and bushy; his hand doubled, maybe tripled in size, with his flesh becoming shades of brown. Seeing all this in a surreal, slow motion was scary and remarkable. Then came the claws. Menacingly long, thick, stretching to thin with sharp tips. They were as black as the night around us and just as daunting. I wouldn't want to be on the wrong end of them. Why? That's what I asked myself. The little I knew of this world, I mean their world. It had to mean something, voluntarily changing like that. It feels weird, with the inclination to respect their job as detectives, but easier when it's less formal. So, I'll call it that way. After all, nothing about this felt 'Law' related. Not no more.

Michael did the same; his hair was lighter, longer, and thinner. No, so werewolf, but more akin to a feral animal. A fox. I'd say. Maybe it's more obvious to obvious, but these moments of the calm before the storm. I was learning as much as I could. Anything to take my mind off what's bothering me the most. Secrets. I don't like them; I was never good at keeping them, and in the last months, I've made it my job, much like Nathan, to uncover the reality behind them.

Look where it got us. George and Michael, though, were bothered right now. I was busy craning my neck and looking for the obvious when something weird happened to me. That bar is uniquely high for me, but this... I was propelled back through the eyes of the killer. Not literally, but those heightened feelings and senses. I could hear heartbeats. That might sound like my stress was getting to me, and it was my hearing. It wasn't. I could hear the double pacing of our supernatural friends in the front. Nathan's was steady, low, almost a sleeping rhythm; he'd withdrawn far into himself and his dark thoughts. Just like I experienced in that vision, George rolled his window down; I watched his head tilt, inhaling to catch a scent. I hate to be rude, but I'd only seen that with a dog. Thank god these were no dogs. His ears twitched, too. My nose began going, too; I picked up on it all. Overwhelming in all its stinking glory. The toxic diesel spewed from our car, a dampness showing rain coming.

That shudder came again; I drifted back in my seat as I felt it. Death. That's what it was. The long, bony hand of death stroking my grave. Vibrant and deadly, it came in ferocious waves carried on the bitter breeze. Death blended with sulphur was travelling toward us, which had George alert. Michael was slower to it, I noticed. Again, why? I asked myself, why was I experiencing this? I shook off the chill in time for another wave. Chills, that is. This was different; I knew what came next. Seems the pre-cursor to our dark standoff.

A finger-like brush of my cheek, then with the usual cold, melancholy, 'Are you ready, Gerald, ready to finally give in? Embrace it because what's coming? You'll need me. Now...Let...me...in. Let the darkness in and own your bloodline and its burden. No crosses need bearing. A curse doesn't need to mean a curse.'

"I can't; I'm not evil. I've seen evil, and that's not me if I let the darkness in. I become the one killing and looking to turn this world on its head." I whisper but caught George's eyes staring at me in the rearview. Not once have I said yes or embraced it. I came close in the basement, but I didn't. So why am I experiencing what I am? Why did the darkness help me at the farm and the basement, teasing me with all the heightened nonsense?

There's no manual for it, and my father ran from it. Nathan's parents, too. The more I dwelled on that puzzle and startling reality, with that melancholic calling hitching a ride with that ever-present terror bobbing on the tiny boat through my sanity. The river had become a tumultuous sea rife with monsters. All waiting to devour the boat, its passengers become captive to them, beasts.

A world of eat or be eaten. Kill or be killed. To compound my impossible choice in this 'most dangerous game', the boat had lost its steering rudder long ago. Broke loose when I watched Nathan's mother have her jugular cut through and his father, a sword clean through his heart. I guess what I'm saying is that at least two of the four bloodlines have run or attempted to hide from this, and they've ended up dead. Would doing the opposite have the same outcome? That's not me deciding to give in, more 'devil's advocate' playing blackjack with a losing hand, deciding whether to stick or twist.

I'm sure this all seems like the rambling of a man who's finally lost his mind, having skirted close for a while. Perhaps that's why the call came at this moment, when morale was low, heading into the unknown, surrounded by the 'undead' staggering through the streets, dripping their decomposing flesh all over the place.

'Why such one-dimensional thinking? If a mundane is inherently evil, it is in their nature that when the opportunity is within their grasp, they will become evil. If a mundane is inherently good, trod a righteous path all of their life, even when opportunities have presented themselves so willingly and that mundane still walks that righteous path. It will be their nature to be good.'

"So, what are you saying?" I say. It was probably my tired brain. I thought I understood the basics and the point, but then I kept looking for hidden meanings. When is evil ever truthful? I asked myself? Nathan continued twitching. I still heard his ultra-calm heart while Michael and George sounded as though readying for that deathly sulphur stench.

'If a mundane is naturally good, like yourself. Look at this crusade for the truth you've been on. I've watched it all; I hear your thoughts, and I know your doubts. I also tantalisingly know your potential. A mundane in pursuit of good. So, why would you think evil would be your path?'

Was I being reeled in? While something approached that I sensed was nothing good, the darkness whispered a sales pitch that made me think. "Are you implying that just because I embrace the darkness, that sounds very much hauntingly evil? I mean, the clue in the word 'darkness' speaks volumes. It doesn't mean I will become some crazed killer like the other guy. I mean, what the hell is he?"

'Finally, the penny drops. I knew mundanes were sometimes slow, but with you, I had hope. As for him, he has become one of the fallen knights; there are many other names or titles, but those like him have fallen from the cause, much like the two that hold your detective friend's girl. They were The Knights Templar at one point, until they became Baphomet chosen or the Eternal vigil because at anyone time there's two Knights watching over, creating chaos and evil in the world.-' I butted in as the last sentence hit me hard.

"What? What do you mean, watching over and creating chaos?" I say, forming a picture that these knights have been the spark for many a conflict that blights our world.

'You see, there's always been that hope, that quest to resurrect all the Knights slain centuries ago when their allegiance to Baphomet was leaked to the King of France. Who ordered them eradicated? Including their General Francois, Louis Philip the second. As evil as they come before embracing the devil. One day, the required relics would surface, and one day, a bloodline would give in to the power. Or they will go mad as so many over the years have. Now, there's a hungry killer playing puppet. While thinking he's playing chess. Mostly, in your life, he has. Suppose those Templars are broken out of hell with the demons? There will be an unstoppable army of undead led by some of the fiercest soldiers ever to walk your earth. To answer your question, the Knights need the right environment; they feed off it. You mundanes are easy to manipulate, and by them creating a world ripe with evil, it's like a drug. A highly intoxicating drug that fuels them.' I was stunned into silence. Although I had been whispering, I knew George was listening.

"What would that make me?" I ask. They say curiosity killed the cat. Well, I say better the devil, you know. Corny, right?

'That's one of life's mysteries, I told you; if you let me in, you will experience all the power you can imagine. But... that doesn't mean you have to fall, too. Could well be a true Knights Templar, one to restore faith and order.'

"But in the beginning, you made it seem you wanted me to kill and do bad. What happened?" I ask, thinking back to when the haunting began.

'What's one of those four-legged beasts in the wild? Oh, a LEOPARD. That's right. A leopard has spots. Those spots cannot change—you mundanes and your humanity, those inclinations, mostly to do bad. So, in general terms, you are all leopards, too. I thrived off your anger, pain, and hatred. So, to me, you were just another leopard with power within reach. There is no use in trying to make spots or stripes. Since then, I've watched and listened as you've strived against the pain and adversity. You can be what you want to be. Until then, I would be on guard; something is coming.'

The whispers stopped abruptly, and the chill was gone, but I could still feel that presence this time. I say darkness because it feels that way. If what it alluded to was true, I had hope, and the girls were swaying me. I could never forgive myself if it went wrong and they came to harm. The reality is, I've been a kite dancing in a hurricane, and lighting was stoking the skies with all its terrifying, strobing might.

Those heightened senses had stayed, too; the nearer we got to Kingsley, the death felt. My ears twitched, which was odd. Getting a taste of what the detectives go through. For good reason, though.

'BOOM, BOOM, BOOM,'

My hand tingled; I looked, and I could see real close as the tiny black hairs ruffled to attention, like wind through fields of straw or a forest of trees. Tiny pimples popped across my flesh beneath; My heart was flying, causing my throat to tighten, and Fear was taking over to the tune of a beating drum. That's how loud and what I heard first before each one thinned out. They were wings flapping. Hundreds of them building to a deafening crescendo. Much like the layby, I saw the piercing blue next. It was bloody scary. A horizon was becoming a nightmare. Except for Nathan, who'd stayed oblivious, we all knew what was coming without uttering a word. More importantly, how? Were they following from afar, or did they know much more about this game than we realised?

With everything the darkness preached, I couldn't help but feel disheartened. The lengths to which these evil bastards go to. Manipulating us mundanes, as we're called. Stirring the pot, creating a world ready for them to enjoy. Sure, there's a lot of evil to go around in various forms. What scared me more was letting loose all those Templars and their general. Nowhere would be the same.

George rolls the car to a stop at least two hundred feet from the road sign 'Welcome to Kingsley'. The horde of deathly ravens swooped toward them, their beady eyes glowing brightly before they seamlessly moved, becoming one of those creepy knights. His face rippled in the moonlight, looking more like a walking corpse. Patches of flesh had long since decayed, allowing his skull bone to show through. I could feel the hatred dripping from him. Stepping slowly, the heavy heels of his shiny shoes clapping against the empty road, echoing a sinister tune.

"What are we doing, Georgie?" Michael says, glancing anxiously toward his friend.

"Fucked if I know. How did they even find us?" George says, thinking like I had while checking on us in the rearview.

'We can end this now. Hand him over with the puzzle piece and the box. He joins us and you lot can go on your merry way. The lovely Ellena included.' The creep spoke as though he were sitting with us in the car; his voice sounded that close. I shuddered again, shaking through the chill. Everything about this morbid Freakshow curdles my blood. I had no intention of going anywhere and hoped George was on the same page.

"I trust you can hear me, so hear this. No way in 'hell'." George says. I couldn't resist a chuckle—a poignant choice of words.

"Ooh, nice use of the word Georgie." Michael quips.

"Why, thank you. I thought you'd approve."

'You think you're so clever? This ends one way, with your death, and the same goes for everyone around you." It may have been a trick of the moonlight or the car headlights capturing in front of us: the street sign, the scenic view of endless trees, and the creepy Knight. I could've sworn his eyes changed; pearlescent black became blood red.

"Hey guys, not to rush you or anything? But do you have a plan for dealing with something centuries hellbent on killing us?" I say, noticing George look at Michael as they exchanged smirks, as if sharing some inside joke I wasn't a part of.

"Well, we've had a little experience with old things. Michael experiences it every Saturday night down the YMCA chatting up the elderly."

"Hey, you dick. That was one night I volunteered to help run the bar for a friend." Michael says, laughing. I'm looking at these two, so calm and cracking jokes in the face of all this danger. How do they do it? It must be bloody hard on their families. The Knight widened his stance, braced to charge at us; what he thought he would achieve was anyone's guess. His right foot dug into the gravel, twisted, and he powered forward.

"Georgie... erm Georgie. In case you missed it, there's a scary-looking knight charging at us. Do something." Michael says, eyes raised, waiting for an answer.

George jammed the car into gear, and with the handbrake on, he throttled the life out of the engine. The car was rocking and vibrating; I shuffled backwards in my seat, feeling the rumbles beneath me; loud wheel spinning filled the air. His claws gripped the wheel tightly. "Fuck it," George says, "Let's go through him." Michael frantically grabbed at his seatbelt, checking he was strapped in. Still, Nathan was oblivious. The three litre engine rocked the chassis some more. I toyed with being brave. There's nothing brave about crashing through a windshield if everything goes wrong.

I'm fighting against the tension to the best of my ability. My eyes dart to the front. The Knight is picking up speed, his coat flails wide, his deathly hand breezes to the butt of a sword. My eyes flick to my belt as I struggle, George unleashes the handbrake and hi BMW beast. The chassis twists and turns against the torque. Burnt rubber teases my senses. My eyes dart to the front again. We're flying; the Knight is too.

Finally, the tension releases, and I yank the belt into its lock. I'm looking on in fear and awe that this creepy Knight was taking on a car now doing fifty miles per hour. Bizarrely, the Knight seemed just as fast. Then... everything slowed. Or looked that way. The front of our car connects painfully with the Knight as he draws his sword. A loud banshee shriek rocks the air; thunder claps in the sky. What happened next scared the living daylights out of me? As we plough into the Knight, he crumbles, not into ravens, but more like decayed pieces of his body. Each part phases ghostly through our vehicle.

His horrifying face was full, gritted teeth, blood-red eyes, his sword comes through as the rest of his body was still in pieces. Then I feel it. The darkness rapidly forms a barrier around me; all those gruesome body parts ricochet off me. The sword whooshes past, and the scary part is that the Knight smiles as he blazes through, phasing through the rear of our vehicle. George slams on the brakes, screeching tyres roar in the night, and the chassis sways side to side until we stop. My hands immediately pat over my body, checking for wounds while struggling to rationalise what just happened. There's nothing. The detectives swivel in theirs, looking shocked; I look out the rear; the Knight was now fully formed, sliding his sword away. Everything went silent.

'Blood...'

I could smell blood—and death and sulphur. But the blood was closer, a lot closer.

"Cuh...Cuh." What just happened, Gerald, I hear beside me. I turned slowly, realising where the blood was coming from. Nathan had a puncture wound to his stomach, his white t-shirt swelling with red and then black. I didn't understand. Judging by their faces, the detectives didn't either. There was another smell, poison, I assumed. It smelt rancidly toxic.

'Your friend has twenty-four hours before the poison reaches his heart. Find the box and surrender yourself to the puzzle piece and the box, and we'll let your friend live. You have my word as a knight.'

"what about your murdering friend?"

'That fool has another quest to fulfil. Don't worry; we'll allow you to uncover who they are. It's only fair to know who has tormented your family, after all. Tik Tok.' Before I got to respond, the Knight crumbled into the blanket of Ravens filling the sky. I'm staring at Nathan, watching black track lines spread through his skin as his wound wreaked of the toxin. Twenty-four hours, that's all we had to decide the world's fate. What do I do?

KINGSLEY

42

'Gerald.'

When does this end? The same darkness blanketed the remaining road into Kingsley. I felt growing, the kind that seemed to drift in on all sides, choking out our headlights and hope. The night air was thick with the lingering stench of death and decay that wouldn't leave us be. The Knight had left a greater imprint in our vehicle than Nathan's wound; I noticed black scorch marks throughout the cream roof lining.

At first, that's all I saw: haphazard strips of burnt black. My eyes seemed to re-focus without trying to map the pattern and shape... It was...the symbol of 'Baphomet', ominously hanging over us. Pain-filled, yawning echoes of the undead still haunting the back of my mind. Matching those carried on the chilly breeze from behind us. Nathan's condition was rapidly deteriorating, the poison spreading through his veins like wildfire; those black tracks were thicker already. I couldn't let him die. Not here. Not now. He'd already suffered so much in a short amount of time. All because I asked him for help. That's where I was laying the blame squarely on my shoulders.

Michael and George were tense, their supernatural senses heightened to a razor's edge, and their claws stayed on the show as we rolled from the asphalt of the country lane over the grilled metal of a cattle grid, squealing and creaking under our weight before churning through the gravel of a ghost town. Thick dust bucked and sprayed through the air; I was still getting used to the heightened sense of smell, wondering how long it would last. Every scent was vibrant and equally grotesque because of where we were.

Kingsley was eerie; quiet was shattered by a flutter of wings that made me jump, looking around, fearing the Knight's sudden return for round two. Ahead, twenty feet to our left, set amongst what would've been thick green bushes once. The kind with sharp stabbing ends fortified like a wall but now dead, with decaying flakes skittled to the winds. A looming tree, its fierce branched arms just as dead as the village, carried two bright blue eyes. We still had company.

"We need to get Nathan some help," I say, my voice strained with urgency. "We can't let him die. We need a bloody plan."

George nodded, his face grim. "We need to see what was so important about this place that it would be marked on Nathan's father's back. The Knight wasn't bluffing about the poison. It smells so strong."

Michael was already on it, looking at the map and tracing a finger through the darkened lanes. "There's an old church not too far into this place; maybe that's what that tiny cross meant in the square," he says. If there's any place to start, this could be as good as any. The Templars often used churches to hide their treasures, secret vaults, and whatnot.

"Look at you, the history buff," George quips, a little surprised.

"Well, you had a book just sitting there, and I was bored waiting while you were on the phone, so I got curious," Michael says a little sheepishly.

The car continued through the deserted road; the surrounding landscape was bleak, full of shadows and shapes. The tension between us was palpable, each lost in our thoughts. I glanced back at Nathan, his breathing shallow, his skin pale. The black veins creeping across his body were a horrifying reminder of the ticking clock.

"Hang in there, Nathan," I whisper. "We're going to save you."

Further into the mouth of Kingsley, the outlines of the old church came into view, its gothic spires piercing the night sky. The place had an ominous aura.

We parked on a side road, which concealed our vehicle. My attention was being pulled away, and I was nervous about the 'stray' watching us. It's creepy head twitching left to right. The chill was cutting as we exited the car, jarring. The occasional rustle of leaves and the distant caw of that raven had us all on edge. Nathan hung from my shoulder, sobbing with pain. It was now I hated the heightened sense of smell I'd gained. Death, that's all I could inhale, seeping from his pores. So tangible I could taste it. Adopted or not, he didn't deserve this, all because of a bloodline curse. None of us did.

"Stay close," George mutters, his claws still out, his face part wolf, eyes scanning the darkness. We don't know what we're walking into.

We moved as a unit, and every step was measured carefully. The church doors creaked open, echoing through the stillness, and we slipped inside, our flashlights cutting through the gloom. The interior was just as ominous as the exterior, filled with shadows that seemed to move and writhe. Panic sweat pooled around my brow, and all I could hear in my head were Father and Charlotte, their shadow versions that had me strangling Nathan. Which reminds me, why, if I could use the darkness for good, did it make me do that?

Currently, there are more cons than pros, and I don't like it. Details like that had me thinking it's all a ploy. Evil is coming at me from both sides. You know, good cop, bad cop. Something I'm sure Michael and George are well versed in. And I reckon Michael is the mean bastard. Not that I don't think George has it in him. He's a werewolf, for Christ's sake. But he is full of empathy, as though he's treading these painful paths many times before.

Straight in front are dusty pews, a cracked altar, and ancient stone walls. I couldn't shake the feeling we were being watched beside the raven. Hairs on the neck jumped on end. Every creak and groan of the old building punctured my spine.

"Look for anything out of the ordinary," Michael says, his voice calm. "Symbols, hidden compartments, anything that could lead us to the box or the puzzle piece."

"We don't know if this is the right place, and it could be a waste of time. Time, Nathan doesn't have." I say, coming across as flippant, but my friend was dying.

"AARRGGHHH." Nathan cries out loud and torturous.

"Georgie, come on, help him."

"How?"

"You know how like you did for me." There was silence, and George looked troubled. "Come on, George, he's struggling. You can do it. George... George? Bloody hell, George, stop ignoring."

"QUIETTTTTT." Suddenly, George shouts a phonically loud 'Quiet' that rocks around the church. We are stunned to a standstill. What is more shocking is Michael's behaviour. He responds out of instinct, cowering on the spot. His eyes glow bright yellow, and George's an even brighter red.

Eventually, Michael shook it off and stood upright. "Michael, it's not that I don't want to. I'm scared, too. Like many things since Scotland, I don't know what is too far anymore," George says, moving to Michael's side.

Michael took George's arm and placed it on Nathan's. "You have a big heart but are so bloody stupid; I would never let it go too far, especially with that venom. The boy is struggling. Just try," Michael says, speaking ever so softly he'd broken through.

George's eyes changed, becoming a blend of black and red; his fangs seemed bolder, and then it happened. I was stunned. That black tracking began reversing, travelling down Nathan's arm and up George's like little black bubbles under his flesh, travelling up. Nathan was improving, seeming to be in less pain and less pale. George was feeling it all. Sweat was pouring from him, his skin greying, and he looked in trouble, gasping for air. Michael lunges at his arm, yanking him free. Both landed in a heap on the hard grey stone floor. George was returning to normal, and Nathan seemed more comfortable... For now.

"Georgie, now's not the time for the wolf to go asleep," Michael says, pulling himself up. Nathan was breathing easier, but I was worried about how long it would last. I was grateful, of course. Michael got my attention with his comment, and he was right. George had fully turned normal.

George goes to stand, his legs wobble, and a foot slips across the dusty floor. I hear a resounding 'clap' as he drops, hands slapping against stone, trying to support himself. He was weak, really weak. I could hear his heart; it was going full tilt, and more worrying was the breathing. It's raspy, congested, almost filled with fluid, exactly like Nathan had been moments before.

"Georgie, are you okay?" Michael says, reaching to grab George's arm and help him up. I'm looking on, worried. I question how wise that move was. Michael shouldn't have pushed if George didn't feel right. I appreciate helping Nathan, but now we're down a weapon to help us.

With Nathan supporting more of his weight on his fight but still hanging around me, I walked over and saw if I could do anything. Not that I knew how this stuff worked and the supernatural. I was useless, but it's the natural thing to do, right? If I thought it would help or that George could do it, I'd offer to take the poison from George, or he could drain some of my energy.

"Micky, I'm fucked, I don't know what that poison is, but I'm tapping against the red, and it feels like I'm getting weaker," George says, trying to hoist up with the help of Michael, but he can't stand. His legs slid from beneath him.

We'd left the church doors open, and I could see right out to the tree and the raven was still there, watching. Wind howled around us, hissing through the gaps in dilapidated timbers and boarded windows. Paranoia was taking root in my mind, knowing we were weaker by two now and stranded somewhere we didn't know, looking for things we didn't know where to start. Every rustle, creak or rattle of wind chimes hanging at a house across the way had me jumpy. I could feel the goosebumps popping up one by one. Every second I look to the shadows,; I expecting them to come alive. My heart bounces against my chest bone; I can see the flesh thrust out each time. Exaggerating, of course, but that's how it seemed.

Michael rakes his claws anxiously through his hair; George is lying on the floor, propped up by his elbows. I feel a tickle at the back of my neck. Not from the darkness, a sixth sense overreacting, again thinking we were being watched. I'm staring so hard into the darkened corner of the church that I swear I see movement. Not the shadow, a slight glint of an eye or something. I don't know. Nothing felt right about being here; was it a trap? I ask myself. Then why would Nathan's father have it on his flesh? I counter. Then it happened again. More spookily exaggerated this time, like the outline of a person. I feel on the verge of freaking out when Michael pipes up.

"WWED," Michael says aloud. George looks at him, screwing his face up, confused.

"What?"

"What would Ellena do if she were here?"

George chuckles, his grey face looking sickly to overshadow his brief amusement. "She'd say, get the hell up, Wolfie, you got shit to do and people to save."

Michael grabs a black wallet from his pocket. "She'd then give you this, her version of-"

George butts in. "A supernatural first aid kit." He catches a sweet or something. Seriously, candy? Right now? I selfishly grumbled. He smirked, looking at me and chewing away. My jaw dropped. It had to be steroids because his eyes blazed brighter than I'd seen them before. The wolf was back. I got to see his features change—another slow motion moment. I had to savour something so awesome, yet freaky. All the black track marks faded, and his claws came like a flick knife as they scraped through stone, levering himself up.

No one else would believe me if I told them. Okay, perhaps now, but pre-undead roaming around the village. I'd be sent straight to the looney bin. With George shaking off the last of the poison, he strolled over to me. My eyes closed, and I prayed he didn't come to have a go at me over the selfish comment he clearly heard. The shout and Michael cowering as he did, sod that for a laugh.

"It's okay, you weren't to know," George says, smiling, but looks where Michael is and whispers. "But we must talk."

"What for?" He had me confused.

"I can sense it, you know." I look at him blankly, thinking, 'he must've bumped his head' before I force a wry smile.

"What? My fear? Is it surprising?" I say, trying to bluff. I never have been good at cards. Ask Nathan.

"It's Okay. You're a good person, and I don't think you have it in you to go bad." Now I was amazed, lost for words. For real. I went to speak, but nothing came. For mind reading another werewolf superpower? If so, I wanted in. A damn sight better than a crazed killer,

I'm really confused now. There's a demon in me? I thought, checking my backside.

"What?"

"That darkness you're fighting against. It's already taking root, infesting within you. It's sharpening your senses. I know the signs, such as head tilts and ear twitches. It began in the car. I think it could work for us." George was amazing; he didn't judge. He's just been through the wringer; He was trying to put me at ease. Didn't make me less confused though. Yeah, I realised my senses and figured it was a little 'suckup' trial run. But amalgamating with me, and it's a demon. Maybe the term 'darkness' should've been a giveaway. Hearing it sounded evil.

"How? How do you know the joining and demon?" I say. It probably sounds stupid, but I was distracted. There was another ripple, more than one outline.

"Because I'm part demon, too. And I'm not evil. So, maybe be prepared to embrace it in desperate times. I think it might surprise you. Now let's fucking keep moving. I believe we have company." George says, his eyes darted to the left corner. Where I saw the ripples, just under some pillars and crumbles walkway above. At least I wasn't seeing things.

"I thought I saw a couple of ripples in the shadows, but then thought it was me being paranoid."

"You need to trust your instincts. Whether you like it, you will join us in the supernatural. You'll have many changes and weird experiences. Don't worry; I will help where I can. As you can see, we're a bunch of misfits, nothing. We have three shapeshifters, a druid and maybe a witch, as part of our unit in London. So, you're not alone." I was blown away; what I was experiencing didn't seem so strange now. Then I catch a look at Nathan, knowing he wasn't a bloodline, and now he's dying. We're bragging about special skills and none of that... Nothing we have... Nothing... fuck, I can't even get the words. Right, I go again. There's nothing in all this fantastical world or abilities from shapeshifters and would-be demons which could save my friend if we're too late.

"What about Nathan? What if we run out of time? He doesn't deserve this, especially with what we know. Even that could shatter his world." I say; Nathan grumbled, stretched a little. I hoped he didn't hear. Michael joined us, slowly scouting the nearby walkway. My guess is that he was stalling. Sure as hell, if George can hear, he can, which was kind of nice, not to pile on the pressure. Meanwhile, the wind whistled through with haunting intent, hellbent on shaking us... Okay, me up. Michael looked at George, made a biting motion with his fangs, and pointed to himself. George raised his eyebrows as if to say, 'Oh, yeah, really?'

Much like cards, I'm crap at charades, but that didn't need interpreting. Suppose I've watched enough horror movies with werewolves. Usually, a bite or claws deep can make another. I think. What Michael imitated was a bite, whether he would do it or George bit him. I'm not sure. Maybe there's a backup plan after all.

Michael kept rocking his head around, bothered. He was sensing company, too. The how and why were details to bother us, but in the dead of night, carrying one wounded and Georgie barely fighting fit again as we traipse through this rundown church looking for a supernatural needle in a holy haystack.

"Michael, guard behind; I'll flank Gerald and Nathan. For all we know, it could be the 'homeless', but the read is off." George says, back to his werewolf form, head twisting anxiously. The initial boost Nathan had was already wearing off. I could feel him leaning on me more and more than we shuffled across the uneven stone. I'm looking, searching every crevice for something, without knowing what to look for. A bit backwards, right? Grey flag stones rested beneath our feet, at least a hundred years old. I was surprised they were still there. The type of things usually stripped for value. Then again, we don't know why the village is a ghost town.

It seemed a little purposeful, a rundown place, too dark and scary looking for anyone to go snooping. Maybe there is something for us to find here after all. Not necessarily this church, but somewhere in this god-forsaken place. If only Nathan were alert, with all his investigating, he could've come across a detail that seemed nothing. But now, it could be important. Dust was settled everywhere I looked, and there were no signs of anything major being disturbed by Nathan's parents or anyone they saw fit to help.

We're moving; the shadows hold the detective's attention. Those ripples continued. Each time they moved, it appeared they were circling behind us toward the doors. All the surrounding architecture looked amazing, run down and left to rot, but I'm sure it was breathtaking in its heyday. Admiring glimpses with each pillar, we passed. I'm no architect, but these seemed wider than usual. I counted four on either side, a few holding nothing. One stood out. Aside from looking cleaner, it had a symbol partly carved, partly screwed in place. It's the 'Templar' cross. The original history book version. Except it was upside down.

I'm focussing as hard as possible, feeling whatever's in the shadows, waiting to make their move. We were more surprised that it was taking so long. They could've had a go while George was down. It was all too confusing. Nathan grew heavier by the minute. These track marks had grown again; they were thicker now. 'Inky' veins pulsated in the gloom. Even the supernatural didn't help him.

An icy breeze hissed towards me the closer I got; I checked the floor around the base, but nothing out of the ordinary. Thick with dust, like the rest of the stone floor. That 'hissing' continued. I was acting like a 'mundane' forgetting what the darkness was doing to me and my senses. My vision. I focussed like a child playing with new toys. A faint line caught my eye; it rose from the ground, six feet up the pillar, curving the pillar before back down to the floor again. A hunch was forming, and I wasn't sure how I felt about it. I'd found either a concealed cupboard or a false door leading somewhere. The 'Cross' pointed down. It had to be a hint, yet as it's screwed in, I had a theory the cross needed turning. 'Righting' again. I was too drawn to figure out the logistics when a sudden 'whoosh' past made me jump.

That cursed raven flew through, landing on a rather damage 'Jesús on a cross'. It's creepy blue eyes blazing on us. Every twitch gave me chills. I must look; the blue looks brighter, pulsating with an allure that scares me, yet I must stare it out. I'm not afraid... I'm not afraid. Those bastards can't get to me; there's nothing they can do that will sway or get under my skin. Look at it: nothing but a flying rat. Those eyes, though. I bet there's all manner of secrets behind them, the reasons for all this death and bloodshed. I can't look away... I feel so cold... So cold...

'Hush, little baby, don't say a word. Mama's gonna buy you a mockingbird.'

"Charlotte?"

'And if that mockingbird don't sing. Mama's gonna buy you a diamond ring.'

"Charlotte? Is that you?"

'And if that diamond ring turns brass. Mama's gonna buy you a looking glass.'

"It can't be you. I know it can't be. Surely?"

'And if that looking glass get broke. Mama's gonna buy you a billy goat.'

"What's going on? Why's this happening? Those blue eyes, it's you, isn't it? Where is everybody? Where's this fog come from?"

'And if that billy goat doesn't pull. Mama's gonna buy you a cart and bull.'

. "I don't understand. This differs from last time, and the shadows are different. What the hell is going on? Christ, everything feels... so... heavy... Look at those blue eyes."

'And if that box and piece don't show. Mama's gonna make Nathan go.'

"What? That... that's ... not... how... how it goes."

'And you if you just wanna give in. Mama's gonna show you what you win. Our new life will just begin.'

I can't see anything through the thick fog. It's freezing; every hair on my body is on end, but I can't keep my eyes open... Oh, those haunting blue eyes, are they doing this to me? I... i... I can't breathe, my throat feels tight. 'cuh.. cuh' There's movement through the fog, several shadows moving, help... somebody help. I can't, I can't... Keep your eyes open...

"Hey, it's time to wake up now."

"Urgh, just five more minutes. It's too cosy. And you're so warm I don't want to move." My eyes reluctantly open; I'm so groggy. Wow, this hangover is kicking my arse.

"Well, you need to get up now, silly. We have the rest of our lives for cuddles, but the girls need to get to your mothers and get to work."

"Charlotte?"

"Of course it's me; who else would it be? Blimey, you and Nathan were hitting the bottle last night, weren't you?"

"I... I guess yeah." I say; my head was pounding, daylight beamed through the curtains, and I didn't want to move. Charlotte was so warm and soothing. Her smile made my heart pound harder. Yet, something was bothering me. A weird sensation... I didn't belong, but I can't remember why or what I did last night, for that matter. A sudden chill swept through everything felt close, too close. My neck hair bristled with a shiver. Out of nowhere, I was irrefutably consumed by fear. Why?

Face of Death

43

'Détective Reynolds—Back to my worst moment,'

I find myself somewhere strange yet eerily familiar. The smoke clouds my senses, bringing me back to one of the worst moments of my life where it all began. There's no light I can feel, only the scrape of my hand against a flaking wall and the clutch of a wooden bannister. My nightmares replay in my mind, each creak of timber a haunting symphony before I discovered Chris. But this time, I'm not barefoot, and I'm not alone.

Listening past the whistling wind, I strain to catch heartbeats, hoping for sounds beyond ours. Skip and Michael are ahead, but someone is down there, and their heartbeat is faint. Michael sparks a lighter; the little yellow flame dances as we move, illuminating strange symbols—Latin, just like the box left in my car. The descent grows darker, and the rancid smell of burnt flesh intensifies.

Full of nerves, I bounce from one problem to another. I recall a giddy feeling that turns my legs to jelly, praying they won't give out as we hit the stone, dusty floor. Like my dreams, my feet kick through the dirt, sending a shower through the air.

"Oh my God, that's freaking vile. Can you smell that? Butcher's meat gone rotten," Michael says, retching, sickly saliva dribbling down his chin.

"Welcome to hell."

"What, Skip?"

"That Latin as we came down, it's a welcome to blooming hell."

All I see is a looming, flickering silhouette cast by the lighter. The space feels larger than

I imagined. I stand in the same spot, spinning around in a daze, letting the smouldering air fill my lungs until the goosebump chill from my nightmare becomes real—a speaker. Heavy iron chains pound against the concrete, sending a metallic clang rippling through the air. Once... Twice... Three times... It's the ghost of my Christmas past.

'How does it feel, Georgie? Is anything coming back to you yet? I can always shed some light on you. Let you revel in the horror before the fun begins,' the puppeteer's voice echoes around us, adding to my trepidation.

I step back, reaching for the bannister; burnt blood swirls through my lungs, and drool pools around my gums, feeling the lust build up. Loud clicking rocks around us before a dim light flickers on. We all gasp, staring in horror; Skip stumbles backwards, falling into a craftsman's bench with a vice. Pinched within is a bony hand, rotten, more bone than anything else. Blood sprays chaotically throughout, enveloping the thick dust and grime.

Four adult-sized bodies are beheaded in kneeling positions. Hands and feet are bound in chains, with the remains of thick tape melted across their mouths; they couldn't move or call for help, even if they wanted to.

They are more than decomposed and burnt, masking the clothing. The puppeteer has arranged the bodies around a circle, an old etching touched up to look new. Two triangles, one upright, the other inverted—devil worship. Just as Skip saw it twenty-five years ago.

My stomach rumbles with the lure of blood I can't escape and the urge to spew its contents among the dirt. The bodies are fresh, only a few days old, with remains of ordinary torched clothing. I'm glued to the depravity, trying to understand where this game is going.

All we have so far is Harkes dead and these unfortunate souls caught up in the chaos. I stare so hard that all I see are the heads on the floor; everything else becomes a blur. The jagged edges of protruding charcoaled flesh with short throaty gristle and neck cartilage. Each flailing is of a different length and width, not made by a knife, axe, or any other symmetrical blade—at least not in the beginning. No, these are claw marks, much like the ones on Lewis, made by a bladed glove. Not claws, as the killer wants us to believe.

My pulse pounds in my temple, throbbing in my ears; I'm lost in darkness, different from what we descended into. My arms are heavy, dragged down limply, feeling a tightness around my wrists. I look down to see thick, chained clamps. Only my arms aren't my own; they are smaller, covered in burnt red-black skin, bubbling and breaking. A pair of bolt cutters hover close and break the chains; I'm lifted like a rag doll before being covered in a sheet. I'm being carried; a haunting red glow in the corner is coming my way. It's a nightmare, and I have nowhere to go.

"You ok, Georgie lad?"

"Huh. Y... yeah, I think so."

Skip calls to me; my eyes clear, and I'm back, staring at the stranded heads, sockets exposed with eyes popping. I can barely see strands of hair on any of them. One, two, three, four, and five. No extra fingers this time; I'm not dreaming. Not this time. But I'd seen myself being carried away, breaking from darkness; it felt more than a horrible dream, more a memory, but so real. Nightmarishly real. The way my arms looked and smelt rancid, almost a nightmare within a nightmare. This was Charlie, tormenting me over the past.

'Surely you remember now seeing my little masterpiece? Volunteers recreating what happened, showing you how my parents, my sister, and my grandmother died. How you were lucky to survive. The rest you'll get if you complete the game.' The motive that drove that bastard was awful—murdering innocent people to make a point and push us around. I can feel the venom in his words thumping around. Chains rattle again on the far-right side, still in the shadows. I strain to look; all I see are dirty brown pillars made of solid wood that have weathered over time—Latin symbols carved into each one with slight differences. It's crazy.

"Skip, any ideas?" I point to the nearest pillar. Much like the strangeness of the box, a few resemble letters from the alphabet, only with extra squiggly lines.

"Well, it's old Latin, I think. I'm not that smart, lad: daemon, esto subjecto voluntati meae. Demon, submit yourself to my bidding. Something like that."

The puppeteer's family didn't mess around looking to summon demons. Not so long ago, I would've laughed that off as nonsense. Now, anything is fair game. The next pillar, ten feet to my right, has a similar inscription.

"What about this?"

"Ad ligandum eos pariter eos coram me. To likewise bind them before me. That's the gist; when the stupid sods delved into this shit, they created sigils. They wanted to trap whatever they summoned and use it. But remember, I told you about that big bloke at the hospital? He's something like that."

Another bump in the road: the newspaper clipping, Skip's bedtime story, and Charlie's tall tale that he gave him in the box. They all have different stories about this, and I was gullible, especially regarding Charlie. Michael has moved to a row of wooden shelves, mould smothering the sides, and his curiosity and screwed-up face. The longer we linger, the more we see. I tick off a mental checklist, comparing the things I've been told.

While Michael is examining the shelves, I see another horrifying detail. Jars, row after row of wide, dusty glass three-quarters full, containing sickly body parts swimming in a dirty green liquid. Some are limbs from babies, including a head, only different—small fangs and two lumps on the forehead, beginning horns.

Michael moves; his leg wobbles beneath him, his once immaculate posh shoes scraping through the dirt. The day has taken its toll, and we are nowhere near done. I can feel the tension in his bones as I pull him to his feet; his arm shudders within my grip, and I hear a sudden rumble as a fluorescent light stutters on. It's not bright, but enough to know where our game is. The back of my eyes warmed slowly, blood vessels boiling with a throbbing in the sockets; I want to rip them out, stop their need to bleed.

Little Piggy Three, dressed in a boiler suit, suspended horizontally, thick silver chains clamped to the limbs and pulled tight. Another chain wraps around the head like a noose—the same for the abdomen. Each feeds two cogs in different basement parts; power cables run to a big junction box on the wall—lo-and-behold, another keypad. Besides that, the annoyingly familiar red smiley face, large, dripping down. More blood.

"Is this bastard for real? That looks bloody medieval. How the hell do we solve this one? More to the point, do we agree that this twisted wanker isn't working alone? How else would he do all of this?"

Michael is traumatised, and Skip isn't much better. That case was awful. It took me to where it all began. A child snatched from his parents and dumped into a seedy foster home that experimented on children. Except I was born a werewolf, and they made me something else. I got to relive it all and remember so much that I'd blocked out, including the fire that should've killed me. Look at me now, doing my best to ensure none of the same happens to anyone else, even if it involves stopping the gates of hell from being opened. We have to do something. I stand looking at all the same devil trap markings and blood. Skip and Michael freeze. The floor crumbled, fading and changing. Everything around me was doing the same. In no time at all, I was back in the tunnel. Nathan, Michael, and Gerald were still knocked out. Confusing, I got to thinking about the Templar order; the original ones were prestigious knights and their secrets, until this day, are sought after. So, that could have been a test to see if I was worthy to carry on. All I can do now is hope that Michael's alternative life choices don't screw him up.

'Michael,'

Bloody hell, that was a trip and a half. One minute I'm in a tunnel, the next I'm back in time, one I bloody don't want to relive. The Kanaima one where I had my throat ripped out, and I should've died. It was also the moment that changed my life for the better. I'm at the Spitalfields warehouse, watching the standoff unfold.

This killer and its master were deadly, with a trail of bodies left in their wake. It was so bloody tough. A twitch, eyes shifting between normal and Kanaima green. Claws came and went. Georgie got in his head. Jack turned to Melanie, grimacing. Georgie thought he could save us all at once.

"Don't think about it. I control everything; press this button, and toxins are released immediately. I know you won't control anything in a minute because of the blood."

Claws slid out; Georgie hid his hands, catching Ellena's eyes. Georgie didn't want to freak her out, let alone Locke find out. He watched helplessly. Georgie was about to try his luck but got hit by a thunderbolt of pain, dropping to his knees. His hands were in sawdust; they'd changed.

'It's okay, Georgie. Let it happen,' Ellena whispers, tears trickling. "I...I... I can't," Georgie struggles, bones breaking around us.

'It's ok, I know... I trust you,' she whispered. Locke nodded in approval. Did he know too? The pain had Georgie wanting to scream; instead, a roar as his fangs grew, shaking the warehouse. Melanie stepped back with fear.

He saw red until his vision settled—beads of sweat on Melanie's forehead. The Kanaima's eyes held black streaks in green. Jack was conflicted. The human side was scared for his life. Georgie was changing, but he had to hang on, halt it. The demon side was assimilating with the wolf; heightened wouldn't do justice.

Power surged, and Georgie sensed Melanie's fear for the first time. There was a vibration in her throat, and her pupils darted, seeking exits.

"Don't be stupid, Georgie," Melanie quivered. Jack worried, flaws fluctuating. Now was his time. Lights off again, darkness. He flew past, yanking drips out, landing on the platform, knocking Kanaima and me apart. The lights are back on. We'd landed feet apart; I'd forced Kanaima's claws into its abdomen, injecting its toxin. Hoping the books were true.

Georgie dragged his angry self from the dust, looking up. Melanie stood over my body—blood pissing from my throat. The Kanaima ripped it out. I remember feeling so cold, ever so quickly. Shock mixed with the realisation I may have had my last done. I was choking on blood, trying to talk, trying to tell my friends that I regretted nothing about being wrapped in this new, dark world. I couldn't.

My body writhed as sawdust soaked the pool of blood. "Aww, you killed the 30 seconds, man. Tut tut. Another lesson I learned from the books. Always have a Plan B," she says, holding the remote. "Don't do it. The game is over."

"Not yet; it ain't. While you decide who to save, I'll take that key and be on my way," Melanie says. The button compressed. A blast of wind; the Kanaima was still stricken. Who would've thought how much joy hearing four little words could bring?

'Hey-up Georgie, lad,'

Georgie turned toward the booming echo of his old Skipper and 'Beta' Andy Morris. "What the hell, how?" Georgie gushes.

"I heard you call, so I came. Now save them," he beamed.

My skin turned pale, lying in a pool of blood slipping away. To the tables behind were two other drips rigged with toxin; Melanie assumed the obvious. Georgie ripped the needles out and flipped the tables flat, tearing through the straps. Returning to me, I was dying, and Georgie didn't know what to do. I'd lost so much blood we'd never reach the hospital in time.

"Skip. Please... tell me how," Georgie pleads. We stopped Melanie, but it's cost Michael his life. I was helpless and drowning.

"Bite him, lad; there's no other way," he says, gripping Melanie tight. I looked at her face, and the rage inside me wanted him to do it.

"I can't; what will everyone see of me?" Georgie screeched.

"You can save him, lad," says Skip.

"It's ok, Georgie," Ellena whispered. Locke stared. He was the unknown.

"Do it, George. Save him; we don't have long," Locke surprised Georgie.

He grabbed my arm; the pool grew, and my heart slowed to the last beat. 'Fuck it', before biting deep into my arm. His fangs pierced my skin and flesh, nicking a vein. A small spray of blood spurted over Georgie's face as he held on. His eyes blazed red, brighter than ever before. Every fibre in his body was alive with blood lust.

"That's enough, Georgie," Skip pleads. Instead, Georgie bit a little harder, causing me to squirm.

Air grazed past; Ellena came to our side, gently touching Georgie's neck. Her face breezed close, lips inches from his ear.

"That's enough, Georgie; let go now. I'm here for you," she cooed into his ear. Her words echoed, a bewitching effect. Georgie's jaw loosened, his eyes dimmed, and he slowly let go, falling backwards, feeling ashamed.

"I'm here for you," she whispers. Georgie tried to hide his face, but Ellena had none of it. She gripped his clawed hands, looking at him deeply with a caring smile. 'You don't need to hide anymore,' she whispered.

I groaned; my neck had healed. I could feel life ebbing back and then some. Colour seeped back into my skin. It was working. My veins were on fire, everything was repairing, and little knocks and issues I had endured through a long life were mending and getting stronger. I was getting stronger. I felt like a bloody kid again, from nearly dying to exhilaration.

"What the hell happened?" I croaked.

"You were all but dead. Now stop lying around; come arrest this bitch, will you?" Skip boomed, rocking me to my senses.

"What? Really?" I say, gathering myself.

"Yeah, Georgie saved you; he saved us all," Locke interrupts, lumbering up.

"So, you had to bite me? Does that mean I must be flea and wormed every month now?" I say, finding the energy to joke.

It was nearly midnight, and Georgie's problems were far from over as the demon gradually took hold of his body. The Kanaima stirred, and everyone stepped back. That smell of death was still here. The Kanaima dragged out its claws. Georgie was about to jump up when a surge of electricity rippled through the lights, and clouds of black smoke breezed through, causing panic.

As easily as they disappeared the other day, those two demons reappeared.

"Don't fear. We mean no harm," says the one in khaki trousers.

"What do you want?" I say.

"'To take the Kanaima back to where it belongs,"

"We are its guardians, making sure it stays imprisoned. It cannot be killed but can be trapped in this." They showed a relic, the one Melanie stole.

"How?"

"That's for us to know. These people disturbed a sacred crypt with their greed, bringing death. The last time cost thousands of lives, so count yourself lucky."

"How will you do it?" Georgie says, feeling confused.

"Like this," in a swift move, the demon in jeans drove a dagger into Jack's stomach. Black smoke arose from Jack and poured into the gem. They slotted the gem into the base of the relic. The demons vanished again in black clouds, leaving us speechless and Georgie dropping backwards in a painful daze.

It was finally over, except for Georgie. An alarm signalled midnight. 'The witching hour.' His body looked ready to explode; it took him to be on all fours. Bones were cracking, blood was boiling, and there was a rage like no other. Making everyone around him his prey. I know I was scared. Until a sharp needle jammed into his neck. Ellena grabbed the paralytic needle to nullify him until it was over. She whispers, 'Sorry,' Georgie drops to the floor, watching the world fade into darkness. I was so relieved and still understanding how my body was feeling.

It was over, and we'd stopped a serial killing demon, and I'd survived. We could finally rest, heavy eyelids trying to flap shut. Battling in the shadows against something nobody would know about, at least for now.

This case, our first as a new team, was betrayed by someone we least expected for horrific reasons, if true. Battered, bruised, and a little bloodied. Okay, a lot bloodied. We had to dig deep, being pushed to our limits.

Now, the fallout. We beat the clock, and the future would be the only way of knowing how different I am. The darkness is where we live now because this world isn't the same as it once was. All the while, the circle of who kept our secrets had grown. That bite saved and changed my life in ways I can't put into words, but our fight to stop the darkness from taking over continues, and I will fight for the good people until the end. Staring at my blood on the floor, feeling lucky to be alive, everything began crumbling and changing. Before long, I was waking up in the tunnel with Georgie standing over me. Gerald was still out with Nathan.

'Gerald,'

Well, that wasn't in the brochure; that smoke or chemical cloud had us all out in seconds. I've woken in darkness, and I smell cigars. I'm in a house—my grandparents' house, full of musk and staleness that comes with their age. I've ended up in a room. It's their spare bedroom from when I used to sleep over. A glimmer of moonlight ripples through the curtains, catching the far-right side of the room. There's me, the young version of me, at least. I'm no older than twelve. The clock on the wall shows a little after 1:30 a.m., and I have to say, this scenario confuses me.

There is little I remember from then, and nothing jumps out. I look peacefully snuggled beneath my 'Batman' duvet cover. Most of the room is quite bland, except the walls are boyish blue. More posters pay homage to the same 'dark knight' that keeps me warm. A football and a cricket bat are in the corner, and a tiny television sits on the dresser. Still, I'm searching for answers, wondering why I was here and now. We were running out of time to save Nathan. Assuming we could. If that toxin overpowered a werewolf, my faith was being tested.

Any minute now, I muttered, hoping, then I saw the ripple of a shadow moving through the hallway. I barely caught it, thanks to a dim light at the bottom of the stairs. It was tall, like a man, unless I was seeing things, another hallucination, hoping to see something to end this situation. There's silence and then a crash caused by a lamp being knocked over and the bulb exploding. A loud scream from Nanna followed that drama, and then Grandad shouted, too inaudible to understand but loud enough to shake the young me awake.

My pale blonde hair swung across my bleary eyes and quickly brushed out of the way as another shout rang out. In matching Batman pyjamas, the young me jumped out of bed, dashing for the cricket bat and out of the door. I followed my little legs, still not remembering any of this. Their bedroom is at the end of the hallway, their light on, and I can see a shadow looming by the doorway. Young me had no fear. Charging headstrong into the bedroom, we barely broke stride over the threshold. I'm stunned. It's the 'whispering man.' He's stood over my grandparents, huddled in bed, facing down the sharp end of a sword. His deathly face had wisps of charcoal flesh peeling from his jawbone. How did this not terrify me back then? Perhaps that's why I couldn't remember.

The 'whispering man' turned to see young me, his demonic eyes piercing its deep, garish red through to my soul. His dirty trilby stank of dead blood, its peak casting a shadow across his haunting, menacing face. At least a metre long, a gleaming mix of metals. I smelled sulphur and then that potent toxin that was ripping through Nathan as I endured this 'trial or test.' What else could it be?

The 'whispering man' smiles before plunging the sword forward. Young me jumped through the air, landing on the bed. My little arms wielded that cricket bat as if it were a sword, too. It windmilled through the air, overhand, crashing down on the sword mid-plunge. The sword veered wide, burying into the headboard, but the bat followed through, and as the sword bounced and bowed before snapping, metal shards splintered through the air. Shocked, the 'whispering man' turned, retreating. "Death will come soon enough," he says, becoming a blur out the door.

Young me saved my grandparents and locked away the memory. The sword's tip still wobbled in the headboard before crumbling away, infecting everything it connected to. My grandparents, young me, and then the room all disappeared. I was back in the tunnels. Michael and George stood over me, waiting.

"About bloody time, matey," Michael says, looking at his watch.

"Sorry, but I didn't know what was going on."

"Well, we need to move. Since our little experiences, the twenty-four hours are nearly up." I was stunned, quickly hoisting Nathan to his feet. His body is on fire. We were losing him and any chance to stop what's coming. How the hell had we lost so much time? All the smoke and mirrors were gone, and a clear path awaited. We all experienced something, but none of us spoke of it. Instead, it weighed us down as we trudged toward destiny or hell. Now I know when I first met the 'whispering man'. More fear provoking for me, was not remembering or deep down, my brain made it into a nightmare, because the truth was too scary.

Smoke and Mirrors

44

'Detective Reynolds—Back to my worst moment'

I'm somewhere strange and familiar. Whatever that smoke was, I'm experiencing one of the worst moments of my life where it all began. I remember it clearly. There was no light I could feel. One hand scraped across a flaking wall while the other clutched a wooden bannister, mulling over my nightmares. Each creak of timber was a haunting symphony before I discovered Chris. But this time, I wasn't barefoot, and I had company. Listening past the whistling wind, I strained to catch heartbeats, hoping for sounds beyond ours. Skip and Michael were ahead, but someone was down there, and their heartbeat was faint.

Michael sparked a lighter; the little yellow flame danced as we moved, illuminating strange symbols—Latin, just like the box left in my car. I couldn't see much on the descent, but I knew we were approaching the bottom. The rancid smell of burnt flesh grew stronger.

Full of nerves, I bounced from one problem to another. I recall a giddy feeling that turned my legs to jelly. I hoped they wouldn't escape from under me as we hit the stone, dusty floor. Like my dreams at the time, my feet kicked through the dirt, sending a shower through the air.

"Oh my God, that's freaking vile. Can you smell that? Butcher's meat gone rotten," Michael says, retching, sickly saliva dribbling down his chin.

"Welcome to hell."

"What, Skip?"

"That Latin as we came down, it's a welcome to blooming hell."

All I could see was a looming, flickering silhouette cast by the lighter. The space felt larger than I imagined. I stood in the same spot, spinning around in a daze, letting the smouldering circle my lungs until the goose pimple chill from my nightmare came true—a speaker. Heavy iron chains pounded against the concrete, sending a metallic clang rippling through the air. Once... Twice... Three times... It was the ghost of my Christmas past.

'How does it feel, Georgie? Is anything coming back to you yet? I can always shed some light on you. Let you revel in the horror before the fun begins,' the puppeteer echoed around us, adding to my trepidation.

I stepped back, reaching for the bannister; burnt blood swirled through my lungs, and drool pooled around my gums, feeling the lust build up. Loud clicking rocks around us before a dim light flickered on. We all gasped, staring in horror; Skip stumbled backwards, falling into a craftsman's bench with a vice. Pinched within was a bony hand, rotten, more bone than anything else. Blood sprayed chaotically throughout, enveloping the thick dust and grime.

Four adult-sized bodies were beheaded in kneeling positions. Hands and feet were bound in chains, with the remains of thick tape melted across their mouths; they couldn't move or call for help, even if they wanted to.

They were more than decomposed and burnt, masking the clothing. The puppeteer had arranged the bodies around a circle, an old etching touched up to look new. Two triangles, one upright, the other inverted—devil worship. Just as Skip had seen it twenty-five years ago.

My stomach rumbled with the lure of blood I couldn't escape and the urge to spew its contents amongst the dirt. The bodies were fresh, only a few days old, with remains of ordinary torched clothing. I was glued to the depravity, trying to understand where this game was going.

All we had so far was Harkes dead and these unfortunate souls caught up in the chaos. I stared so hard that all I could see were the heads on the floor; everything else became a blur. The jagged edges of protruding charcoaled flesh ended short of the throaty gristle and neck cartilage. Each flailing was of a different length and width, not made by a knife, axe, or any other symmetrical blade—at least not in the beginning. No, these were claw marks, much like the ones on Lewis, made by a bladed glove. Not claws, as the killer wanted us to believe.

My pulse pounded in my temple, throbbing in my ears; I was lost in darkness, different from what we came down to. My arms were heavy, dragged down limply, feeling a tightness around my wrists. I looked down to see thick, chained clamps. Only my arms weren't my own; they were smaller, covered in burnt red-black skin, bubbling and breaking. A pair of bolt cutters hovered close and broke the chains; I was lifted like a rag doll before being covered in a sheet. I was being carried; a haunting red glow in the corner was coming my way. It was a nightmare, and I had nowhere to go.

"You okay, Georgie lad?"

"Huh. Y... yeah, I think so."

Skip called to me; my eyes cleared, and I was back, staring at the stranded heads, sockets exposed with eyes popping. I could barely see strands of hair on any of them. One, two, three, four, and five. No extra fingers this time; I wasn't dreaming. Not this time. But I'd seen myself being carried away, breaking from darkness; it felt more than a horrible dream, more a memory, but so real. Nightmarishly real. The way my arms looked and smelt rancid, almost a nightmare within a nightmare. This was Charlie, tormenting me over the past.

'Surely you remember now seeing my little masterpiece? Volunteers recreating what happened, showing you how my parents, my sister, and my grandmother died. How you were lucky to survive. The rest you'll get if you complete the game.' the motive that drove that bastard was awful—murdering innocent people to make a point and push us around. I could feel the venom in his words thumping around. Chains rattled again on the far-right side, still in the shadows. I strained to look; all I saw were dirty brown pillars made of solid wood that had weathered over time—Latin symbols carved into each one with slight differences. It was crazy.

"Skip, any ideas?" I pointed to the nearest pillar. Much like the strangeness of the box, a few resembled letters from the alphabet, only with extra squiggly lines.

"Well, it's old Latin, I think. I'm not that smart, lad: daemon, esto subjecto voluntati meae. Demon, submit yourself to my bidding. Something like that."

The puppeteer's family didn't mess around looking to summon demons. Not so long ago, I would've laughed that off as nonsense. Now, anything is fair game. The next pillar, ten feet to my right, had a similar inscription.

"What about this?"

"Ad ligandum eos pariter eos coram me. To likewise bind them before me. That's the gist; when the stupid sods delved into this shit, they created sigils. They wanted to trap whatever they summoned and use it. But remember, I told you about that big bloke at the hospital? He's something like that."

Another bump in the road: the newspaper clipping, Skip's bedtime story, and Charlie's tall tale that he gave him in the box. They had different stories about this, and I was gullible, especially regarding Charlie. Michael had moved to a row of wooden shelves, mould smothering the sides, and his curiosity and screwed-up face. The longer we lingered, the more we saw. I ticked off a mental checklist, comparing the things I'd been told.

While Michael was examining the shelves, I saw another horrifying detail. Jars, row after row of wide, dusty glass three-quarters full, containing sickly body parts swimming in a dirty green liquid. Some were limbs from babies, including a head, only different—small fangs and two lumps on the forehead, beginning horns.

Michael went to move; his leg wobbled beneath him, his once immaculate posh shoes scraping through the dirt. The day had taken its toll, and we were nowhere near done. I could feel the tension in his bones as I pulled him to his feet; his arm shuddered within my grip, and I heard a sudden rumble as a fluorescent light stuttered on. It wasn't bright, but it was enough to know where our game was. The back of my eyes began to warm slowly, blood vessels boiling with a throbbing in the sockets; I wanted to rip them out, stop their need to bleed.

Little Piggy Three, dressed in a boiler suit, suspended horizontally, thick silver chains clamped to the limbs and pulled tight. Another chain wrapped around the head like a noose—the same for the abdomen. Each fed two cogs in different basement parts; power cables ran to a big junction box on the wall—lo-and-behold, another keypad. Besides that, the annoyingly familiar red smiley face, large, dripping down. More blood.

"Is this bastard for real? That looks bloody medieval. How the hell do we solve this one? More to the point, do we agree that this twisted wanker isn't working alone? How else would he do all of this?"

Michael was traumatised, and Skip wasn't much better. That case was awful. It took me to where it all began. A child snatched from his parents and dumped into a seedy foster home that experimented on children. Except I was born a werewolf, and they made me something else. I got to relive it all and remember so much that I'd blocked out, including the fire that should've killed me. Look at me now, doing my best to ensure none of the same happens to anyone else, even if it involves stopping the gates of hell being opened. We had to do something. I stood looking at all the same devil trap markings and blood. Skip and Michael froze. The floor began crumbling, fading, and changing. Everything around me was doing the same. In no time at all, I was back in the tunnel. Nathan, Michael, and Gerald were still knocked out. Confusing, I got to thinking about the Templar order; the original ones were meant to be prestigious Knights and their secrets, until this day, are sought after. So, that could have been a test to see if I was worthy to carry on. All I can do now is hope that Michael's alternative life choices don't screw him up.

'Michael'

Bloody hell, that was a trip and a half. One minute, I'm in a tunnel; the next, I'm back in time; one, I bloody don't want to relive. The Kanaima one where I had my throat ripped out, and I should've died. It was also the moment that changed my life for the better. I'm at the Spitalfields warehouse, watching the standoff unfold.

This killer and its master were deadly, with a trail of bodies left in their wake. It was so bloody tough. A twitch, eyes shifting between normal and Kanaima green. Claws came and went. Georgie got in his head. Jack turned to Melanie, grimacing. Georgie thought he could save us all at once.

"Don't think about it. I control everything; press this button, and toxins are released immediately. I know you won't control anything in a minute because of the blood."

Claws slid out; Georgie hid his hands, catching Ellena's eyes. Georgie didn't want to freak her out, let alone Locke find out. He watched helplessly. Georgie was about to try his luck but got hit by a thunderbolt of pain, dropping to his knees. His hands were in sawdust; they'd changed.

'It's okay, Georgie. Let it happen,' Ellena whispers, tears trickling. "I...I... I can't," Georgie struggles, bones breaking around us.

'It's okay, I know... I trust you,' she whispered. Locke nodded in approval. Did he know too? The pain had Georgie wanting to scream; instead, a roar as his fangs grew, shaking the warehouse. Melanie stepped back with fear.

He saw red until his vision settled—beads of sweat on Melanie's forehead. The Kanaima's eyes held black streaks in green. Jack was conflicted. The human side was scared for his life. Georgie was changing, but he had to hang on, halt it. The demon side assimilated with the wolf; heightened wouldn't do justice.

Power surged, and Georgie sensed Melanie's fear for the first time. There was a vibration in her throat, and her pupils darted, seeking exits.

"Don't be stupid, Georgie," Melanie quivered. Jack worried, flaws fluctuating. Now was his time. Lights off again, darkness. He flew past, yanking drips out, landing on the platform, knocking Kanaima and me apart. The lights are back on. We'd landed feet apart; I'd forced Kanaima's claws into its abdomen, injecting its toxin. Hoping the books were true.

Georgie dragged his angry self from the dust, looking up. Melanie stood over my body—blood pissing from my throat. The Kanaima ripped it out. I remember feeling so cold, ever so quickly. Shock mixed with the realisation I may have had my last done. I was choking on blood, trying to talk, trying to tell my friends that I regretted nothing about being wrapped in this new, dark world. I couldn't.

My body writhed as sawdust soaked the pool of blood. "Aww, you killed the 30 seconds, man. Tut tut. Another lesson I learned from the books. Always have a Plan B," she says, holding the remote. "Don't do it. The game is over."

"Not yet; it ain't. While you decide who to save, I'll take that key and be on my way," Melanie says. The button compressed. A blast of wind; the Kanaima was still stricken. Who would've thought how much joy hearing four little words could bring?

'Hey-up Georgie, lad,'

Georgie turned toward the booming echo of his old Skipper and 'Beta' Andy Morris. "What the hell, how?" Georgie gushes.

"I heard you call, so I came. Now save them," he beamed.

My skin turned pale, lying in a pool of blood slipping away. To the tables behind were two other drips rigged with toxin; Melanie assumed the obvious. Georgie ripped the needles out and flipped the tables flat, tearing through the straps. Returning to me, I was dying, and Georgie didn't know what to do. I'd lost so much blood we'd never reach the hospital in time.

"Skip. Please... tell me how," Georgie pleads. We stopped Melanie, but it's cost Michael his life. I was helpless and drowning.

"Bite him, lad; there's no other way," he says, gripping Melanie tight. I looked at her face, and the rage inside me wanted him to do it.

"I can't; what will everyone see of me?" Georgie screeched.

"You can save him, lad," says Skip.

"It's okay, Georgie," Ellena whispered. Locke stared. He was the unknown.

"Do it, George. Save him; we don't have long," Locke surprised Georgie.

He grabbed my arm; the pool grew, and my heart slowed to the last beat. 'Fuck it', before biting deep into my arm. His fangs pierced my skin and flesh, nicking a vein. A small spray of blood spurted over Georgie's face as he held on. His eyes blazed red, brighter than ever before. Every fibre in his body was alive with blood lust.

"That's enough, Georgie," Skip pleads. Instead, Georgie bit a little harder, causing me to squirm.

Air grazed past; Ellena came to our side, gently touching Georgie's neck. Her face breezed close, lips inches from his ear.

"That's enough, Georgie; let go now. I'm here for you," she cooed into his ear. Her words echoed, a bewitching effect. Georgie's jaw loosened, his eyes dimmed, and he slowly let go, falling backwards, feeling ashamed.

"I'm here for you," she whispers. Georgie tried to hide his face, but Ellena had none of it. She gripped his clawed hands, looking at him deeply with a caring smile. 'You don't need to hide anymore,' she whispered.

I groaned; my neck had healed. I could feel life ebbing back and then some. Colour seeped back into my skin. It was working. My veins were on fire, everything seemed to be repairing, and little knocks and issues I had endured through a long life were mending and getting stronger. I was getting stronger. I felt like a bloody kid again, from nearly dying to exhilaration.

"What the hell happened?" I croaked.

"You were all but dead. Now stop lying around; come arrest this bitch, will you?" Skip boomed, rocking me to my senses.

"What? Really?" I say, gathering myself.

"Yeah, Georgie saved you; he saved us all," Locke interrupts, lumbering up.

"So, you had to bite me? Does that mean I must be flea and wormed every month now?" I say, finding the energy to joke.

It was nearly midnight, and Georgie's problems were far from over as the demon gradually took hold of his body. The Kanaima stirred, and everyone stepped back. That smell of death was still here. The Kanaima dragged out its claws. Georgie was about to jump up when a surge of electricity rippled through the lights, and clouds of black smoke breezed through, causing panic.

As easily as they disappeared the other day, those two demons reappeared.

"Don't fear. We mean no harm," says the one in khaki trousers.

"What do you want?" I say.

"To take the Kanaima back to where it belongs,"

"We are its guardians, making sure it stays imprisoned. It cannot be killed but can be trapped in this." They showed a relic, the one Melanie stole.

"How?"

"That's for us to know. These people disturbed a sacred crypt with their greed, bringing death. The last time cost thousands of lives, so count yourself lucky."

"How will you do it?" Georgie says, feeling confused.

"Like this," in a swift move, the demon in jeans drove a dagger into Jack's stomach. Black smoke arose from Jack and poured into the gem. They slotted the gem into the base of the relic. The demons vanished again in black clouds, leaving us speechless and Georgie dropping backwards in a painful daze.

It was finally over, except for Georgie. An alarm signalled midnight. 'The witching hour.' My body would explode; it took me to be on all fours. Bones were cracking, blood was boiling, and there was a hunger like no other. Making everyone around him his prey. I know I was scared. Until a sharp needle jammed into his neck. Ellena grabbed the paralytic needle to nullify him until it was over. She whispers, 'Sorry,' Georgie drops to the floor, watching the world fade into darkness. I was so relieved and still understanding how my body was feeling.

It was over, and we'd stopped a serial killing demon, and I'd survived. I could finally rest, heavy eyelids flapping shut. Battling in the shadows against something nobody would know about, at least for now.

This case, our first as a new team, was betrayed by someone we least expected for horrific reasons, if true. Battered, bruised, and a little bloodied. Okay, a lot bloodied. We had to dig deep, being pushed to our limits.

Now, the fallout. We beat the clock, and the future would be the only way of knowing how different I am. The darkness is where we live now because this world isn't the same as it once was. All the while, the circle of who kept our secrets had grown. That bite saved and changed my life in ways I can't put into words, but our fight to stop the darkness from taking over continues, and I will fight for the good people until the end. Staring at my blood on the floor, feeling lucky to be alive, everything began crumbling and changing. Before long, I was waking up in the tunnel with Georgie standing over me. Gerald was still out with Nathan.

'Gerald'

Well, that wasn't in the brochure; that smoke or chemical cloud had us all out in seconds. I've woken in darkness, and I smell cigars. I'm in a house—my grandparents' house, full of musk and staleness that comes with their age. I've ended up in a room. It's their spare bedroom from when I used to sleep over. A glimmer of moonlight ripples through the curtains, catching the far-right side of the room. There's me, the young version of me, at least. I'm no older than twelve. The clock on the wall shows a little after 1:30 a.m., and I have to say, this scenario confuses me.

There is little I remember from then, and nothing jumps out. I look peacefully snuggled beneath my 'Batman' duvet cover. Most of the room is quite bland, except the walls are boyish blue. More posters pay homage to the same 'dark knight' that keeps me warm. A football and a cricket bat are in the corner, and a tiny television sits on the dresser. Still, I'm searching for answers, wondering why I was here and now. We were running out of time to save Nathan. Assuming we could. If that toxin overpowered a werewolf, my faith was being tested.

Any minute now, I muttered, hoping, then I saw the ripple of a shadow moving through the hallway. Thanks to a dim light at the bottom of the stairs, I barely caught it. It was tall, like a man, unless I was seeing things, another hallucination, hoping to see something to end this situation. There's silence, and then a crash, caused by a lamp being knocked over and the bulb exploding. A scream from Nanna followed that drama, and then Grandad shouted, too inaudible to understand but loud enough to shake the young me awake.

My pale blonde hair swung across my bleary eyes and quickly brushed out of the way as another shout rang out. Young me jumped out of bed in matching Batman pyjamas, dashing for the cricket bat and out of the door. I followed my little legs, still not remembering any of this. Their bedroom is at the end of the hallway, their light on, and I can see a shadow looming by the doorway. Young me had no fear. Charging headstrong into the bedroom, we barely broke stride over the threshold. I'm stunned. It's the 'whispering man.' He's stood over my grandparents, huddled in bed, facing down the sharp end of a sword. His deathly face had wisps of charcoal flesh peeling from his jawbone. How did this not terrify me back then? Perhaps that's why I couldn't remember.

The 'whispering man' turned to see young me, his demonic eyes piercing its deep, garish red through to my soul. His dirty trilby stank of dead blood, its peak casting a shadow across his haunting, menacing face. At least a metre long, a gleaming mix of metals. I smelled sulfur and then that potent toxin that was ripping through Nathan as I endured this 'trial or test.' What else could it be?

The 'whispering man' smiled before plunging the sword forward. Young me jumped through the air, landing on the bed. My little arms wielded that cricket bat like a sword, too. It windmilled through the air, overhand, crashing down on the sword mid-plunge. The sword veered wide, burying into the headboard, but the bat followed through, and as the sword bounced and bowed before snapping, metal shards splintered through the air. Shocked, the 'whispering man' turned, retreating. "Death will come soon enough," he said, becoming a blur out the door.

Young me saved my grandparents and locked away the memory. The sword's tip still wobbled in the headboard before crumbling away, infecting everything it connected to. My grandparents, young me, and then the room all disappeared. I was back in the tunnels. Michael and George stood over me, waiting.

"About bloody time, matey," Michael said, looking at his watch.

"Sorry, but I had no idea what was going on."

"Well, we need to move. Since our little experiences, the twenty-four hours are nearly up." I was stunned, quickly hoisting Nathan to his feet. How the hell had we lost so much time? All the smoke was gone, and a clear path awaited. We all went through something, but none of us spoke of it. Instead, it weighed us down as we trudged toward destiny or hell.

Light will come from Dark

45

'Gerald'

A dead end. Nothing but thick grey stone. Did we do this for nothing? Wasting time that could've been spent trying to save Nathan. By doing something, we stood a slim chance of succeeding. Michael and George searched every inch in the thin hope of another way.

I was listening; the only good thing I could do was hear echoes, drips, and footsteps. Still, that image stuck in my mind. The 'whispering man' trying to kill my grandparents. Thick moss was everywhere, but vine leaves only grew in one spot, the far left wall beside the dead end.

If the smoke scenario taught me anything, these 'Templars' liked games and tests. Nothing is ever as it seems. Much like our grimy, bloody village. How the hell are we going to put all the 'undead' genies back in the bottle? How do we come back from this? Any ideas? If so, scribe it in blood somewhere; we'll stumble across it, eventually. Hell, be artistic and make it out-of-body parts; there's enough to go around.

I'm following the vines, seeing where they lead. They had to go somewhere, and they looked likely to be up. The damp swarmed the upper corner, swelling over a jagged cluster almost resembling an angry face. Who could blame it, like a mushroom kept in the dark? Does that make us mushrooms, too? As we're always surrounded by darkness.

It was the rocky pattern to the right of it that grabbed my attention the most. A strip straight to the floor, it was much lighter than the rest and dryer, too, as if warmer. I nearly forgot my vision was enhanced until a timely reminder.

'What you see isn't, what is'. The chill still gets me, and so does the weepy tone; it wouldn't be so bad if he cheered the fuck up a bit. I hadn't dared to ask if it was the same one I saw in my grandparents' room. It couldn't be, could it? Perhaps a conversation for later, if we survive. How bloody cryptic, though.

It wasn't just the dry strip, though. My head lurched from side to side, doing some weird dance with my head enough to get Michael's attention. Who stared at me, confused? I wasn't losing my mind; that may have already happened. The rocks had a pattern along that strip, which was easily missed. I guess that's the point. When you look face on, nothing, a little to either side, and you see steps. I couldn't tell how wide, but they went up, fading into black.

"Guys, check that wall; looks like steps," I say, getting George's attention too. They both moved close with their glowing eyes. Another weird thing that gets to me. Will anything be normal again?

"He's right. It goes up, matey. A hatch of some kind made of stone." Michael says, glancing at George. Who, judging by the constipated expression, was trying to work out the logistics.

"Right, Michael, you head up, open the hatch, then reach down to me, and I hoist Nathan up for you to drag through. Remember to go easy; he's fragile," George says, formulating as good a plan as any. That's the difference between us 'mundanes' and the supernatural. Fragile. Perhaps we should carry signs, 'careful we break easy'. However, the least we needed was Michael sending Nathan. Tossed around like a rag-doll, through the air or smashing his head on the roof.

It was all going too well. The scared part of me was expecting trouble. For us to be blindsided. Like the 'young me', only less bravado. I wish I knew where all that went. I needed it in spades now. They were through; I was dragging myself up slowly, cold stone scraping through palm flesh. My head finally popped through the hatch, thrashed by a wave of cold, dead air. No other way to put it, 'dead', stale, pungent swirls. It's dark; I hear footsteps pacing frantically. Judging by the short gate, it's Michael, looking for a light, I assumed.

With a flicker and a clicking of a lighter, Michael found a candle. Its warming aura adds a touch of 'spooky' lashing around an immense room. More a museum or art gallery. Wall to wall of stone, suits of armour, weapons and statues. I'm looking, but felt it was nothing more than a 'Templar' façade—a shell. I was expecting another twist, finally, up amongst the relics and all the 'Templar' stuff. Nathan was rested on a bench; everything else looked ready to fall apart if they ever saw the light of day again. On another occasion, I may have even found it amazing. Instead, I expected one of those creepy knights to poke his 'dead' head out of the shadows.

There are more pillars, but no fake doors, no 'Christ' on a cross, and the floor is flagstone until I see six man-sized and detailed tombs seamlessly blended four feet up. They represented KNIGHTS, dressed in armour with a 'templar' symbol on their chests, hands clutching swords. With every second of information I took, a sudden realisation hit me: another puzzle. Starting back at the pillars, there were only five or twelve statues, three suits of armour and six tombs. There are so many more. What combination and where did they go? The altar to the far right had four-digit dials, all showing zero.

"It's a number game," I say. George breezed close, looking from my viewpoint.

"I see what you mean. Not what you think, though. It's too obvious and too many; the combination could be anything." George says he was right, of course. Who was I to think it would be that obvious?

"Look, on the tombs, there's a small number three on that one's chest," I say, pointing to the fourth knight in the bank of six. George spins on the spot, and Michael, too.

"There, the statues on the back wall, the statues opposite the tombs, a seven down on an ankle," Michael says; that meant two digits out of four. In what order, though?

"One has a 'two' on it by the doors, the shields, the centre of the stack." George ran over to be sure. We had two, three and seven.

"Quick, there, 3 o'clock, the flag mounted to the wall, a nine in the corner," Michael says. We had four digits, but in what order?

"Now what, play lucky dip?" George says in jest, but it felt…

"Wait, Michael, you said 3 o'clock. It's all a bloody clock. Look how it's all positioned." I say, noticing there was a grouping of artefacts at every clock point: conveniently, six tombs at 6 o'clock, statues at twelve, and so on.

"So we enter them clockwise, right? Two, seven, nine, three." George says, looking at me with eyes raised. I wasn't getting the impression they wanted me to test it. Bit of a joke, considering they can heal. I'm a bloody mundane, for Christ's sake.

Well, I may struggle with my fears and be haunted by the 'whispering man'. Come to think of it, I'm not a fan of the dark, eerie shadows, death, the Walking Dead or those creepy knights. That's quite a list without thinking too. Deep. That little 'boat' weaving through the 'sanity river' feels more like a battleship with each passing hour—small steps, feeling the hard stone beneath me as if vibrating into my soles. I heard every heartbeat; Nathan was barely a blip. Rodents scurried between limestone crevices, and the wind howled outside. A ferocious, intimidating beast on the rampage, looking for weaknesses and a way in. This room may be stone, and the doors re-enforced iron; the surrounding cocoon whistled like timbers yawning and crying at the torture.

An unrelenting assault, roaring, wanting to tip us on edge, wanting us to feel every nerve as it shreds by the ticking seconds. I looked at my watch. We had less than thirty minutes left to save Nathan, and we still didn't have the other piece. Let alone know where Father hid his. Tentative step after step, daydreaming on the watch face, thinking Father. He wondered what he would do in this situation or if he had any inkling that this could be the future. The nearer I was to the altar, the more the watch went crazy. First, it stopped, and I shook it like a madman, thinking, 'Rolex's' didn't do that. Then, the arms spun wildly in reverse before landing at the original time.

It made no sense, much like most of the horror that's unfolded or weaved through my life. Father told me on the tapes that our bloodlines were cursed. Is that why I could see 'death' all these years, or was there more to me? Nathan's father alluded to a Plan B, someone strong enough to break free from these 'evil shackles'. I can't shake what happened in the tunnels. I'm stalling near the altar, searching through Nanna's encyclopaedia of stories to see if any may have been that awful night.

'Did you know nobody moves on?' Nanna says. 'They all stay behind the curtain, waiting to peek at us when we sleep. They hover over us with long, pointy fingers of wrath. Hoping one of them can see and feel their torment'. She'd say. 'Our house has had a few. Yours too, I've seen them. I've seen a lot of things. My mother called it a 'gift', able to see both sides of the curtain. Imagine walking into the bloomin bakery, only to see my great aunt Agnes cutting bread. That silly woman stripped down some stairs at work and broke her neck twenty hundred years ago. Nanna said she always sounded like she was telling a few stories at once, and her years were a jumbled mess.

'Two', I spun the dial until the magic number. I heard nothing, no click, nothing. I don't know what I was expecting, but surely something.

'Seven'. The next one is done, but still no click.

'Nine'. Again, nothing. I looked at the others; Michael was pacing. George raked his fingers through his hair, and his face blushed red. Nathan looked greyer, knocking on 'death's door' with a sledgehammer. His breathing was erratic, sharp, struggling, and shallow. My hearing was laser-focused, his lungs were full of mucus, and I could hear the toxins ripping a pathway through every vein, artery, chamber, atrium, and god knows what else. A battle ensued with my best friend, and he was losing. His chest bounced like a vibrating bass drum; a curious little corded chain slipped from beneath his top, an odd vial in an hourglass frame without split chambers. The fluid was bright red, akin to fresh blood, and resting on it on a pearlescent back. You heard that correct liquid resting on another—oil on water.

Maybe it was something their family was into, carrying a piece of each other with them. Or belonged to his actual parents. If that last act of bravado from Nathan's father was true. Still, that trinket was mesmerising, of all moments, for it to catch my eye. 'No. You can't, we won't. Anyway, did you think there wouldn't be a backup plan? We know there's one of us strong enough to break the curse, break what they're meant to become and will use it to stop your stupid, reckless and suicidal plan.'

I replayed the words again. They were two statements, not one speech—a backup plan. Then, we know there's one of us strong enough to break the curse, break what they're meant to become and will use it to stop your stupid, reckless and suicidal plan. It was a two-pronged jab at the 'killer'. Could that weird liquid be a backup plan and involve Nathan? How was my brain even making such drastic leaps? It could simply be a harmless trinket that caught Nathan's eye. The tiny remaining, rational 'grey-matter' was looking for bright 'silver linings' within that 'near-constant haunted cloud'. We needed a Hail Mary.

'Here goes nothing', I mutter, getting back to task. 'Three', I held my breath; my chest ached to the point of burning, tensing my stomach, expecting something, anything. I don't know… Like a statue coming to life or a tomb pops open to reveal what we seek. Then… A faint hiss in the background, not the wind outside. From the pipes running throughout the perimeter. Then 'whoosh' air burst out, only it wasn't fair, another cloud, this time 'lilac', quickly filling the space above in a thick fog like a bitter-smelling cloud. We fell into a trap. It was a simple mistake; perhaps the sequence was too obvious. Michael and George were already detecting what it was, covering their mouths while throwing themselves as close to the floor as possible. Neither spoke, too scared to bother in case they inhaled the cloud.

I was stuck. Nathan would usually be my soundboard, but I sure as hell wasn't asking the voices in my head. I know that sounds equally crazy. Frantically, I ran the numbers again, the positioning going 'clockwise'. It had to be the code. True to 'Templar' puzzlement, it carried a sting. A rare lightbulb moment happened. I looked at my watch, moved it close, and it spun again in reverse.

'In reverse', I mutter, spinning the dials, 'three, nine, seven, two'. This time, a click. A loud reverberating click. The pipes closed immediately, and a vacuum kicked in, inhaling the cloud away within seconds. Michael and George scrape themselves off the floor, uncovering their faces. Both were shellshocked, none more so than me. I pissed in the wind, and luckily, the winds had changed just in time—all thanks to Father's watch. I like to think he was with me at that moment. He sent the watch crazy, a hint at what to do, but it probably wasn't; I like my version better.

"Well?" Michael says impatiently. I understood the reasoning but not the timing. That was all on me, and for want of a better phrase, I pulled a fucking rabbit out of the hat. Obviously, not really fucking. Now, that would be rubbish timing. In all seriousness, I was flying by the seat of my 'scared' pants, and they were turning fifty shades of brown at the minute. I'm still sitting by the altar, emotionally and mentally drained. I can hear 'cogs' whirring—not the tired, rusty ones in my head. First, within the altar, then somewhere under the floor ten feet from me, a gap similar to the others. My sweaty face was inches from the dials, and I wished I could rest and catch a break.

'Pssssst.' I hear it. It's ominously quiet, the noise a mundane uses to get another's attention without drawing attention. I'm looking slowly, doing just that, trying not to get attention or cause worry. It was close, that much I was certain. Dare I say it, from behind the dials. My gaze lingers on the dials momentarily. I see dust peacefully drifting. A thin sheet of mist. However, it appears to change direction. Another hallucination? I wondered. Nothing was off the table these days. There was something cosmic about it. Anyone who likes to read up on planets can see some have misty rings around them. Don't ask me which; I'm not one of those stargazers, but I've seen a few pictures. Anyway, it looked like that, and it was looping towards me.

There was plenty of time to move; I should have. Again, it's the little things that draw me in. The details other mundanes overlook. So I didn't move. It's almost a Schrödinger's cat moment. Leave the box closed and, in my case, move away. In my mind, the cat is alive, and this mist is nothing. Or open the box to see, likely knowing the cat is dead, and I allow the mist to come and see what makes it change direction for me. I opened the box, and the mist dazzled my eyes. I've never done drugs, but I imagined the sudden lightheaded, spaced-out feeling was what it could be like. (Step away from the drugs, kids. Drugs are bad.). Everything is hazy. Okay, it's like a mist wrapped around my eyeballs.

My foot slips lazily across the stone floor; I hear gravel. I'm relying on other senses as my eyes slowly clear. Blood swims through the air, lots of it. My stomach turns; I drag my foot back but knock on something else. It rattles across the floor; it's long. I can almost see a faint white and black outline. It's bone. Beside it is a round object of the same colour. Oh my god, it's a skull. A mundane skull. I stood, shaky but stable enough when I can finally see...

My eyes twitched. A deep, soul-disturbing burning began through my optic nerves. It pulsated to behind my eyeballs. A fire sparked. None of that happy campfire stuff. This was a raging forest blaze engulfing the blood-red flesh lining around the sockets and lids. The whites bubbled and boiled until a bloody-white goo melted, oozing from my sockets until nothing but the nerve ends were left, swinging in the breeze. The horror before me was that evocatively sickening.

As far as I dared or could see. What was once a mundane village, varying blankets of gloom, had become a terrifying swamp of blood. That 'Willen River' flowed over, drenching normality and anything that used to resemble tragic, mundane life. That boat drifted freely through the blood-covered streets, crunching through the endless jumble of skeletons strewn, having been stripped at an all-you-can-kill buffet.

A crunch rattled beneath me with every step, and a horrific sound wormed through my ears. In the distance, wading through intestines, bladders, and the copious other organs, a stumbling army of 'undead' ripping other mundanes apart. Anyone that dared rebel. Army tanks lay impaled in shops and homes. A line of those creepy knights flanked the dead and sat atop equally striking horses in all the worst ways. Red eyes blazed from horse and creep alike, piercing a brooding black sky lit by a blood-red moon. Their gaze fixed in my direction.

A heavy rumble roared through the soaked ground beneath; I was wobbling, barely keeping on my feet. There were no fault lines anywhere near here and none through the U.K. that I knew of. The first fracture was slight, easily tearing through the sidewalk on my right, allowing a luminescent purple-red glow to break free, throbbing. The ground was alive; the fracture grew, and the loud crunching of stone struggled to outstrip the haunting of bone ripping. That fracture destroyed phone booths, benches, and any street furniture in its path.

A shiver and a curdle of my blood drained my energy to my feet and rooted me to the spot. My life was tormented by the 'whispering man' and twisted by what Nanna called a 'gift.' Able to see both sides of the curtain. Nothing prepared me for this. Out of that fracture slithered black clouds with red eyes: smoking, swirling clouds of evil. Demons were breaking out of hell, and with everyone that tore loose, the fractures grew, gathering speed, splintering more and more like a menacing tree, shredding a path to bring hell on earth. I can't do this; I can't be a part of causing or dragged into the middle of this if that's what's coming. My daughters already lost their mother; I lost my wife and a father because someone thought it would be a great idea to 'shake things up a little.' There's so much death, so much evil. Sulphur is so strong that it's squeezing the life out of my lungs. All this blood before me, surely it can't be true.

What if it's a result of our meddling, not evil winning? We could surrender, and they'd spare most mundanes. That could work, right? I'm soaking in the horror, watched by the evil knights, streets littered with death and bones… Who am I kidding…Whether we want it, this is coming on the wings of fury. I may only be mundane, with no strength, speed, or anything like Michael or George, but if they're willing to face all this without a moment of thought, how can I turn and run? Even if I reached my girls safely, I'd never be able to look them in the eyes and say I did everything I could to save their future. Save everyone's future. Hell will come, and we will meet it head-on. That thought spun through my brain, watching in terror as the massacre unfolded. The whole time, it felt like a standoff.

Could they see me? Or was my fear making me paranoid? I nearly had the second option locked in when faint whistling travelled on the 'bloody breeze'; even that sounded fucking scary. Every hair on my body was on end, and I mean EVERY hair…That torturing whistle soon took a turn for the worse. Tears swelled in the corners of my bleeding eyes, my heart throbbed, clutching my breath in my throat. It was Charlotte's voice again. Rippling in the wind, I could feel my heart breaking again.

'Hush, little baby, don't say a word. Mama's gonna buy you a mockingbird.'
'And if that mockingbird doesn't sing. Mama's gonna buy you a diamond ring.'
'And if that diamond ring turns brass. Mama's gonna buy you a looking glass.'
'And if that looking glass gets broke. Mama's gonna buy you a billy goat.'

By the time Charlotte sang the fourth verse, the knights kicked into the sides of their demonic horses, nothing but bone, flaking skin, and a blood-coloured fire acting as their lungs within decayed rib cages. Those sick bastards had to have seen me; they charged towards me with sinister intent, and I still couldn't move. I was stranded amidst a nightmarish crimson sea, and that 'tiny boat' was thriving in my turmoil. With nowhere to go, I felt like a 'mundane kite' twisting adrift in a hurricane of evil. Horse hooves blazed a path of hellfire, flying at me. The knights drew their swords, gleaming under the red moon. Each thrust aloft and then to the front. Thunder savagely tore through the broken streets, their galloping pounding the brittle stone beneath, closing in.

Was this it? Had I been fed to the demonic wolves, a last roll of the dice from the Templars, as a sacrificial lamb? Surely not. I tried summoning the darkness within. Nothing. I was all alone. Something I'd got used to, this though, wasn't how I expected it to go down.

'Thump, thump, thump,' came the gallops. My heart screamed for help, screamed for it to be quick. The deadly line of evil flew at me, deafened by the pounding. All I could do was close my eyes and hold them tight, just as their swords rampaged within a couple of inches. Wind tore through me, but that's all I felt. Daring to open my eyes, my gaze met a whirlwind of sulphur and pain. Not theirs. It was akin to a million screams at once, all melded within them. Moments like these are hard to describe as mundane and not well-versed. I can only imagine and dread what the detectives have been through.

The nearest way to put it is, as well as the screams and pain. I almost felt who and what they were, names being hollered, calling for help. Tormented souls cannot get to where they should be. If I guessed, over the centuries, these things would kill and would immediately absorb their essence. No doubt making the knights stronger. Every single one, all tearing through me. Victims were ripped apart and swallowed up. Sick bastards—the mundanes' souls, all of their emotions. There is so much torment. It wasn't fair. No one deserves to suffer in life and after death.

No sooner had I felt the last pass through; everything changed a lot quicker this time. I was crying, full-on sobbing; the pain lingered. Their fingerprints in life. Everything was back to normal and with the others. I couldn't stop, as if they were still travelling through me. Is that even possible? Each soul toyed with every fibre of my being. I haven't felt it. Torture. I didn't speak, I couldn't. How could I put all that evil, blood, and death into words without destroying what fragile hope we had?

Not much had happened when I endured that preview, premonition, or a scary glimpse of everything we feared could happen. I'm sitting in the same place, cold stone seeping a chill through my flesh. Another downside of being mundane, unlike George and those like him. They don't seem bothered by trivial details like that.

I still felt the aftereffects of all those souls using me as a waypoint. So much blood and death. How was I going to break the news? Nathan had less than fifteen minutes now.

"Right, we've dodged another bullet and completed this fancy puzzle. What the hell happens next?" Michael says, calling to me, yanking me from those gory thoughts. I'm getting sick of them using Charlotte to taunt me and that flipping nursery rhyme of all things. The girls loved that, and Charlotte had it down to a nightly ritual—one of the few normal regularities in Willowbrook.

As if by magic or just the next phase in the cycle of the Templars dangling the carrot in front of us. Which is getting rather annoying. Besides, I'm not a fan of carrots or much of any veg, to be honest. I'll stomach peas and broccoli at a push and only after a lecture from Mother, as always. I hear those cogs whirring again ahead of me. One large flagstone in the centre of the grouping and in line with the path to the main doors began rumbling. I saw a thin veil of dirt and dust jumping with each rumbling. There's no cement lining the perimeter, unlike the rest—stone grated against stone. There's movement.

The whole slab is rising slowly, still rumbling, showering the air with pent-up nostalgia, history and more dust that cut a distinct feeling in the back of my throat. A little sickly for my liking, the others too. The price we pay to know still, absolutely fuck, all about what to do next. An old and heavy-looking stone pedestal stuttered its way above ground.

"Is this some bloody joke, matey boy? There are 10 minutes to live and not a prostitute in sight for a 'happy ending'. There's dead roaming the streets, and some creepy fuckers want this guy for some reason. And this is what we get? A fucking fortune cookie riddle." Michael says, red-faced and pissed off. I get it. On top of the pedestal, there's an engraved plaque slotted within the surface. I see a slight glow, a gleam of light forcing its way out from the edges.

'Light will come from the dark. One less than whole possesses the 'might' to rise for the fight. The prize is granted to thee, with the fortitude to climb from the ashes of death and embrace the 'Knight'. What lurks as evil in the haunting black can shine against all in the white.'

George paced side to side, his eyes glowing bright red. He was checking every angle of the pedestal, clutching his chin, thinking. The cryptic verse had me as confused as ever. A constant state for me these days. All was quiet except Nathan's erratic, clammy breathing. He was close to gone. I saw the movie 'The Living Dead'. How quickly the assistant declined after inhaling the fumes from the 'dead guy' drum: the clammy 'dead' grey, the blackened mouth, thick black rings around sunken ghostly eyes. Every juddering breath produced white vapour plumes. His skin was shrinking, thinning as if bodily fluids like water beneath the flesh rapidly evaporated.

"He hasn't got long," George says, glancing at me.

"I know, less than ten minutes."

"That's not what I meant. Use your enhanced sense. Focus on the surrounding smells; picture them like an IMAX cinema. So overwhelmingly strong but tangible, you can move through them like objects, shoving one after the other out of the way until you find your target. In this case, Nathan. You'll see what I mean," George says, whispering with a touch of resignation in his voice. He was only saying what I'd been too scared to acknowledge.

Closing my eyes, I did just that: focussed, inhaled and meandered through the vibrant jungle of aromas until Nathan. Rotting. Nathan was rotting from the inside out. His organs were slowly dying. I could hear each one tightening. Veins, fibres, ligaments, and stomach lining were all decaying. Suppose I was asked to describe the metamorphoses as a feeling or emotion. It was as if all the joy and colour had been sucked out of life. Everything is bland and tasteless, a million shades of grey: no fun, no happiness, just death.

"Fuck... Ere Gerald, that's got to be for you. You know, fate and all that malarky. All the clues and talk of one from your bloodline nonsense, being strong enough to change things. Especially if you lot are descending from them Templar arseholes." Michael says. Looking pleased with himself, my guess is George does most of the thinking for him. Not in a bad way, but seems more clued up on all this dark stuff.

He was on to an idea, though, aside from being highly coincidental. Judging by the flagstones, nothing had been touched in a long while. How would they know? I moved closer, hovering my hand near. I'm staring at the words but not taking any of it in. Have you ever had that? Stare so long at something that your eyes get foggy. Except there was no fog. I was captivated. The nearer my hand moved, the glow around the edges pulsed. Getting quicker and quicker. All eyes were on me.

Cold metal sent a chill through my fingertips. Everything was silent. My head was in an empty black room... Nothing but the quick beating of my heart. Static rippled through my fingers. I could feel the tiny hairs on my arms buzz, trembling over the unknown. My fingers trace each letter, lighting it up like the pulsing glow—word after word. I look at the detectives for reassurance, hoping they'd steady my nerves.

It's darkness...

Each breath was a flurry of white cloud...My brain citing each word off by heart, 'The prize is granted to thee, with the fortitude to climb from the ashes of death and embrace the 'Knight'.' Stood out, mulling over 'embrace the Knight' and that particular spelling.

'Hush, little Gerald, don't say a word. You'll never see mumma again to get that mockingbird.'

'And when that mockingbird don't sing. Death will come for everyone you're missing. Charlotte's voice cut through the darkness and deep into my bones. Terrifyingly cold and gargled. My thoughts jump to the girls, hoping by me not knowing the location. The evil Knights couldn't find them either. My hand wouldn't stop shaking, searching for any hint there could be a secret button. The door in the pillar has me questioning everything now. Still, nothing moves. I reach the last part, having gone over the rest. Trail from the last letter, there's a click. I feel the plate shudder against my hand. I jump, and the plate lifts. There's a wooden box. Exquisitely carved with sigils that I recognised but can't place. The wood is dark, an 'Ash' of some kind, has a sweet smell, is slightly floral, and is strong enough that Michael and George are backing away.

I grab the box. It's heavy, but in my haste, I didn't think about the true 'Templar' theatrics. Air whistled, and cogs spun. First, the shields shook, and several fell, clattering to the floor, making Michael jump like a cat on a hot tin roof. Statues wobbled, and then the whole room shook. A loud squealing set the tone before we felt movement. We were on tracks—steel ground against steel. Michael and George displayed the worry I felt.

"This ain't good. I didn't think we were still underground." George says, looking at the doors. He was probably wondering what I was. Were they even real? I heard the wind whistling earlier, giving the impression of a normal room. Okay, as normal as it gets.

"I reckon we should get our game faces on." Michael flicked out his hands, they instantly became furry with his sharp claws, while his face morphed to the fox, his body more muscular and a yellow strobe grew around him, continuing until formed the outline of a large fox, at least seven foot tall, wrapping over Michael like a shield. I hadn't seen this yet, not properly. It was amazing and scary. I wouldn't want to tangle with him, that's for sure.

George was next, far more intimidating, size, fangs, claws, the works. It's the eyes though, deeply disturbing red. I still can't get over seeing him fully phase to a wolf when we escaped the farm. All I could hope for was that the toxin was fully out of his system. We eventually ground to a halt, loud grinding of metal, before a flurry of metal sliding bolts triggered, releasing the doors. The detectives simultaneously reached for the backs of their necks... Trouble.

Time Fly's

46

'Gerald'

Michael hoisted Nathan on my shoulder, with the box tucked under my free arm. He and George stayed in front as we moved. I hadn't dared look inside the box yet, us stopping, and Nathan's slower, wheezing breaths distracted me. Not too much the early warning system from the detectives. The doors swung open, sounding like a strangled cat. (Disclaimer: I never have ever done that or seen it done, nor would I condone it) but boy, have I heard them fight, high-pitched squealing, loud enough to make my ears bleed. Great, we're mushrooms again. It's dark.

Twenty-four hours have nearly gone in the blink of an eye. We were still in Kingsley, by the looks of it, a lot further in. For Christ's sake, another farm. The room we travelled in slotted neatly into a large rustic garage; anyone looking in would be none the wiser, and no doubt the room would travel back as soon as we exited. We sat ducks with too many run-down buildings and street debris to hide behind. For all we knew, the place was surrounded, waiting. Those creeps have been on our trail throughout, and that raven in the church did a number on me. I imagine they already knew of this place, but something stops them from getting access. This means I was the puppet on strings, and Nathan was paying with his life. The detectives were on edge, trying not to make me worry; they were ruffled. I'd rarely seen either of these knocked out of their stride, even when George endured the toxin. Michael remained calm, and the pair even joked. Now, though, they seemed to be 'touching cloth', and that's not good.

A sudden change in the wind brought it howling our way, with it the unmistakable 'Eau de death', followed by the latest in 'killer-sheek', 'Eau de blood', and for those little special occasions, 'Eau de sulphur'. Michael tilts his head, inhaling. George's eyes blazed a more blood red now, scanning the shadows. I see further, but I didn't know how much longer. I wished mine were a bit more fancy and would change colour like George's, maybe allow me to see different heat signatures. At least if mine went red or even yellow like Michael's, I could pretend to belong. Fake it until you make it, right? It's a bit like me feigning normalcy for years. You could say that ship has well and truly sailed. Likely on its way down the swollen 'Willen River' with my good friend 'the tiny boat', AKA 'HMS Fear'.

Jokes aside. A lot of death is coming, and I feared how the cards lay once the dust settles. That peek behind the curtain has me rattled. Even now, looking at the dry, muddy rubble stretch before us and the uneven track littered with creaking flared trees yawning their arm-like branches to the chaotic winds. There are flickers and sporadic flash images of blood. Bones, pungent blackened organs and shredded flesh were used for nothing more than stepping stones amongst the crimson canvas. Intestines stretch purposefully from the lowest muscular 'oak' forearm, creating a swing with a seat from stretched torso flesh.

This is a nightmare view suited to any horror movie. Bordered by a sky, I didn't think it could get any darker. How wrong was I? A blanket of wings, whipping the chilly air, swooped in from beyond the semi-peaceful horizon. That haunting, piercing blue set the ominous mood lighting of impending doom.

My throat squelched at the swell of saliva I hadn't dared to swallow out of fear of being heard. My heart set the anxiety rhythm throbbing between my ears. Nathan was now dead weight, flopped across my shoulders, his clammy flesh now a deathly cold. He was knocking on heaven's door.

'Hush, the little baby, don't say a word; mamma's gonna make your screams heard.'

'And if those screams aren't loud enough, your mamma's gonna get torn up.'

A scarily hypnotic chorus of that tormenting rhyme chose the wrong moment to bellow through the skies. Charlotte's words were as menacing as those beady blue eyes. It grew louder, more piercing, and my ears throbbed painfully; the rhyme felt so close and smothering until my head felt like a needle was jabbed through my eardrums. I hung my head, finding it unbearable; the others were unaffected. George was looking at me like I was going mad. The torment was driving me close, and I found it odd that only I could hear it, especially with their super hearing. Then it halts.

"How far do you think it is to the car?" I ask naively, shaking off the ringing. If we could get Nathan and the box safe, there would be two fewer distractions from what I feared would happen. I assumed those ravens would let us move anywhere.

"By the looks of it, at least half a mile. Too far to try. Besides, I reckon they have other ideas." George says, pointing to the menacing flock in the sky. I glance at Nathan's grey head, flopping forward. Life was all but drained from him, barely able to breathe. That corded vial swung into view as I shuffled further on my shoulder for better support.

The cord had tiny black symbols throughout its edging. They were sigils. Not that I knew what any of it meant. We hardly had the time to pop into the library for reference. There were more on the wooden casing of the vial. I was about to return focus ahead when I saw tiny letters etched on the thin lip, 'Plan B', which made me think of Nathan's father and the backup plan. What was it, though? It had to concern Nathan. Otherwise, it could've been hidden with the blade in the cabin floor. We're all waiting, but nothing's happening except for the ravens looming.

"Might be wise to move along the path by the house there, with more shelter and obstacles between us and whatever comes our way. Nathan can rest on the metal bench on the porch." Michael says, pointing to the big farmhouse next door; the right side was shielded by the side of a tin barn, limiting access to us, and the porch was wide like a corridor, and the roof blocked that crap from above.

We shuffled along the dirt track; the detectives shielded Nathan and me. We only had to make it fifty feet, and Nathan would be safer. All I could hear were the wings whipping above us while the constant breeze ushered blood, death and sulphur to follow us. The first step, 'crack', Michael crashed his foot through the rotten timber, nearly sending him flying. Every movement had me thinking the house could fall. What happened to this bloody village for it to be deserted?

Naathan's safely laid out on the bench; Michael and George flare their claws sharply, looking ahead. I hear rustling by the bush line by the bottom of the path. I prop Nathan's head on the armrest, checking his breathing. I turn to join the others...

'Whoosh!' I hear a quick fizz through the air. George darts his claws in front of my face in a flash. He catches a long black arrow between his claws—an inch from between my eyes.

'Arrrgghh,' George growls out, showing his right palm, which is bleeding. The sides of the arrow have been adapted with blades, and they're dripping a yellow fluid. The wound on his hand is infected, and yellow track marks weaved up his wrist. He weakened immediately, stumbling sideways into the crumbling railing, nearly falling through.

"Wolfsbane," Michael says, grumbling through gritted fangs. He tosses what could be a lighter but looks like a mini blow-torch. George catches at the second attempt, thumbling—a quick click and a powerful blue flame jets out. And I mean 'jets', like a fighter plane gearing up for takeoff. There was no messing around; George let it rip into the blood pooling in his palm. Much like the flare incident, he burned the wolfsbane out of him. Who shot the arrow and how they knew about Wolfsbane? Yellow clouds drifted from his hand, the track marks receding in the nick of time, too.

"Hey Georgie, when you're done playing with fire, get over here." I didn't need to look. Painful yawning and churning filled the air. 'Undead' were approaching, and lots of them.

They swarmed from everywhere. Any point that could be a hiding place they came from. We were 'bottlenecked' as the farm's muddy road rapidly filled. Each one groaning, prickling my skin with goose pimples. So loud, so much pain. My mind flashes to the vision and how that felt—all those souls.

"Holy shit. Look at the front." George points his now healed hand, looking lively again. I see Grace, the librarian, staggering; her skin is peeling. All of those cuts from the barbed wire that I saw in my nightmare were pissing blackened blood. I glance nervously at Nathan. There were only a couple of minutes left.

The beating wings above quickened. The blanket of ravens was now flying in circles, their spooky blue twirling in the sky. Like a tornado, they spiralled into a funnel, swooping down with a thunderous boom, quickly morphing into death; the two creepy Knights, without breaking stride, landed a fair bit ahead of the 'undead'. Both had the butts of their swords tipping past their dirty cloaks towards the night sky. Each nonchalant stride jettisoned black clouds of sulphur drifting from their feet. Every footprint made, sizzled, blue fire rippled from the edges. Gone were the bony clear faces, no facades.

Their true selves were haunting—just bone. Old, grey remnants of flesh stretched thin like melted rubber across decaying bone, their eyes gleamed sinister blood red thirst for pain, sunken deep into the bottomless, soulless black of their eye sockets. Their evil smiles chilled me to my core; no lips or gums. Only rotted teeth. George looked worried. Glancing at Michael, I heard him whisper, 'where's Ellena?' No mundane woman was alive amongst the horde, and unless she was hidden behind their cloaks, 'Ellena' wasn't here.

"Whatever you do, stay by your friend and that box," George says, looking me in the eye. I see fear. I know the feeling well, and George swam in it. He and Michael walk towards the creepy knights. My stomach tensed. I needed to pay attention to two places, Nathan's health and the horror at the front. Every wheeze Nathan forced out felt it could be his last.

"Baby, is that you?"

Her voice is close, and it's... "Charlotte? Is that you?" I see flowing blond hair shimmering under the moonlight, a vibrant pale face, and rose-coloured pouting lips on the sweetest smile I've missed for six months.

"It's me, baby. I'm free. I've been given a second chance." Charlotte looked alive and real. Tears were brimming in the corners of my eyes; I had an uneasy lightness nestled in my chest. It had to be her. Dressed in a fancy white blouse, a black pencil skirt, and a white porcelain coat. Exactly how she looked the day she died. Her tiny feet made the floorboards creek. It had to be her. The sweet scent of Chanel No.5 coasted through the air.

"How did you get a second chance?" Charlotte stopped in front of me. Her warm hand took mine. Her green eyes gleamed, but with a slight ripple—watery, maybe—a quiver that seemed to alter the retina. And then normal again. It had to be my fear playing havoc with my brain, translating the information wrong.

"How do you think, silly? Because of you. Of course."

"What do you mean?"

"Being so brave to find the box. They wanted to reward you. They said you're a god amongst mundanes. Did you hear that, baby? They think you're a god. See, I always told you baby, you're meant for more. You can do so much more. Don't quote me, but they want you to work for them." Everything Charlotte said felt confident. Her heart was beating and steady. It's what Charlotte said that made my balls twitch.

Charlotte drifted her hands up my arms, static rumbling over my skin. Her eyes, though, I couldn't take mine off them. Emerald green, tiny tree bark patterns throughout. The pattern seemed to spin. I didn't want to move. I couldn't.

"They want to reward me."

"Yes, baby, doesn't that sound exciting? Look what you've done to help make this mundane world better already." Charlotte's hands cupped my mesmerised face, turning it to face from the porch, slowly helping me get a better view, rocking my body closer to the steps to see nothing by wide open spaces, bounding green hills, horses running in a paddock, prancing happily. Our daughters are throwing a frisbee for our dog. Our cute Labrador mix is fast as shit off a shovel. Our girls are happy; everything looks peaceful.

"Did I do this?" I say, whispering.

"Hush, little baby, don't say a word. Mamma's gonna buy you a mockingbird. And if that mockingbird don't sing. Gerald is about to lose everything."

"And if that diamond ring turns brass. Mamma's gonna destroy Gerald's world and kill him last."

That rhyme came again. Charlotte's singing it. I'm still mesmerised, staring at the tranquil green and the girls. Something's wrong. My eyes, whatever I'm seeing, are glitching. The view shudders, flicking between different images. There's green... no, it's dirty mud and rundown homes. No, wait, it's blood... it's lots of blood, it smells so strong and coppery and... and the pain... there's so much pain. The blood is everywhere.

No, it's green grass and hills. The girls are laughing. No, wait, it's muddy, there's sulphur and screams. Why is everyone screaming? It's so loud. My ears hurt; they want to bleed. It's all quick, unnerving and painful flashes. What's real? Is Charlotte real? Am I real? What if I'm hallucinating again? Oh god, the blood, there's too much. Can somebody stop it? Please... I can't breathe. My chest. My fucking chest is tight. It hurts. It fucking hurts. Sharp stabbing pain, my heart, it's... so... much... pressure. Something is squeezing my heart. I... I...can't take it anymore. My face is boiling... I... Can't breathe.... Please make it stop. Make the pain stop.

"Oh, baby... why would you want that? You'd miss all the fun. After all, you said I would have your heart forever. Fuck... It feels so squishy... I can feel blood trying to pump around your body... And if I put my finger on this little tube like so. You lose all feeling in the left side of your body, colour and life is all forced to one side. Damn... you look like two face."

Warm breath polluted by sulphur grazes my right earlobe with each word. The voice is hardened, raspy. There's so much pain, I can't feel my left side. I can't stand on that leg. I need to fall over, but whatever is crushing my heart is also holding me upright. The flashes are quicker now; I feel so confused. It's a dream. No, it's a nightmare. Where am I? Who am I? Arrgghh, what's that piercing my back?

"How does that feel, a mundane meat puppet, a little flick of the nerves through the spine to your brain, and you don't know what day it is or if you still wear nappies? Damn, this is so much fun. If only I knew I could do this sooner. My dear, sweet Gerald, so kind of you to help. You remember helping, right? And you said for your reward, you'd like to know how it feels to be helpless and vulnerable, knowing your heart is literally in the palm of my hand."

"I remember helping."

'Gerald, let me in. Let me in now, before it's too late. That's not Charlotte. What you see is an illusion. A clever, evil illusion. Let me in, and the pain will stop.'

I hear weeping.... Its cold, melancholic wails. It's familiar to me, but I can't think why. It sounds inside of me and all around. The flashing images are slowing....

"Oh, baby, you still have some fight in you. Let your dear Charlotte take that burden from you... Wait, what's going on? What is this sorcery? Let go of me. Gerald, help your Charlotte.... Stop that... So, it's like that. Let's leave a little mess to clear up; how's a broken rib, and a punctured lung sound?"

'AAARRRGGGHH!' Searing pain ripped through me; my brain was settling. My top right rib is snapped, and all air is ripped out of me as the rib tears into my lungs. Pressure rips out of my back. I lose my balance, and my blood sprays the floor as I fall. I hear a familiar gravelly laugh. I hit the deck, drained and struggling to breathe. A tall, obscured shadow looms over me, stepping forward from the moon's glare.

It's the 'whispering man'. It's the killer. The one who murdered Nathan's parents, Grace, and most likely the others... His gaunt, deathly face, wisps of charcoal flesh peeled from his jaw and cheekbones. Those demonic eyes pierced their deep, garish red vibrancy through my mind. That dirty, bloodstained trilby is covered in more blood now. While I struggle to breathe, blood pooling beneath me, I'm locked onto his haunting aura, part terrified, reliving all those moments over the years. All the glimpses, shadows and the black cloud breezing to stand over my grandparents. And my act of childish defiance. I'm part curious. I don't know why, but I sense something familiar and not haunting. I fell for it again, and now I'm at the 'whispering man's' mercy. Blood seeped into my lungs, making me cough it up. Another nail in my coffin came quickly; his long, bony hand drifting inside his cloak, swiftly unhooking a large object before producing the proverbial rabbits from the hat. The 'whispering man' had the box.

A quick flick opens the lid, and a glowing rubric cube-sized artefact appears. If it could be called that, an aura that looked more like a slither of space, stolen and wrapped around its edges. Black with a white glow and a ton of tiny white speckles. Each side had tiles that slid to make up sigils, with one small space on four sides for our puzzle pieces. The 'whispering man' reaches into his pocket, producing a third piece, covered in blood, which he wipes on his cloak.

'click' is slotted in.

I noticed the time: Nathan's twenty-four hours were up. I couldn't hear him breathing, and I had no strength or room to move so I could reach him and try that vial.

'I can help you... If you just let me in.' The darkness calls again. I don't respond. Not straight away. I look at the thing that's plagued me, taunting that he now had Pandora's box. I couldn't see what was going on with the Detectives. I turn to Nathan, remembering the farm and when we were trapped in shackles.

"Help him, and we'll see. The vial around his neck tip the fluid down his throat." I say, clinging to the last of my hopes as I struggled to sit upright, slipping in my blood. Whatever happened with the undead, the Knights and the Detectives, there was a lot of noise, the occasional bone-jarring roar. I was too limp and clammy to fight on. I felt it leave me, an odd thing to say considering I was swimming in blood and as near death as Nathan now. A branch-like spiral of black drifts unnoticed from my side. It snaked low until it reached the bench, coiling and twirling up the leg towards the armrest and Nathan's head. The darkness lasso'd the cord in a remarkable yet spooky performance. The vial hovered mindlessly, drifting towards Nathan's mouth, which hung slightly ajar. I cautiously look to the 'whispering man', amazed at how inconsequential some deem the little things. My tormentor was busy gloating to notice. The darkness sizzled and struggled, trying to release the cap. I felt every ounce of the pain; I was burning up. It had to be the sigils; the darkness continued, gripping tight. If I wasn't in enough pain, this had me on the ropes and was dancing a jig on my grave.

Finally, the cap came off; the liquid glowed bright, and now it was exposed to the air, the darkness tingled from it. Whether this thing that so desperately wanted to be a part of me was anything demonic, it had a connection to the essence of the fluid. Dripping freely into Nathan's mouth, all that was left was hope.

"So, now most of the fun has been used up. Where's the puzzle piece?" My attention is snapped back, a wasted attempt because I didn't know.

"I wish I knew. Now fuck off."

"Still, a fighter to the end. I have to admit, it wasn't meant to happen like this. They had designs for you. What can I say? I got carried away. Trying a new trick, and I wanted to feel your life in my hands. Oops."

"Looks like you were premature; probably the story of your life. No doubt they'll make you pay." The 'whispering man' grabbed the butt of his sword, swings it wide before lunging forward. I catch the sword in my hands, the blade pushing through, tearing into my flesh, spilling more blood. Its tip pressed on my bony chest over my heart. I could feel it pushing and pushing. Having lost so much blood already, I was too weak and could feel it slipping, piercing my chest. The darkness had returned, and Nathan was in God's hands now.

Clinging On

47

'Détective Reynolds,'

You've heard thunder, 'clap'. Now imagine that noise in the thousands, swooping down, morphing into two sinister, medieval Templar Knights, gone to the dark side. How they've survived this long, the number of centuries and the changes they've witnessed. The carnage they've instigated, it defies thinking about. Even if we physically overcome these two, we don't know how many more are waiting to be thawed.

It's not like they have some 'Templar test-tube baby production line', do they? Fuck, what if they do? In all seriousness, if we fail, and the gates of hell get opened, there's no telling how many got slaughtered when the French king at the time declares the Templar order had grown too powerful and wanted them 'culled'. I have to admit; when I first heard the extent involved in this case was more than the typical serial killer, I was a little sceptical. Now, their history intrigues me. Especially how dark the order has got. Even if we succeed, I don't think we'll escape soon. Some of us may not make it at all, and I sure as hell will move heaven and earth to get Ellena back. Second chances like ours are rare. I can't let that be snatched away to be used as a pawn and collateral damage. I know Little Lamb is brave and mentally stronger than me most of the time. Watching these freaks entering without her was worrying unless she was hidden nearby.

I've tried locking onto the scent of her coconut shampoo, but nothing. In Scotland, I could filter out so much and find her a distance away and in the nick of time; otherwise, she would've gone off the cliff. The point is, I don't think she is anywhere near, and that scared me. The Knights had ditched their suits. Both had the butts of their swords tipping past dirty cloaks towards the night sky. Each nonchalant stride sprayed black clouds of sulphur from their feet. Every footprint made, sizzled, and blue fire rippled from the edges. Gone were the bony clear faces, no facades.

Their true selves were ugly as fuck. Just bone. Old, grey remnants of flesh stretched thin like melted rubber across decaying bone, their eyes blazed blood red, like mine. Only theirs looked hungry to inflict pain. Sunken deep into the bottomless, soulless black of their eye sockets. Their creepy smiles were something that only a mother could love; being as theirs kicked the bucket long ago, they were shit out of luck. No lips or gums. Only rotted teeth. It made Michaels look healthy. No lips or gums. Only rotted teeth. It made Michaels look healthy.

All I could hear were the chilling, mindless yawns from the 'undead' staggering slowly behind. There are hundreds of them. A cruel abuse of the natural process of things. These should be left to rest. I see Grace, the victim from the library; her body is ripped to shreds and oozing blackened blood. If she's here, the others will be somewhere, and that had me on edge because I couldn't see them. Translation... There's another plan afoot.

Michael and I stood our ground; the wound on my hand had finally fully healed, raising the question, who fired the air? It couldn't have been the Knights, they were too busy show boating in the sky. Unless the 'undead' suddenly regained the use of their brains, then it couldn't be any of them.

"This was a fight you didn't have to join Mr Reynold's."

"Ah, well, we're here now. Besides, you kind of made it our business, letting your little pet run around killing people. Didn't you consider a little training, you know, to show a little restraint? He's like a stray dog humping anything that moves. Maybe that is your method, after all. To live vicariously through him? I imagine it's been a while, nothing but dust and a million therapy sessions. For the other party, of course."

"There you go again, hiding behind your mundane jokes. Failing to realise, the game is already over."

"If it's already over. Why are you before us, flapping your gu... I guess you call those teeth? Either way, why all the theatrics, then?" I'm looking around, noticing the undead numbers had grown considerably. They'd gradually drifted around the space between the house, the dirt road and the run-down shacks opposite. I was a suddenly a 'B-List' movie star and had the leading role in a low budget horror flick that could give 'The return of the living dead' a run for its money. Everything about that movie mirrored our lives at the minute. Except for no army experiments gone wrong. Or calling out for 'brains'; instead, these are soulless, thoughtless empty vessels.

I believe Gerald called it earlier... Nathan... He mirrors the young warehouse guy and the old man's boss when they bust the toxic waste drum with the zombie body in it. Nathan's decline mirrors, and by the look of these smug pricks in front of us. They have no intention of a cure. What I haven't told Gerald, in case I'm wrong, nor Michael for that matter. There's something different about Nathan. Unfortunately, I don't think he knows either. It's the demon part of me. I find it hard to explain the feeling, kind of like the rumble of my hackles when danger is near.

With the demon bit, there's a burning at the back of my eyes. The red glows brighter. Imagine the flashing of headlights to allow the driver opposite to pass or turn. My eyes react like headlights. It's involuntary, and no one notices. Took me a while to figure it out. But was made all the clearer at the cabin when I was searching, and the standoff with the killer, or should I say Gerald's 'whispering man'. All nightmares get warped and changed, and as much as he's been plagued by the darkness calling to him. I fear the glimpses he had may have been the killer stalking him. It's clear he's one of the other bloodlines, dressed all dark and scary with the trilby hat. I reckon that's the universal 'designer sheek' once they embrace the darkness. What a fucked up dress code, eh?

The giveaway was Gerald's father on the VHS tapes. The shadow was his 'darkness' haunting him like what's going on with Gerald. So, these fuckers in front of us had the killer on Gerald's case for a long while. Probably crushed his father with the scaffolding, too.

"A few loose ends. Needed yourselves to retrieve the box. Only someone of Gerald's standing. Would've been allowed to retrieve it. All we need now is the puzzle piece and judging by the looks of it. That won't take long." The Knight drifted with a bony, decaying hand, pointing to the house.

My eyes had to be deceiving me. I must've blinked 8 or 9 times even so. I saw the same. Gerald stood on the porch smiling his head off, holding his arms up around waist height. If I didn't know what I know, I'd say he finally snapped because he looked to be holding someone—hand in hand or arm in arm. Gerald alluded to hallucinations and whatnot. This looked personal, someone or something dear to him. I've been there, seen my share of ghosts, some so real it's hard to know what's going on. Thankfully, we didn't have Casper and his crew knocking around, too. There's plenty of dead to go around. Having ghosts would be the straw to break the camel's back.

Looking at 'happy' Gerald was unnerving, not least because these creeps seemed happy about it, too. And their smiles were giving me the 'ick'. Gerald was rocking side to side, almost dancing, tilting his head, listening. This went on for a good thirty seconds until Gerald was facing us on the mud track, again smiling his head off.

"Right, cut the crap, matey boy. What's going on? This circus is getting old and I'm gagging for a pint." Michael says, firing shots across the creeps bow.

The Knights smile, their red eyes gleaming. I could feel the undead closing in. "Keep watching." One says, his long, menacing fingers toy and then wrap around the handle of his sword. The other did likewise. They were waiting for their moment to attack. Michael and I shuffled backwards, kicking through the rocky mud, nearly tripping with our eyes trying to be in two places at once.

Gerald's face began changing, alternating between happy, sad, and then scared. It was spooky. All we could do was watch and listen to the undead yawning in sickly unison. Their stomps a chorus of impending doom, causing me to picture them as an army marauding the streets filled with blood, likely even now, while we're in no-man's-land. Gerald's face stretched, turning pale as his eyes widened until the 'whites' blazed bright. His mouth moved, making all the actions as though he was shouting, but nothing came.

I shuffled my foot, ready to run to Gerald's aid. A knight wrenched his sword free. It glistened with that deadly toxin. I stayed, looking down the tip if the blade, wanting to send it where the sun doesn't shine. Even the slightest must now, caused the undead to step closer.

"Nothing rash, George. You'll miss the best part."

Gerald grimaced and in the blink of an eye, his body contorted, arching backwards as if wounded in his back. A few seconds later, his upper body buckled sideways. He was in agony. Then, with no rational reason, Gerald is thrown backwards in a heap, 'blood', lots of it. I could see it spray across the porch floor. I was desperate to help him. The Knight knew this, pushing the sword inches from my chest.

When I think I've seen everything, or as much as any sane person can digest in such a short amount of time. I'm blindsided by the 'whispering man', appearing. Dripping blood from his cloak, that haunting grey, menacing face breezed up to Gerald, ripping the box from Gerald's struggling grip. A blood river flowed. My eyes zoomed in to watch the crimson tide travelled across the breadth of the crumbling wood, trickling over the steps, slowly at first. It soon became a bloody waterfall. One step after the other. Gerald clambered backwards with his life depending on it, struggling to pull himself onto his elbows. The killer, as I prefer to call him, lifted a cube from the box. It glowed, encasing its edges with what appeared to resemble 'space' in all its twinkling glory. It was breathtaking and scary. I could feel the power emanating from it, all the endless darkness that didn't belong here, not in this world.

My anger simmered, waiting to explode. Michael too. The killer swiftly weald his sword, thrusting it at Gerald's chest. Gerald caught the blade but couldn't hold it. The sword was tearing through his palms. I couldn't stand and watch this. How could we stand by and let Gerald be run down like this? If that wasn't enough...

"His heart just stopped?" I say, whispering to Michael, feeling helpless. I hate that feeling.

"Yeah, I just noticed. All of this is happening and we're conveniently tied up. Gerald is pissing blood and facing down a sword. We're amongst this shit. Another move and that blade is in your chest. We run, they're probably as quick. Then there are these dead fuckers. I hate to say it matey, but our backs are against the wall and I don't know how this nightmare ends." Michael was right, of course. Every angle I looked at this mess from ended in bloodshed. Likely ours.

"Oooh, whispers, I like this game. How about I show you how this ends?" The Knight, not holding the sword, breezed beside me. He leans in close. Never have I felt so powerless. In moments like this, he was more haunting up close, sulphur and death teased the tip of my ear as he whispered. I was so off guard by his sudden movement. I didn't expect what came next. Distracted my his nightmarish face, I wasn't watching his hand. Those creepy, long fingers whipped to behind my neck. Deathly cold. His razer sharp nails scythe into my flesh, penetrating deep into the nerves leading to my brain stem...

Electricity strobed through my body. My claws were full and thick. Searing heat burned through my brain, bright flashes and blood. It hurts, everything hurts, everyone is in pain. Their screams fill the air. Thousands of lost souls are in agony. I have to make it stop. It has to stop. No, don't do it.... Don't do it. A sea of red covers the streets. I see a knight with a mundane at his mercy, buckled to the floor. He's battered and bruised, but that's not enough. The Knight stares at me; he lifts his shiny, pointed shoe, hovering over the mundanes head. The knight lets rip with a bloodcurdling laugh, and then...

'crunch.'

My eyes clench tight, my fangs grind hard, pushing out the sadistic sound of the mundanes skull crushing. The pressure did not relent, his skull collapsed like 'sink hole', his eyes exploded from the sockets. Their whites became dribbling mush mixed with the retinas. Two poached eggs popping, squelching as flesh ripped in half down the centre and through the nose. Its boney bridge splintered before the final few lbs of pressure shattered teeth, jaw and gums. A gooey pancake littered with bone sank amongst a pool of blood. All the while, the mundanes body twitched and writhed a few more seconds. A fish out of water, flopping around.

It's the same everywhere, streets ripped in half and glowing, air raid sirens echo through the darkness. Oh, my god… There's Ellena… She's lashed to a giant tree in the centre of the village. Her head hangs limp, blood pours from open wounds, too many to count. She's guarded by undead, with others terrorising fleeing mundanes. Any strays that are too fast get swept up by the Knights, despatching them with the ease of that crushed head. I want to go to Ellena; I need to, every fibre in my being longs to save her from this nightmare, but I can't. I can't move forward. I'm being held back by more than this vision or hellscape. A part of me thinks it's my mind too. Psychosomatic. Black smoke shaped like people, pour from the glowing cracks in the street, screeching a piercing shrill that shook my hackles. They wreaked of sulphur.

They're swarming the skies, weaving through the rain, looping past Ellena, lashing out, leaving claw marks in her flesh. Blood-rain fell from the sky. Hell had taken over. I need to stop this. It can't be allowed to happen. What if I hurt the wrong person? Scotland still has its claws in me and I needed to remove them. My fear could cost me Ellena. If I don't stop, it could cost the world.

I have to embrace my nature again. The Knight scrapes the remaining brain juice from his shoe, takes another look at me and bolts. He's a black blur with two red dots. He's nearly here. What do I do? His path was scorched with his footprints. He was getting close, too close. All this torment has to stop… NOW.

His blur slowed, the more I focussed. Within the ripples of black smoke, I see him clearer. Wind catches his shirt, the middle button flapped loose under the pressure from his speed, revealing a bony, almost vampiric dead chest, and something else. It appeared mechanical, plunged deep and in the area his heart would be. Obsidian in colour, with baphomet's symbol in the surface, the goat's head too, except it's made from a blood-red stone. The gap closes. I stop holding back. Feeling all that pain from those souls, all of my regret from Scotland, and I drop my right fist with claws fully out. Still seeing the Knight within the blur, I grind my foot down and power forward, punching my claws through the smoke and the red stone. His chest caves in, the stone shatters and the Knight explodes into flames, quickly becoming ash, scattering to the wind. The electricity rumbles again and I'm bolted back with the sword poised at my chest.

I feel the knight's claws withdraw quickly. Something was different. I smelt it too, fear. His hand shook, nails catching my neck. He blurs back near the other knight, except he'd moved a few paces further back. Michael noticed it too and then looked at me. I felt different, lighter, almost freer. I check my claws. There are shards of that red stone, caught within my fur. How did I bring it with me?

"What happened?" Michael says, doing his best to whisper even lower.

"I don't know. I think it was a preview of what's coming. It was fucking awful. They had Ellena strapped to an enormous tree." I say, holding back about the stone and symbol in the chest. It had to be their weakness for that knight to combust the way he did. This Knight that spiked my neck saw it too, and that's what has him worried. I believed I've found the weakest link, the chink in the evil Templar armour.

"Oh... Th...that was exactly what's coming." The shaky Knight spoke up, involuntarily reaching for his chest, checking. I had my 'mark'. Yet, like all good ideas, especially ones by us, they never go according to plan. I was about Revell in my renewed confidence and give Michael the green light to cut loose and get bloody. When I hear a loud scream coming from Gerald. The 'Whispering man' was winning the battle, his sword impaling Gerald's chest little by little. I could feel Gerald's pain. Pure agony. A tear bubbled at the corner of my eye, watching. Michael too. It's crazy how pack dynamics work, feel each other's pain... Wait... What did I just say?

Pack dynamics and feeling pain, we could feel Gerald's. How was that so? The only way that's possible was if he wasn't a mundane at all. More than the darkness within him. He's different. That's what could turn the darkness on his side. I bet he doesn't know, same with Nathan, yet also different. To me, a pack is more than being the same supernatural creature, the same colour fur or the same country the shapeshifter was formed. No, to me, it's family. It's friends that will drop everything at the first hint of danger. They look to protect one another from what may come.

It's also new friends that began on opposite sides of the law, with a common interest and will go toe to toe, side by side to stop 'Hell on Earth'. One thing is for sure, Gerald and Nathan were more than they know and their parents hold the secrets. Some may have taken them to the grave. If there's any constant I've noticed in this world, nothing is truly dead. Gerald let loose with another loud scream. Something was happening to Nathan, too. His heart had stopped, but I sensed his core body temperature rising, and fast.

"Georgie? Georgie?... What are we doing? It's now or never."

A quick look around, weighing up the options, the undead, Gerald and the Knights. "Now, fly right." Eyes glowed and claws flared. The undead swarmed us, closing the circle of death... For them... Again. I dodged Grace out of pity, shredded my claws straight through a line of the undead. Their bodies were brittle. I took their heads clean off. Black blood gushed through the air. This is what I call, 'do or die', with a liking for the first option. Gerald screamed again... weakening. I glimpsed his head dropping as the 'whispering man' buried the gleaming blade through his chest. Gerald's hands clung to the sword...The last trickle of life...

'Gerald,'

Every scream was agony, barely breathing as it was, with my rib using my lungs as a pinata. The 'whispering man' had me pinned. An added incentive, not that sadistic murderers needed one, but if he was the same one, I stopped from murdering my grandparents. I'm sure he was enjoying himself. The sword's blade slid deeper, cutting through flesh, muscle, tendons, and bone. I could feel the point dangerously close to the side of my heart. My saving grace was that he'd missed. I was sitting in a pool of my blood, trousers soaked through, and I could barely stop my hands from slipping off the blade.

Nathan's heart had stopped. As far as I could hear, anyway. I wanted to be angry. I wanted to explode into a fit of rage and seek revenge on those creepy bastards that poisoned him with no intention of coming through with the cure. There was no guarantee that one even existed. The darkness did what I asked of it, tipping the vial down his throat. For all I know, that was a joke, some inter-family thing and Nathan had to wear it... Fuck, I can't even come up an alternative story for it. My brain was all but done. My lungs swam in blood and any attempt at bravado in the face of death led to me choking, spraying mouthfuls of it on my lap.

Everything we did or tried was for nothing. Michael and George were in the middle of some 'undead' death match. I know that sounded better in my head. The undead swamped them, had to be hundreds of them, all crawling from the termite infested woodwork. Before the pit of doom swarmed, I caught glimpses of a standoff. One of those morbid, 'death-lukewarm' freaks jabbed his nails in George's neck. What I found strange, in five degrees of distant cousins kind of way, I felt it. It bloody hurt. Not as much as being fooled by the image of my dead wife, my heart put in some kung-fu death grip and then have a sword impale me. Still, I felt George's pain. With no reason. Me, a simple mundane.

'Ouch,' Again, Michael just had his flesh shredded through by nails or claws. If I wasn't in such a bad way and position, I'd be intrigued. Unfortunately, fate has other designs for me. Again, if I wasn't so weak, I'd be kicking myself for being fooled again. In my defence, the church was different. One of those bug-eyed ravens messed me up with hypnosis. Charlotte looked, sounded, and smelt real. Even dressed the same way as the day she died. All the details were too good. Even the sensation of her fingertips tracing my arms. I stared into her emerald green eyes and then... I don't know... I was lost. There were flashes of images, 'the good, the bad and the ugly', manipulating me into position to get blindsided. Now look at me. A stiff breeze short of flopping into hell. Perhaps I'll be scrubbing the toilets in hell. It's ironic when you think about it.

Baphomet and his minions want to get up here for some semi-fresh air and a tan. Okay, maybe not so much the tan. Not in these villages anyway, and it's unlimited shades of grey. You're probably listening to me thinking, why is he so upbeat with what's going on? I'm not. It's more that I've slipped into a state of Delerium. Everything is all sparkly in front of my eyes. It won't be long now if this is happening. Soon, it will be intermittent consciousness where I'll choke to death on my blood.

Through all this, the 'whispering man' is just staring, smiling in a 'nightmare on Elm Street' way. Yes, I quoted that movie again. But seriously, if you watch Freddy smile, you'll get it what he hasn't grasped yet, with all the damage he's done. The fourth puzzle piece is still missing. Speaking of which, I wonder who had the third, who did he slay this time. That thought, though, the missing piece. I couldn't smile.

"What the hell do you have to be happy about? Have you not realised I'm in you?"

"Erm, no offence, and not even while I'm on my deathbed. That would never happen. Never ever. Not judging at all. If that floats your boat, good luck to you. Maybe one of those coffin dodgers will oblige or a coffin escapee. Just not me. Not even if you dress up as Charlotte again." I say, goading him through gargles of blood.

"Funny fucker, are you? Well, I'm surprised you even fell for that, to be honest. How gullible are you? Right, let's get back to business. Where's the piece?" I choked too soon. Still, he'll be disappointed.

"I told you before, and I'll tell you again. I don't know." I say, a little distracted by

Nathan. No breathing or heartbeat, and everything was a struggle, feeling so drained. I heard his organs swell. Not in a bloated death way. Nor had he released his bowels after succumbing to the cruel blade of destiny. Don't ask, I read it somewhere. How true? I'd say 50/50. Not only were his insides deciding on a makeover, I felt warmth. I mean, yeah, I was colder, a numbing kind. That warmth was drifting from Nathan.

"See, I think you do. I didn't go through all this effort to get to here and have you lie to me."

"All of what effort? I'm not lying. What would be the point?" I say, curious about the effort comment, mindful of the undead limbs being tossed through the air, their numbers falling rapidly. Blood flew from every angle imaginable. The two knights watched on, saving themselves. As much as I applaud the detective's efforts, it felt in vain.

Everything was a mess. My preview looked to be coming true, but there were still details that hadn't been lined up yet. If Grace was here, where were the others poignant to our dilemma? What was happening with George's Ellena? And who was the 'whispering man?'. Their true self.

"See, I think you have it on you. I think you know exactly where just being sentimental. The effort? Who do you think scared this shit out of your dear old dad and made the scaffolding collapse? I thought the polaroids were a nice touch. Smear a little of his blood, get photos taken and job done. Fuck, you should've seen your face when they fell out of the file. Priceless. As for lovely Charlotte, tut tut, making her travel alone. All sorts of bad things happen on them big, nasty motorways. A reckless driver here, a nudge there. Next thing you know, she's kissing the windshield. It's great having people willing to do things for money. Sadly, it was getting awkward. You were quite the busy bee. So they had to go. Now, hand over the piece." He says, laying out his crimes. I was stunned. I felt a spark inside, finding the strength to feel angry. No, I was pissed. Yet, still, I could barely hold my head up.

"You sick bastard, if I weren't so dying, I would," –

- "You'd do what exactly. Let's face it: even on your best day, it wouldn't happen. Always too scared. Now, I'll be taking that." He ripped my father's watch from my wrist. I didn't have the strength to fight. He was right; scared has been my second nature. Now, he was interrogating my father's watch with his free, garish, grey-skinned hand. They weren't claws, but the nails were long and fierce-looking. A little like talons. His black leather gloves, covered very little, not least the grotesque peeling flesh. Deep enough to show bone. Definitely a point in the nightmare column. If the darkness meant my flesh would deteriorate like that, I didn't want it.

Michael and George were taking a beating, slowing down. They were still ripping through the undead, but their numbers were too great to sustain their energy. All those groaning yawns had me clenching. It was awful; they had to roam the streets like that, reduced to rotting punchbags. I replayed his bragging over and over. The anger had me clinging on. Then, the watch's underside got ripped off, and the puzzle piece fell, in slow motion, into the blood. I couldn't believe my eyes. I had it all the time. Father had to have known when he gave me the watch. Why didn't he tell me? Another question to add to the list of things Father neglected to share.

A Knight Rises from the Darkness

48

'Détective Reynolds,'

They kept coming but couldn't even see where they were from. My claws ripped through another 'undead' throat. I had to tell myself they were already dead, and it couldn't hurt them. Much like the vampires, a conscience is hard to water down or hide in a box. Every groaning, yawning face had already been through many things. Now, in death, was the devil's playthings.

Whether they're vessels in waiting or a distraction, what we had to do was hard. And we're flagging badly. The killing circle had become a bloody free-for-all. Seeing Michael covered in blood and intestines was comical yet sickening. While our batteries were being drained, the Knights were watching, and the one on the left was bothered by me. His jamming those girly nails into my neck hurt like... excuse the pun, hell. He knew what I saw, and it freaked him out. It was their weakness, and when the moment came which we may only get one shot at, we had to aim there. I was intrigued, though; call it a detective's curiosity. Was that how they maintained such a long life? Obviously, that was the most rational thought, as a wad of trachea goo splatters my face. The implosion was profound and exhilarating; I wished the others had seen it. The flames quickly turned to ash before scattering to the wind. They would've got a much-needed morale boost if we weren't so up the creek without a paddle.

The way his shirt flapped at the right moment revealed the mechanical thing in the Knight's chest, Obsidian, with Baphomet's symbol on the surface. He's a bit of a narcissist, if you ask me, making his prize toys wear such garish things with his symbol. Then again, it's the devil, Baphomet, the prince of darkness, or whatever ridiculous name he gave himself. Talk about being up one's arse: even the bling, a goat's head made from a blood-red stone.

I bet that wasn't cheap. It's not like they can walk into 'Warren Jmes' and say, hey there, don't mind the just dragged out of a coffin look. Can I have a dozen of your finest rubies carved in the shape of a goat's head? Oh, and it needs setting in this devilish pacemaker right here. And I need it yesterday, or you'll spend an eternity in hell. Crap, do you take a Visa debit card? I left my Amex in the other 'bloody' cloak. Imagine the faces behind the counter. The nearest I've come to ruby is, as the cockney prince calls, a curry, a ruby, murry me old Mücka. Damn, where was I? Grace kept coming at me; I know she's dead and all, but after being at her crime scene and all of those cuts she endured, I can't bring myself to... well... kick her while her coffin's re-opened. Oh, that's it,

Just before I lashed out, I felt all that pain from those souls. What's with that? It's a new one for me. Perhaps it's what I've hinted at already about Gerald and being different. Even now, changes are happening to him with a sword in his chest. And will have to experience an ability to deal with lost or stranded souls. If my gut feeling is right, there will be much to sense soon. At that moment, though, I unleashed all of my regret from Scotland, punching my claws through the smoke and the red stone. The way the Knight's chest caved in is no wonder Mr Close and Personal are worried. Not even Ellena has dug her nails into my flesh yet. The chance would be a fine thing. It seems we keep getting pulled apart by death, and blood, and kidnappings, oh and vampires.

I'm surprised she's willing to hang around when it's listed like that. Must be the hairy chest. Please tell me you get that, as my claws eviscerate another bladder and a pile of intestines that are now spewing over the mud that's rapidly becoming a crimson swamp. I shouldn't find it funny, but seeing the hundreds of limbs and heads still moving on the floor, I do. Taking any chance to find humour in this horror is a must. Everything is always so dark. My nightmares are relentless. Although they've come a long way since the demon's eyes in the burnt basement, they're wearing me down.

I haven't told Michael yet. Aside from the recent ones here, they were truly haunting. It's a chest-pounding fear... and involves London and the elder vampire. I keep seeing him. Not in a memory of what happened. Some of these are graphic, bloodthirsty attacks. Yep, there's a theme; no matter where we end up, there's blood. He genuinely scares me, which is hard to admit, but we won't see it coming if he could become anyone he chooses and is fixed on payback. The Knights evoke a different unnerving in me because they're an unknown, yet we're about to get to know each other a little too well the way this carnage is unfolding.

I need to tell Michael that those stones I joked about will shatter if caught properly. The Knights have displayed super hearing, which takes whispering off the table, and we can't share our thoughts, you know, that inner voice thing. Okay, that's a little white lie. There was a brief situation in Scotland when I rescued that 'Alpha', and he jumped into my mind, and we spoke. I don't know how yet. There's so much I need to learn about being a werewolf, let alone an alpha. There's been no time to practise.

Michael and I spin, ripping through another couple of undead each. Blood gushes in my eyes, dripping down my face. I catch a bit in my mouth, too. It's rancid, blacker, dead blood, enough to make me gag. Ordinarily, I'm drooling at the scent of the fresh, coppery stuff, especially on a full moon. This, though, is awful. In our frenzy, Michael and I crash into each other, nearly ending up on the wrong side of some claws. We're panting and struggling. Michael's face told the story in all its vibrant gore. Back to back, shuffling in a circle as the remaining fifty undead close in. Gerald was still fighting; he was weak, but his emotions were everywhere. The 'whispering man' has Gerald's watch, the underbelly is off, and Gerald's face... fuck, he's shocked and angry. Oh shit, that can only mean one thing.

"Michael, did you see?" I say, again trying to keep my voice low.

Michael's panting wildly, wiping blood from below his eyes. "I, er, think so. Does that mean what I think it does?"

"Afraid so, detectives. I must applaud the valiant effort. But yes, it's game over. You've lost. There are no do-overs. We have the box and the final piece. Now, everything you previewed will come true, and then some."

"So, everything I saw is real?" I say, focusing on the stone, not thinking about Ellena strapped to a tree but watching the Knight on the left shift uncomfortably. By the looks of it, it could be every knight for himself when the chips are down. That, right there, is a runner. It is also called Live to Fight Another Day. Something I would very much like to do.

"Everything. Now grab them."

A haunting chuckle follows his words as the undead lunges for us. The Knights draw their swords, breezing towards. We dodge left and right, avoiding waves of rotten, fleshed arms flailing at us. We're almost cornered. I see a sword drive through a gap in the crowd at the last minute as it headed for Michael's throat, who was busing fending off two undead. I've gripped the blade, holding it off, but I'm weak, and the sword is pushed further.

There's nowhere to run or hide, all but tapped out. My hands slip, giving me a sense of Gerald's struggles. Blindsided, the other sword lunges through, tearing into my right rotator cuff. It's deep, and the knight keeps it in. My arm goes limp. I can't use it or move it. Absolute agony. Blood is pissing out. The muscles try to heal themselves, but the knight twists the sword. The other sword rips from my hand but thrusts back quickly. I try to fend it off, but it rips into my chest. Michael has three undead latched onto him as more pile on. The knights know what they're doing, driving down powerfully. My legs buckle. I'm forced to my knees, helpless. Everything is becoming muffled and foggy. I can hear the knights laughing. Michael is down, too.

They keep twisting and pushing the swords. Blood soaks through my top as I languish amongst the pool of guts and dismembered moving limbs. Everything felt lost. Tears filled the corners of my eyes. All I could picture was Ellena. Not her strapped to the tree. It's our first kiss by the canal. She'd accepted both sides of me without hesitation, and I never imagined finding love again. We've been through hell, but one thing is sure: we love each other. How can this be it? I die amongst other body parts at the hands of creepy knights?

If she was here… If she… Oh god, I'm struggling. If she were here, she'd say, get the fuck up and show them who's boss. How? I'm picturing her smiling face. When I feel something weird, I can't describe it other than a small rumble of heat through my hackles. It's coming from Nathan. It's growing more intense. My red eyes suddenly become a brighter blood red.

My gut told me to roll the dice, trust my instinct and… Roar. I closed my eyes, took a deep breath to the pit of my stomach, and grabbed onto all the pain and suffering we've endured and still going through, all the sadness and loss. I pulled it up with as much venom and power as I could muster. Letting rip with an ear rocking, ground shaking, wood rumbling and bone-jarring… 'Rooooaaarrrrrr', emptying everything I had. Trees shook as I sent a mini shockwave rippling through the undead and the knights towards the house. Undead fell to the floor. Michael pulled himself free. His eyes were glowing bright yellow. My head flops forward, spent, but I feel a stirring at the house. That heat dialled up to a ten, and something was happening. Was it too little too late? Or me clutching at straws? There's silence except the groaning, then… 'der-dum, der-dum, der-dum'—a heartbeat.

'Gerald,'

Everything shook; the ground rumbled from George through to the house and beneath. I could feel the wet floorboards vibrating against my limp legs. It rocked the 'whispering man', too. I felt the pressure on the sword ease slightly. My hands were fighting against the slipperiness of my blood, smearing the blade. Whatever that vial was doing to Nathan, George roaring, kicked up a notch. The heat grew and grew.

Watching the detectives struggle in the swamp of body parts and guts, I felt the swords plunge into him, as this one did to me. Searing agony, even the numbness as his arm dropped, losing function. That roar, though, I felt it as a sudden shock. My eyes bolted open wide. Then, as if we hadn't navigated through enough twists and surprises. Nathan's heart restarted. Only small blips, but I can hear it getting stronger. Again, I can't believe I'm saying things like that. I'm at least ten feet away and hear shallow beats as if my ear hovers over his chest.

With every struggle I put up, my strength drained some more. Looking at the smug, horrifying face in front of me was killing me more than the blade. I had the puzzle piece with me all along, and that stings. Because now they are on the verge of opening the gates of hell. A lot still bothered me. If I was dying, I had to know who the killer was—a little closure for the soul.

"Hey, thugly, when you ask for your pay rise or bonuses, perhaps you can ask for enhancements. Like attaching another set of arms, you may find it easier to pat yourself on the back. Maybe they'll throw in a personality for good measure." I say, getting the only reaction I expected. The sword twisted some more, and the blade grazed the right chamber, making me writhe in agony and taking the wind out of my sails.

"Why don't you die already? Your mouth is tiresome."

"Bet the Knights will say that to you soon, no matter how well you please them."

"What's that supposed to mean?"

"Exactly what I said. No matter how much wear you get out of those knees, you'll soon be despatched." I wanted to laugh, but everything was a struggle. I glance at Nathan.

It may have been my eyes weakening, but I would've sworn I saw a slight fiery glow assimilating through Nathan's body. The heat grew, too.

"You cheeky bastard! After everything that's been taken from you, there's no giving in."

"My life has been crazy from the get-go. Nothing has been normal, and you made it worse by snatching what's good from me. Except for the difference between them and you. Is that they will live on in the lives they've touched. In the footprints in the sands of time. You're a footnote in a bad horror movie. Nothing more."

"I'll make history instead of being seen as the weakling everyone overlooks." Did I hear that right? It wasn't the first time, either. The way those photos were described from the folder. I thought it was said as the glimpse of the 'whispering man', but my instinct caused a shiver that was more than another step closer to death.

"History is exactly that, the past full of people that weren't spoken about enough when they were alive. If you're a 'bloodline', why don't you show your face? Your true face. Unless you're scared? You have us beat. Look, we're all on our last legs, and soon, the earth will be smothered by the dead in a sea of blood and hellfire. So, come on, a glimpse. For old times' sake. Or history, as you prefer it." I say, leaning to his need to feel wanted. I had to know the snake who destroyed my world and plagued my life. Everything about Charlotte kissing the windshield turned my stomach and boiled what little blood I had left.

George kept trying to stand against the blades. Each time, those creepy knights forced him back, blazing those evil red eyes. Every yawn of the dead was haunting, triggering flashes of that Red Sea and those bodies—a mundane skull.

The crunches beneath every step, and that line of creepy knights flanking the dead. How could that be allowed to happen? The 'whispering man' smiles in a way that only a demented mother or a dead one could love. He gripped the sword, leaning into it, pushing the blade deeper. If hell had my number, I may as well fall with the face of the truth.

"Be careful what you wish for, Gerald. What was it?... Oh, that's right. Be bloody careful; this is just the beginning... See, I warned you, yet you failed to listen." There was another echo moment—everything I'd just pieced together.

Death and sulphur swirled on the winds of change, creaking the floorboards, rippling against the blade and beneath my fingers. The 'whispering man' drifted his garish grey, decaying face close. To within inches of mine, his eyes were as red as the knights., carried the sum of my hauntings. In this moment, looking deep into them, all I saw was Charlotte's crash, the wreck of her car, fluttering like embers of her dying light in the depths of death incarnate, before me. Then the grey shimmered, and the decay faded, allowing the true visage of my tormenter to face me at long last.

Like nothing I've ever felt, Rage rapidly grew within me, and so did the darkness. I allowed it to. Seeing the detectives struggle, the knights regained composure after the roar. Nathan was, against all odds, stirring, and I found the courage to look the real 'whispering man' in the eyes. Colin. The man we relied on for help with father's autopsy. He lied to my face. He slipped those horrifying photographs into the file. Fuck... and I bet he cut father's flesh to post to us.

"You sick bastard. How could you?"

"Spare me the melodrama. You couldn't care less who helped you and Nathan as long as you got what you wanted. My father was the same, bragging about how he felt like a king among mundanes and that it would be my turn one day. I didn't want to wait any longer, so I took it... The long on mother's face when she found me cutting through the last few fibres of muscle to remove his head. She too, asked how could i? So, I showed her by removing hers. Now, they sit together in the freezer, and I'm the one who is the king among mundanes. And you're the footnote. Now, it's your turn to die. Goodbye Gerald, thanks for making it interesting."

'Let me in... before it's too late. They need you. I will bend to your will.'

Colin smiles, just as evil as the garish façade. He cupped my chin with those long, bony fingers, held my head facing him, and drove the sword deep with a final push. Blood spewed out my mouth, and everything went dark... and cold...

"Well, that was easy. I expected more, and I even hoped for it. It's been a blast terrorising your family and the other bloodlines. Now I'm the one. Finally, the curse means nothing."

Life is full of surprises and twists. Sometimes, it's the least expected that makes the biggest impact. Death is a relentless beast, devouring everything it touches. It lurks in the shadows, waiting until the last flicker of light fades, leaving behind nothing but darkness. Now and then, that flicker has the strength, the last trickle of fight, to spark back to life.

"Wait, what's happening? How are your fingers still moving?"

First came the spasms in my fingers, tapping against the sword and flicking blood. Spasms became a grip. Little by little, my hands pulled towards the handle. My eyes finally opened. It was surreal. Everything was vivid: shades of red, black, grey, and more. I could see the quiver in Colin's lip. His hands shook on the handle.

"How are you alive?" Colin's voice was missing the conviction of moments ago.

"Looks like I finally let the darkness in."

I had boundless strength and energy. I could feel my wounds healing. The blood beneath me was being drawn back into my body. My hands gripped the blade tight, pushing it out of my chest, dragging myself to my feet as the tip finally left. I'm changing in ways I couldn't imagine. My hands grew wrapped in a grey protective wrapping over my arms. I caught my reflection in the blade in time for the grey hood to drift over my head. My face was the same, except for piercing red eyes and perhaps slightly leaner. I was becoming the opposite of the 'whispering man', in shades of grey with a two-tone templar cross, dressing my upper body. The real Templars. Not the evil imitations. It felt profoundly euphoric.

And I had 'him'. Colin, or the 'whispering man', at my mercy. I easily forced the sword up, turning the blade under Colin's chin and forcing him against the railings. Colin was powerless compared to me; anger burnt bright, and I had revenge with reach. This moment was about more than that. If I let him go, he'd come again and again. I had to remove one evil bastard off the board.

The tip pierced his flesh; I felt him tremble; I gripped his jaw as he did to me. "Hey, Colin. Are you still with me? I have something important to say."

"Wh... What,"

"One sec... Okay, here goes... Hush, little Colin, don't say a word. Maybe Baphomet can buy you a mockingbird, but if that mockingbird doesn't sing. Remember this: you were never a king, just a weakling desperate to be heard. All that will be is the screams from a lonely turd."

With a quick thrust, I tore the sword through Colin's chin, all the way through his skull. His mouth cranked open, feeling the blade's width rip through, blood gargled and spluttered, his tongue had been impaled too. I looked Colin in the eyes, feeling my pain slowly ebb as the life left his eyes. Tears filled mine, his body heavier on the sword, and capillaries burst, gushing down his cheeks. Revenge was bittersweet, even if it went against everything I stood for. That was then. This is now. I finally let the darkness in, and it's altered me in ways I don't have time to understand yet. The voice is still there, quieter at the back of my mind. One thing was for sure, I wasn't a mundane any more.

I withdrew the sword, allowing a final spray of blood to paint the floor. Colin flopped limp, dropping. I hear two thuds. I go to see, remembering the box, a black cloud whips forward, sulphur and death. The cloud obscures everything in front. I hear 'yawns of the dead'; they're close.

The cloud vanishes as quick as it came, in its place, a line of undead, including two that helped Colin, Patrick Sheh and Frank Ecklesttone. These seemed different. Their eyes glowed a vibrant purple.

I counted at least ten while I was distracted by Nathan's sudden groan. I was right; that fiery glow had overtaken his body, but he was still out.

'How does it feel?' I hear in my head, forgetting the darkness for a moment.

"So far, so good. What exactly are we?"

'We are one. Your strength of character won me over, essentially a demon, the darkness everyone has but different. We are, I guess you could say... A demon Knight of the Templar order, a true heir to the original folklore that did so much good in the world. It's your turn now,' Hearing the voice like this was so weird, still as melancholy as it had been, but now we were one, and I liked the sound of a 'true heir.' Doing good had to start now—a quick check of Colin's cloak. The box was gone. That black cloud took it, meaning those bloody creeps had it.

We needed Nathan awake so we could help the detectives. And try getting the box back.

"Well, that sounds good, but you'll have to help me as I learn about this new world. First, there's these." I say, looking at Frank Ecklston, his grey rotten flesh oozing that rancid black blood—the word 'Book' etched in his arm.

I surmised that the Book of the Dead may be a trail we must follow if that's the Knights' next step.

'Of course. First, allow me to wake your friend up. I have a feeling he will come in handy,' the darkness chuckles like it knows something. It's surreal to think both of us will be different now after being so close to death. Just what did our parents get involved in, and who were Nathan's parents?

That was another issue that needed to be handled with care. First, a farm drenched in blood, guts and everyone's worst nightmare, the dead roaming free. I feel it again, like when the vial was tipped down Nathan's throat. The darkness slithered from my side, wisps of black that were more grey now, spiralling particles drifting. A sight that will never settle in my mind, I don't think. It became a branch until it lingered over Nathan's face.

The end morphed into a hand; I knew what was next. Nathan had an aura around him now, rippling fire, even the tips of his blonde hair.

'smack,' The darkness let rip with a hard slap across Nathan's face. For a cloud or smoke, it packed a hit.

'ROOOOOAAAARRRRR.'

Nathan jolts upright, creaking the bench, and his eyes rip open wide. It was like seeing two balls of fire. No whites or anything, just fire, the same that quickly engulfed him but not burning. That aura was now a full, fiery body suit, as we saw Michael with that yellow fox. This was something else. I couldn't put my finger on it, but it was kind of a huge beastly hound. You've seen Ghostbusters, right, and the beasts that take over the geek and his love interest. The face was that. Nathan was bigger, too, muscular with a set of huge fucking fangs. This was awesome and so bloody scary. God had finally shone his light on us and gave us a helping hand. Maybe, just maybe, we could turn this around.

Nathan stood, moving quickly to face me, even more intimidating up close. While we had the perfect cannon fodder before us to test our training wheels. "Gerald, what happened? I died. I was in this big empty blackness; then suddenly, I was ripped back into my body, and now this. What am I? More the point, what are you?" Nathan's voice had a menacing growl, and I was so glad he was on our side.

"You could say I finally embraced my darkness. FYI, I died too. And guess who the killer was?"

"Who?"

"That fucking gimp, Colin."

"No way, but he was so nerdy."

"Exactly. But we'll have time to catch up. First, we must destroy this lot, save the detectives, retrieve Pandora's box, and stop an apocalypse."

"So, not much then." Nathan chuckles. It was so good to have my best friend back. And finally, we could make a difference.

Eckleston and Sheh were first up. Sheh defied gravity and common sense, his torso was not connected to his legs, every move had the halves sliding in different directions. Nathan's fire aura glowed as the undead and their yawning groans approached. All it took was a raise of his hands, and fire flew, torching the undead. It was so hot their bodies were reduced to char-grilled black shells glued to the spot. I hear the cracking of crispy flesh. The putrid stink was almost unbearable. Yet, again, I was in awe. It was like watching the 'torch' from The Fantastic Four. I couldn't help but smile. What an upgrade. It kind of had me feeling a little underwhelmed now, which the darkness sensed.

'Don't worry, we have plenty of tricks. Those dead bastards aren't prepared for it. Take out your sword... The one on your hip!' I paused with a chuckle, drawing the sword. Heavier than Colin's. The metal was different, too, with thick leather wrapping around the handle. The butt had a thick round symbol of the Templar cross. There was a smell, too, not the toxin like the Knight's. A gasoline tinge, yet a strange added ingredient. Made me think of the church and its sterile holiness.

We carefully walked down the creaky steps and around the wall of crispy dead, hearing their rotten flesh sizzle. Burnt dead blood smelt even worse. No sooner were we clear. 'Ready'. The darkness says. A blue fire ripped through the sword from hilt to tip, searing heat. Yet it didn't bother me. Nathan was a walking wall of fire, his eyes blazing even brighter, growling as we trudged through the sloppy land of death. Heads yawned. Arms and legs twitched, with the occasional headless body stumbling in circles, their guts spilt like a conveyor belt of butchers sausages.

From that moment on, everything felt in slow motion, weird all the time in the world, feeling as we moved, getting the knight's attention. The one on the left had let his sidekick impale both swords into George while he had Pandora's box, sliding the tiles around to move the coin pieces in place. Three were complete, and we didn't have long. Michael was still struggling against a mountain of undead—a raft of dripping, crumbling flesh staggered towards us. The moment reached within a few feet, George lifted his head, and his eyes flickered brighter. Michael's, too. The same happened to Nathan. I could feel their pain, particularly George's. Whatever our presence was doing, there was a shift. Both seemed to gain energy and renewed strength.

George let rip with another growl, which was not as loud as earlier but still enough to shake the ground. With his eyes blazing, a hand gripped each sword, his fangs bared, he pushed the swords out of him. He'd overridden the loss of feeling in his arm to power through. The knight was shell-shocked. Before long, the undead were coming at us from all angles. I never wielded a sword, yet it seemed I'd held one for years. I moved fast and light, dodging and slicing; blood sprayed the air. Some hit my face. Nathan only had to touch one, and their body combusted.

Nathan ploughed through the pile on Michael, gradually breaking him free, who jumped to his feet, drenched in blood, roaring loud enough to give goosebumps. The blood-covered tide was turning, laying to waste anything that came at us, making up for lost time. I manoeuvred a path towards the knight with the swords. It was our turn to face off.

'Are you ready?' The darkness whispered between my ears.

"No time like the present."

'Don't worry, we've got this. Now let's slay this creepy freak.' It was surprising to hear that from something I'd run from for so long. Life is never a straight path. And this felt like a crossroads, a very gory crossroads. And by the time I ever get some sleep, I'm sure there'll be nightmares.

His peeling grey face grinning, spinning the swords, trying to impress. Every swoosh waved his cloak in the wind; every move filled the air with death. We mirrored each other's movements, wading through the bloody pool. I don't know how or why, but I felt a presence, two. A tingle to the back of my neck, a gentle touch on my shoulder. Charlotte and Father were with me. Not in the haunting ways that have tormented my life. I felt them in that moment and my heart. For the first time, it was full.

The knight breezes towards, swinging. I parry his strike, sparks in shades of blue and black, flew as the blades rattled. "Looks like someone got a makeover."

"Yeah, about that. You need additional help. Your guy doesn't have the chops for the dirty work, nor the brains, for that matter." Our swords ground against each other, slipping, and I dodged his next swing before ducking and swiping my blade across his chest. It hurt him, the blue fire was burning him, black smoke sizzled from the wound. I was getting quicker, to the point. The knights' next few attempts missed. I'm looking down through the end of the blade as it comes. With all the time in the world. Shocking, even myself.

I pivoted on the spot, turning and churning through the blood, my back mirroring the Knight before spinning out with my sword at the Knight's back. I drove it all through, screaming with rage, then dragging my sword free again. Blue fire ripped through his back and abdomen. The Knight staggered, his sword buried into the bloody mud as a support to keep him on his feet. I turn to check on the others, each ripping through the remaining undead.

"The chest, Gerald, over his heart," George calls out, holding two detached arms without breaking stride or giving the Knight any rest. I spun around his hunched body. At that moment, the Knight pushes himself upright. I drag my sword, swinging and drawing back before impaling the Knight's chest. His face was shocked. Glass or a gem shattered, a fire sparked, and the Knight combusted and turned to ash. Scattering to the wind. Catching my breath, I'm looking for the other knight. The others finished the last of the dead. Nathan, Michael, and George stood covered in blood and guts, bewildered. The skies were changing, becoming a lighter purple as the first hint of sun rose. I could see the knight's ashes lingering.

Somehow, we survived and still failed. The other knight was nowhere to be seen. Then we felt it, a rumble of the floor. Soon after, the first crack appeared, splitting through the fight pit, and the blood poured into the ground. My preview was coming true. A light purple light boomed out of the ground. George's face looked in pain. He'd seen something, too. A new dawn was coming, and so was hell. We'd failed. George was in tears, talking to Michael. All I heard was about Ellena, still trapped with those evil fuckers. All four of us had an ability now, some newer than others, while Nathan and I fought back from the dead to slay some. The ground continued to shake; houses fell, not that it would take much. Without a word, a look did enough. We knew the fight had only begun. And we will drag our world from the ashes of hell if we have to. That knight ran scared. We could only hope the message filters down. We're coming.

Rachel - 'Good morning, everyone. This is Rachel Cordwell reporting live for Sky News, coming to you in an emergency broadcast after reports of zombies seen roaming the streets. It's not even Halloween. My pilot, Lenny Chadwick, bless his soul, finally got it up. The helicopter, before all your deviant minds wander. Say hi, Lenny.'

Lenny - 'Hi Lenny.'

Rachel - 'Wow, the old jokes are the best. ' next to me, as loyal as ever, even at this ungodly hour, my cameraman, Jack Casey. Give the viewers a glimpse of you on this bizarre and terrifying day, if true.'

Jack - 'Good morning.'

Rachel - 'That's great, Jack, right Lenny, where are we now?'

Lenny - 'We're coming up on… What in god's name… It's Willowbrook, but not as you may know. Quick look.'

Rachel – Oh my god, it's truly horrifying. The reports are true. If anything, they undersold it. The streets are lined with grotesque, dead walking. Zombies for the want of a horror movie term. Some are fresher than others; some are punching out of their graves as we speak. Oh god, one just lost an arm as they came through. I'm not mincing words or towing the P.R. line on this rare and monumental morning. It's fucking awful. Others are dripping black blood and shedding flesh. It's pure carnage, holy shit, that one is just one arm, a rib cage, a skull and spinal cord. It's dragging itself through a sea of red. Oh god, it was. Now, it's a stepping stone as a chunky one obliterated it. They have no coordination and little balance,'

'With our side door open, even from up here, we can hear a horde of groans and yawning. No words. At least none we can pick up. Their eyes are cloudy and vacant; it's so goddam spooky,'

Lenny - 'Quick Rachel, look, as we head north of the Pennines, giant cracks are tearing through the streets.'

Rachel – 'As ever, Lenny is right, holy cow…town after town, roads, gardens and sidewalks are being destroyed, even farms, as fissures tear through like huge spider webs or branches. Now, if this doesn't evoke thoughts of 'hell' opening up, I don't know what will. Bright purple light beams out with intensity. These cracks are everywhere, getting longer and longer, wider and wider. There's no covering this up as an earthquake or reporting otherwise, CNN.'

Rachel – 'There's just so much blood as more and more is spilt. Oh no, people are fleeing their homes as the ground opens up and swallows them whole. They're not getting far, running straight into the zombies. Who are savagely ripping these ordinary people to shreds. One is even waving a dismembered arm around like a bat. Oh crap, they just bit a chunk out of it. Damn, I think I'm going to be sick. It's fucking awful.'

Rachel – 'Remember, we are coming to you live, my word. This is a first for this reporter. Anyone at home watching this, do not leave your home or open any windows or doors. Keeps the news on at all times for regular updates. This is unprecedented and an awful nightmare. I'm truly stunned and devastated.'

Jack – 'Crap, what's that?'

Rachel – 'And it keeps getting terrifyingly weirder. This is no joke, no illusion. It's straight out of an IMAX-quality horror. Hundreds of body-shaped black clouds with blood-red eyes spewed from the ground. You heard that right: if Casper went to the Darkside and had millions of babies, this would be them. They're filling the air. Wow, some are flying into zombies, and they're changing. Just when you think it can't get any worse, these haunting bundles of smoke make the zombies more mobile and less rigid. Shit, one just ran and caught a human, ripping their head clean off. This is so tragically crazy, I'm almost at a loss for words.'

Lenny – 'Hang on guys, it's going to get bumpy; several fly directly toward us. Oh god, oh god. Duck, one's just flown inside. Aaarrghhh, it... it's got me.'

Rachel – 'Did you hear that? Lenny just said one has flown in. This Is Rachel Cordwell at the heart of the action, people. Wait, what's going on? Lenny just screamed out, that cloud has got him. Oh god. I'm going to be sick for real. We're in a tailspin, Jack, hold on. Shit, did you hear that? It's coming from Lenny. I can hear... It's loud, groaning, just like the zombies.'

Rachel – Shit, he's leaving the cockpit. Oh, no, wait, what are you doing? Lenny is staggering towards me and Jack; he looks dead, his skin has turned grey, and his eyes are jet black. EWWW, there's blood too. It's spewing from his mouth and eyes. Holy shit, no one is flying the helicopter. We're going down. Wait, what are you doing? He's grabbing at the camera. I guess Lenny wants his close-up. Oh, no, this has been reported by Rachel Cordwell and Jack Casey. Lenny has been turned into a zombie by one of those things that came out of the ground. It appears hell has opened its doors and is coming for us. Blood drenches our streets, and we're overrun by the dead. If we don't survive this. Mum, dad, I love you. No, wait, let go, get your face away from Jack.

Dead Lenny - 'We... kill... all.' Arrgggh,'

Rachel – 'You heard... it... here... first. They're looking to kill all. Oh shit, we're spinning out of control. Noooooo, We're going downnnn.'

The End

Acknowledgements

To the family and friends who sat through the countless drafts and listened to my crazy ideas. Even when my confidence wavered, at a crossroads of whether to give up. You inspire me to be better every day and with every novel I create. Especially with this one, and pushing me to let go, stop holding back. Thank you...

Printed in Great Britain
by Amazon